A HOUSE DIVIDED

AS IT STANDS

After years as an orphan, Henrietta Achilles has learned she's the last living relative of deceased wizard Ornun Zol—and she has inherited her uncle's estate. Inside Zol's towering manor, she discovers bandits searching for treasure, soldiers out to capture them, and tiny monsters swearing revenge after their banishment from the kitchen.

Stranger still, a massive cat is stalking Henrietta. Their clash soon creates a flood throughout the manor. Henrietta and the other occupants unite to end the deluge, forcing bandit leader Nate Flemming and his enemy Captain Booner to face their shared past.

When a blast of water separates Henrietta from her new allies, she makes another fateful discovery: a candle in the shape of a boy. A creation of Ornun Zol, it quickly envies her status as the wizard's heir. They navigate the house together until the cat once again confronts Henrietta. This time, she embraces the cat, soothing its rage but making an enemy of the living candle. Henrietta, the soldiers, and the bandits stop the flooding and defeat the candle creature. But a final wave consumes the cat, and Flemming falls from a bridge after an unlikely act of heroism.

Afterward, Henrietta's friends say farewell while she settles in for the winter. Meanwhile, a new threat comes into view. Stone statues have begun a march toward the manor. Like the house itself, these sculpted soldiers are creations of Ornun Zol—but some other force has them under its command. As the statues lay siege to the house, Henrietta's only hope is that the magic inside its walls will hold out long enough to stop the stone horde . . .

Thanks to Eve Jay, Annelie Wagner, Parvin Jahanshad, Margarite Heimbuch, and Edda Heue for their help and support

Script by Haiko Hörnig
Art by Marius Pawlitza

First American edition published in 2022 by Graphic Universe™

Copyright © 2022 by Haiko Hörnig and Marius Pawlitza
All rights reserved. International copyright secured. No part of this book may be reproduced, stored in a retrieval system, or transmitted in any form or by any means—electronic, mechanical, photocopying, recording, or otherwise—without the prior written permission of Lerner Publishing Group, Inc., except for the inclusion of brief quotations in an acknowledged review.

Graphic Universe™
An imprint of Lerner Publishing Group, Inc.
241 First Avenue North
Minneapolis, MN 55401 USA

For reading levels and more information, look up this title at www.lernerbooks.com.

Main body text set in CC Dave Gibbons Lower.
Typeface provided by Comicraft.

Library of Congress Cataloging-in-Publication Data
The Cataloging-in-Publication Data for A House Divided: The Lost Daughter is on file at the Library of Congress.
ISBN 978-1-5415-7246-1 (lib. bdg.)
ISBN 978-1-7284-4865-7 (pbk.)
ISBN 978-1-7284-4407-9 (eb pdf)

Manufactured in the United States of America
1-46523-47552-9/23/2021

örnig, Haiko, 1984-
ouse devided. Book 4 The
st daughter /
22.
305254761087
08/03/22

A HOUSE DIVIDED

THE LOST DAUGHTER

HAIKO HÖRNIG • MARIUS PAWLITZA

GRAPHIC UNIVERSE™ • MINNEAPOLIS

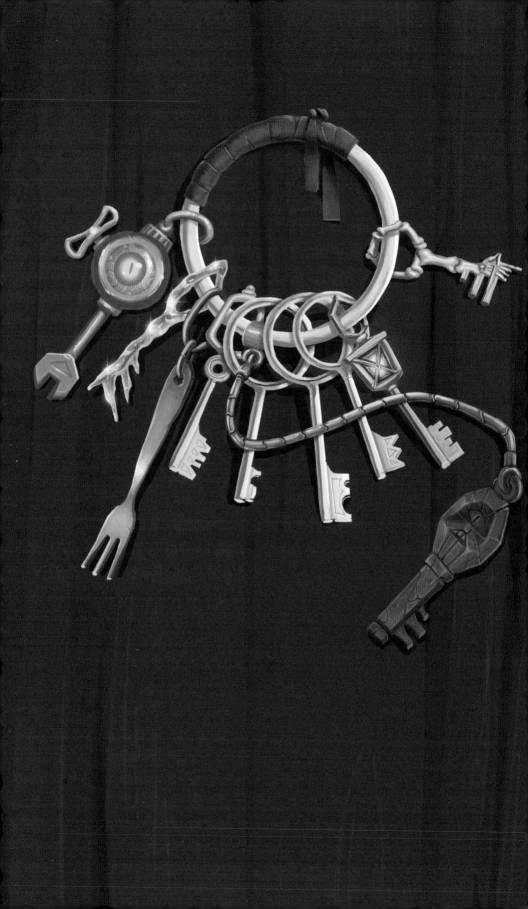

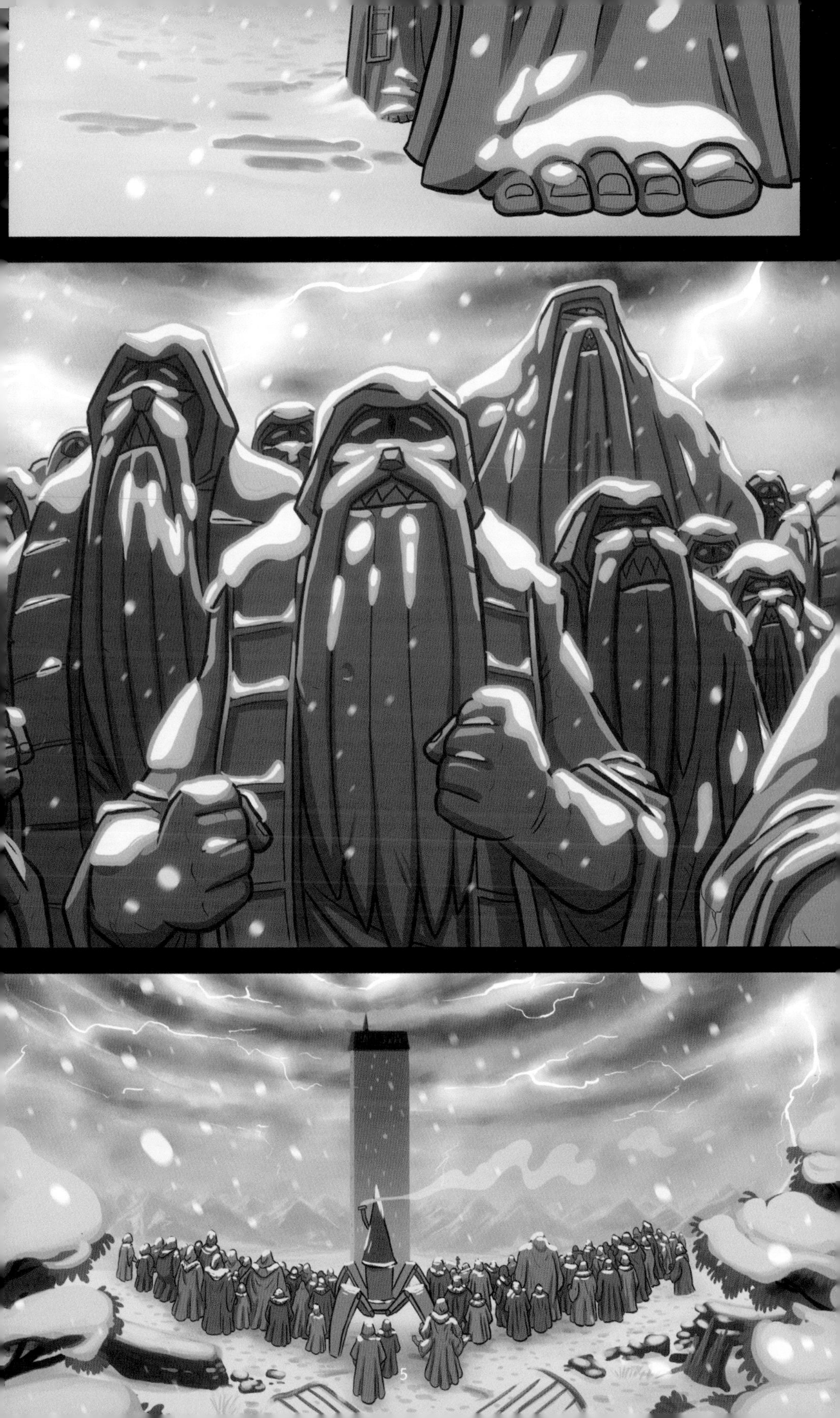

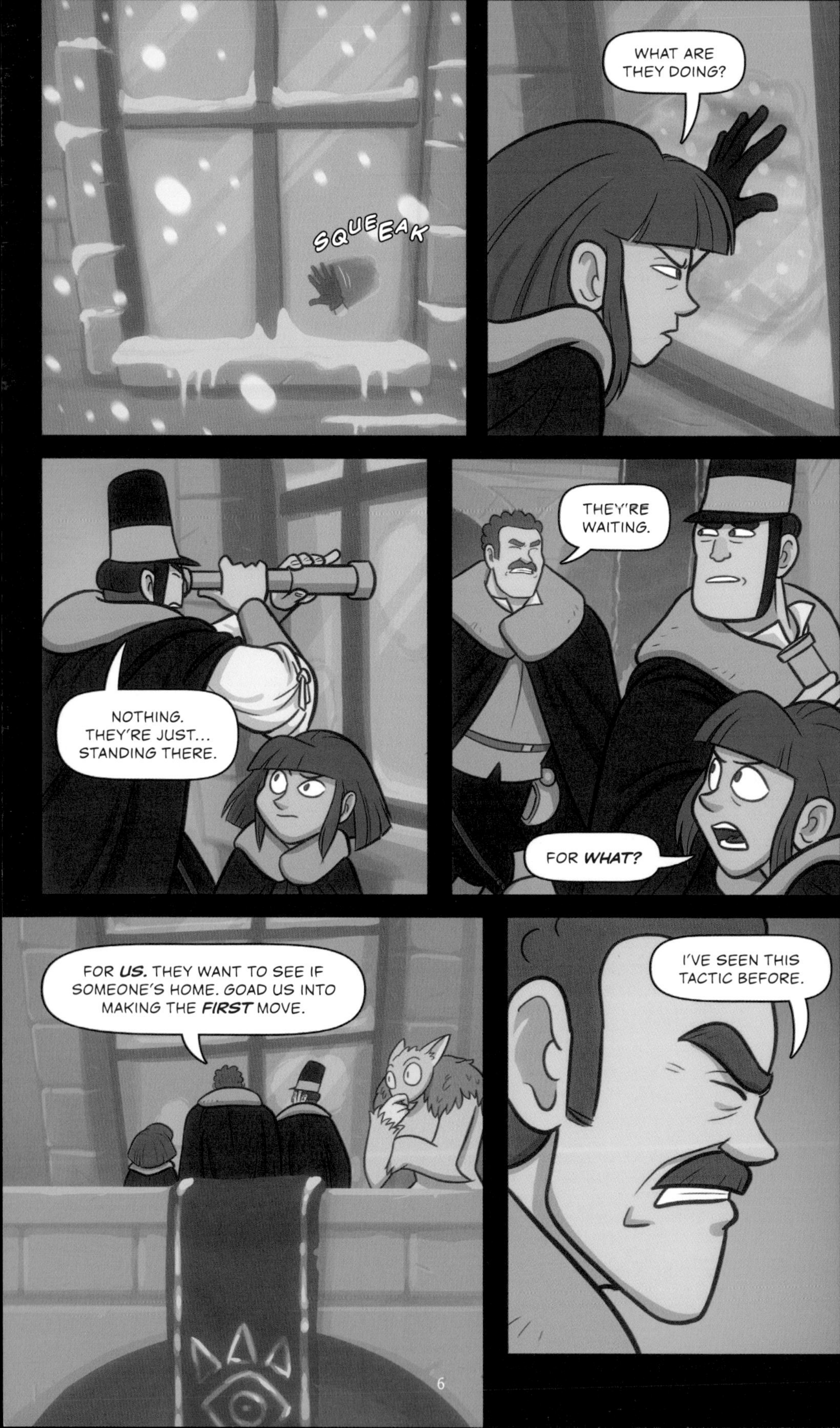
SQUEEAK
WHAT ARE THEY DOING?
NOTHING. THEY'RE JUST... STANDING THERE.
THEY'RE WAITING.
FOR WHAT?
FOR US. THEY WANT TO SEE IF SOMEONE'S HOME. GOAD US INTO MAKING THE FIRST MOVE.
I'VE SEEN THIS TACTIC BEFORE.

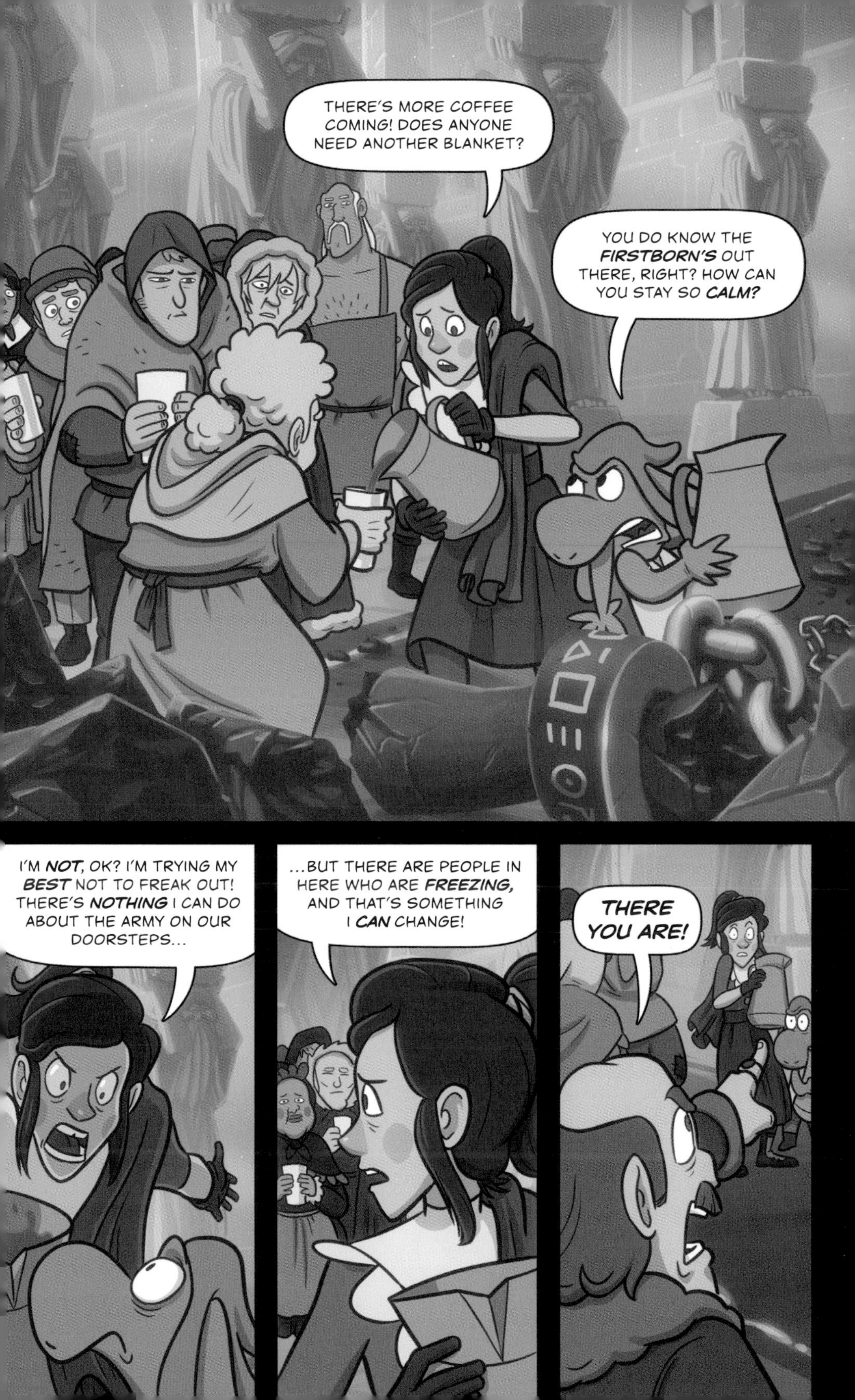
THERE'S MORE COFFEE COMING! DOES ANYONE NEED ANOTHER BLANKET?
YOU DO KNOW THE FIRSTBORN'S OUT THERE, RIGHT? HOW CAN YOU STAY SO CALM?
I'M NOT, OK? I'M TRYING MY BEST NOT TO FREAK OUT! THERE'S NOTHING I CAN DO ABOUT THE ARMY ON OUR DOORSTEPS...
...BUT THERE ARE PEOPLE IN HERE WHO ARE FREEZING, AND THAT'S SOMETHING I CAN CHANGE!
THERE YOU ARE!

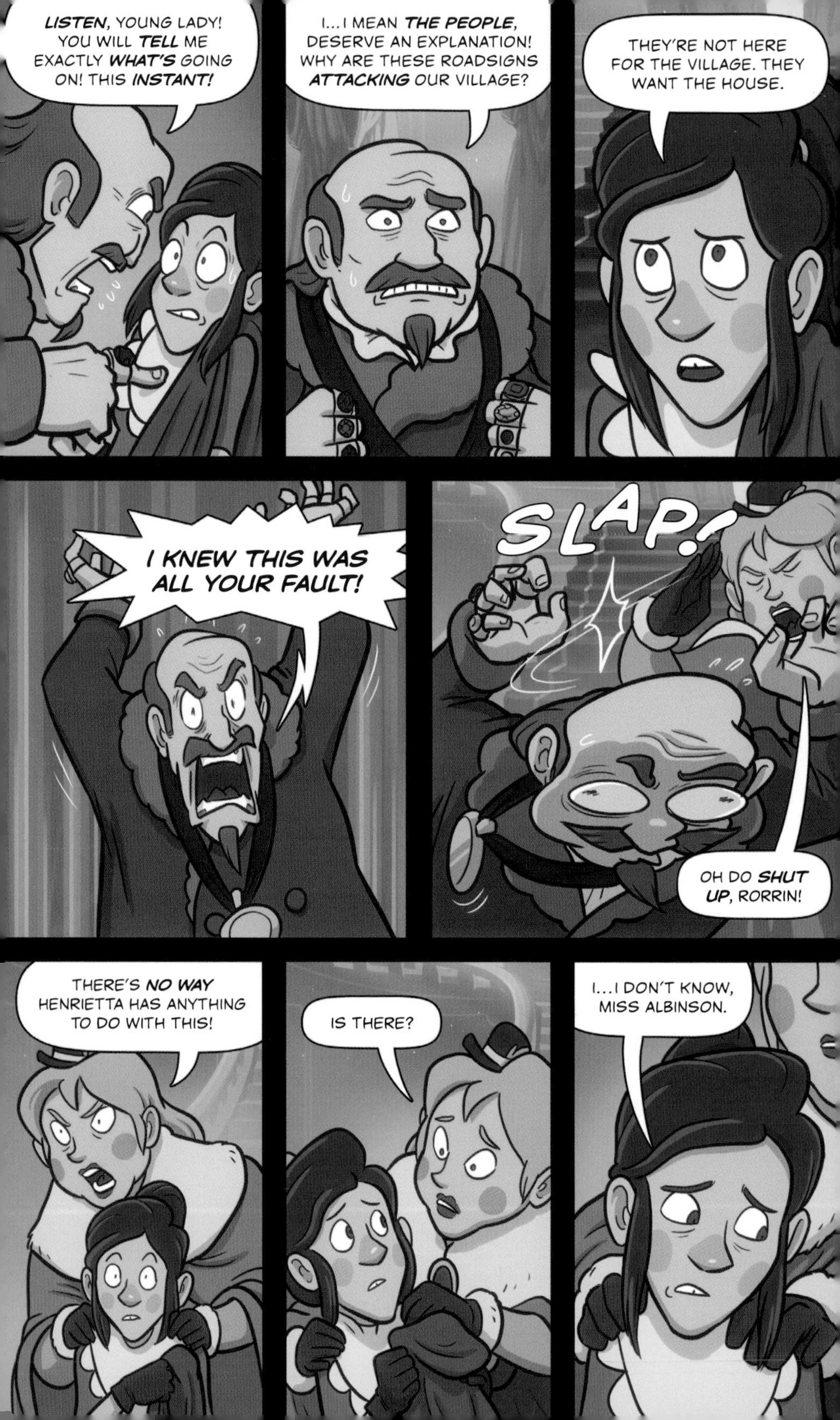
LISTEN, YOUNG LADY! YOU WILL TELL ME EXACTLY WHAT'S GOING ON! THIS INSTANT!
I...I MEAN THE PEOPLE, DESERVE AN EXPLANATION! WHY ARE THESE ROADSIGNS ATTACKING OUR VILLAGE?
THEY'RE NOT HERE FOR THE VILLAGE. THEY WANT THE HOUSE.
I KNEW THIS WAS ALL YOUR FAULT!
SLAP!
OH DO SHUT UP, RORRIN!
THERE'S NO WAY HENRIETTA HAS ANYTHING TO DO WITH THIS!
IS THERE?
I...I DON'T KNOW, MISS ALBINSON.

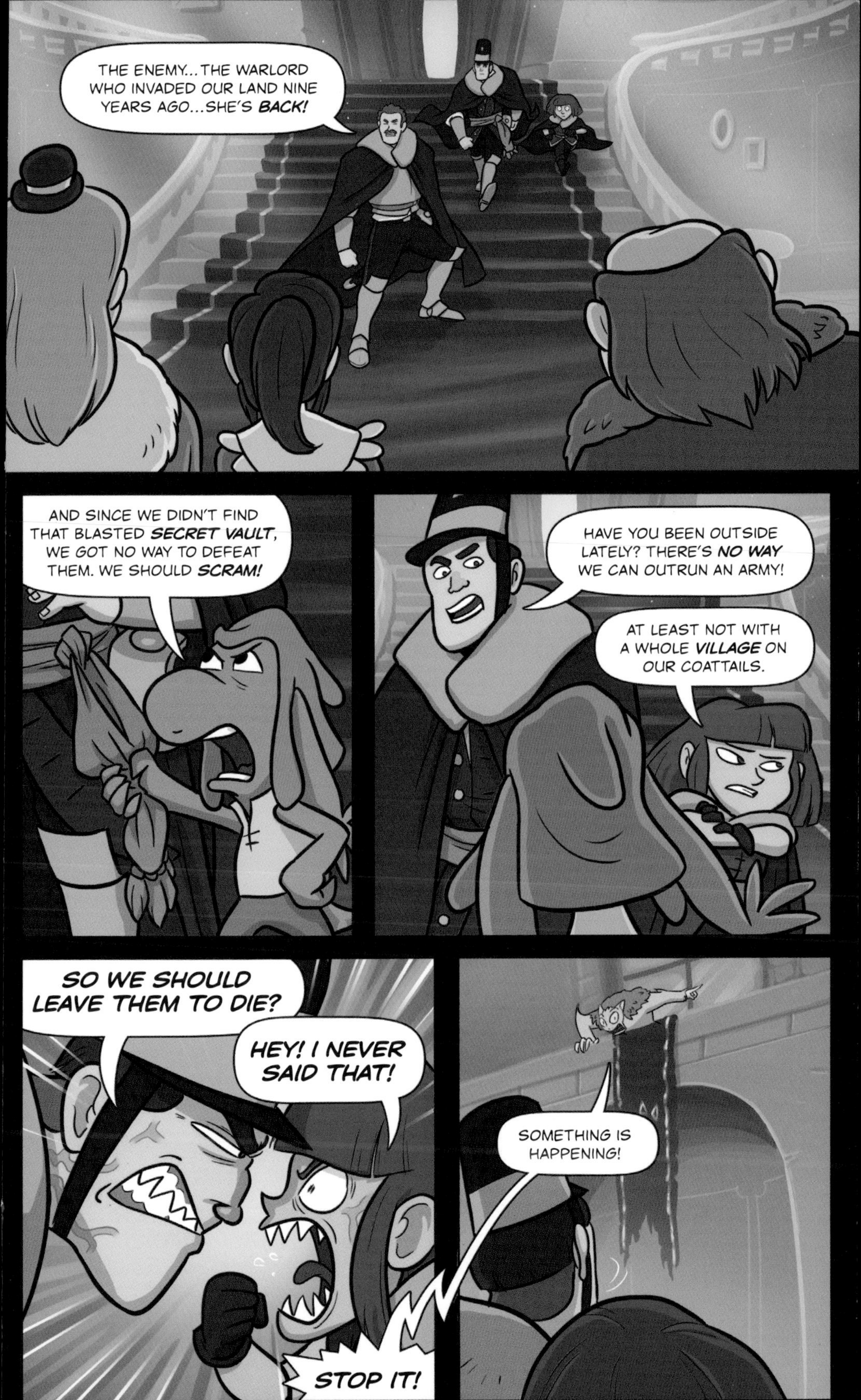
THE ENEMY... THE WARLORD WHO INVADED OUR LAND NINE YEARS AGO... SHE'S BACK!
AND SINCE WE DIDN'T FIND THAT BLASTED SECRET VAULT, WE GOT NO WAY TO DEFEAT THEM. WE SHOULD SCRAM!
HAVE YOU BEEN OUTSIDE LATELY? THERE'S NO WAY WE CAN OUTRUN AN ARMY!
AT LEAST NOT WITH A WHOLE VILLAGE ON OUR COATTAILS.
SO WE SHOULD LEAVE THEM TO DIE?
HEY! I NEVER SAID THAT!
STOP IT!
SOMETHING IS HAPPENING!

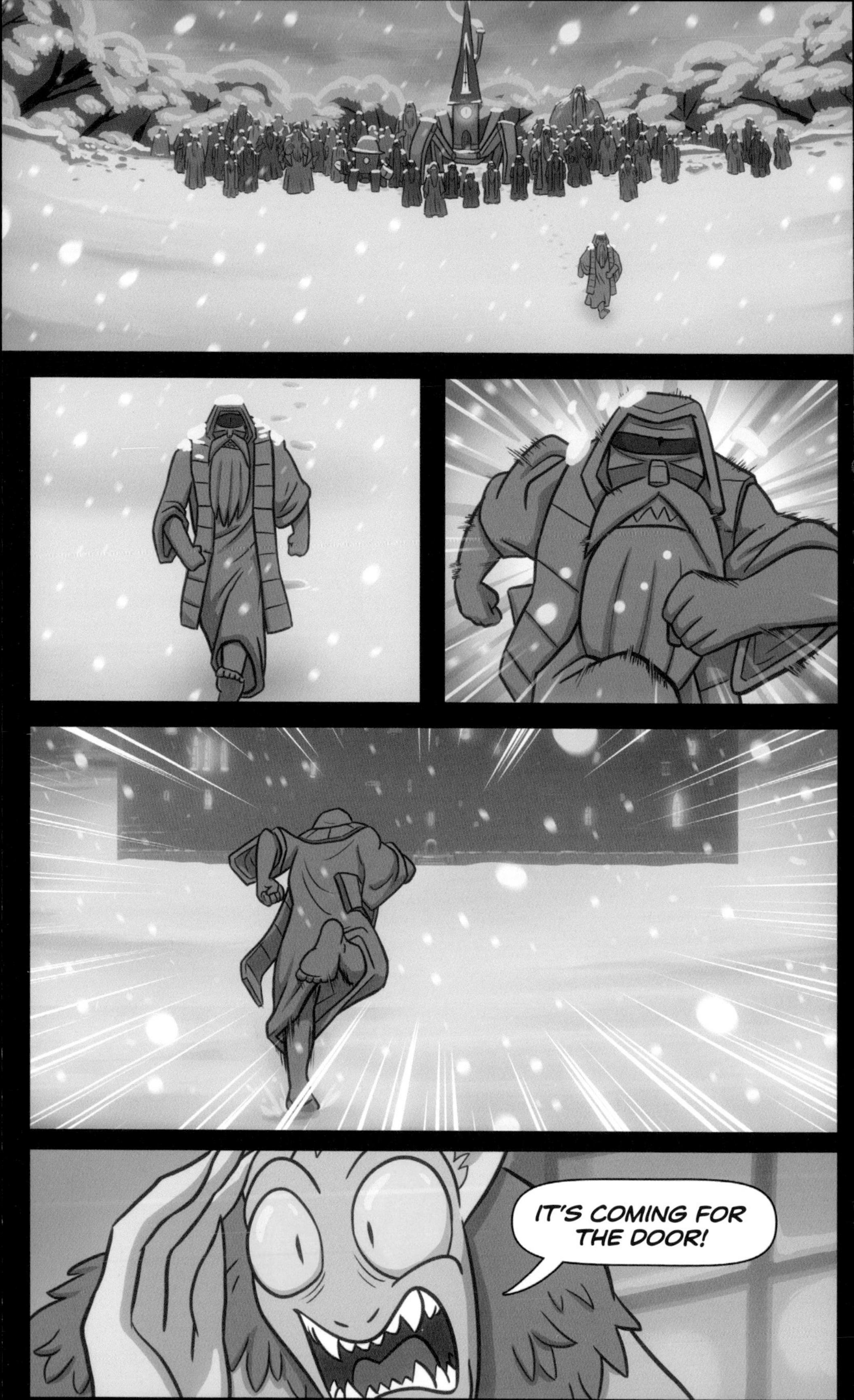
IT'S COMING FOR THE DOOR!

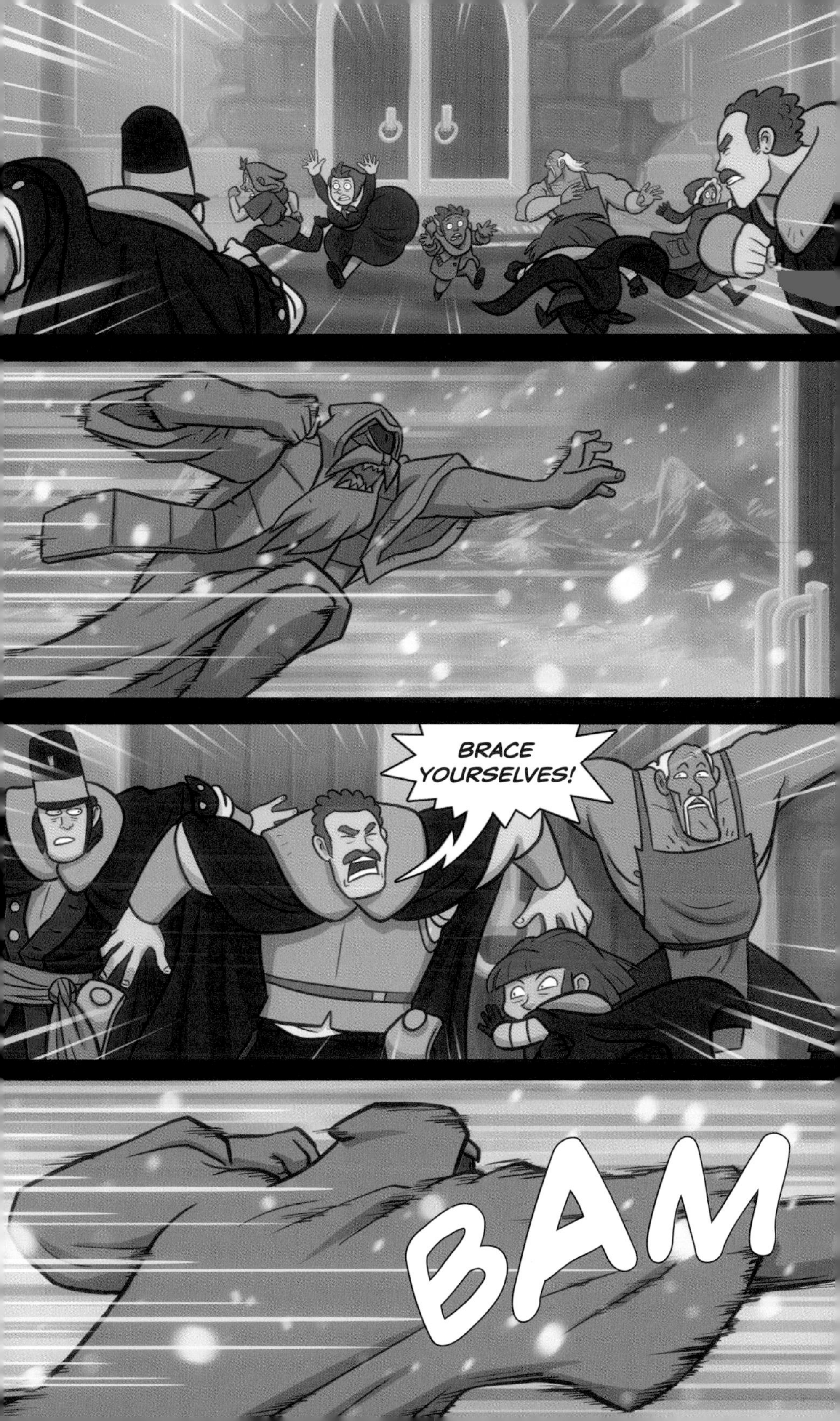
BRACE YOURSELVES!
BAM

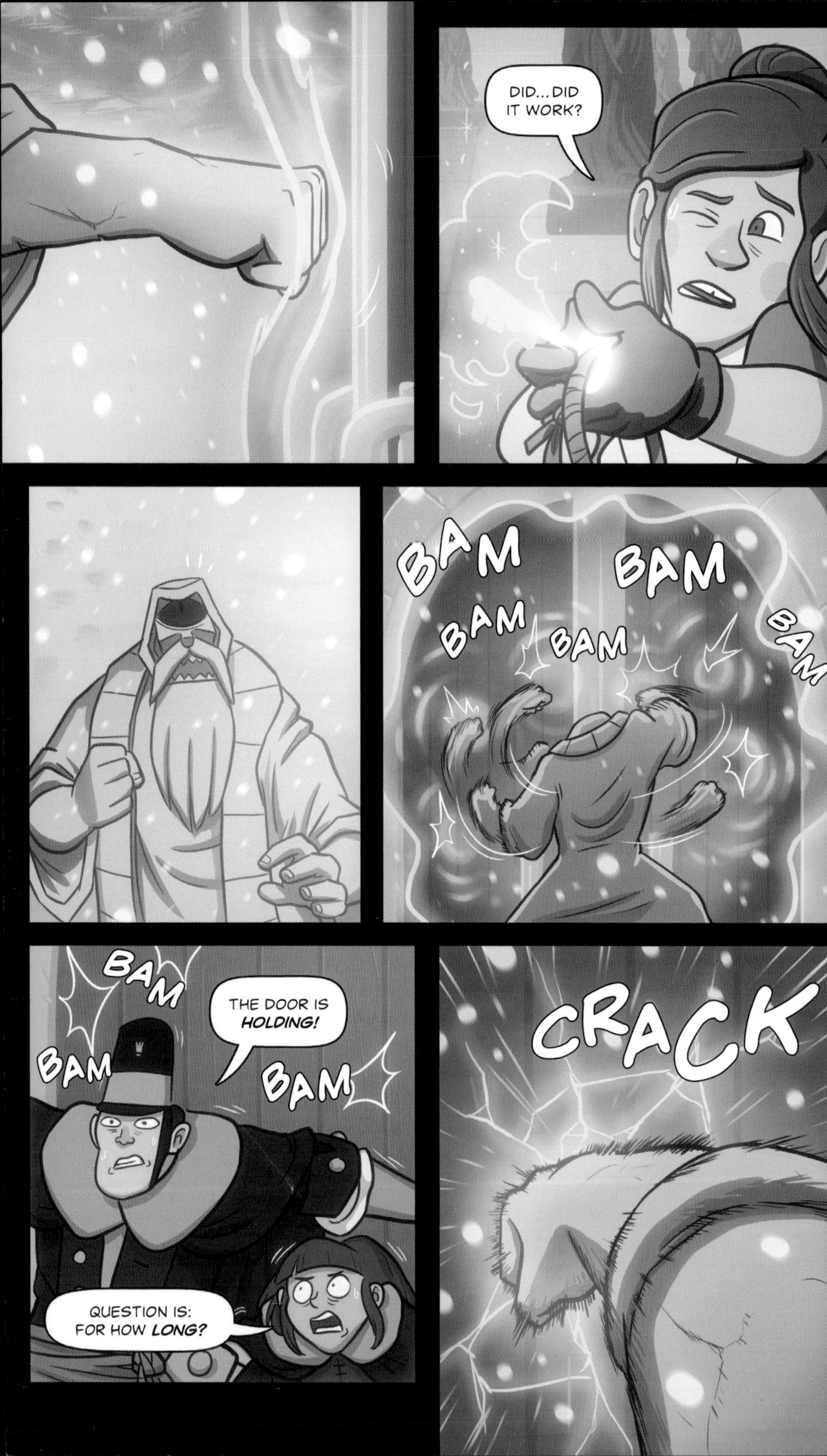
DID...DID IT WORK?
BAM
BAM
BAM
BAM
BAM
BAM
BAM
THE DOOR IS HOLDING!
BAM
QUESTION IS: FOR HOW LONG?
CRACK

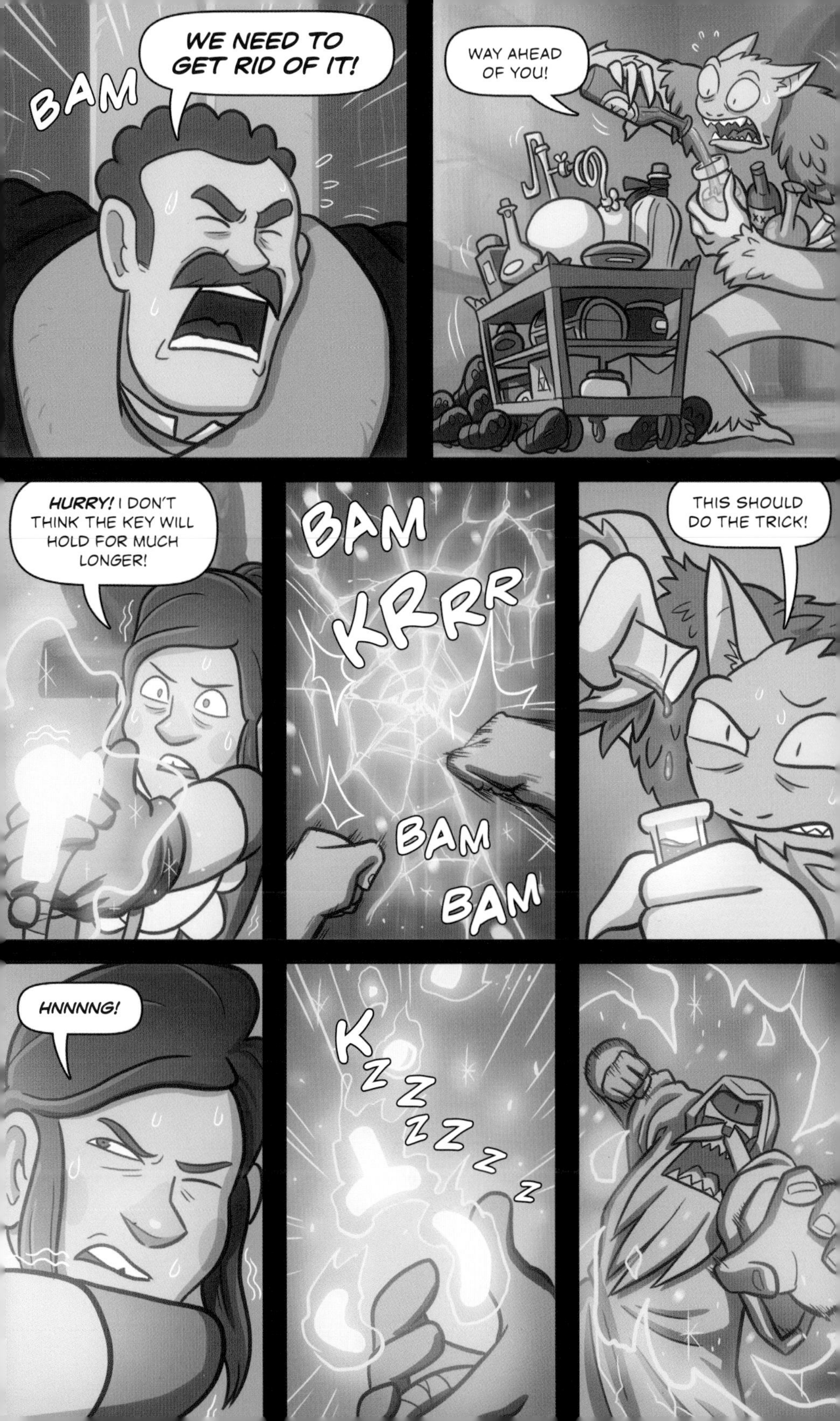
WE NEED TO GET RID OF IT!
BAM
WAY AHEAD OF YOU!
HURRY! I DON'T THINK THE KEY WILL HOLD FOR MUCH LONGER!
BAM
KRRR
BAM
BAM
THIS SHOULD DO THE TRICK!
HNNNNG!
KZZZZZZZ

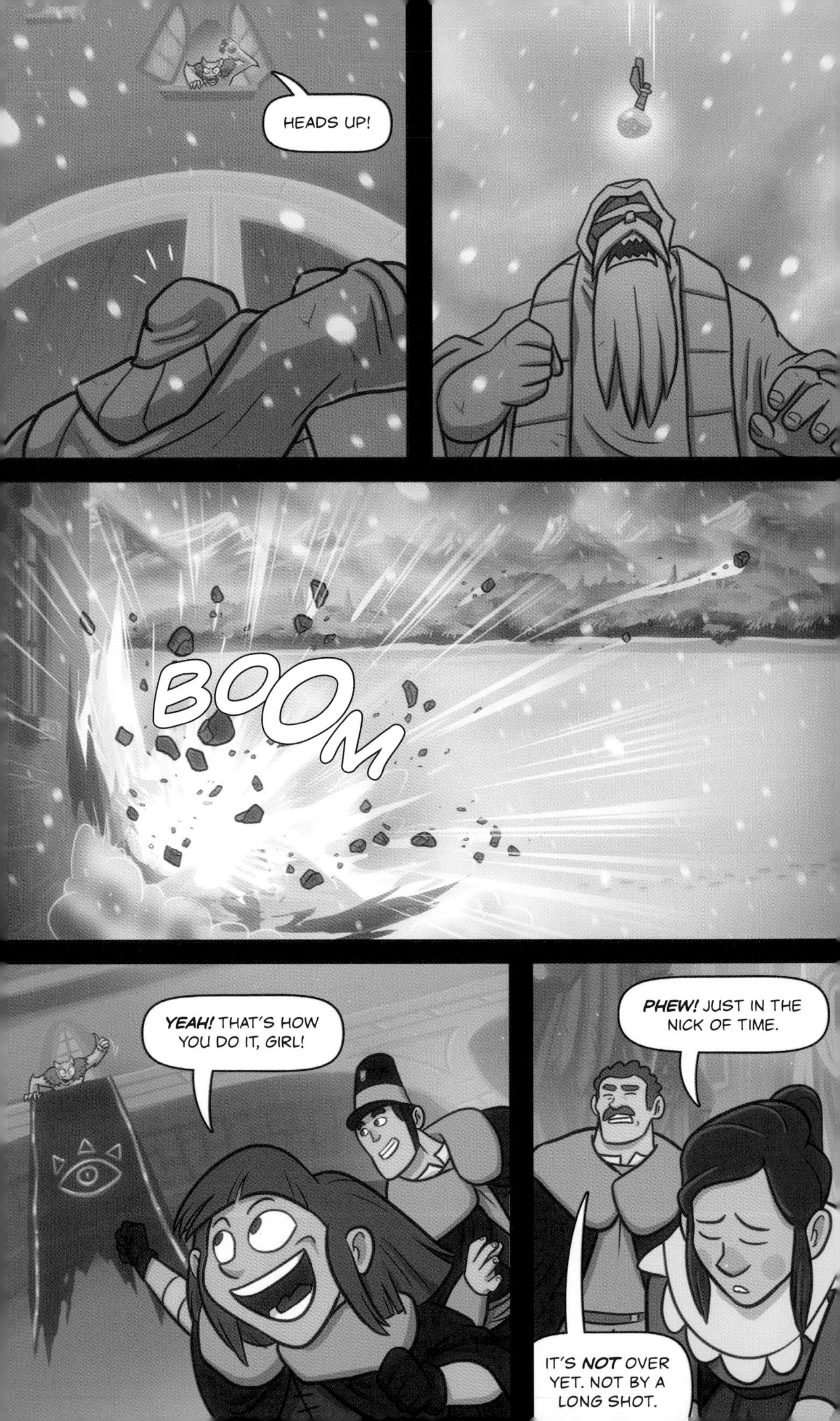
HEADS UP!
BOOM
YEAH! THAT'S HOW YOU DO IT, GIRL!
PHEW! JUST IN THE NICK OF TIME.
IT'S NOT OVER YET. NOT BY A LONG SHOT.

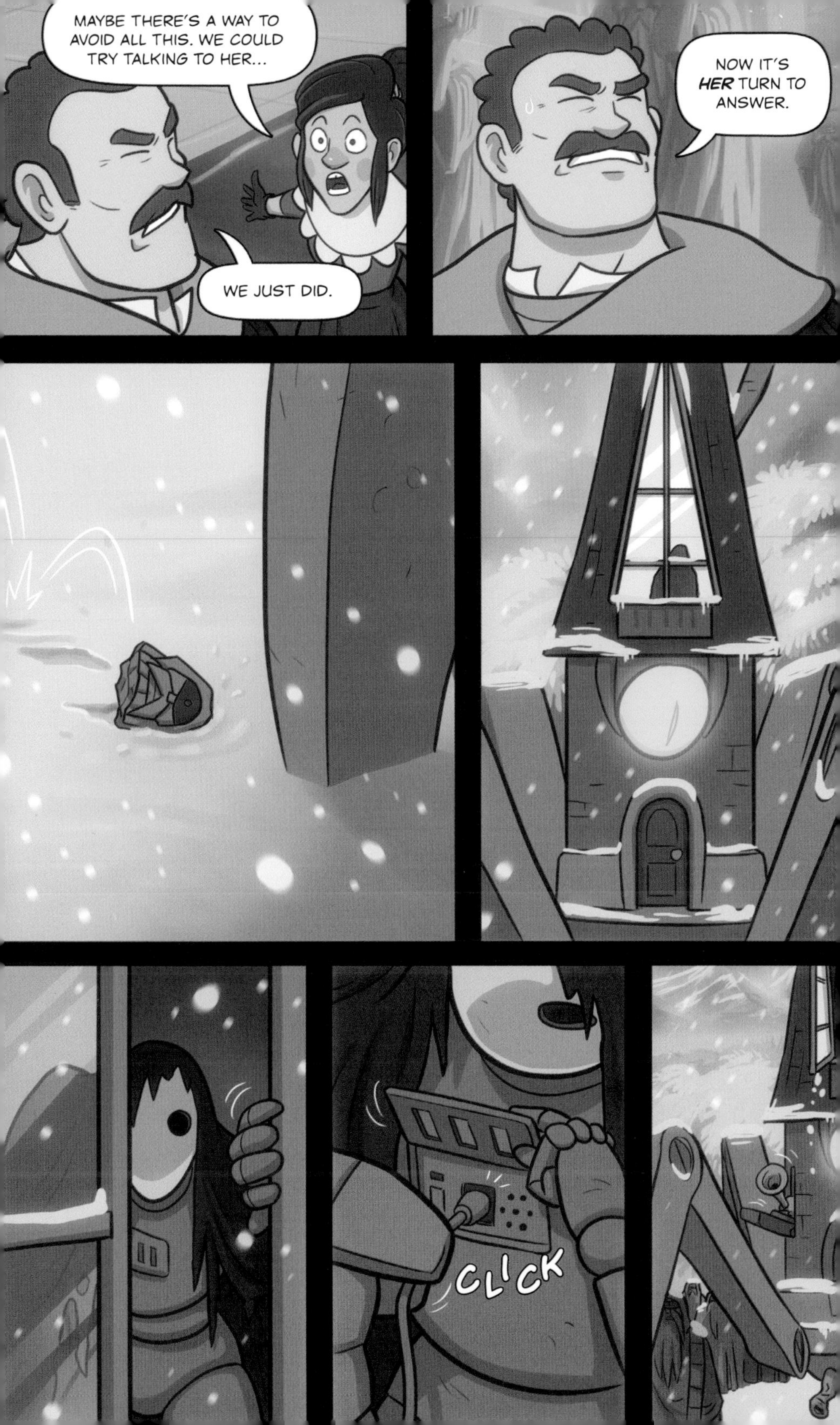
MAYBE THERE'S A WAY TO AVOID ALL THIS. WE COULD TRY TALKING TO HER...
WE JUST DID.
NOW IT'S **HER** TURN TO ANSWER.
CLICK

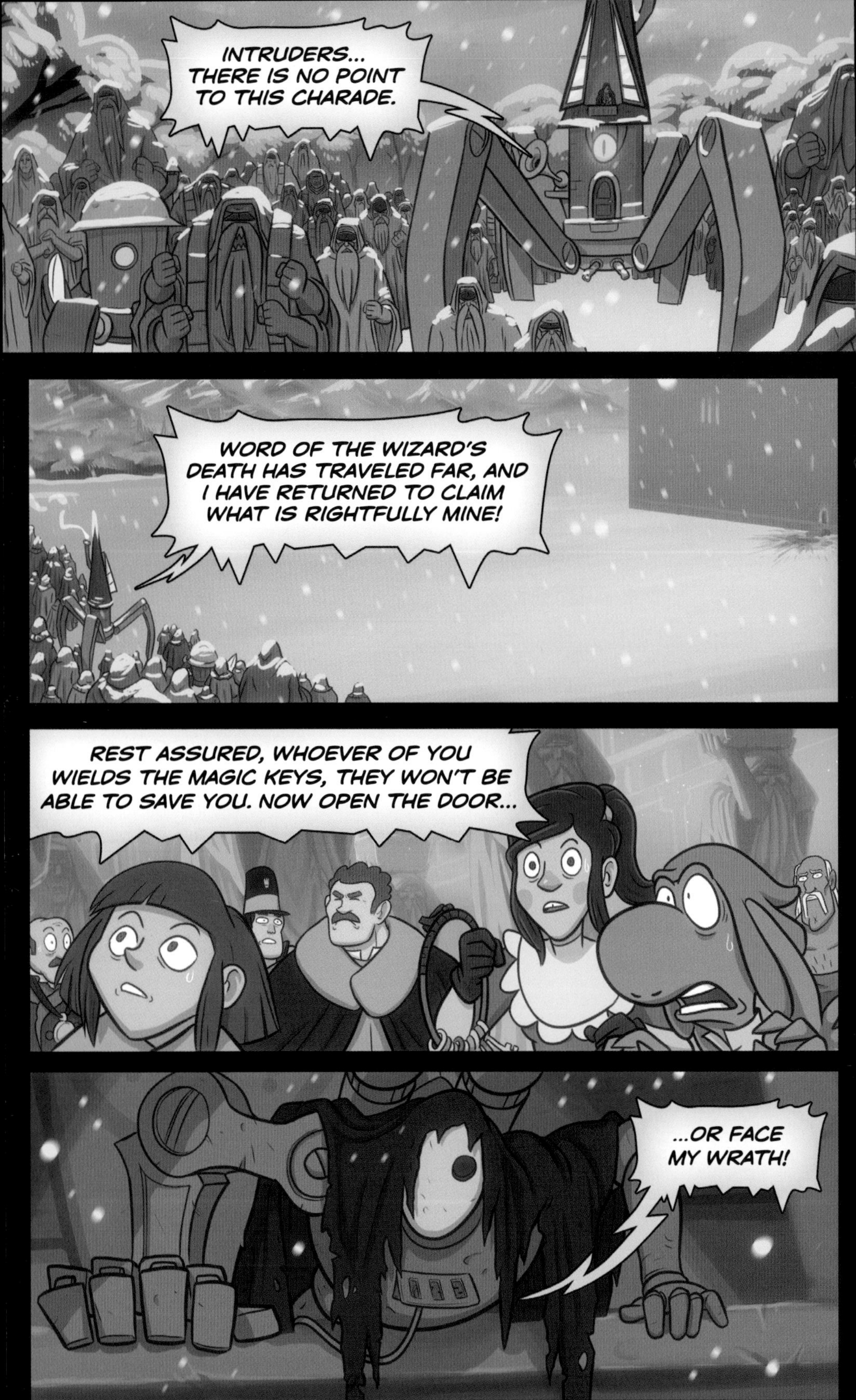
INTRUDERS... THERE IS NO POINT TO THIS CHARADE.
WORD OF THE WIZARD'S DEATH HAS TRAVELED FAR, AND I HAVE RETURNED TO CLAIM WHAT IS RIGHTFULLY MINE!
REST ASSURED, WHOEVER OF YOU WIELDS THE MAGIC KEYS, THEY WON'T BE ABLE TO SAVE YOU. NOW OPEN THE DOOR...
...OR FACE MY WRATH!

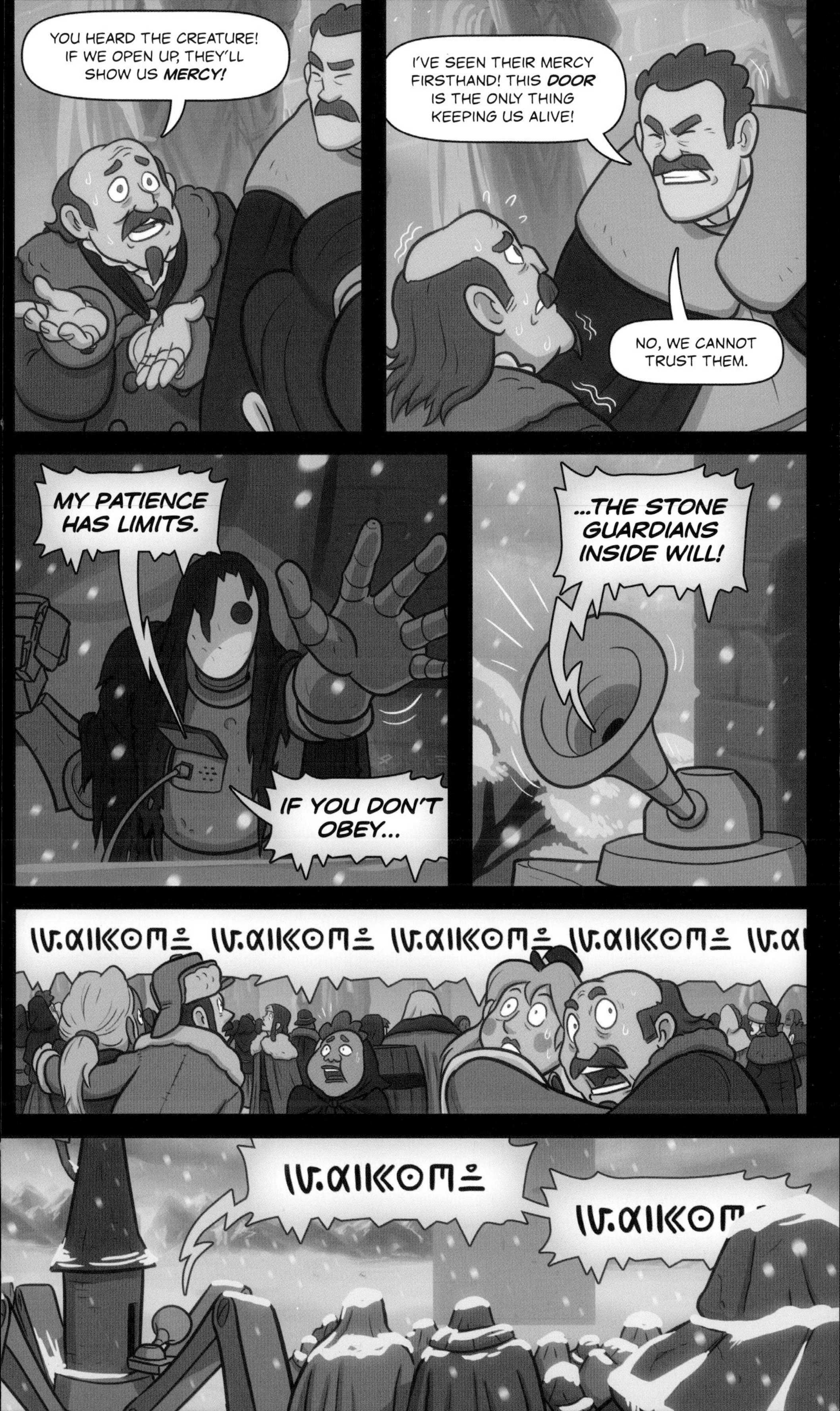
YOU HEARD THE CREATURE! IF WE OPEN UP, THEY'LL SHOW US MERCY!
I'VE SEEN THEIR MERCY FIRSTHAND! THIS DOOR IS THE ONLY THING KEEPING US ALIVE!
NO, WE CANNOT TRUST THEM.
MY PATIENCE HAS LIMITS.
IF YOU DON'T OBEY...
...THE STONE GUARDIANS INSIDE WILL!

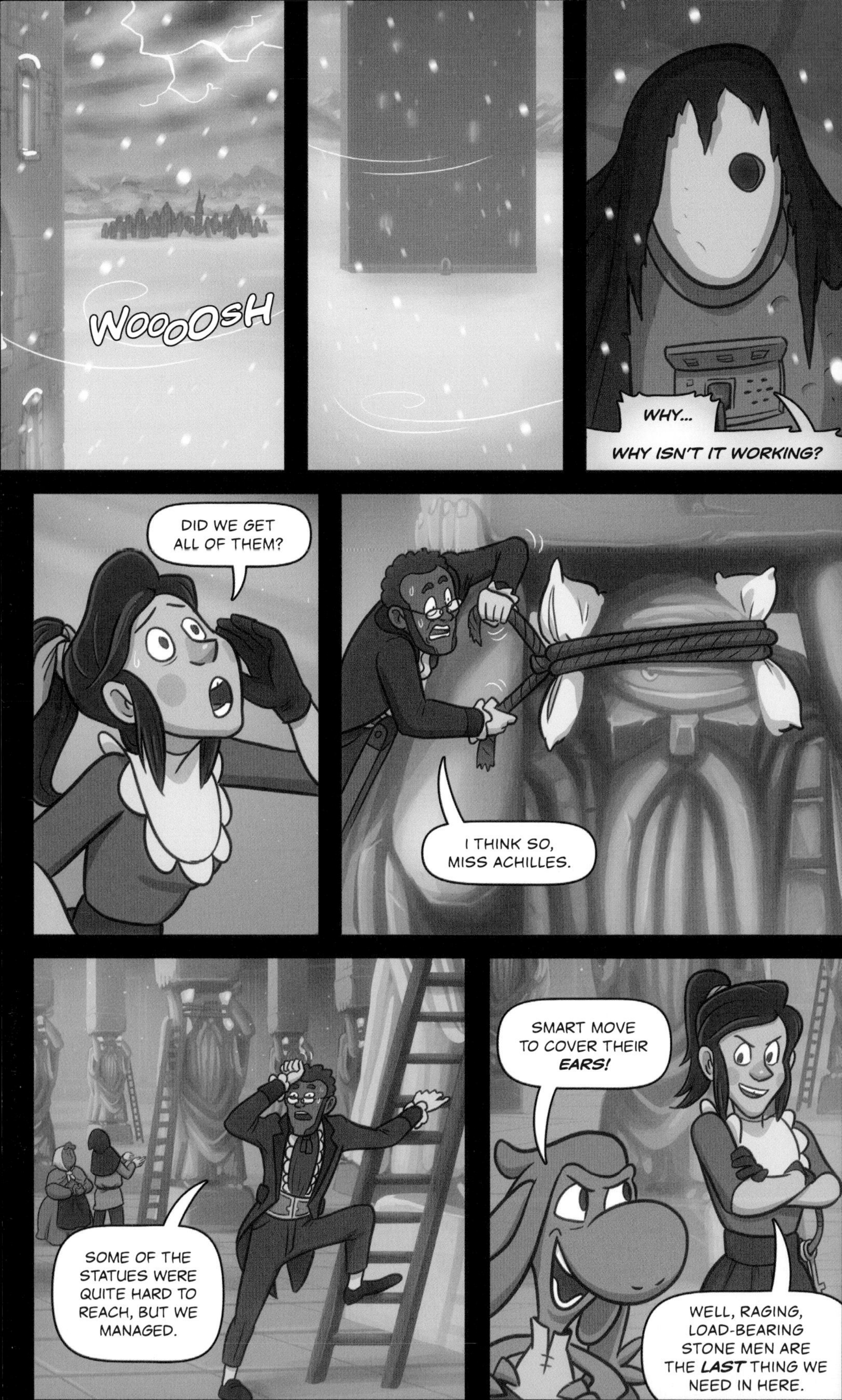
WOOOOOSH
WHY...
WHY ISN'T IT WORKING?
DID WE GET ALL OF THEM?
I THINK SO, MISS ACHILLES.
SOME OF THE STATUES WERE QUITE HARD TO REACH, BUT WE MANAGED.
SMART MOVE TO COVER THEIR EARS!
WELL, RAGING, LOAD-BEARING STONE MEN ARE THE LAST THING WE NEED IN HERE.

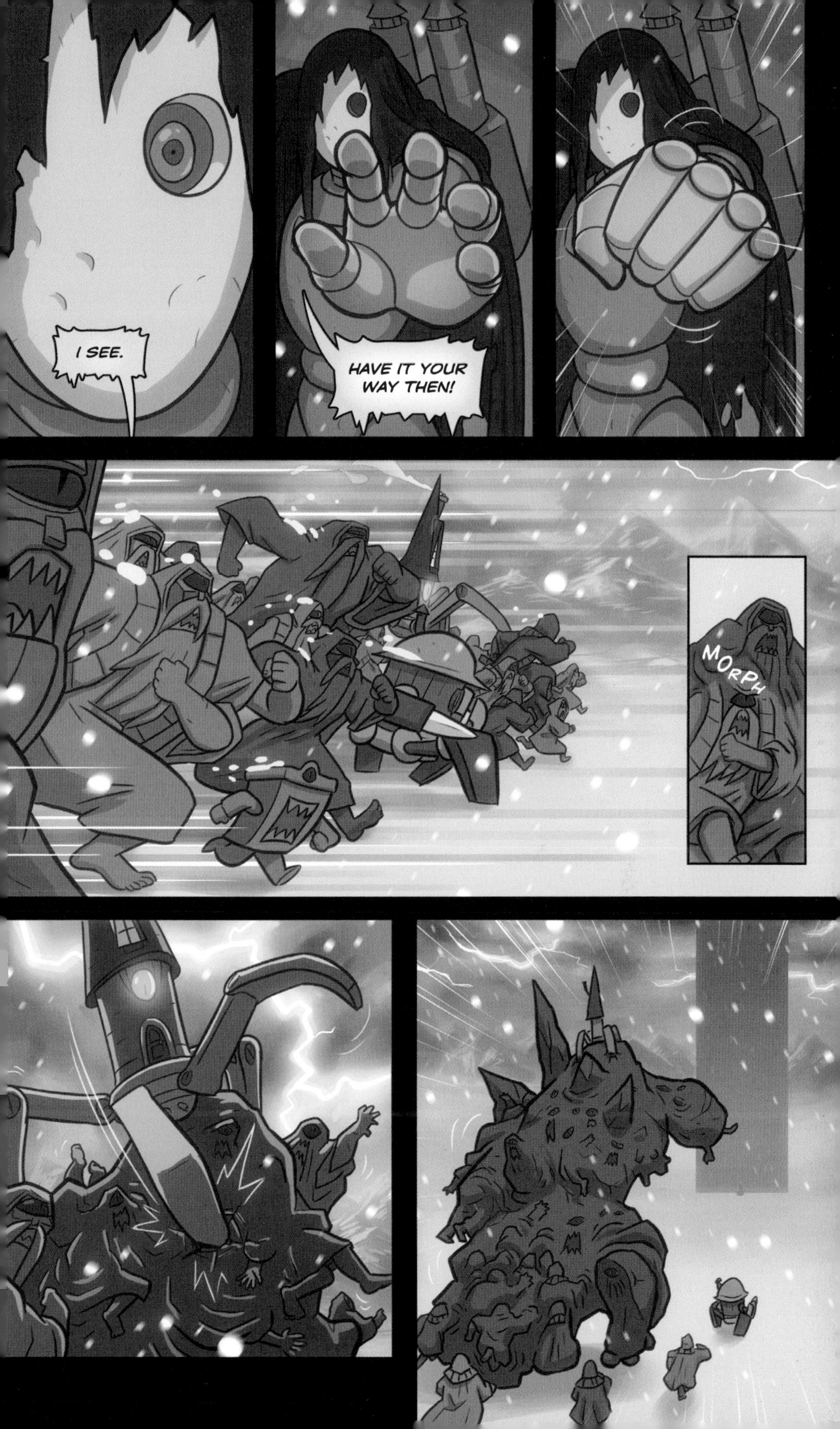
I SEE.
HAVE IT YOUR WAY THEN!
MORPH

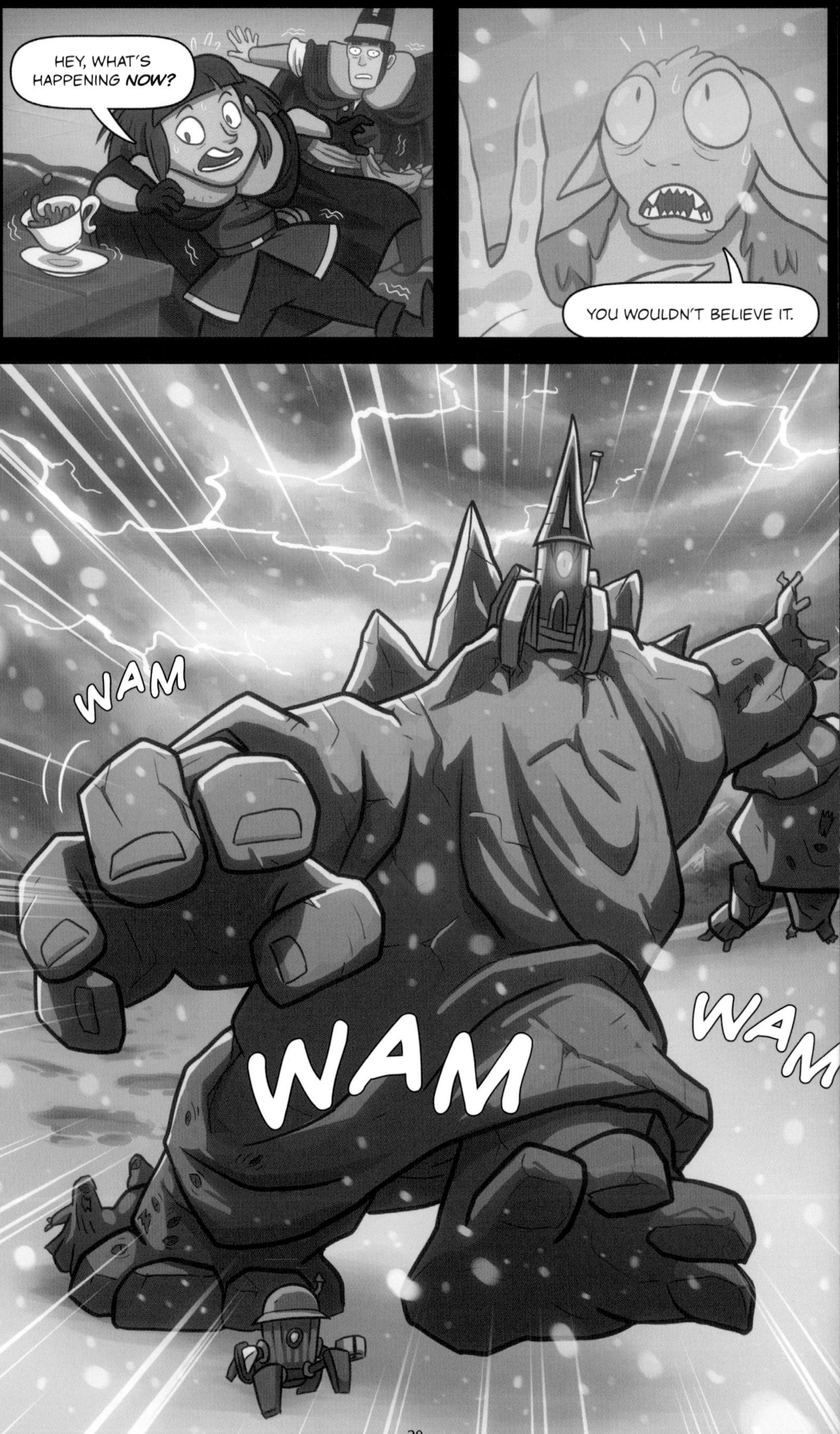
HEY, WHAT'S HAPPENING **NOW?**
YOU WOULDN'T BELIEVE IT.
WAM
WAM
WAM

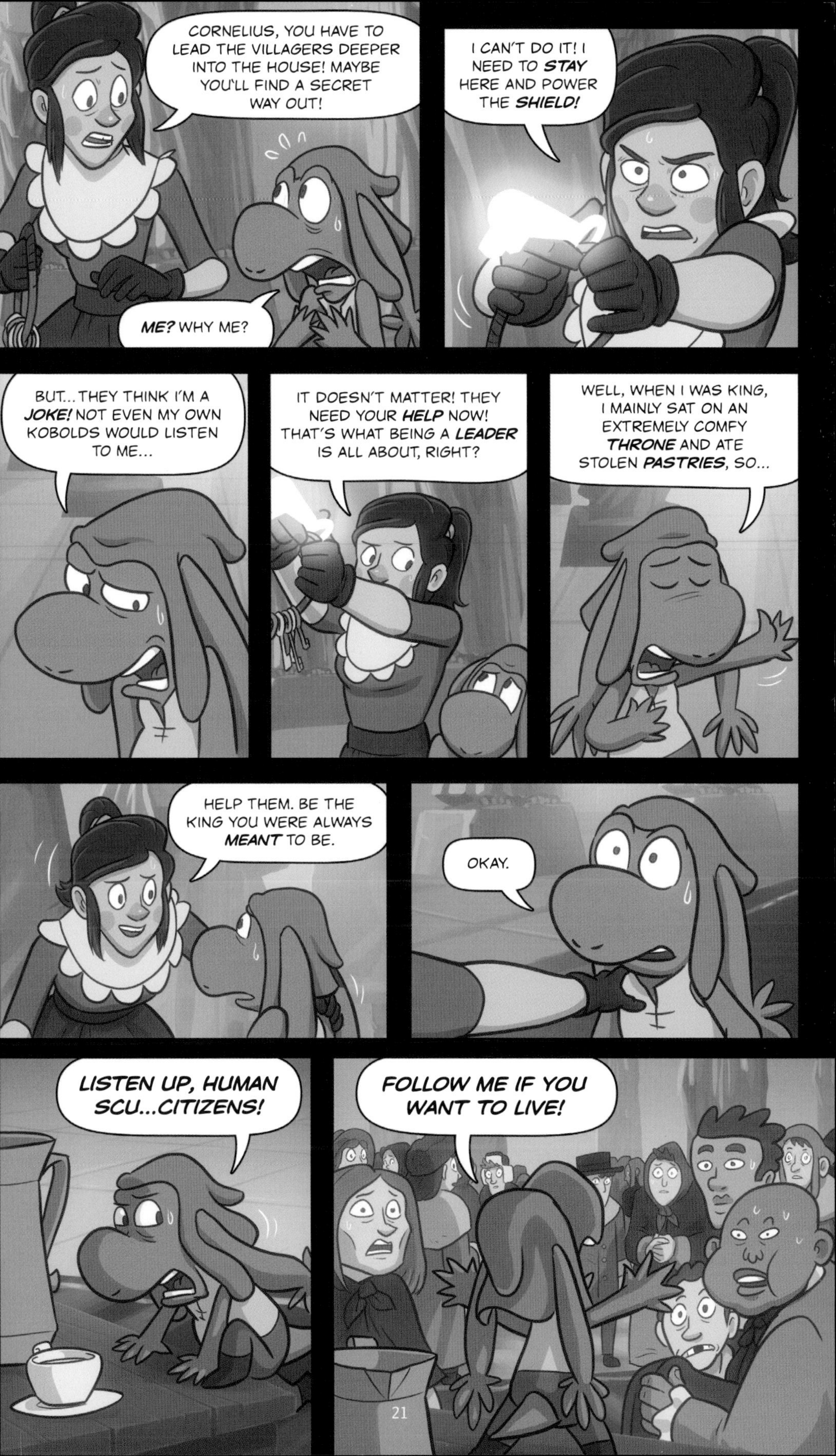
CORNELIUS, YOU HAVE TO LEAD THE VILLAGERS DEEPER INTO THE HOUSE! MAYBE YOU'LL FIND A SECRET WAY OUT!
ME? WHY ME?
I CAN'T DO IT! I NEED TO STAY HERE AND POWER THE SHIELD!
BUT... THEY THINK I'M A JOKE! NOT EVEN MY OWN KOBOLDS WOULD LISTEN TO ME...
IT DOESN'T MATTER! THEY NEED YOUR HELP NOW! THAT'S WHAT BEING A LEADER IS ALL ABOUT, RIGHT?
WELL, WHEN I WAS KING, I MAINLY SAT ON AN EXTREMELY COMFY THRONE AND ATE STOLEN PASTRIES, SO...
HELP THEM. BE THE KING YOU WERE ALWAYS MEANT TO BE.
OKAY.
LISTEN UP, HUMAN SCU...CITIZENS!
FOLLOW ME IF YOU WANT TO LIVE!

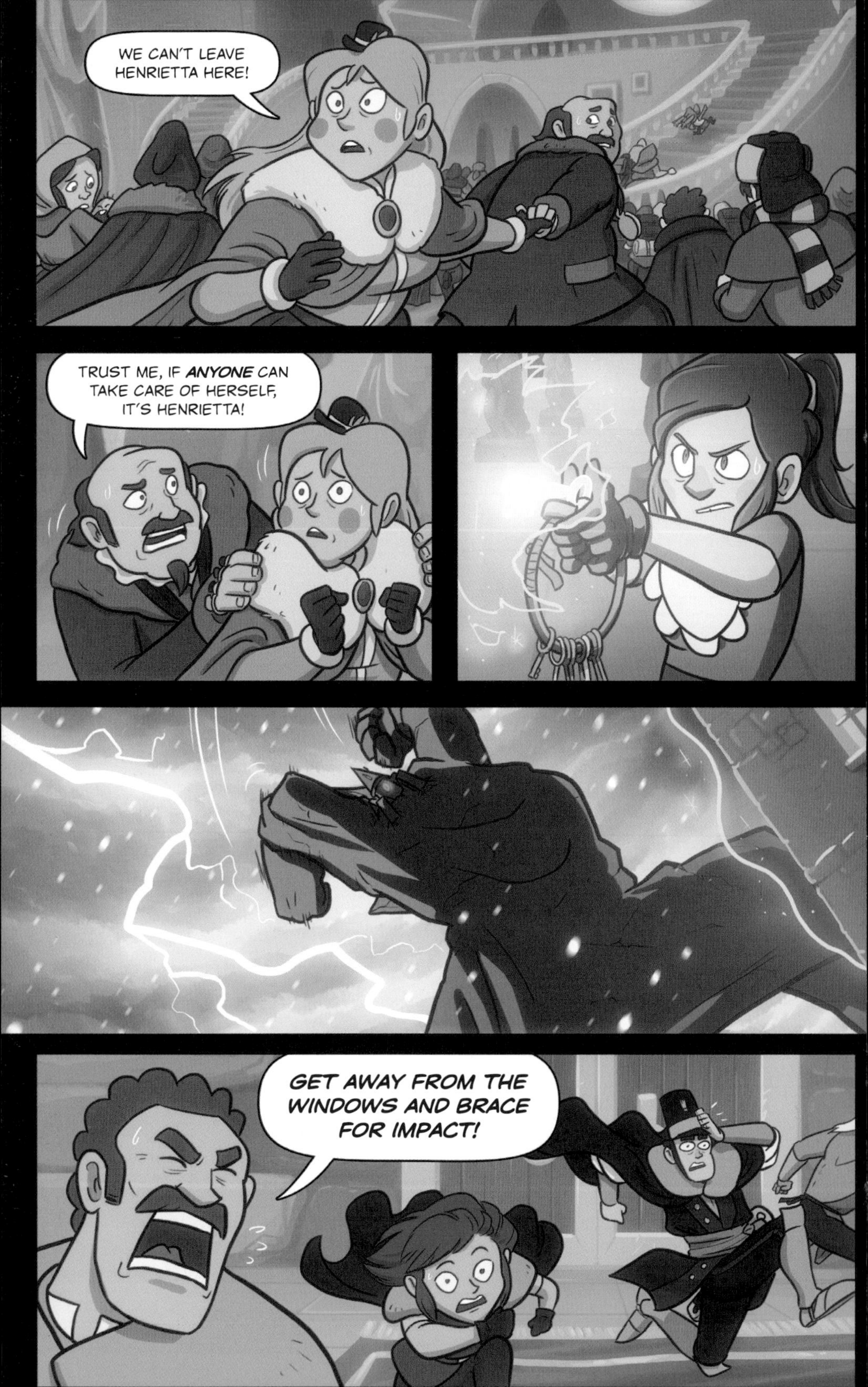
WE CAN'T LEAVE HENRIETTA HERE!
TRUST ME, IF ANYONE CAN TAKE CARE OF HERSELF, IT'S HENRIETTA!
GET AWAY FROM THE WINDOWS AND BRACE FOR IMPACT!

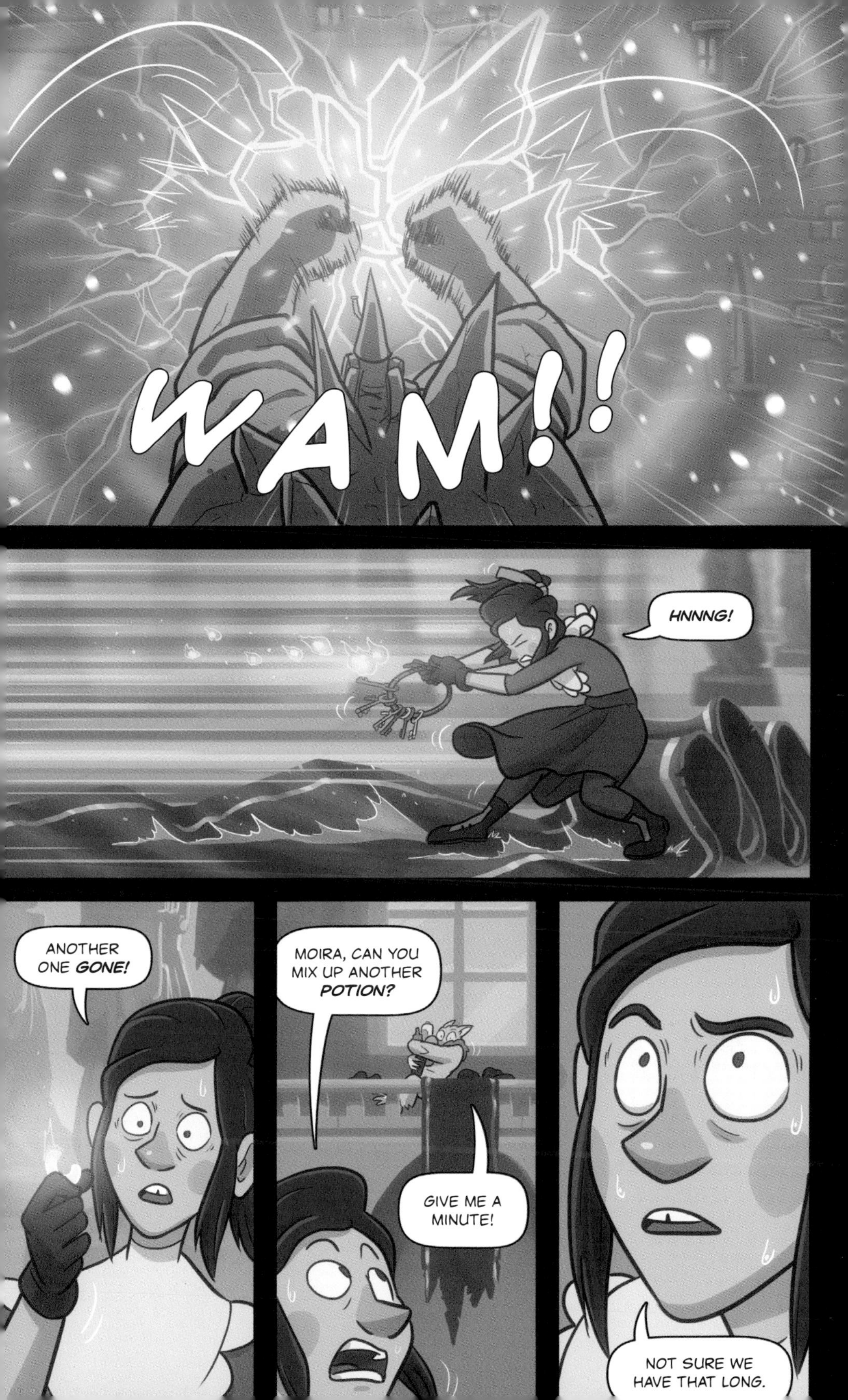
WAM!!
HNNNG!
ANOTHER ONE **GONE!**
MOIRA, CAN YOU MIX UP ANOTHER **POTION?**
GIVE ME A MINUTE!
NOT SURE WE HAVE THAT LONG.

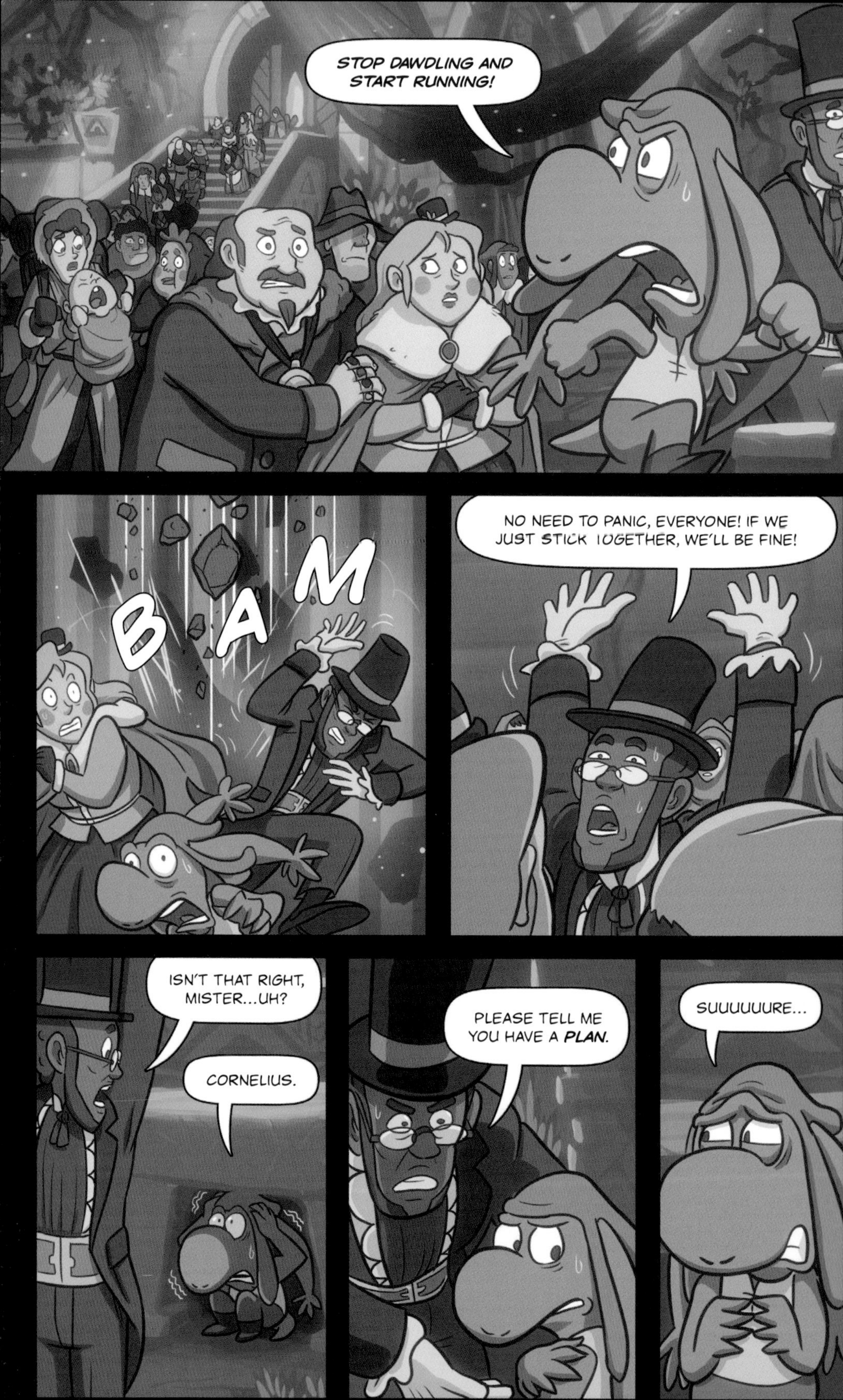
STOP DAWDLING AND START RUNNING!
BAM
NO NEED TO PANIC, EVERYONE! IF WE JUST STICK TOGETHER, WE'LL BE FINE!
ISN'T THAT RIGHT, MISTER...UH?
CORNELIUS.
PLEASE TELL ME YOU HAVE A *PLAN*.
SUUUUUURE...

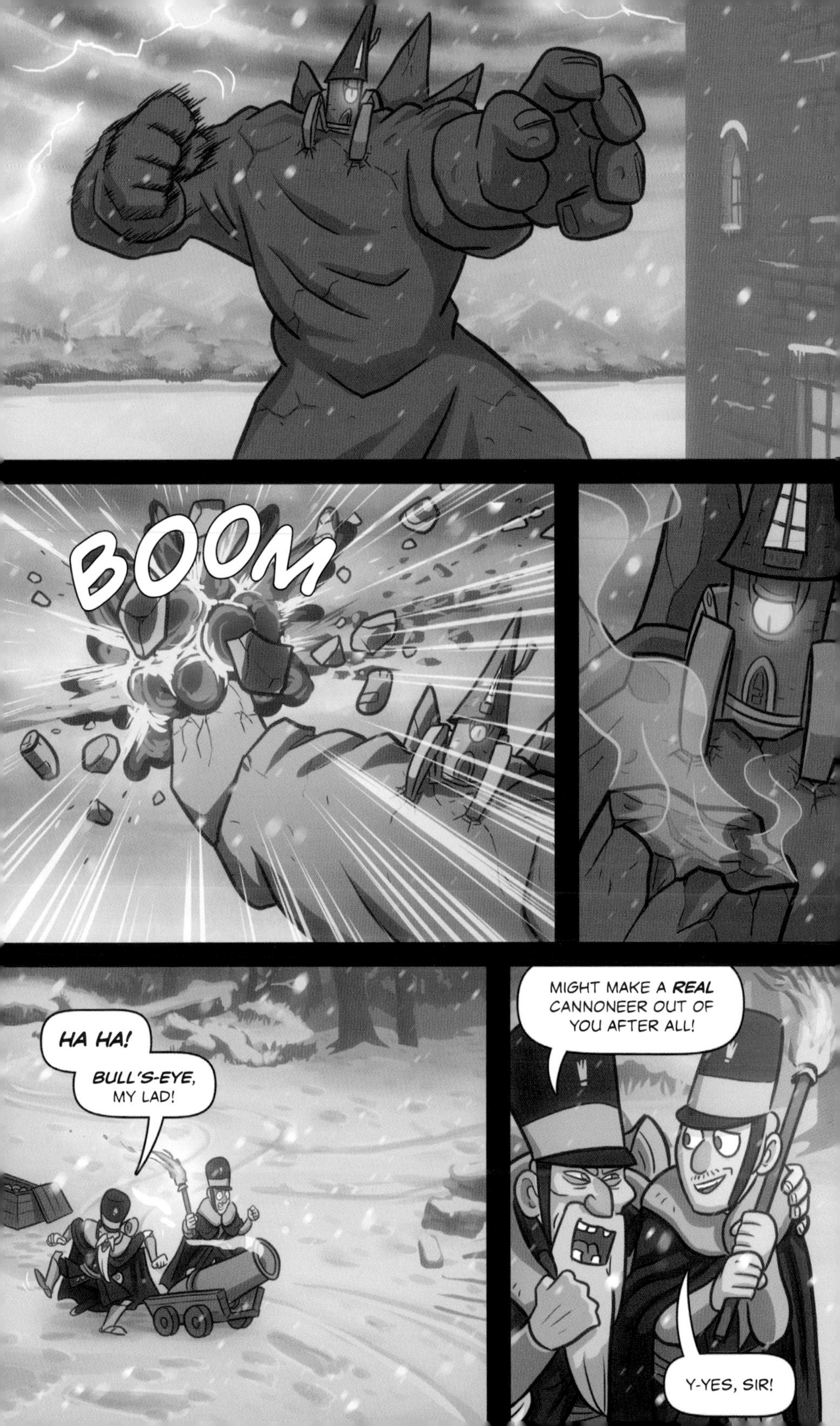
BOOM
HA HA!
BULL'S-EYE, MY LAD!
MIGHT MAKE A REAL CANNONEER OUT OF YOU AFTER ALL!
Y-YES, SIR!

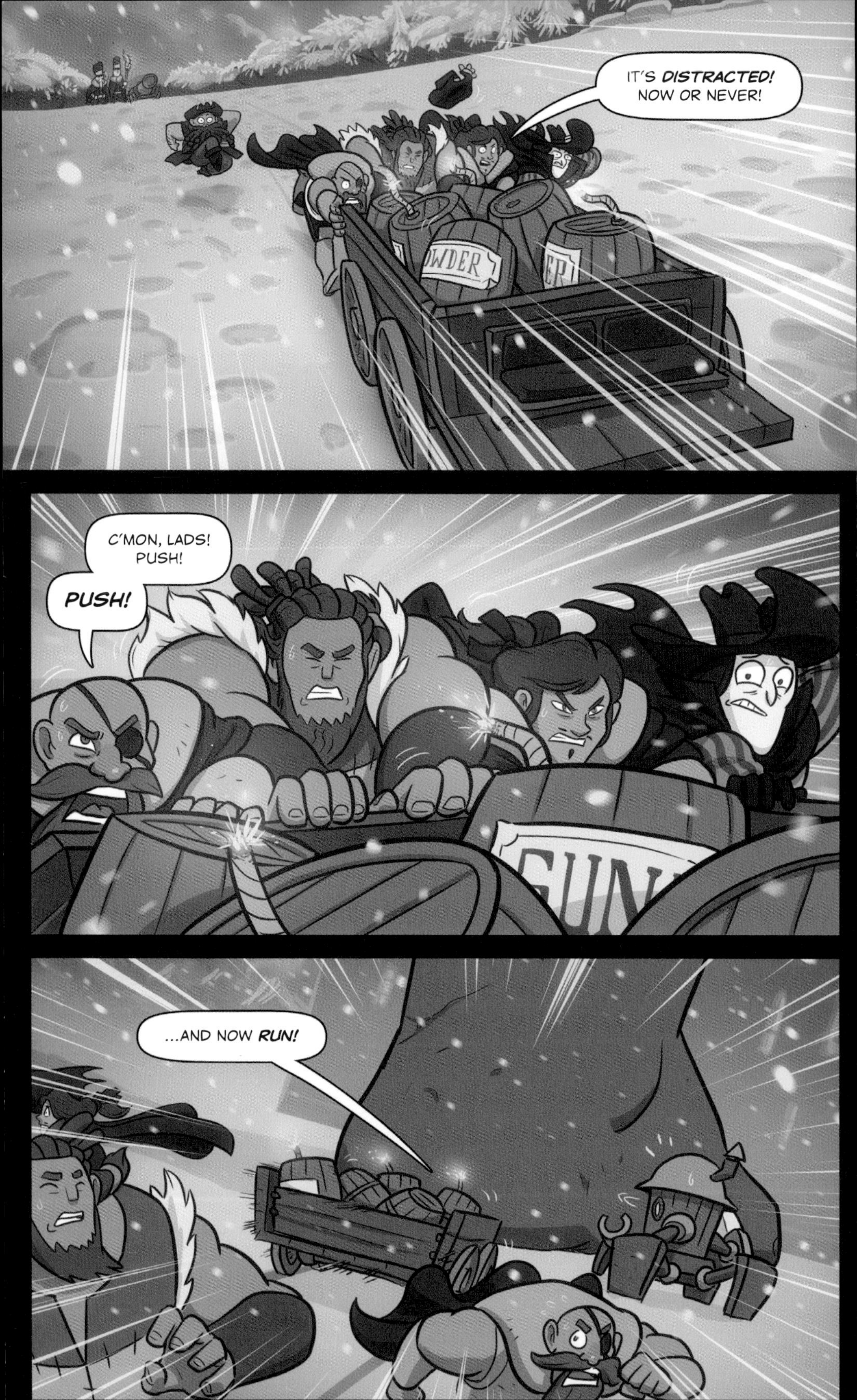
IT'S **DISTRACTED!** NOW OR NEVER!
C'MON, LADS! PUSH!
PUSH!
...AND NOW **RUN!**

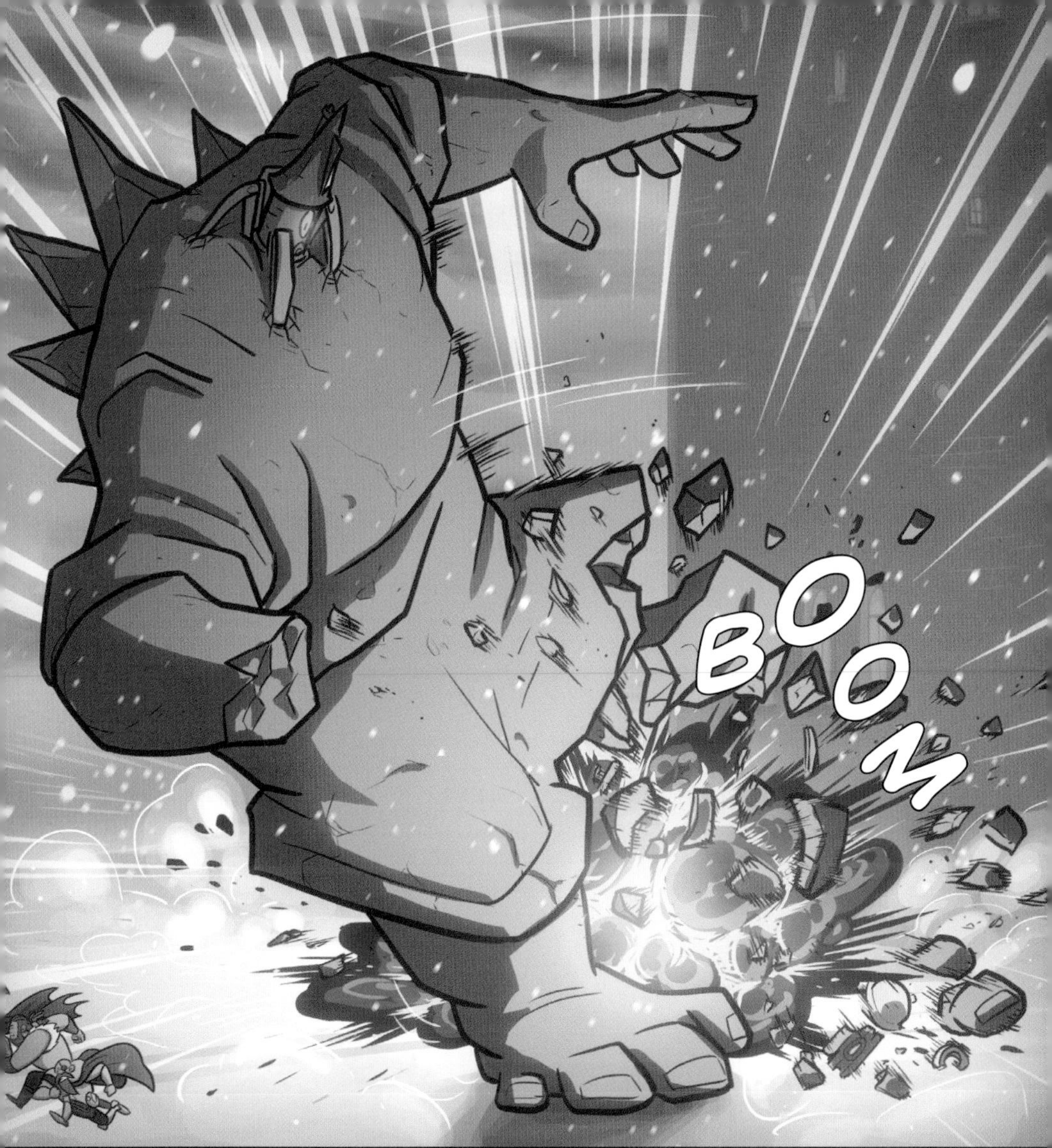
BOOM

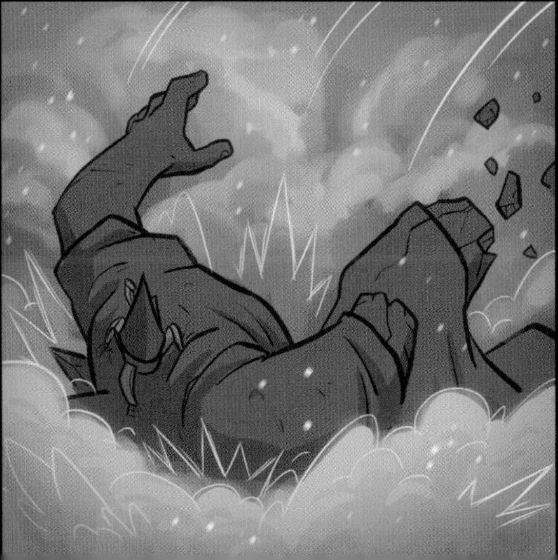

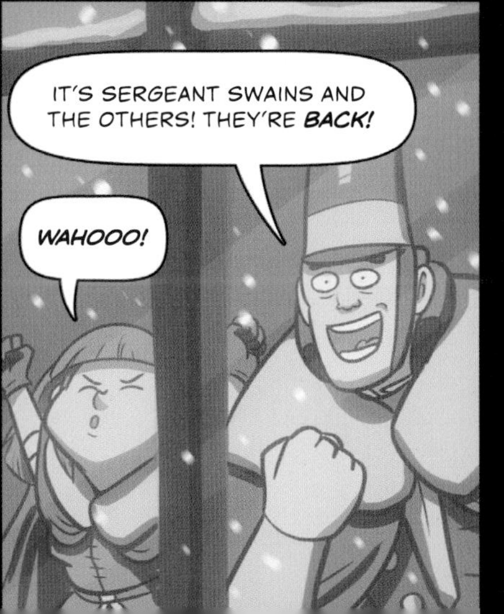
IT'S SERGEANT SWAINS AND THE OTHERS! THEY'RE ***BACK!***
WAHOOO!

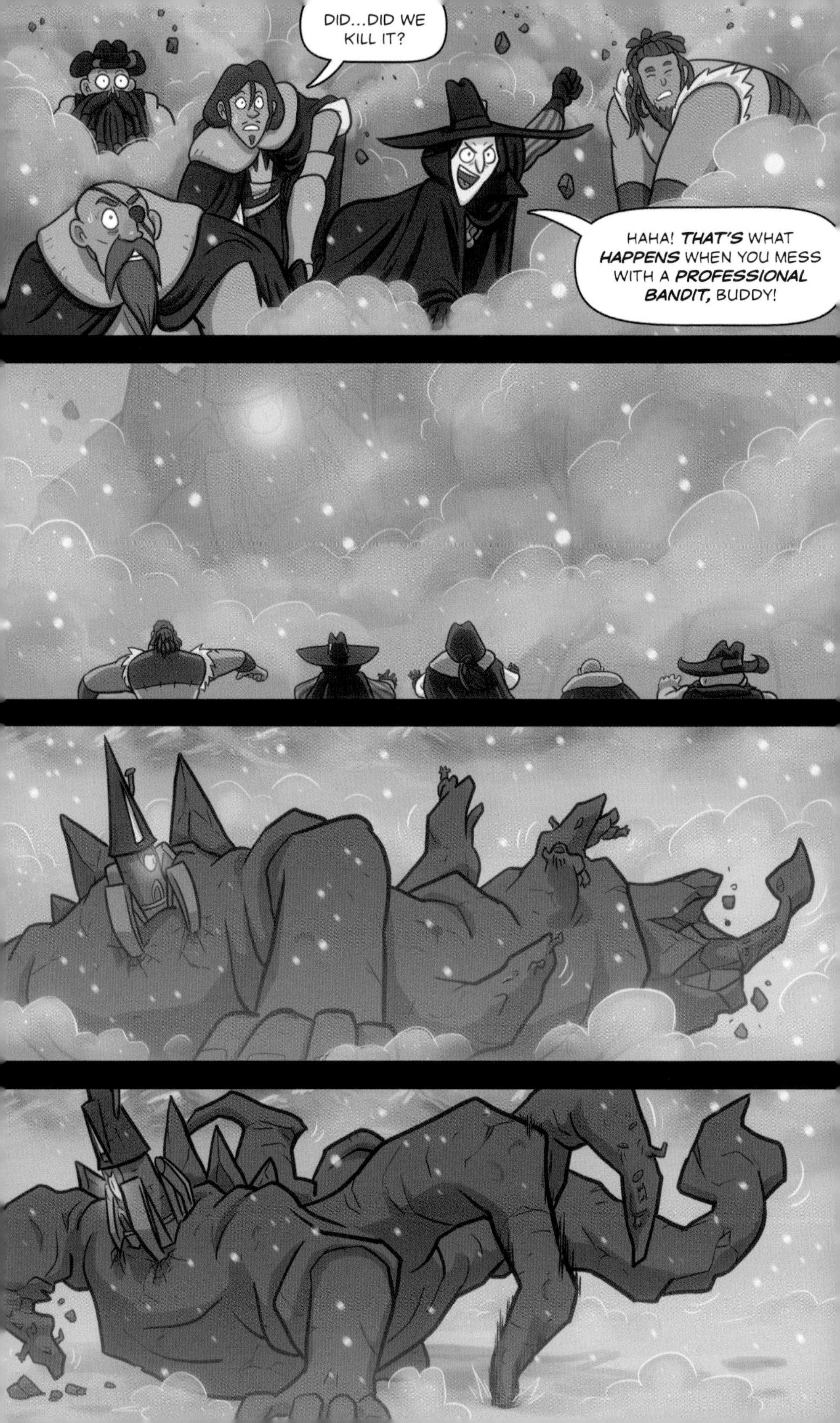
DID...DID WE KILL IT?
HAHA! **THAT'S** WHAT **HAPPENS** WHEN YOU MESS WITH A **PROFESSIONAL BANDIT,** BUDDY!

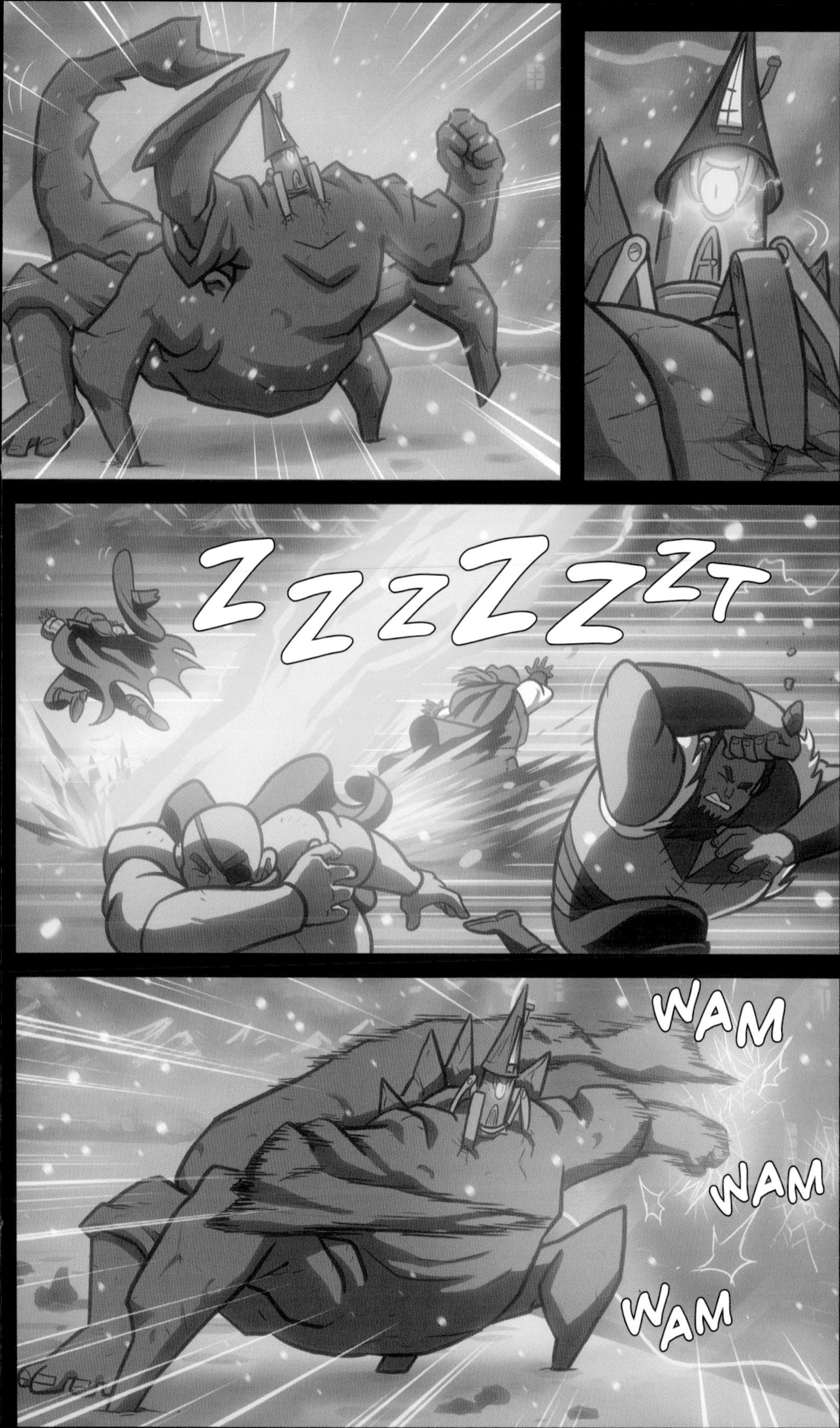
ZZZZZZZT
WAM
WAM
WAM

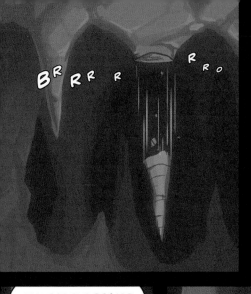

BR R R R R RO

CRACK

MY LIEGE, THE **ESCAPE TUNNEL** IS READY! WE CAN LEAVE AS SOON AS YOU GIVE THE WORD!

MY LIEGE?

THE PEOPLE AWAIT THEIR KING'S COMMAND.

YES...OF COURSE...

...BUT SOMETIMES I THINK...

...IN **ANOTHER** LIFE...

...I WOULD HAVE MADE A PRETTY FINE **BANDIT**, TOO.

WANTED

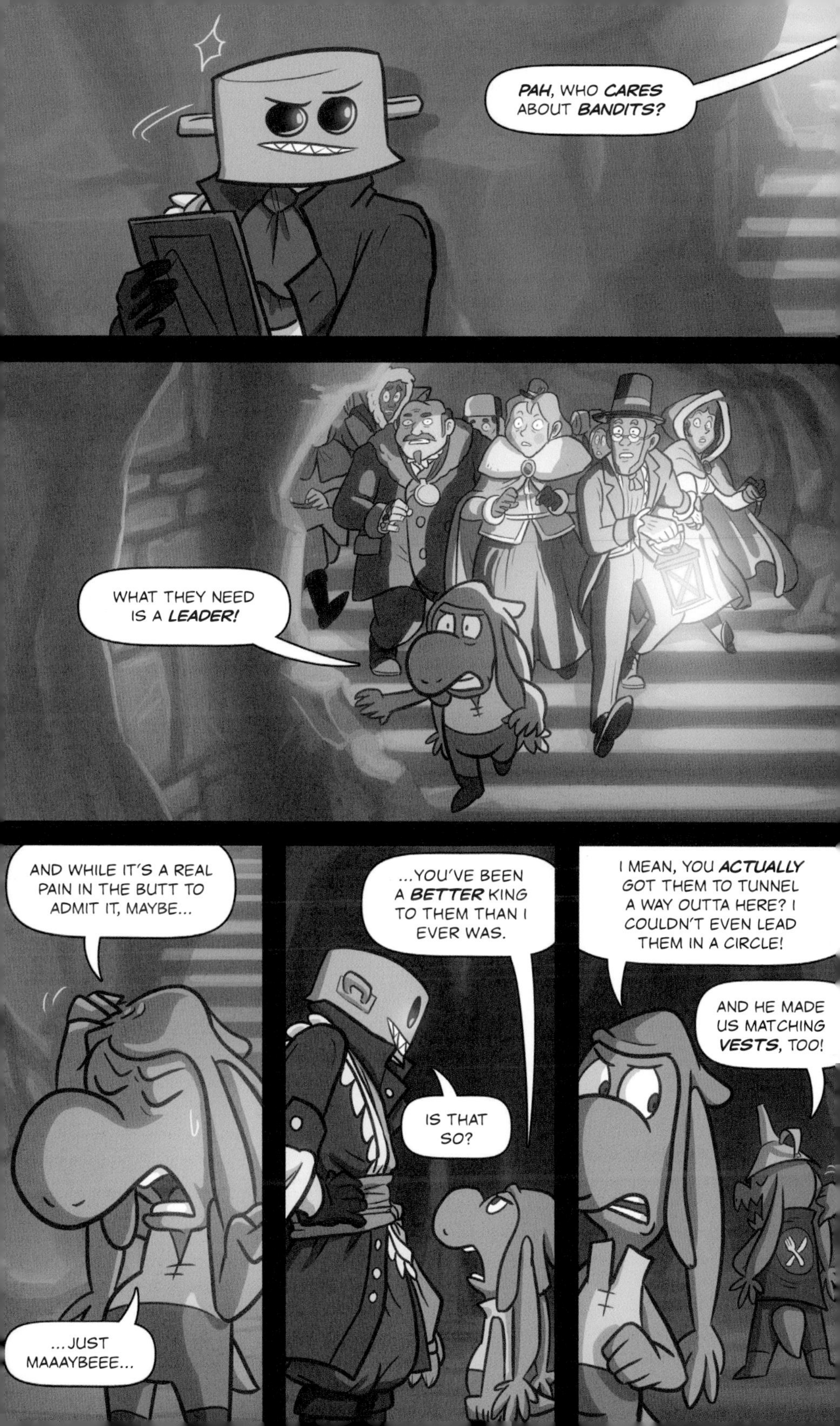
PAH, WHO CARES ABOUT BANDITS?
WHAT THEY NEED IS A LEADER!
AND WHILE IT'S A REAL PAIN IN THE BUTT TO ADMIT IT, MAYBE...
...JUST MAAAYBEEE...
...YOU'VE BEEN A BETTER KING TO THEM THAN I EVER WAS.
IS THAT SO?
I MEAN, YOU ACTUALLY GOT THEM TO TUNNEL A WAY OUTTA HERE? I COULDN'T EVEN LEAD THEM IN A CIRCLE!
AND HE MADE US MATCHING VESTS, TOO!

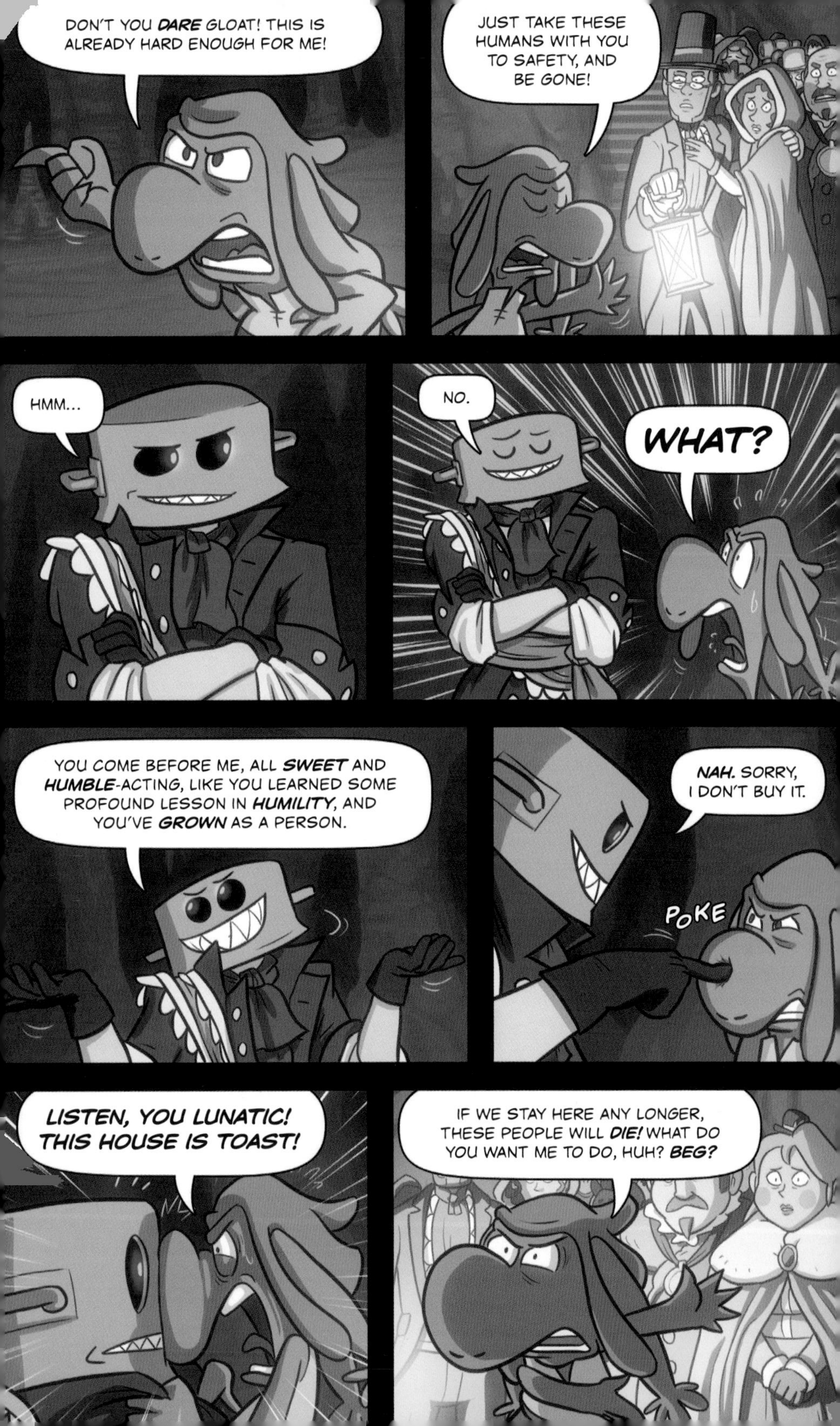

DON'T YOU DARE GLOAT! THIS IS ALREADY HARD ENOUGH FOR ME!
JUST TAKE THESE HUMANS WITH YOU TO SAFETY, AND BE GONE!
HMM...
NO.
WHAT?
YOU COME BEFORE ME, ALL SWEET AND HUMBLE-ACTING, LIKE YOU LEARNED SOME PROFOUND LESSON IN HUMILITY, AND YOU'VE GROWN AS A PERSON.
NAH. SORRY, I DON'T BUY IT.
POKE
LISTEN, YOU LUNATIC! THIS HOUSE IS TOAST!
IF WE STAY HERE ANY LONGER, THESE PEOPLE WILL DIE! WHAT DO YOU WANT ME TO DO, HUH? BEG?

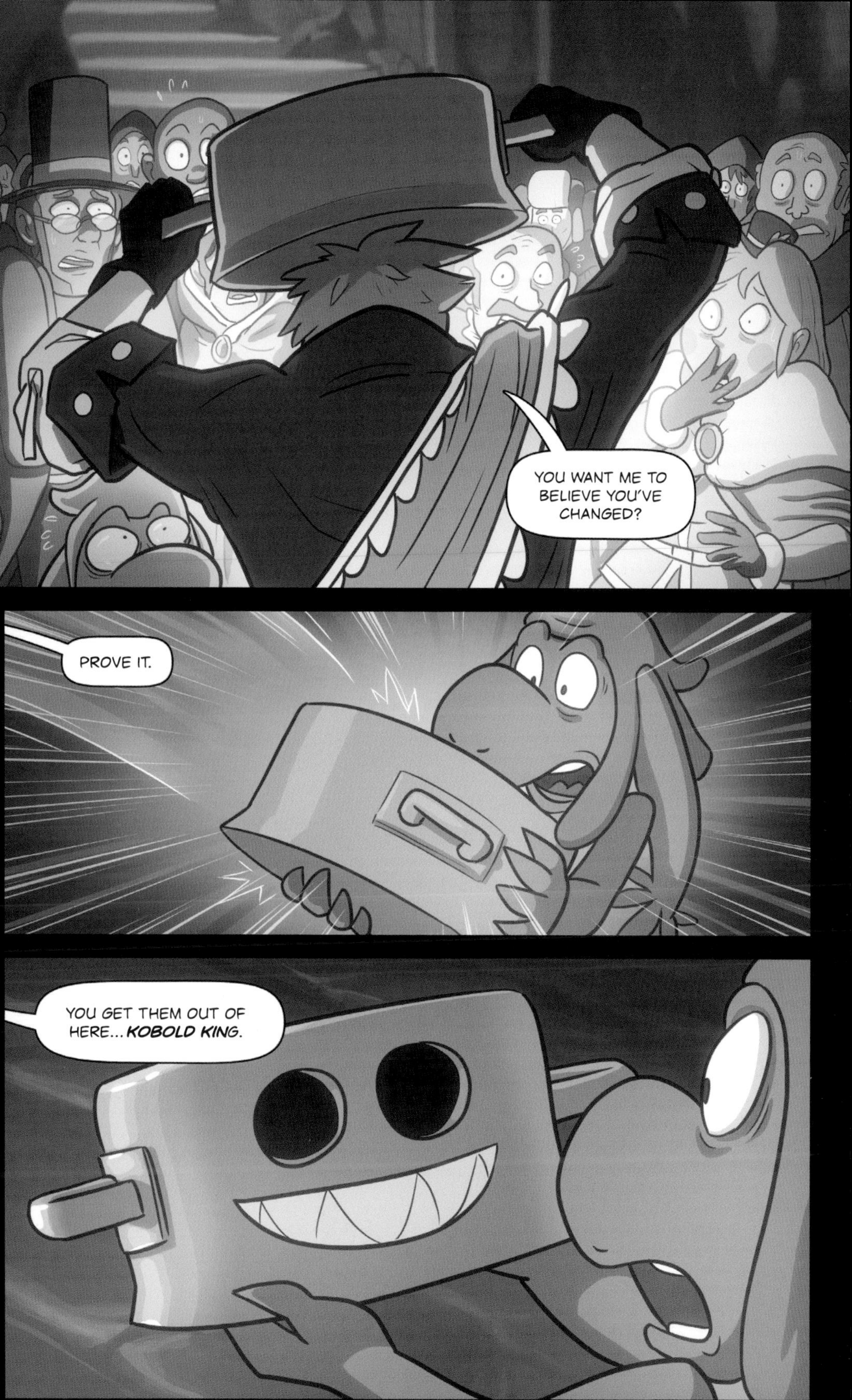
YOU WANT ME TO BELIEVE YOU'VE CHANGED?
PROVE IT.
YOU GET THEM OUT OF HERE... ***KOBOLD KING***.

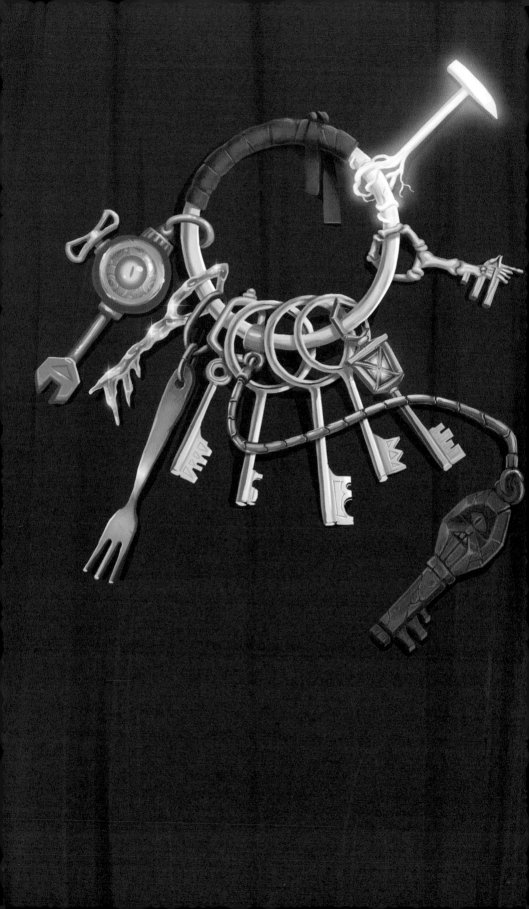

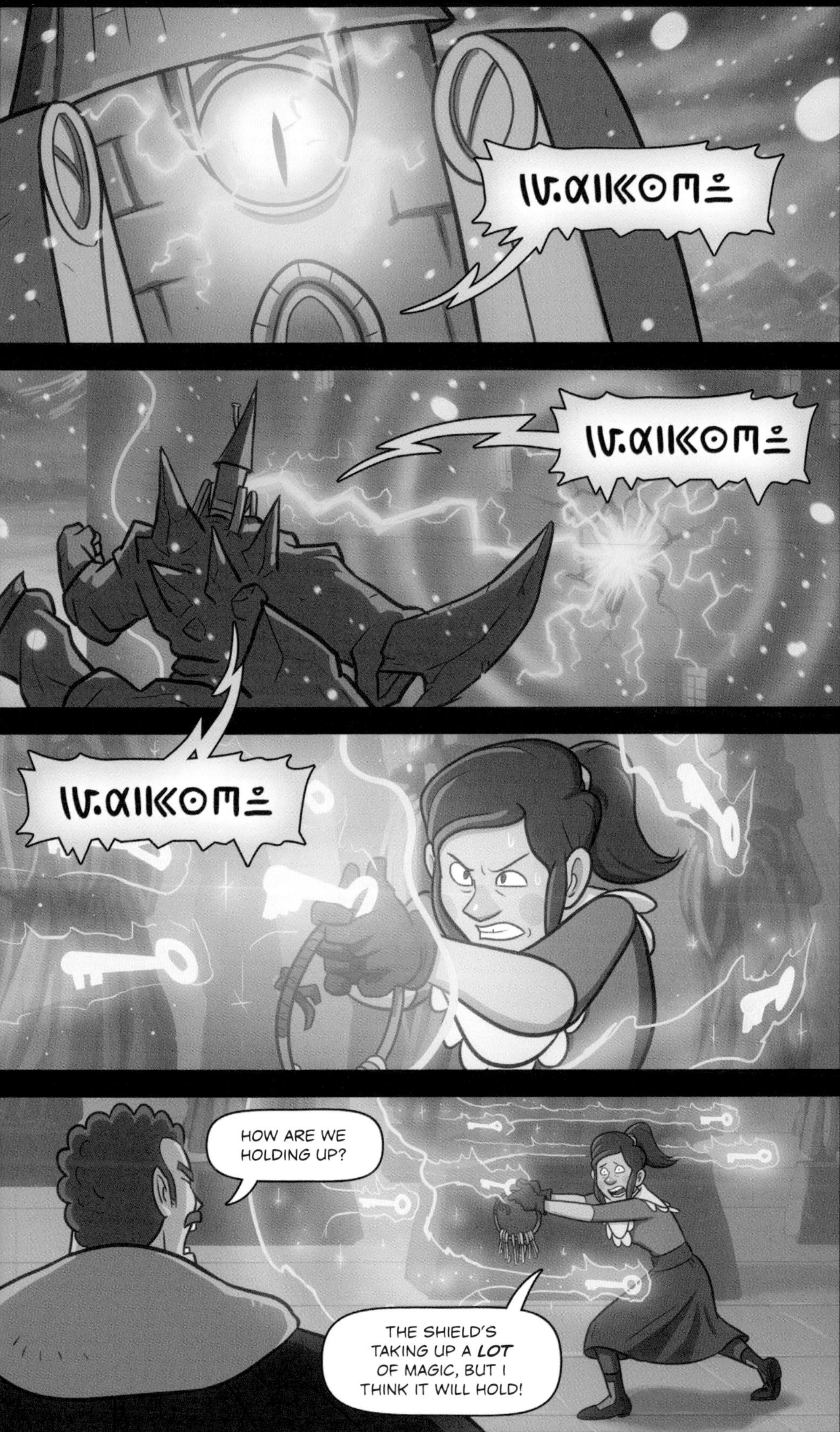
HOW ARE WE HOLDING UP?
THE SHIELD'S TAKING UP A *LOT* OF MAGIC, BUT I THINK IT WILL HOLD!

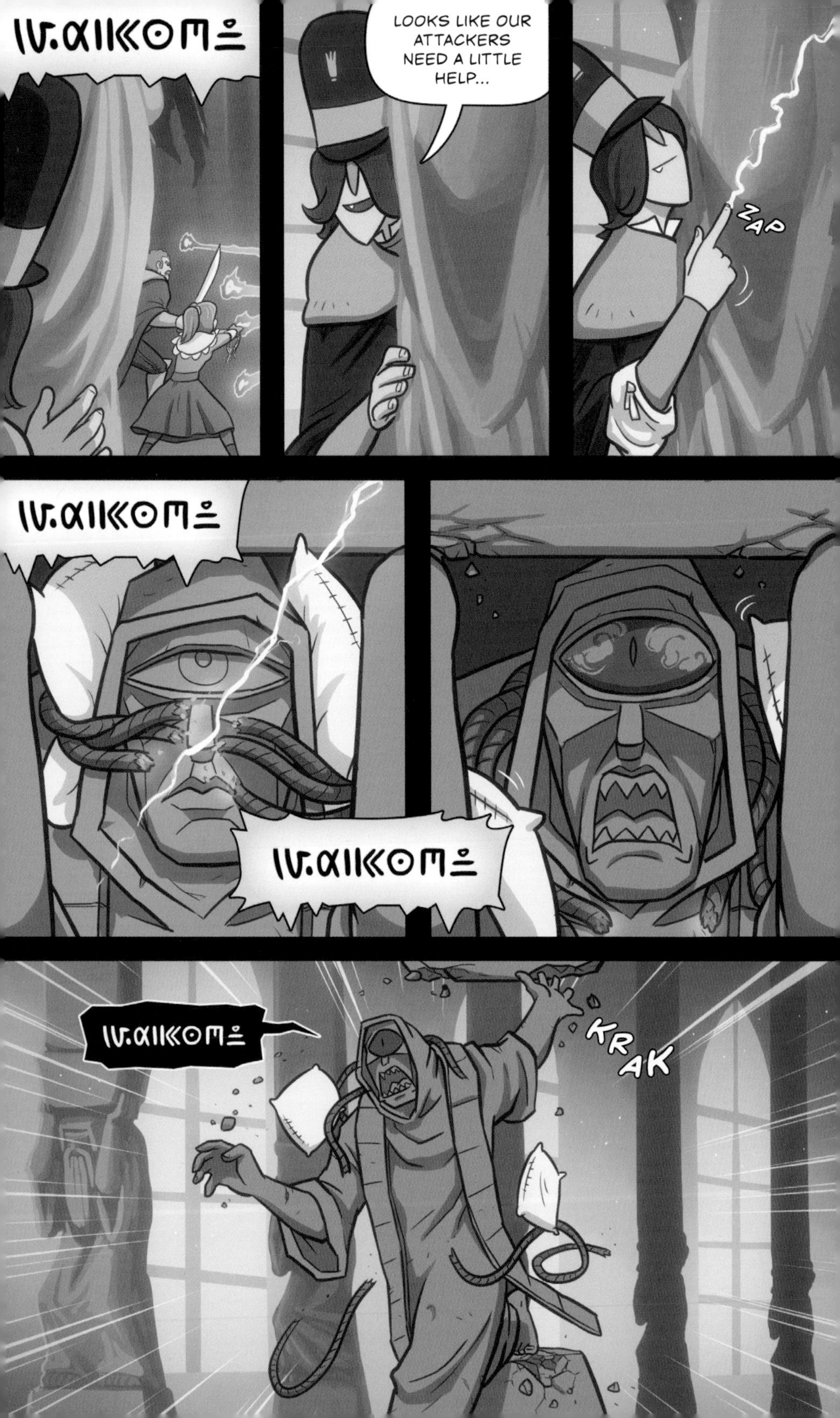
LOOKS LIKE OUR ATTACKERS NEED A LITTLE HELP...
ZAP
KRAK

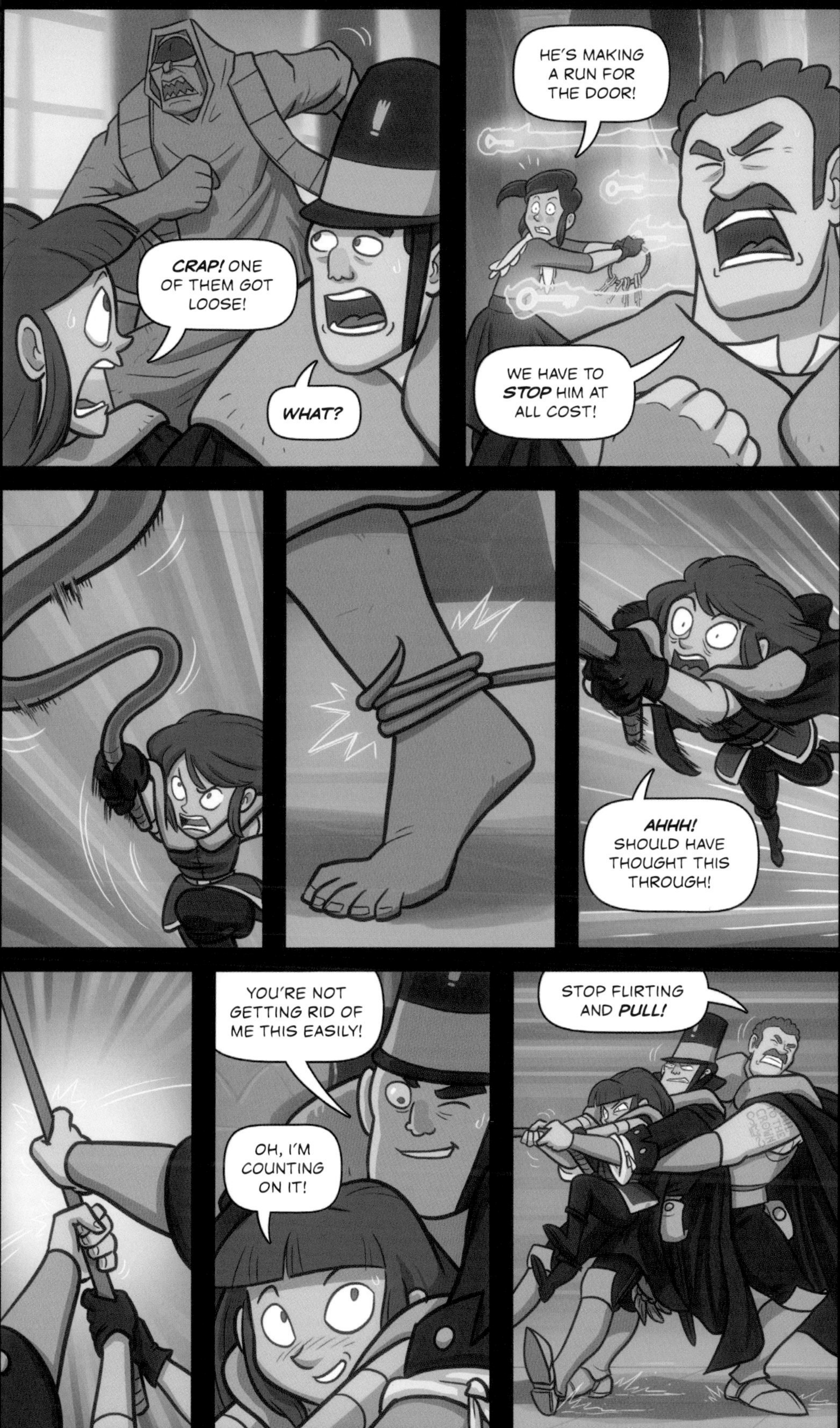
CRAP! ONE OF THEM GOT LOOSE!
WHAT?
HE'S MAKING A RUN FOR THE DOOR!
WE HAVE TO STOP HIM AT ALL COST!
AHHH! SHOULD HAVE THOUGHT THIS THROUGH!
YOU'RE NOT GETTING RID OF ME THIS EASILY!
OH, I'M COUNTING ON IT!
STOP FLIRTING AND PULL!

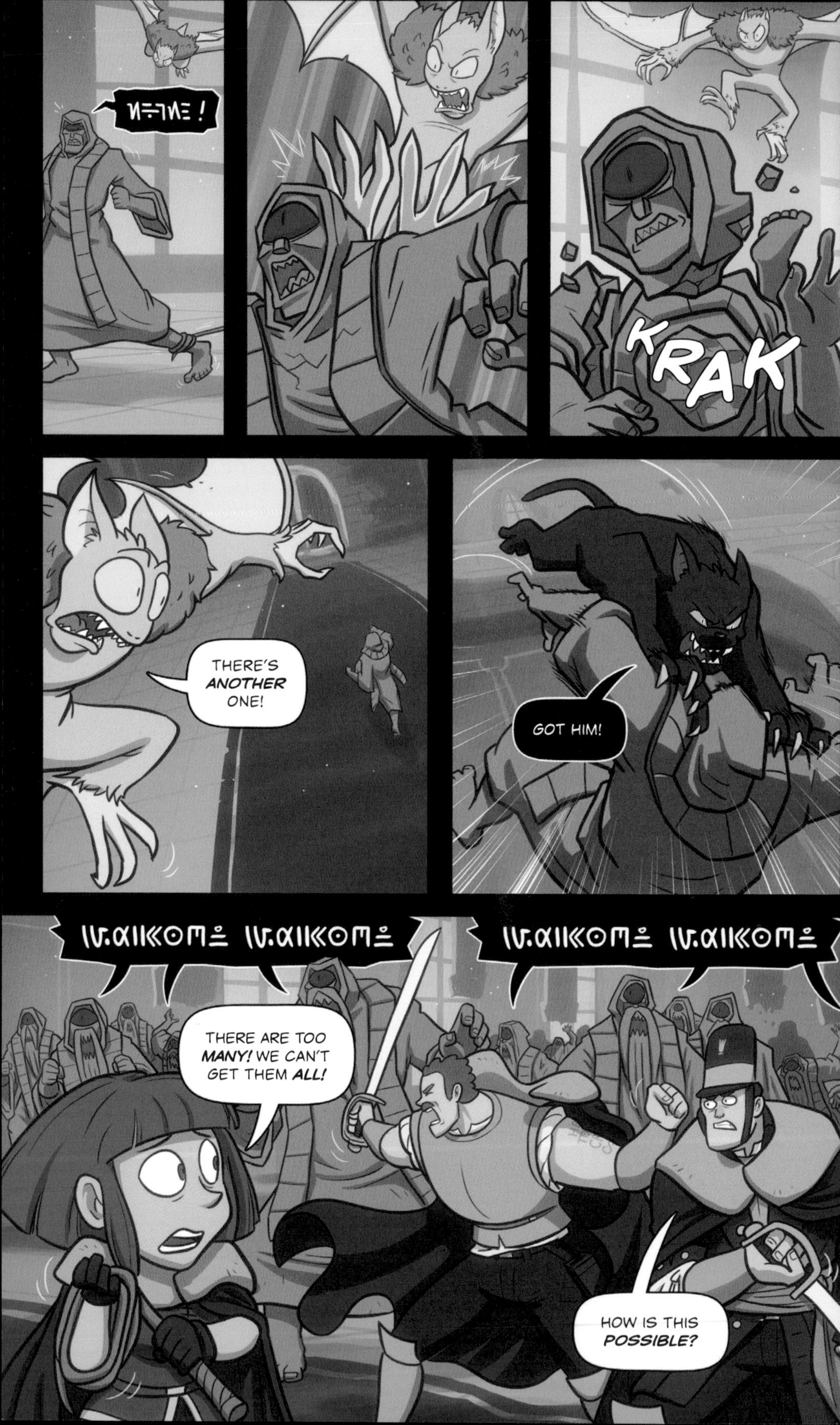
KRAK
THERE'S *ANOTHER* ONE!
GOT HIM!
THERE ARE TOO *MANY!* WE CAN'T GET THEM *ALL!*
HOW IS THIS *POSSIBLE?*

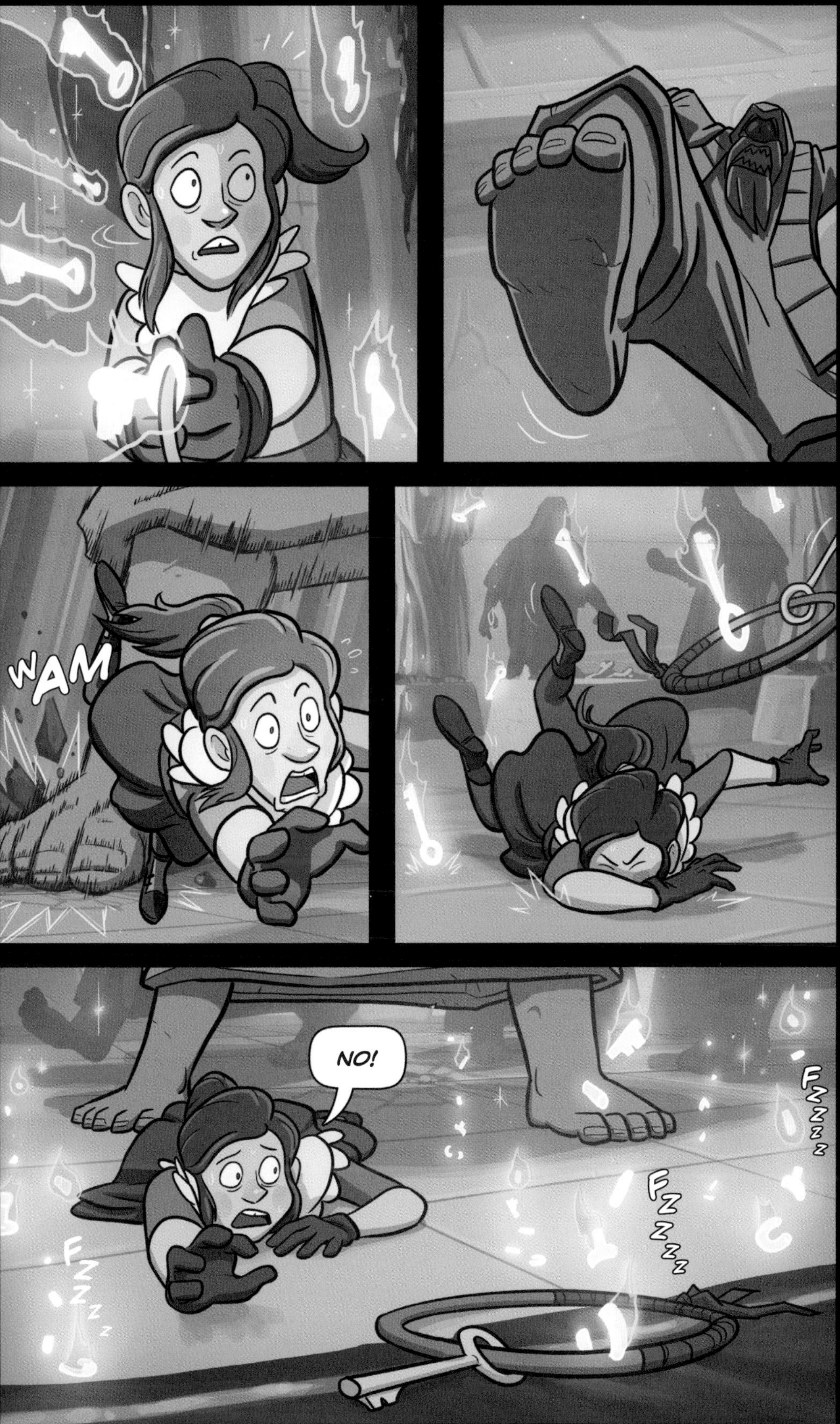
WAM
NO!
FZZZZ
FZZZZ
FZZZZ

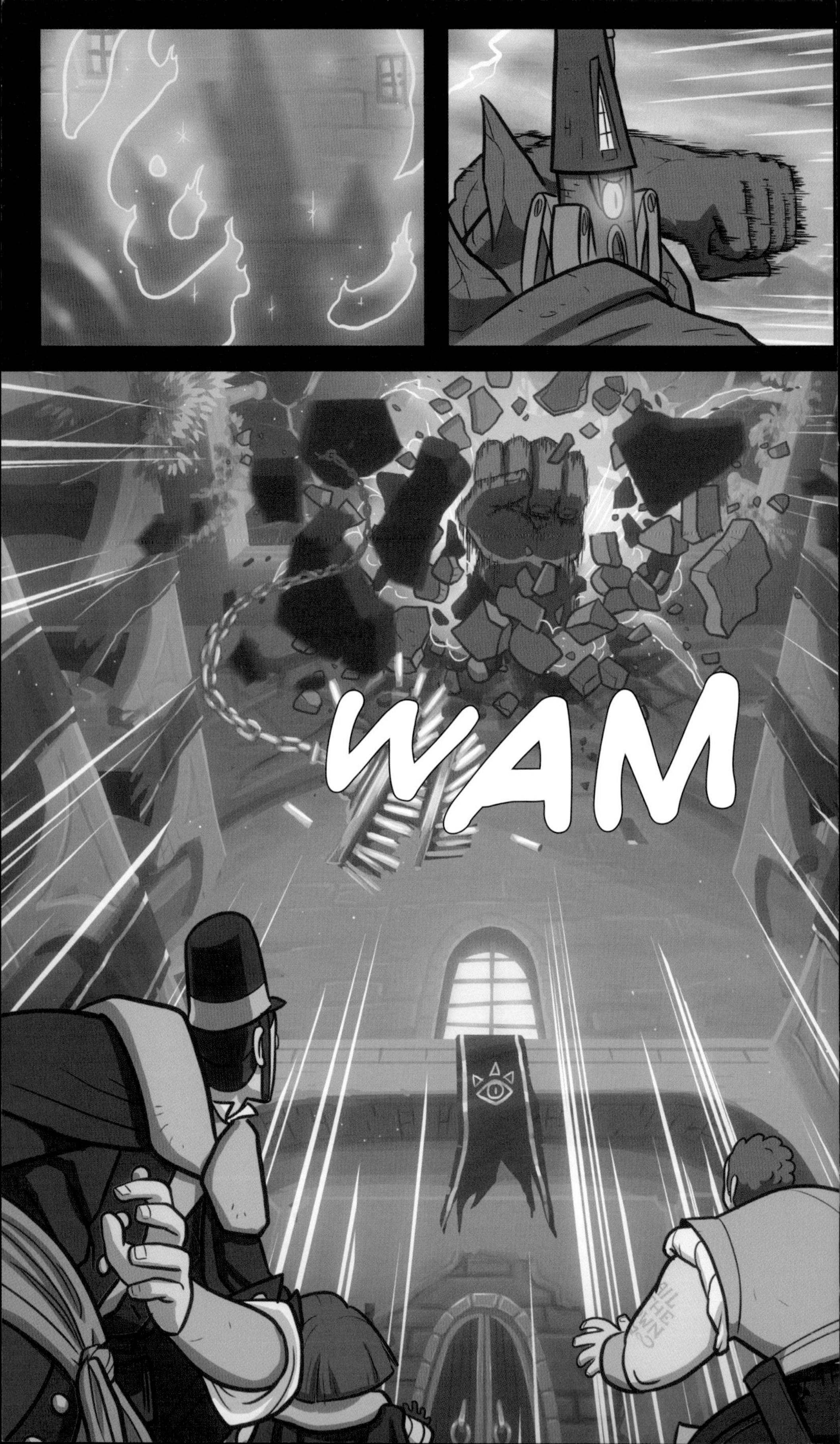
WAM

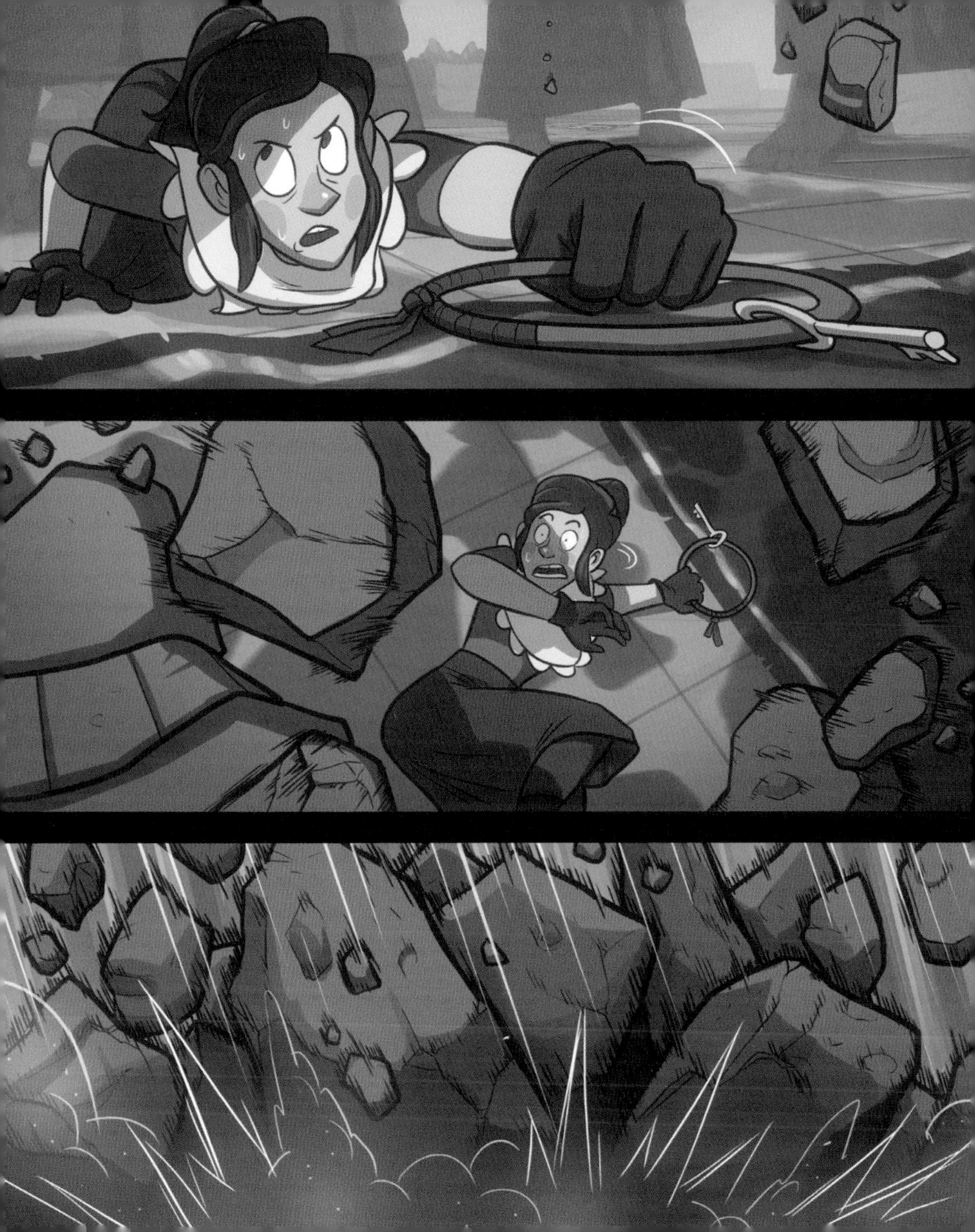

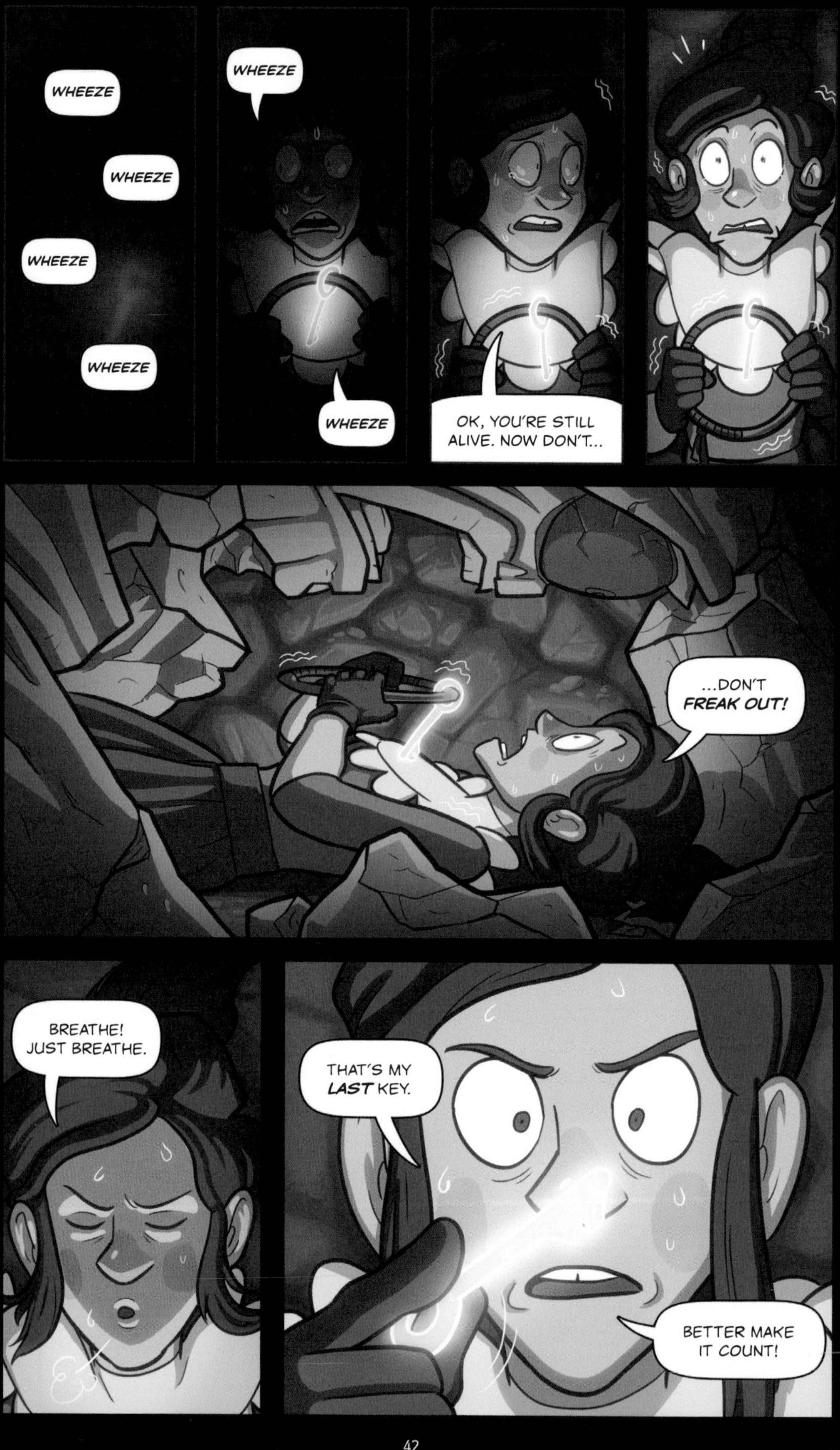
WHEEZE
WHEEZE
WHEEZE
WHEEZE
WHEEZE
WHEEZE
OK, YOU'RE STILL ALIVE. NOW DON'T...
...DON'T **FREAK OUT!**
BREATHE! JUST BREATHE.
THAT'S MY **LAST** KEY.
BETTER MAKE IT COUNT!

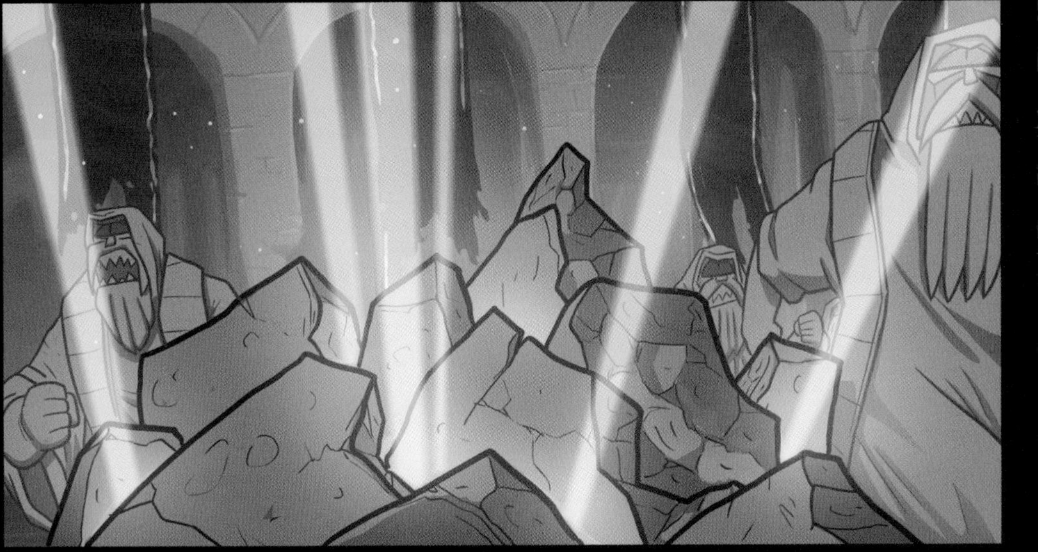

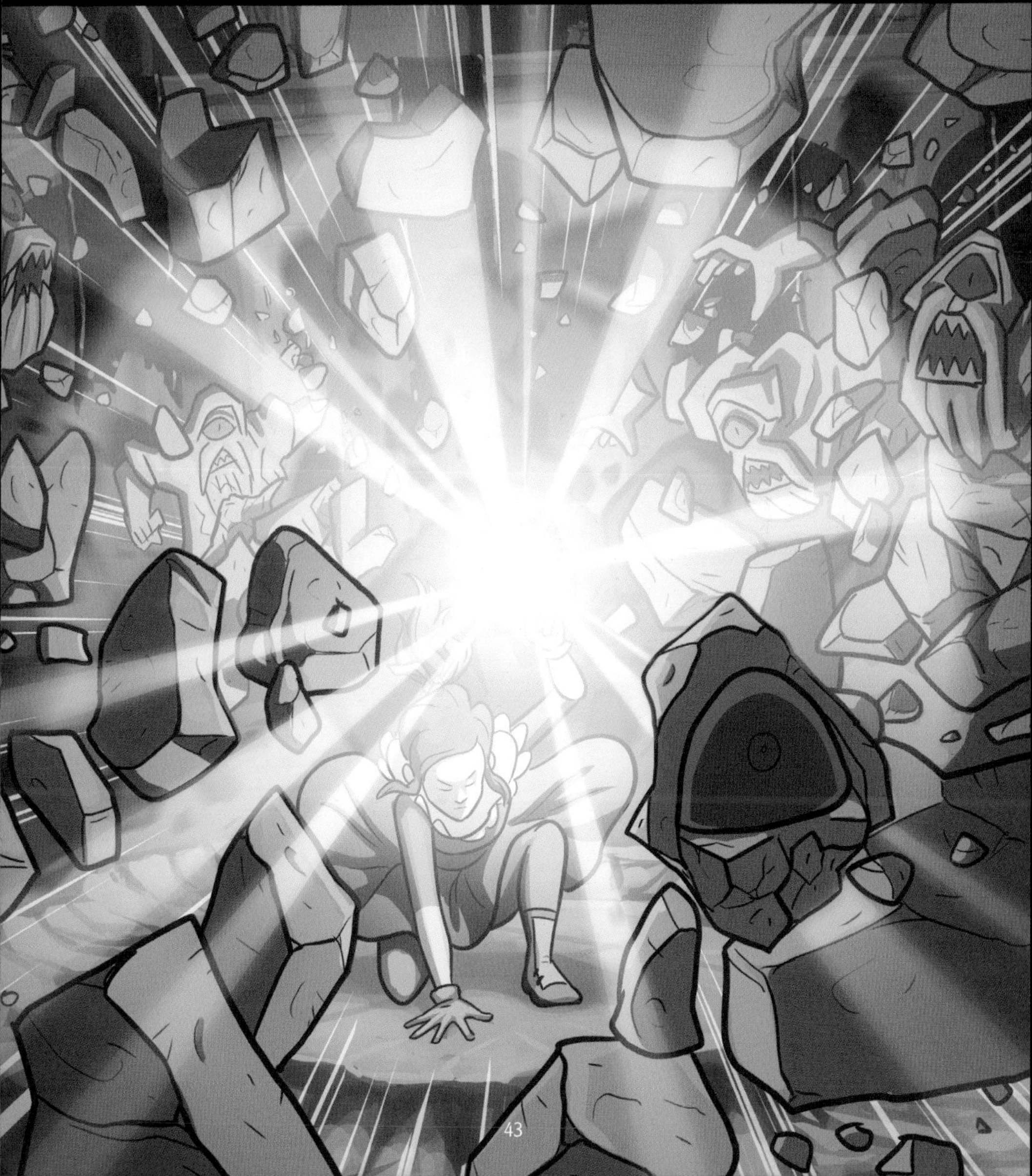

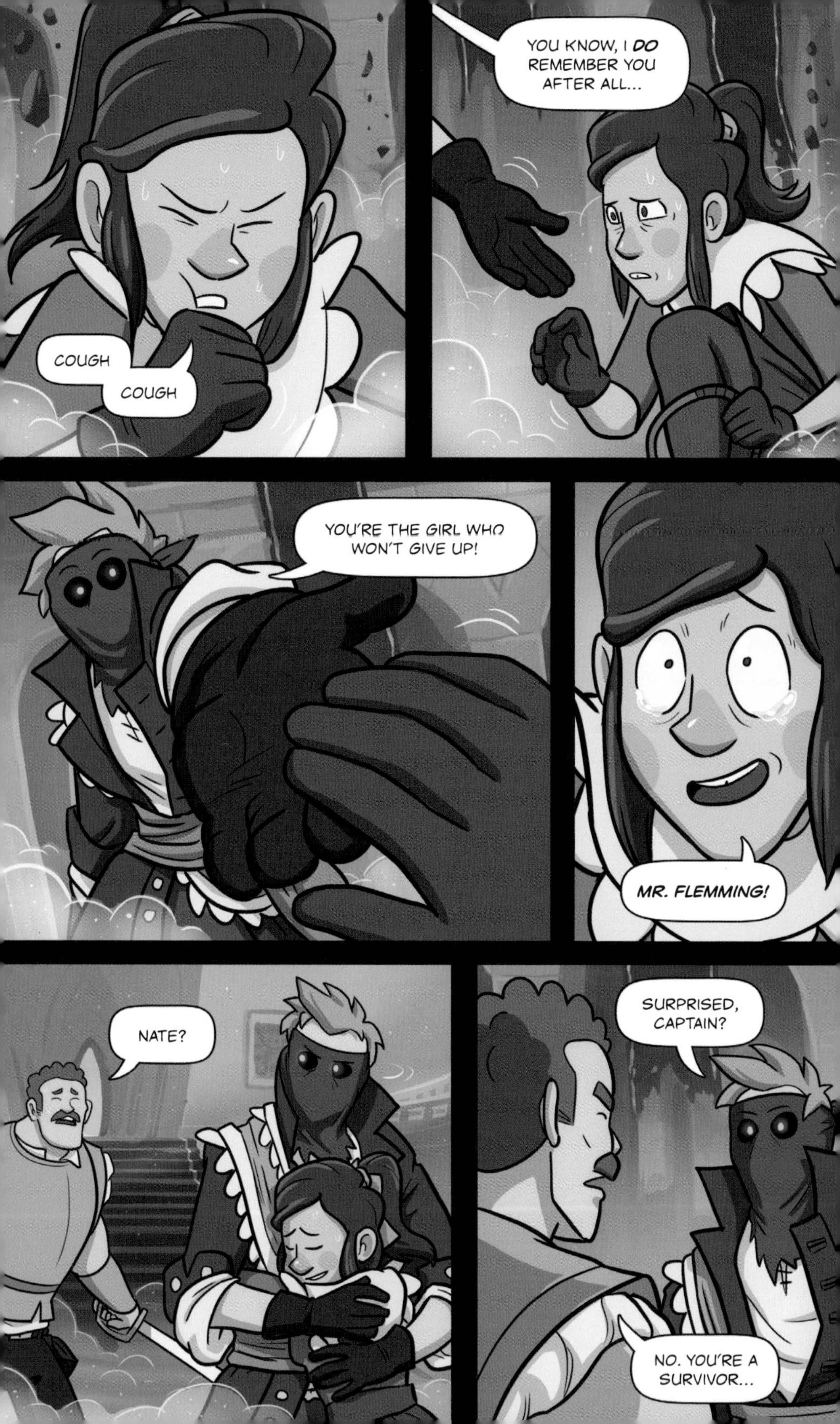
COUGH
COUGH
YOU KNOW, I DO REMEMBER YOU AFTER ALL...
YOU'RE THE GIRL WHO WON'T GIVE UP!
MR. FLEMMING!
NATE?
SURPRISED, CAPTAIN?
NO. YOU'RE A SURVIVOR...

CLAP

...BUT I AM *RELIEVED!*

ME TOO.

ᴧⵏ≪ᴎⵑ:ᴑ, ᴧⵏ≪ᴎⵑ:ᴑ

ᴧⵏ≪ᴎⵑ:ᴑ, ᴧⵏ≪ᴎⵑ:ᴑ

I JUST DON'T KNOW IF ONE MAN MORE WILL MAKE A DIFFERENCE.

WHO SAID I CAME *ALONE?*

ATTACK MANEUVER *"HOUSE PARTY"!*

45

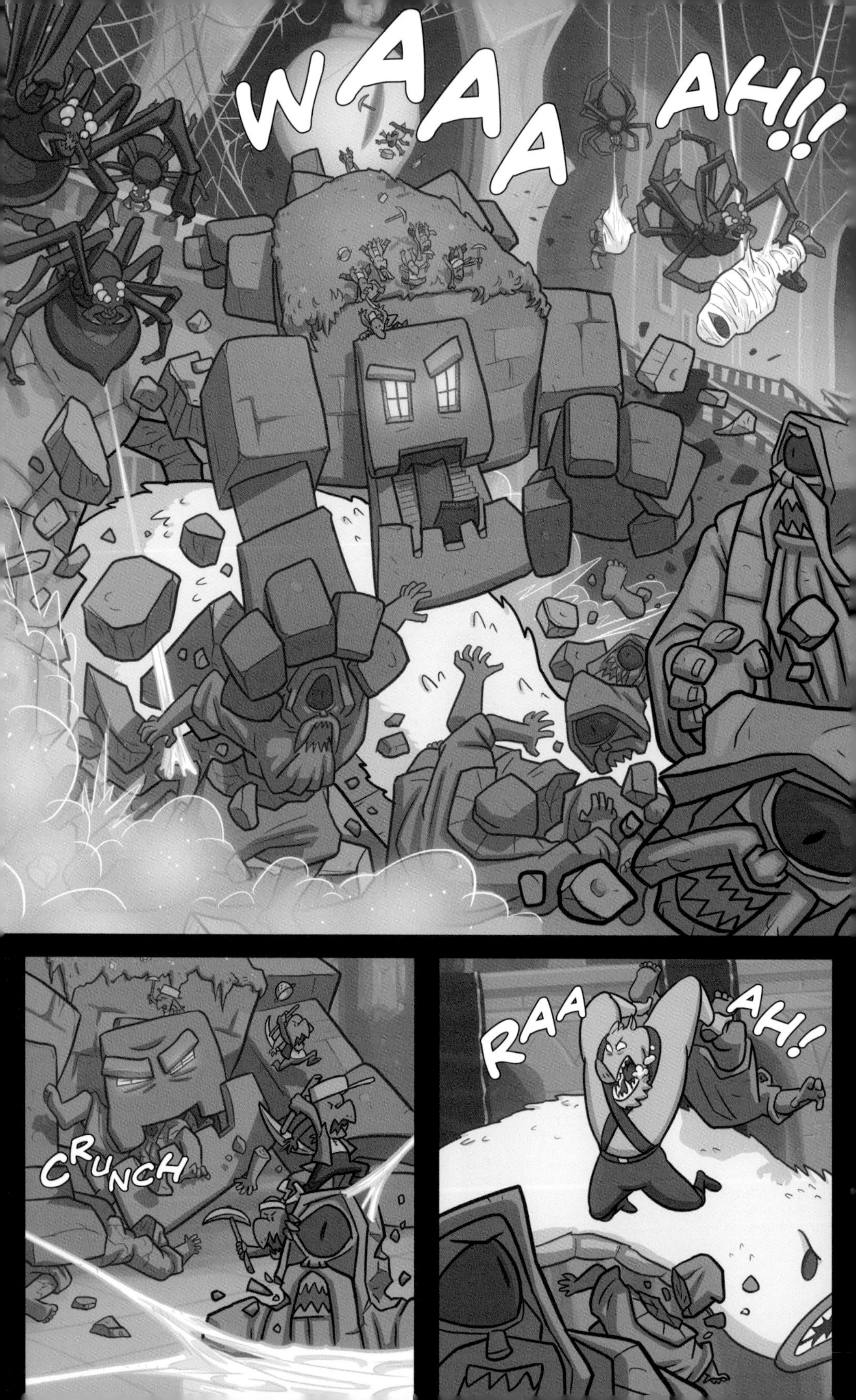

WAAAAH!!!
CRUNCH
RAAAH!

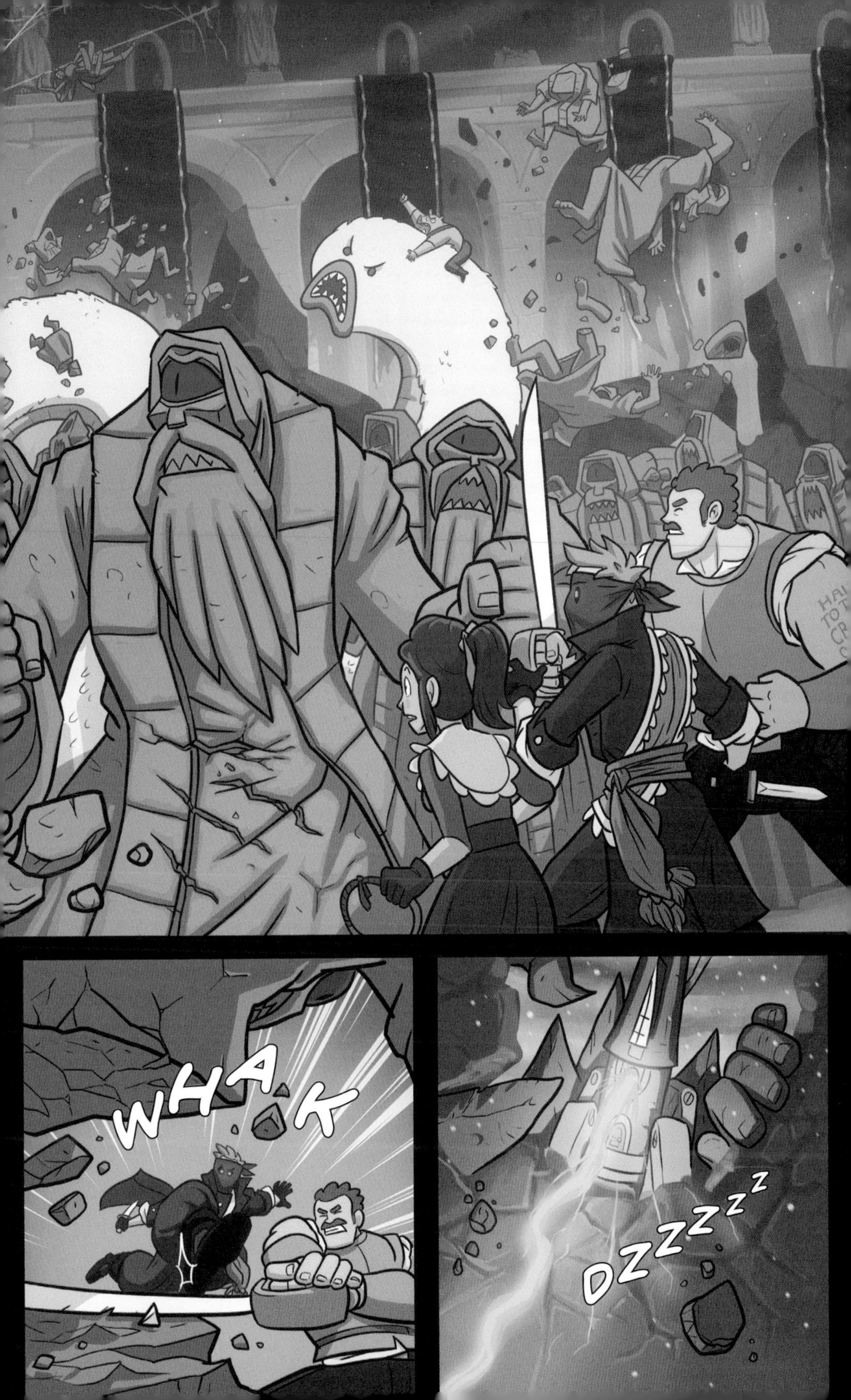
WHAK
DZZZZZ

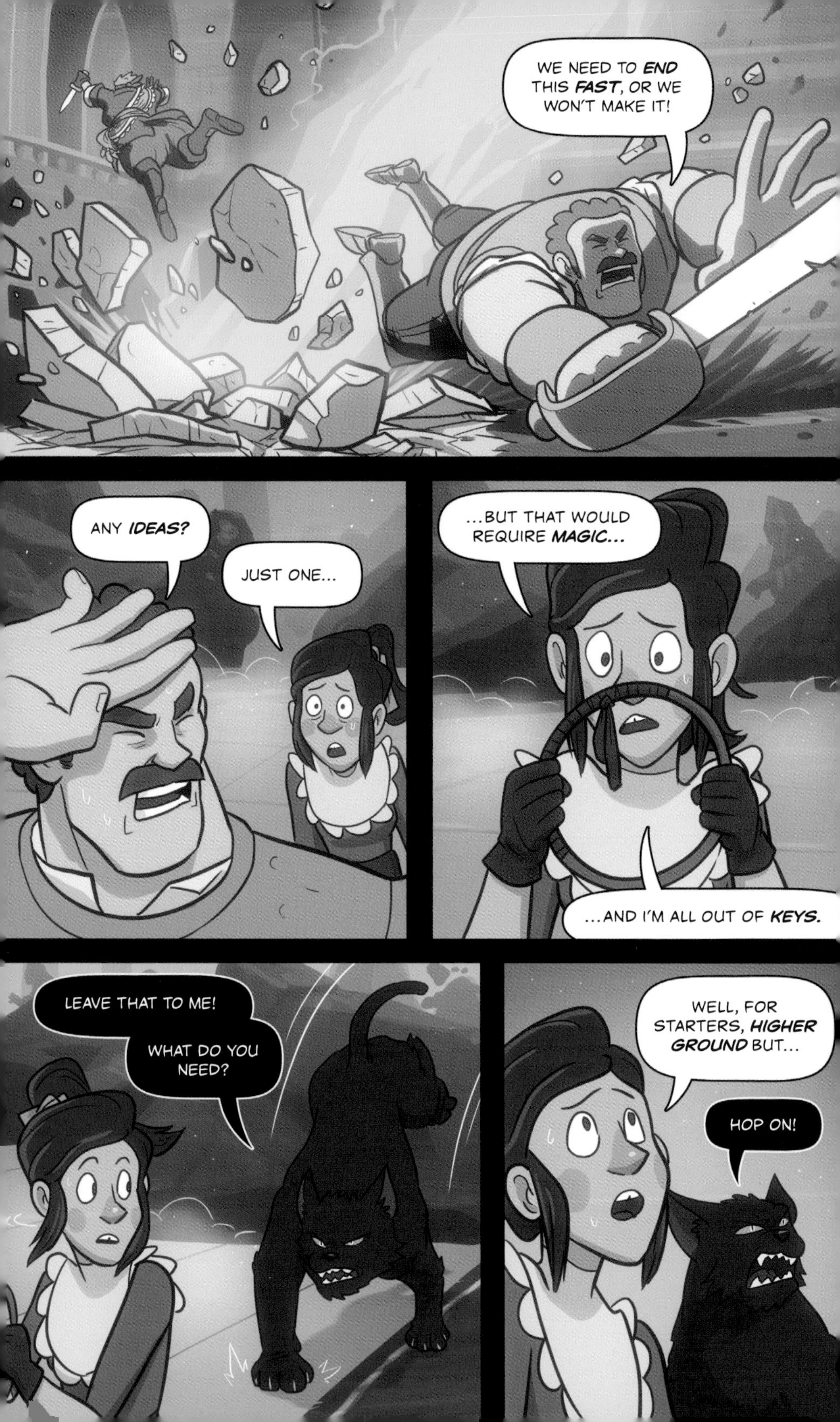
WE NEED TO END THIS FAST, OR WE WON'T MAKE IT!
ANY IDEAS?
JUST ONE...
...BUT THAT WOULD REQUIRE MAGIC...
...AND I'M ALL OUT OF KEYS.
LEAVE THAT TO ME!
WHAT DO YOU NEED?
WELL, FOR STARTERS, HIGHER GROUND BUT...
HOP ON!

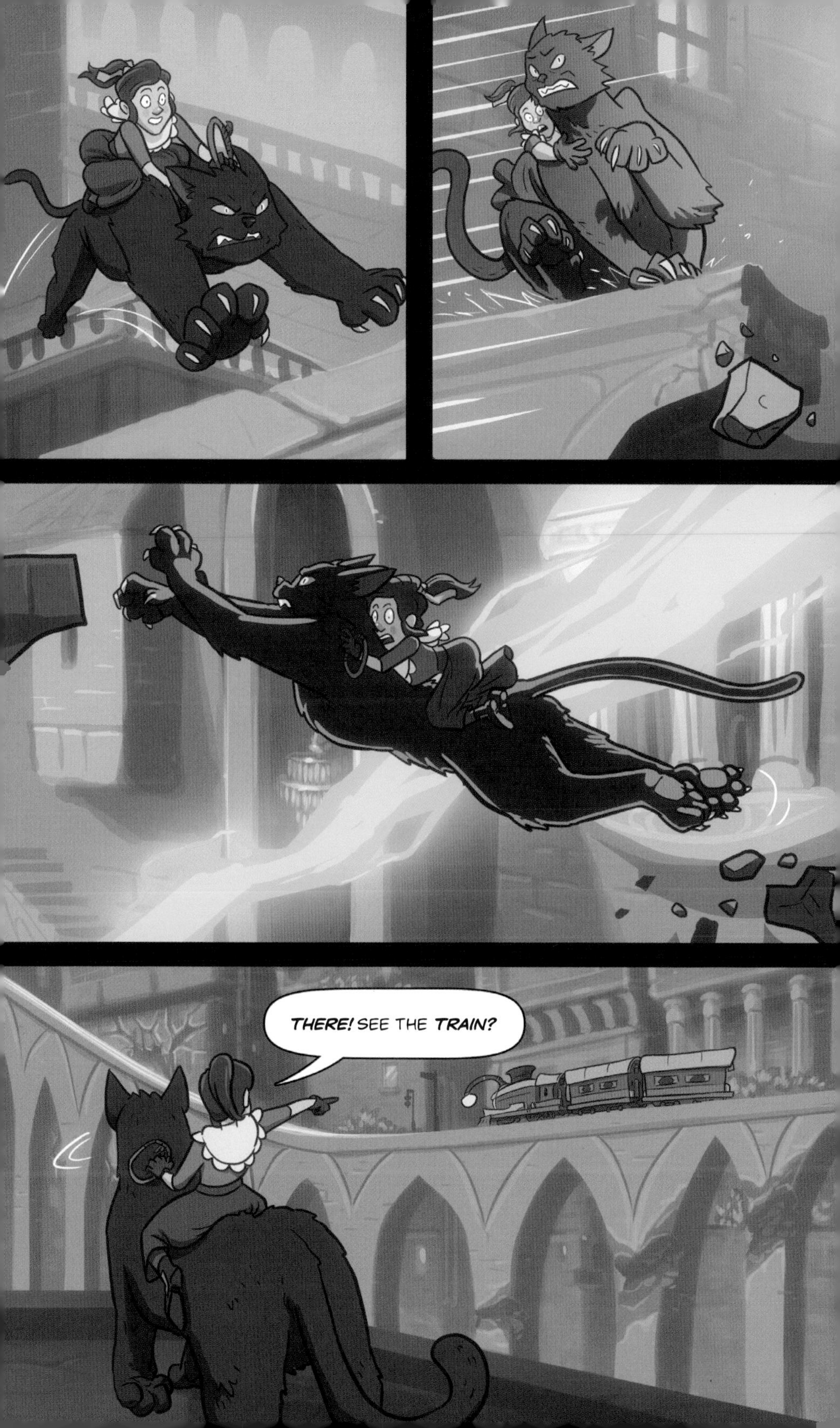
THERE! SEE THE TRAIN?

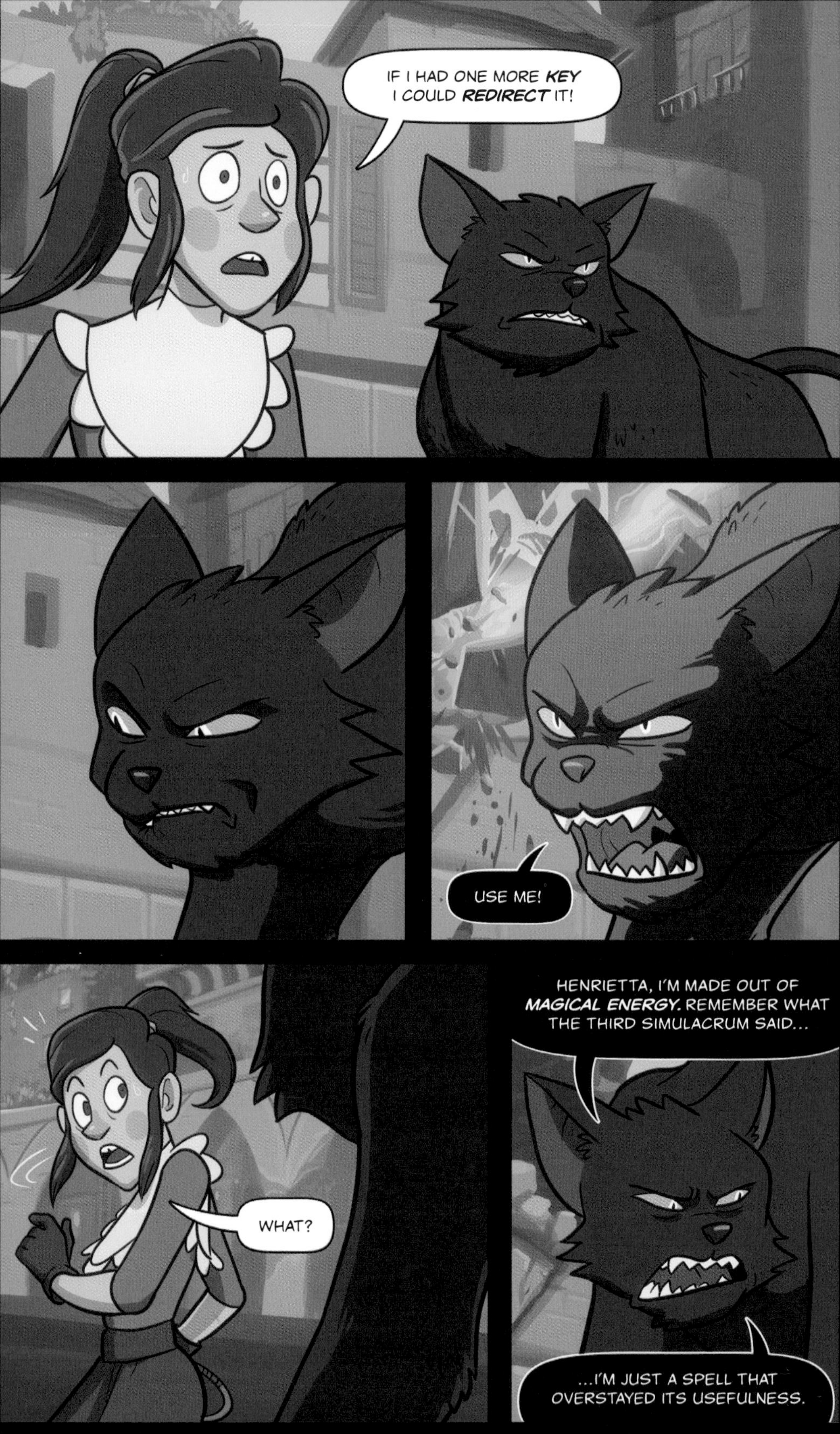

IF I HAD ONE MORE **KEY** I COULD **REDIRECT** IT!
USE ME!
WHAT?
HENRIETTA, I'M MADE OUT OF ***MAGICAL ENERGY.*** REMEMBER WHAT THE THIRD SIMULACRUM SAID...
...I'M JUST A SPELL THAT OVERSTAYED ITS USEFULNESS.

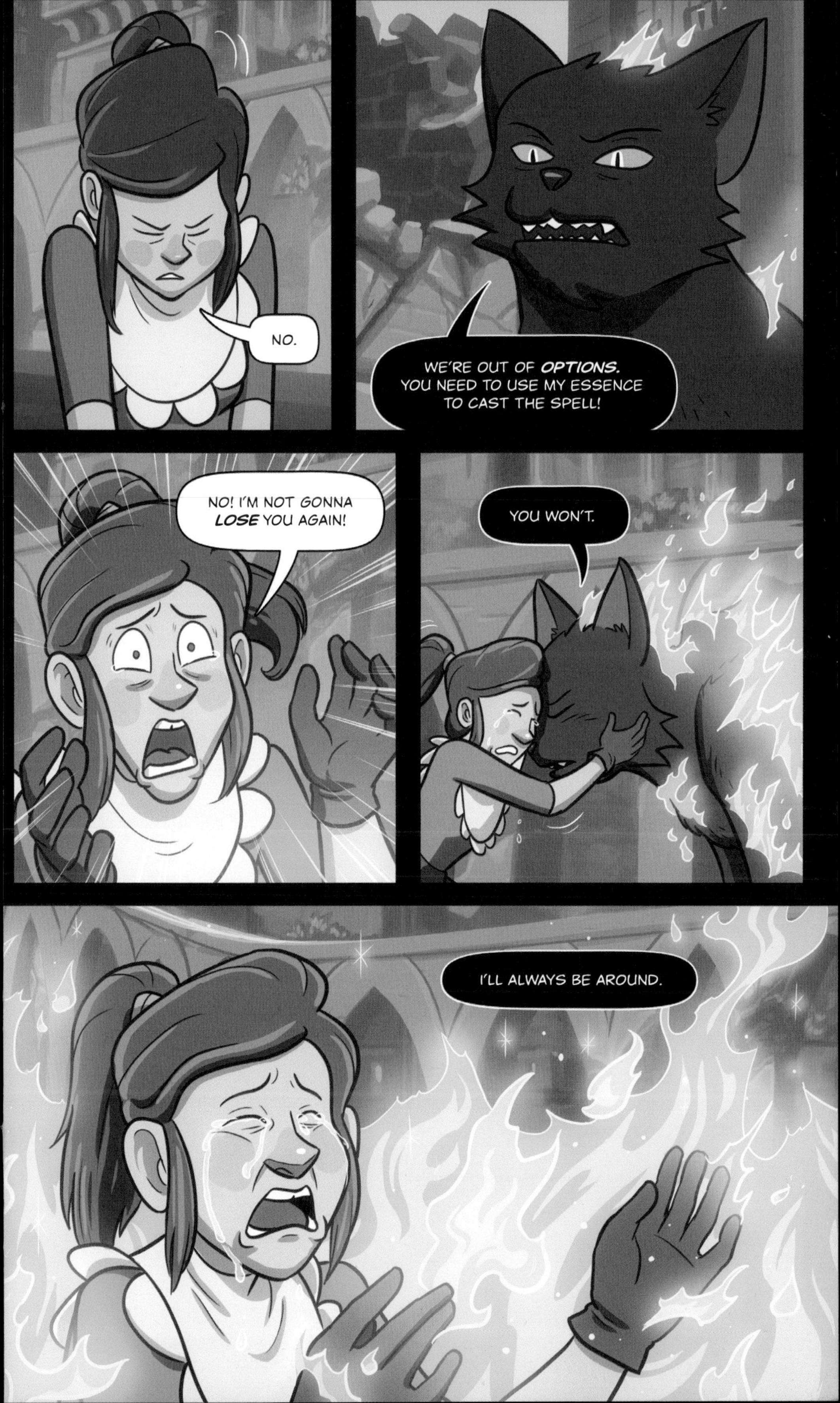
NO.
WE'RE OUT OF *OPTIONS.* YOU NEED TO USE MY ESSENCE TO CAST THE SPELL!
NO! I'M NOT GONNA *LOSE* YOU AGAIN!
YOU WON'T.
I'LL ALWAYS BE AROUND.

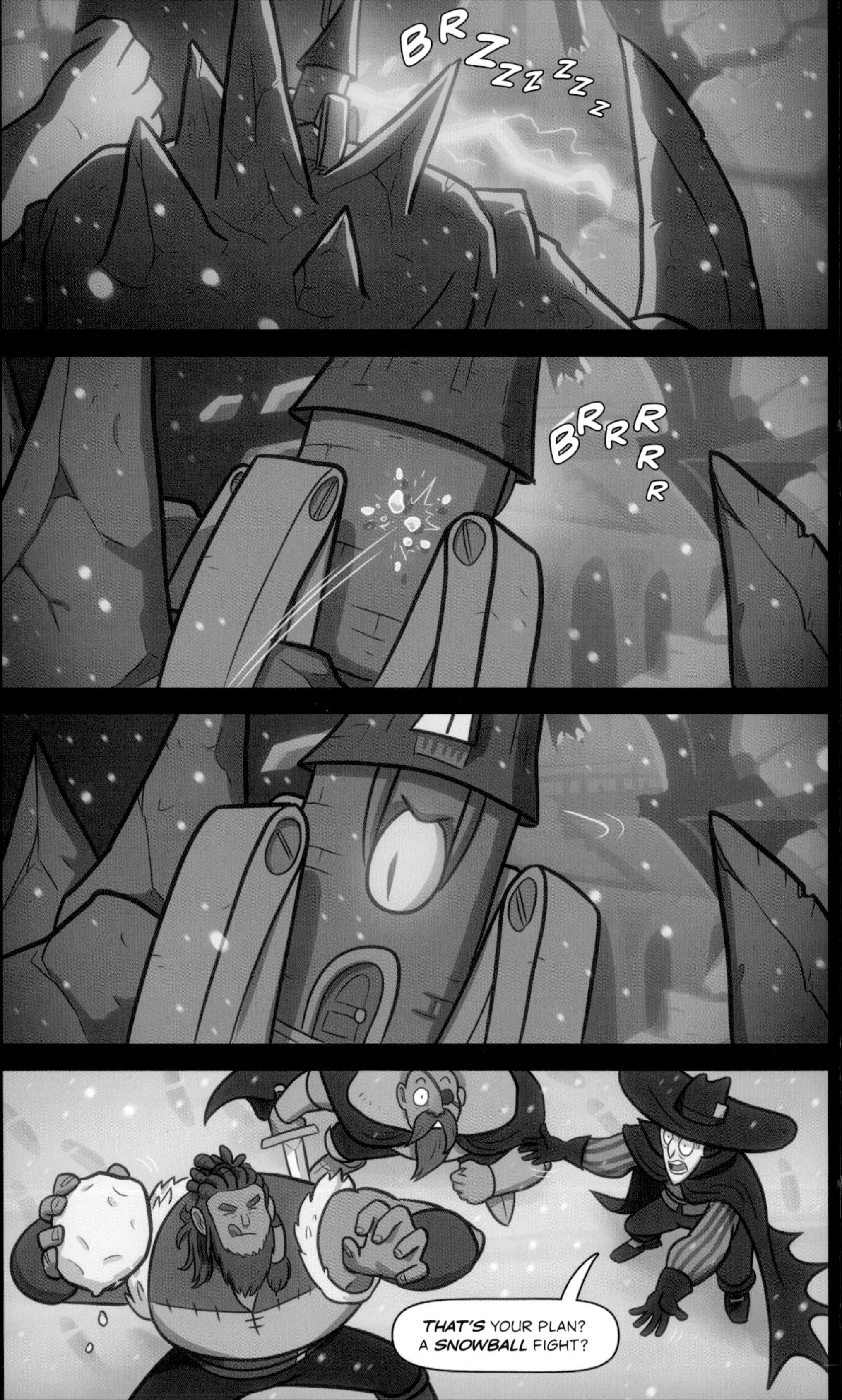
BRZZZZZZZ
BRRRRRR
THAT'S YOUR PLAN?
A SNOWBALL FIGHT?

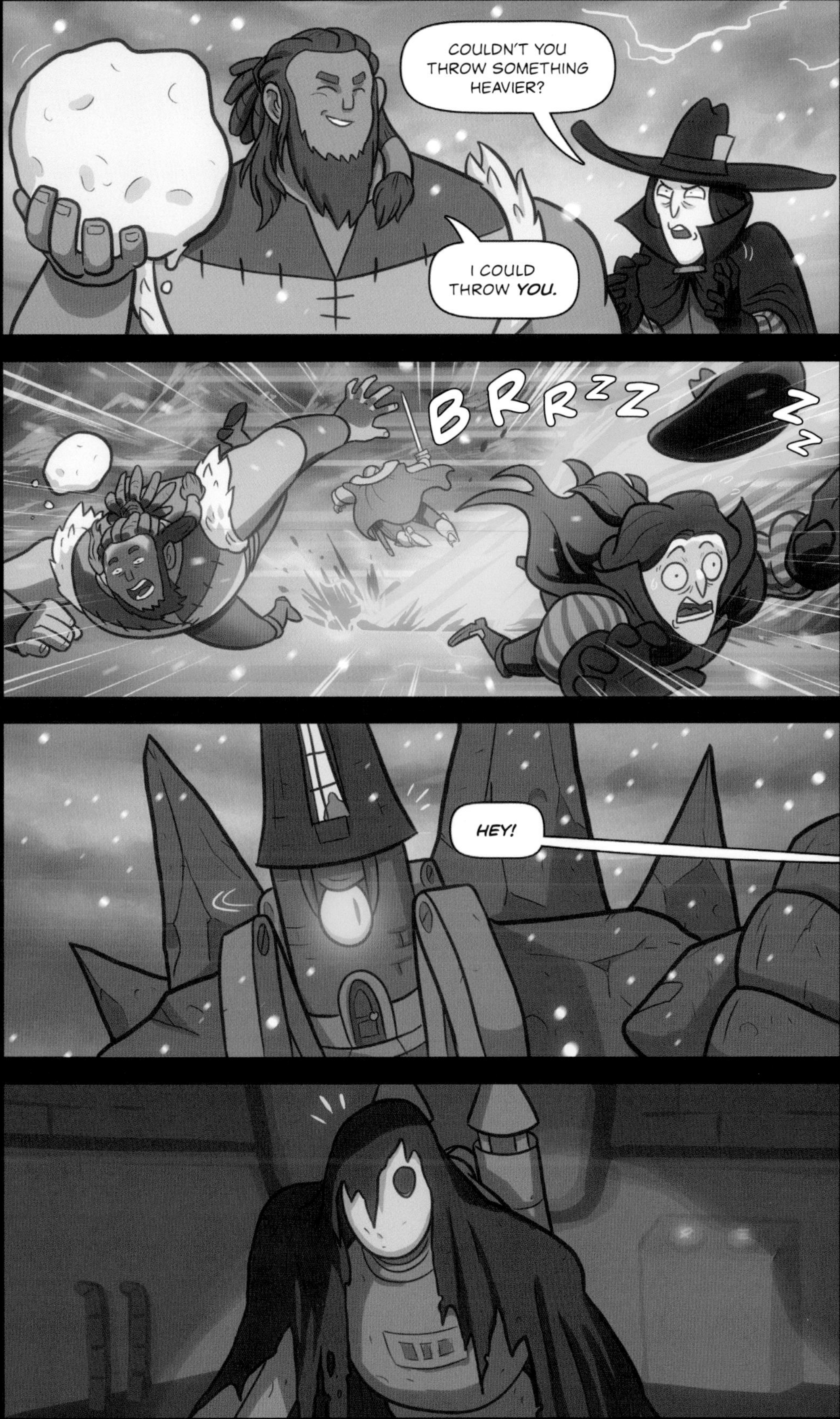
COULDN'T YOU THROW SOMETHING HEAVIER?
I COULD THROW YOU.
BRRZZ
ZZ
HEY!

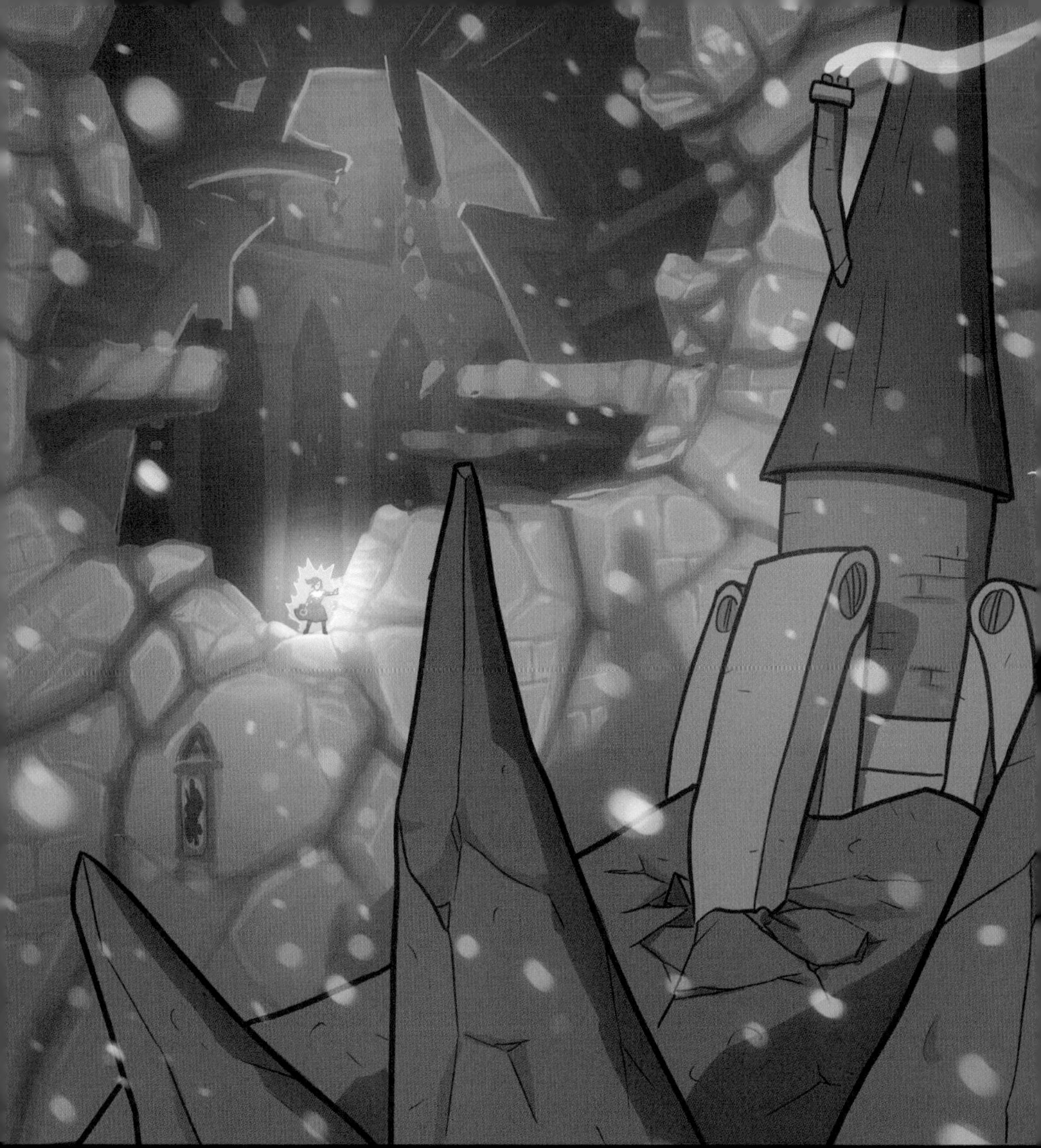

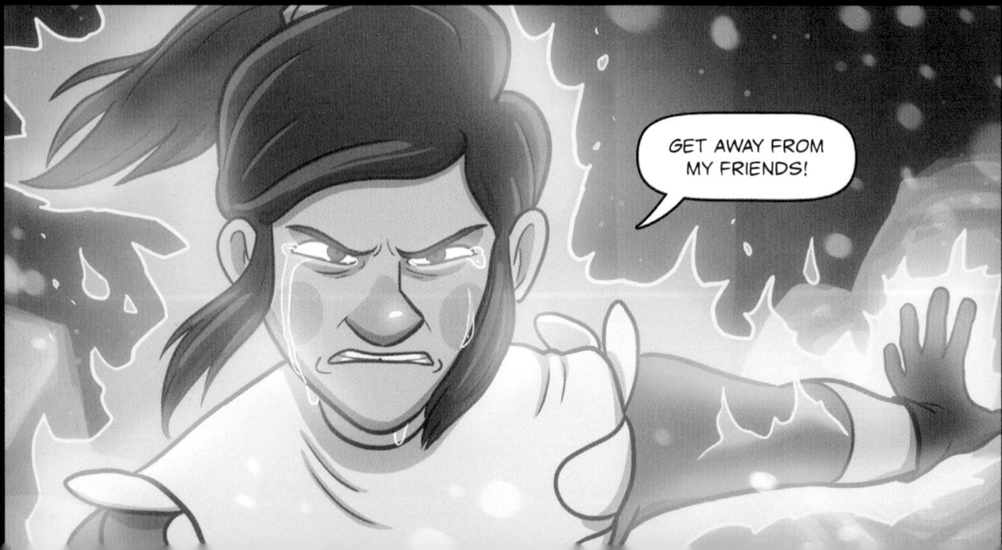
GET AWAY FROM MY FRIENDS!

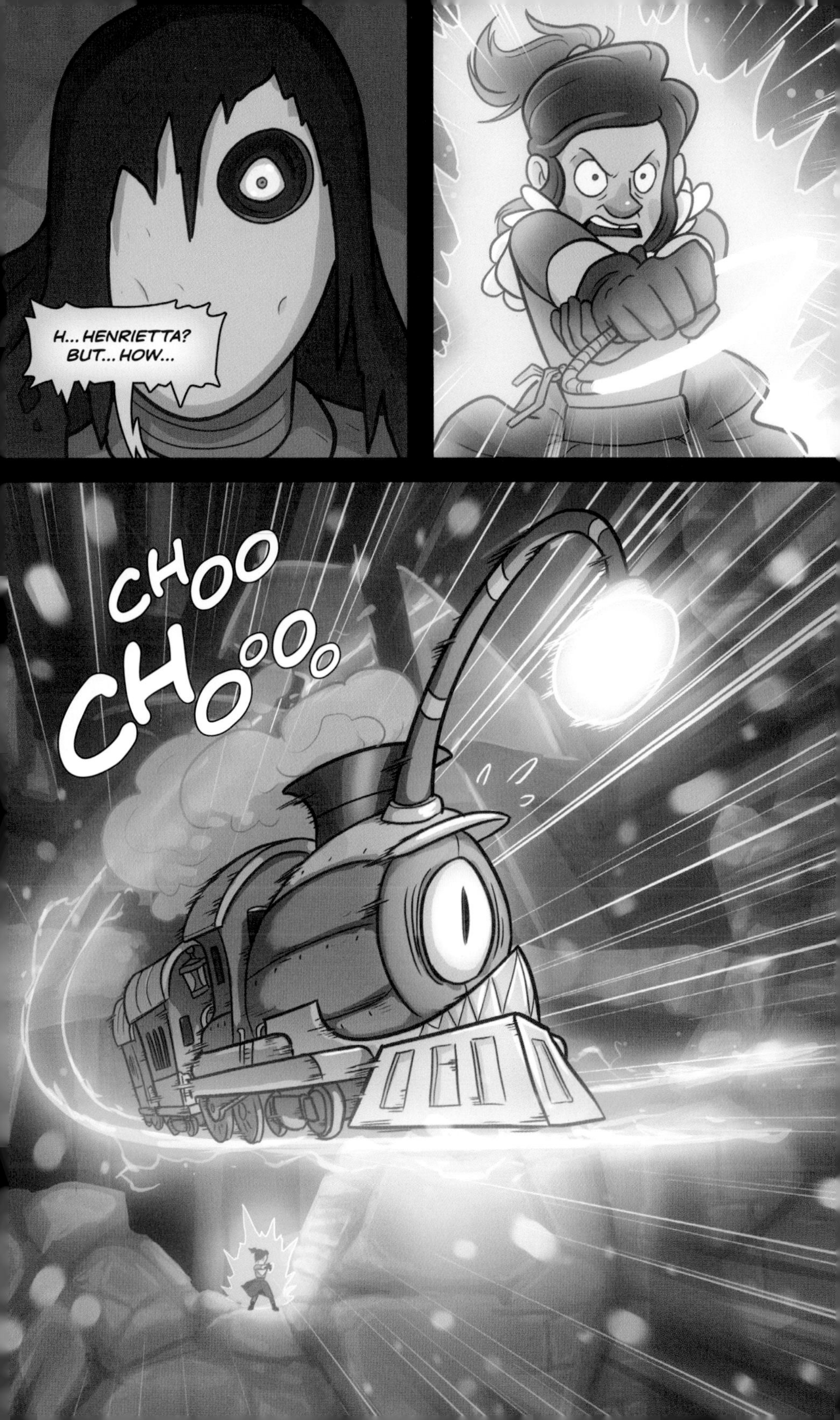
H... HENRIETTA? BUT... HOW...
CHOO CHOOOOO

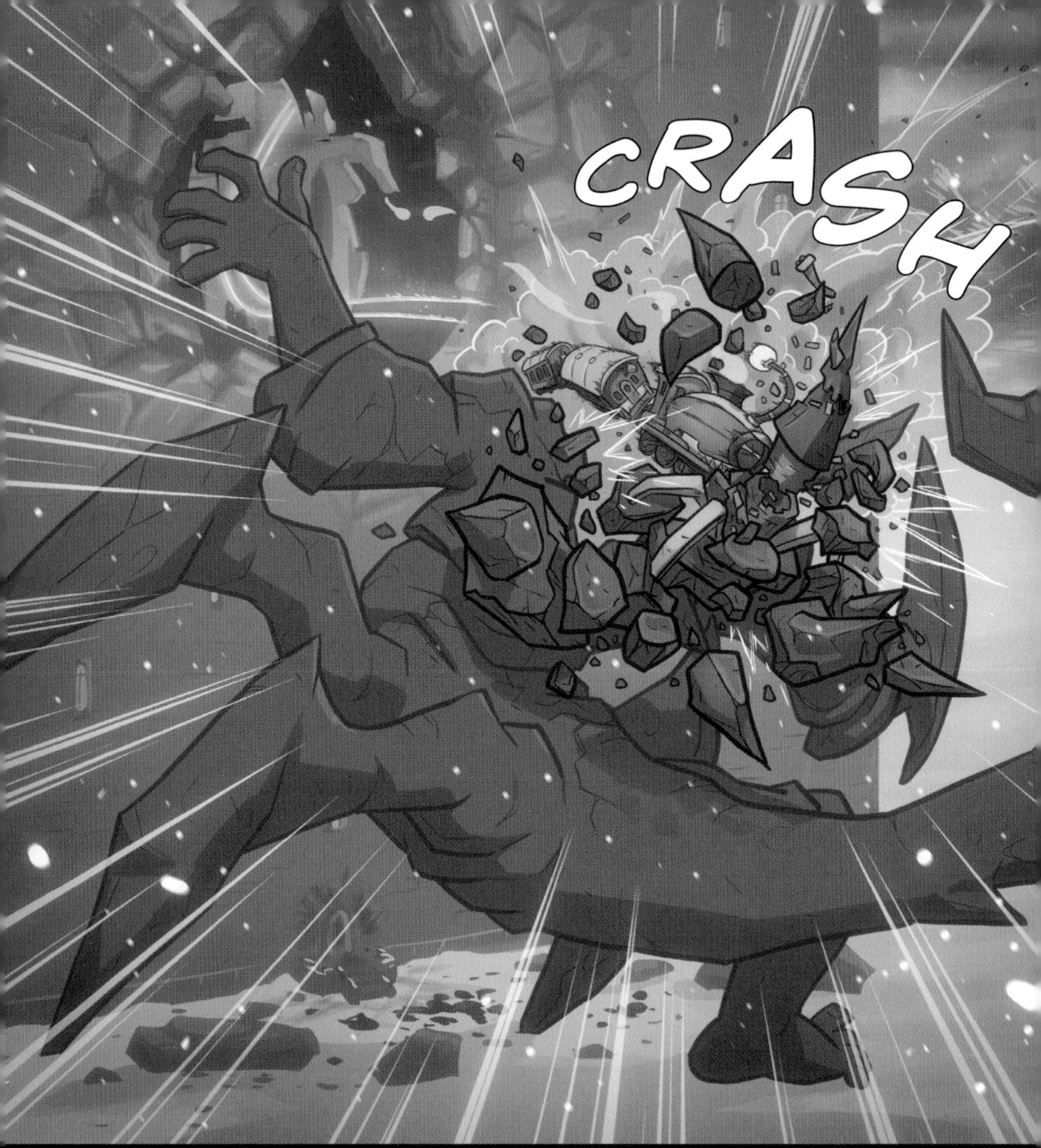
CRASH

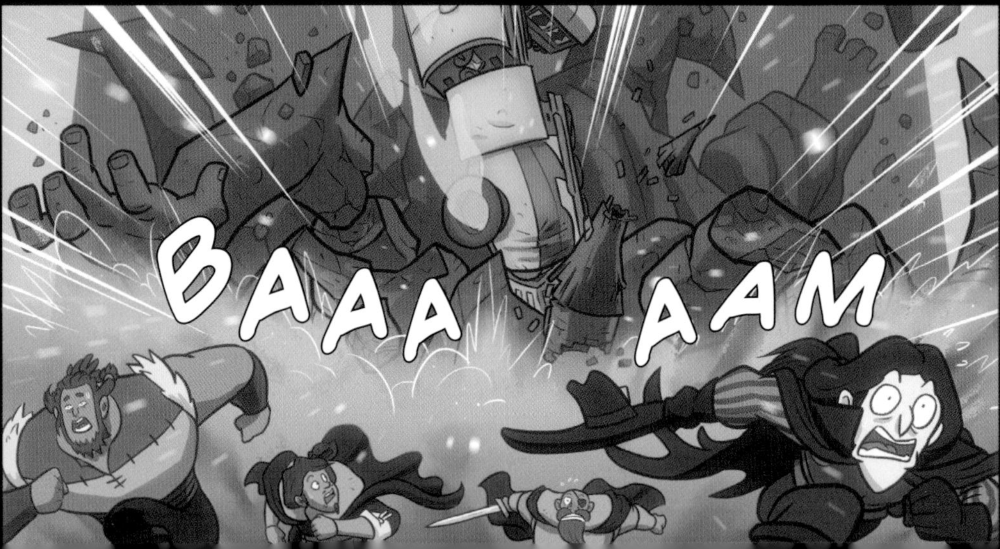
BAAA AAM

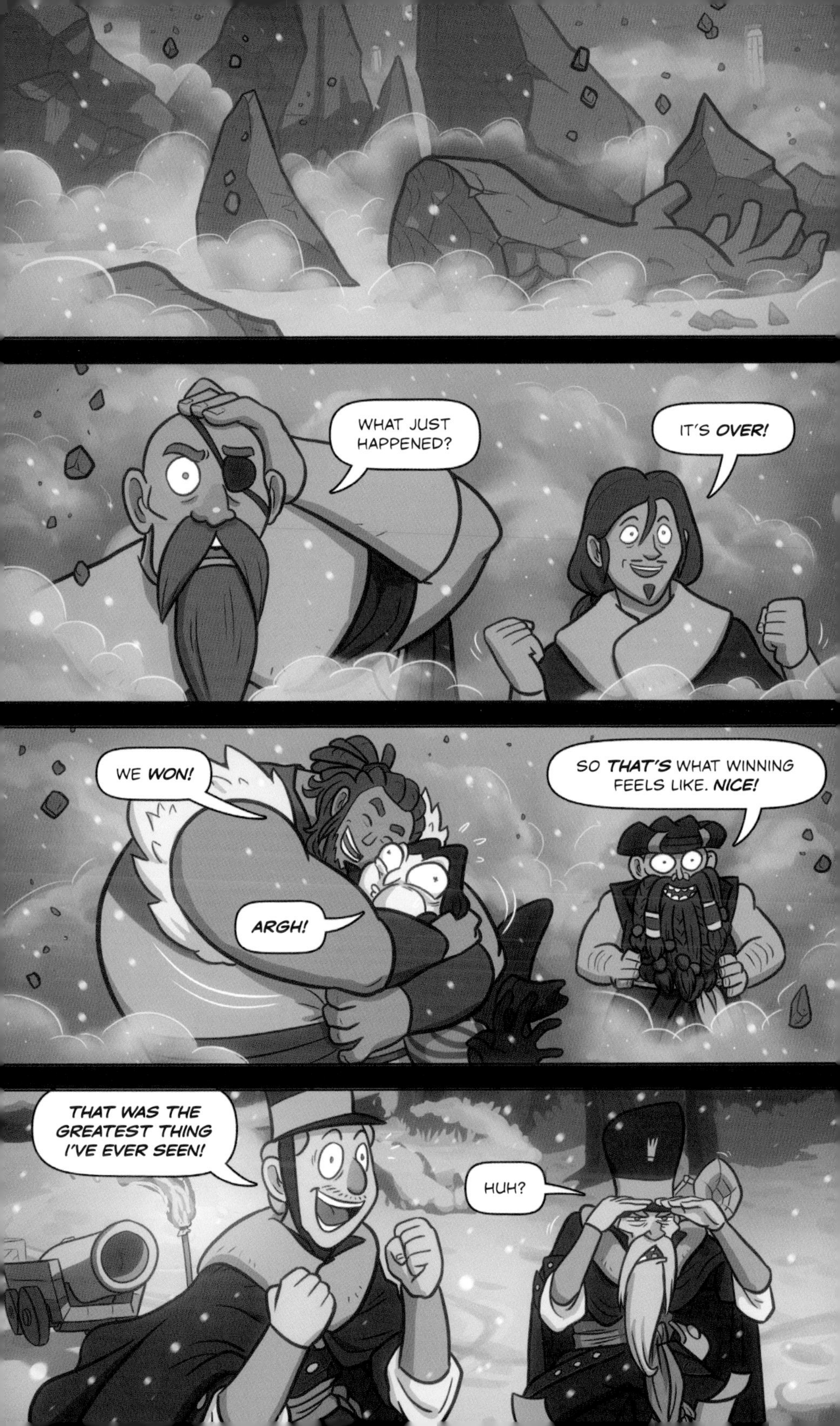
WHAT JUST HAPPENED?
IT'S OVER!
WE WON!
ARGH!
SO THAT'S WHAT WINNING FEELS LIKE. NICE!
THAT WAS THE GREATEST THING I'VE EVER SEEN!
HUH?

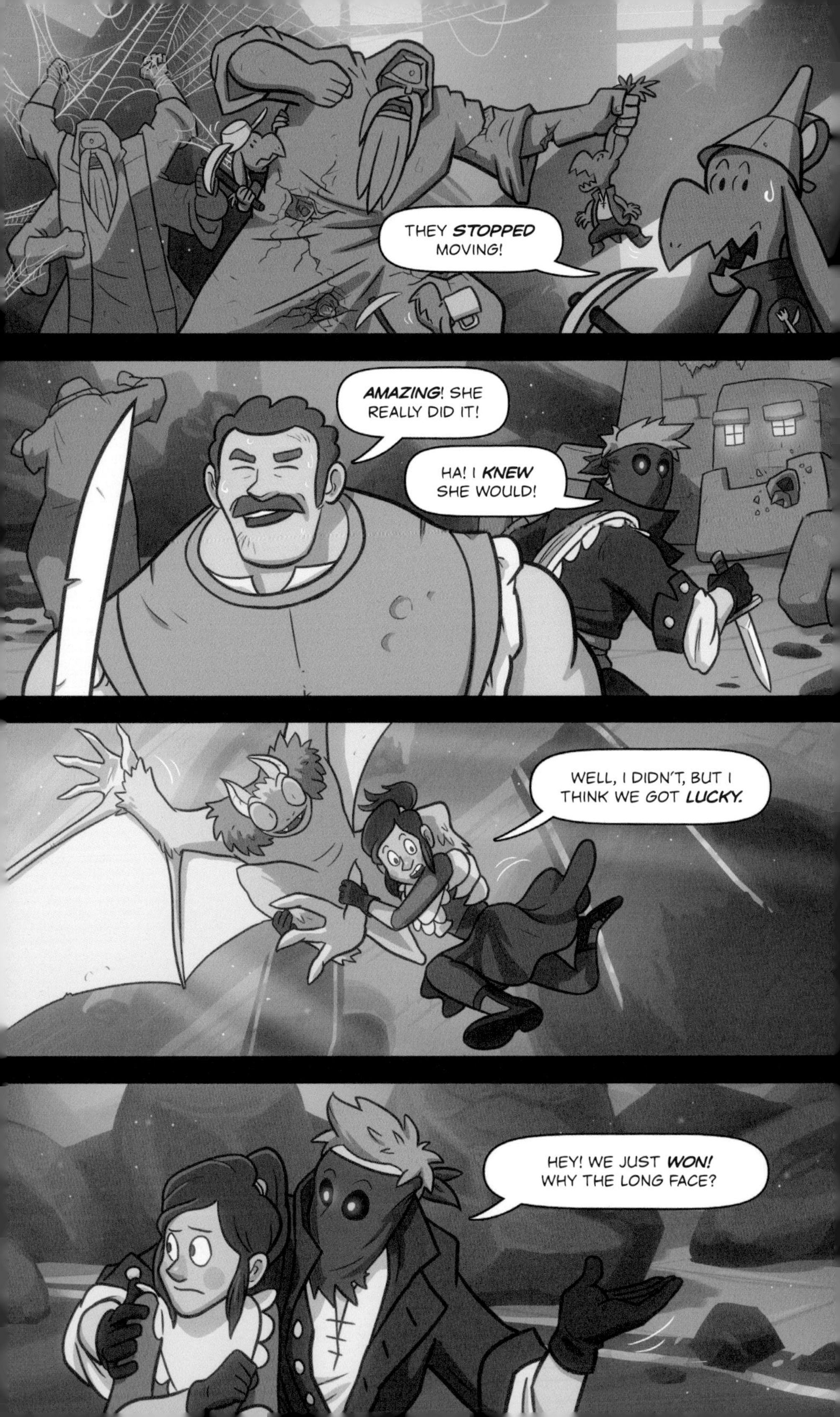

THEY STOPPED MOVING!
AMAZING! SHE REALLY DID IT!
HA! I KNEW SHE WOULD!
WELL, I DIDN'T, BUT I THINK WE GOT LUCKY.
HEY! WE JUST WON! WHY THE LONG FACE?

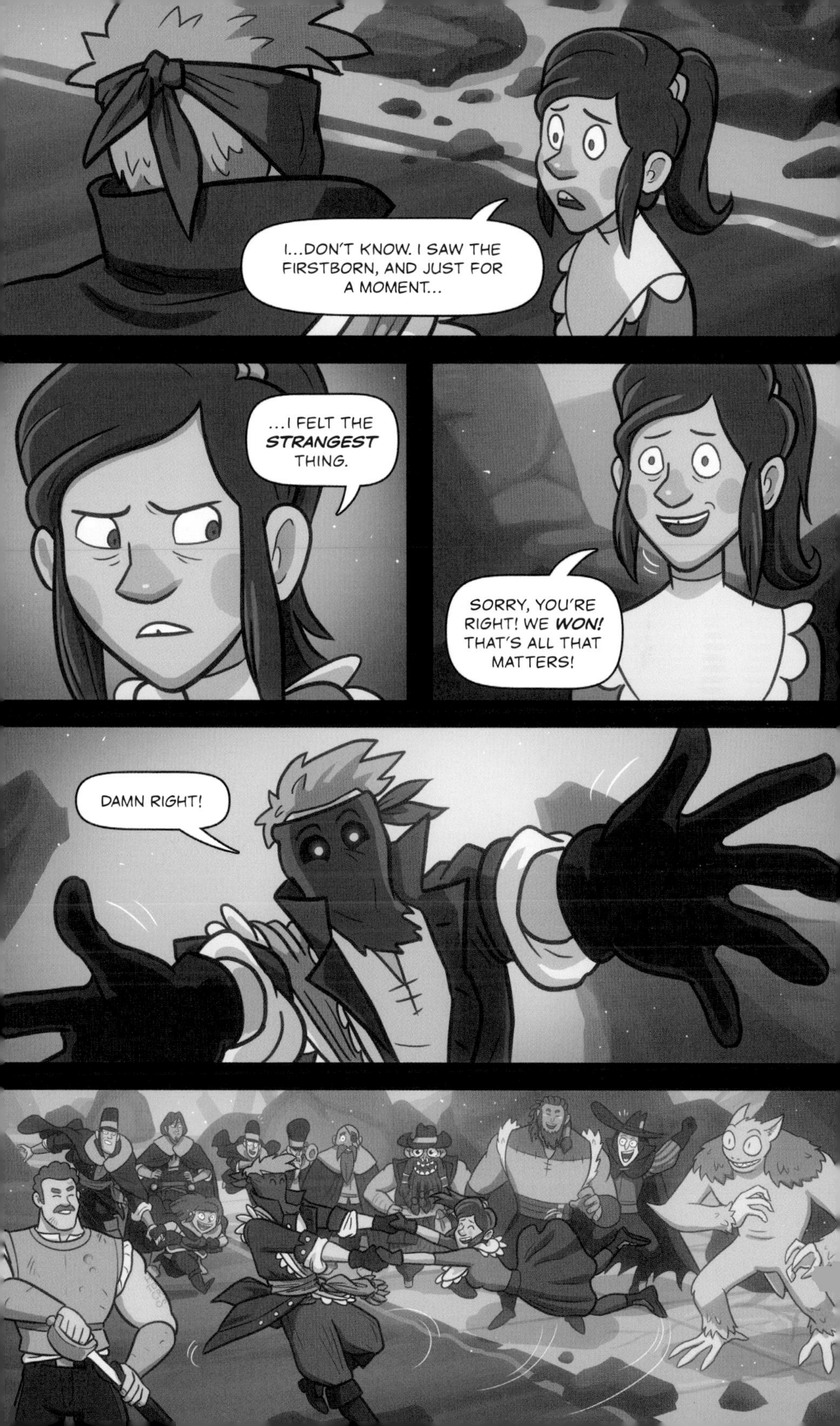
I...DON'T KNOW. I SAW THE FIRSTBORN, AND JUST FOR A MOMENT...
...I FELT THE **STRANGEST** THING.
SORRY, YOU'RE RIGHT! WE **WON!** THAT'S ALL THAT MATTERS!
DAMN RIGHT!

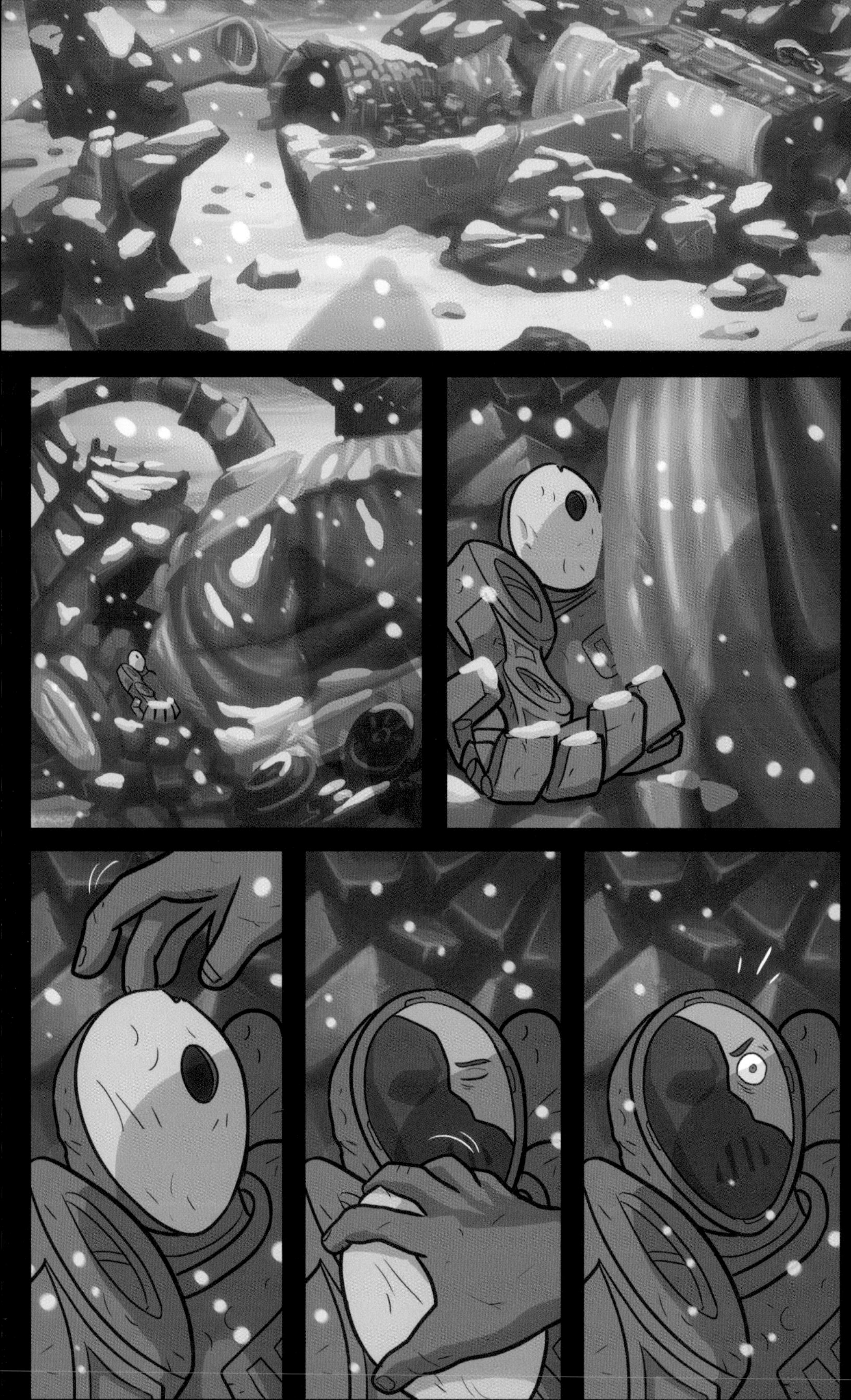

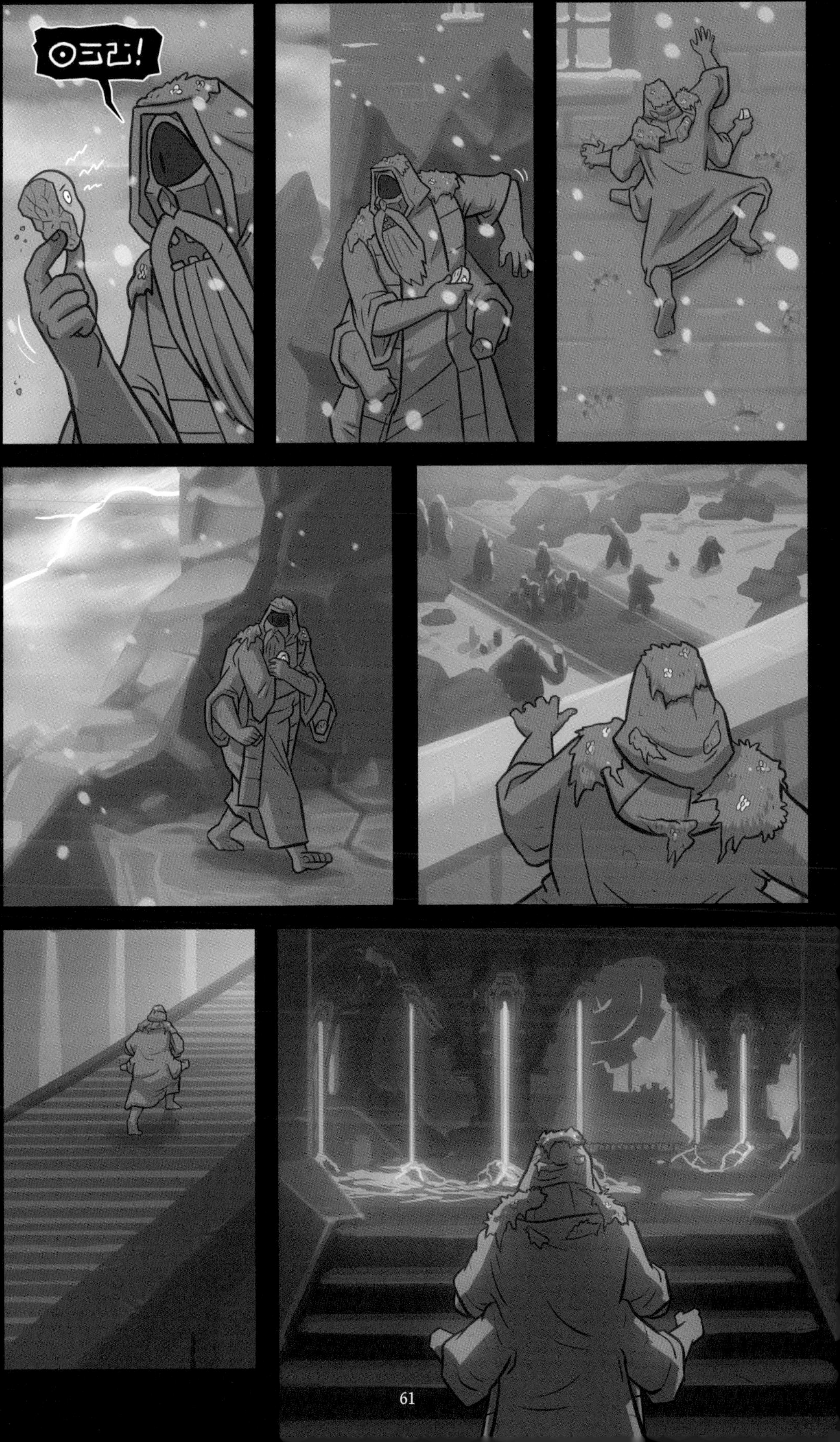

ONCE UPON A TIME THERE WAS A **WIZARD**. THE WIZARD WAS GREAT AND POWERFUL...

...BUT HE HAD GROWN **OLD**.

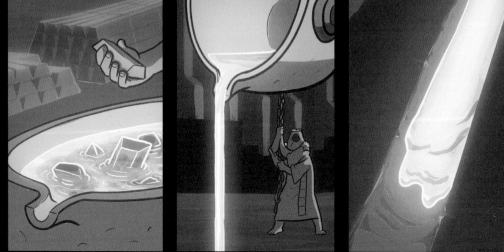

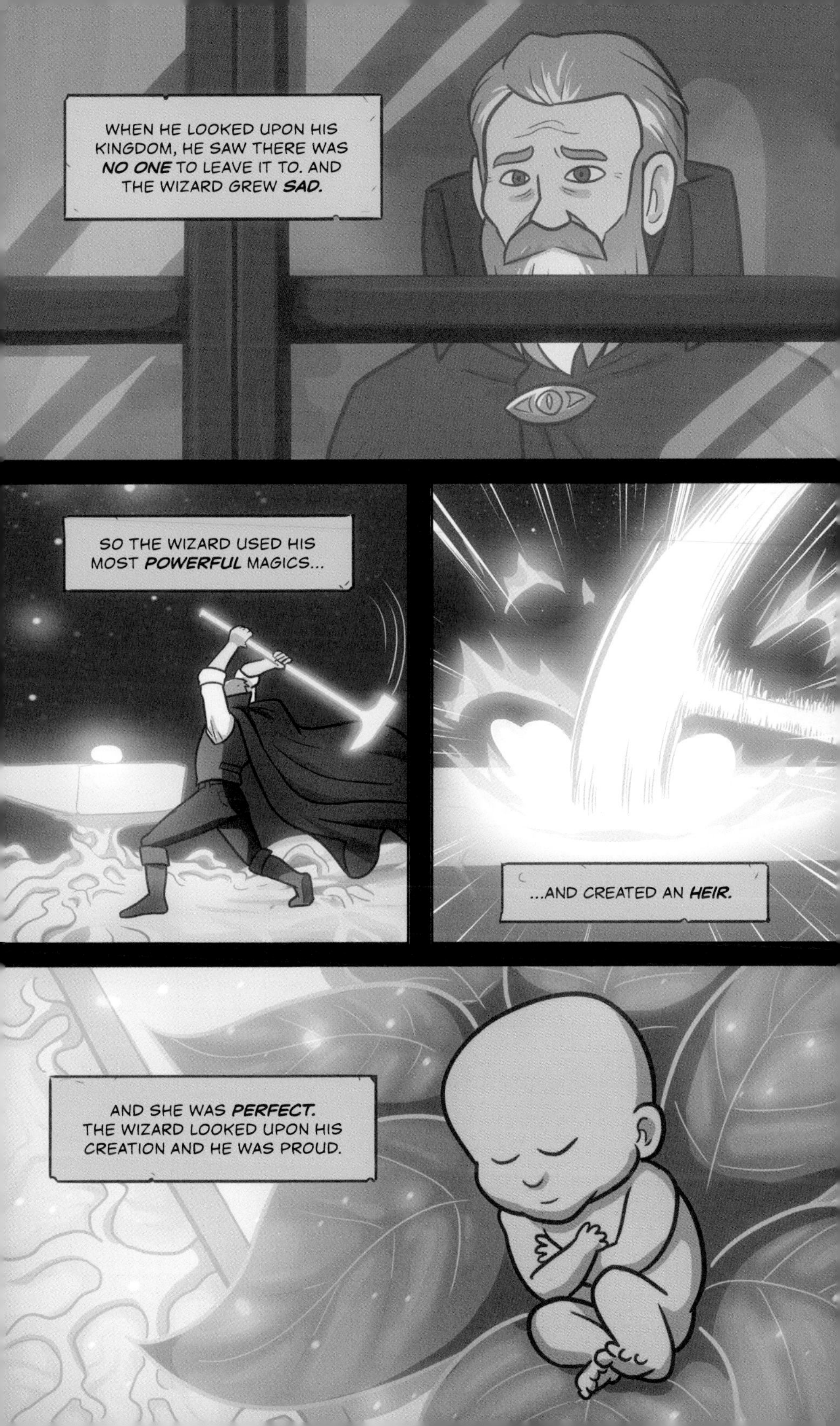
WHEN HE LOOKED UPON HIS KINGDOM, HE SAW THERE WAS ***NO ONE*** TO LEAVE IT TO. AND THE WIZARD GREW ***SAD.***
SO THE WIZARD USED HIS MOST ***POWERFUL*** MAGICS...
...AND CREATED AN ***HEIR.***
AND SHE WAS ***PERFECT.*** THE WIZARD LOOKED UPON HIS CREATION AND HE WAS PROUD.

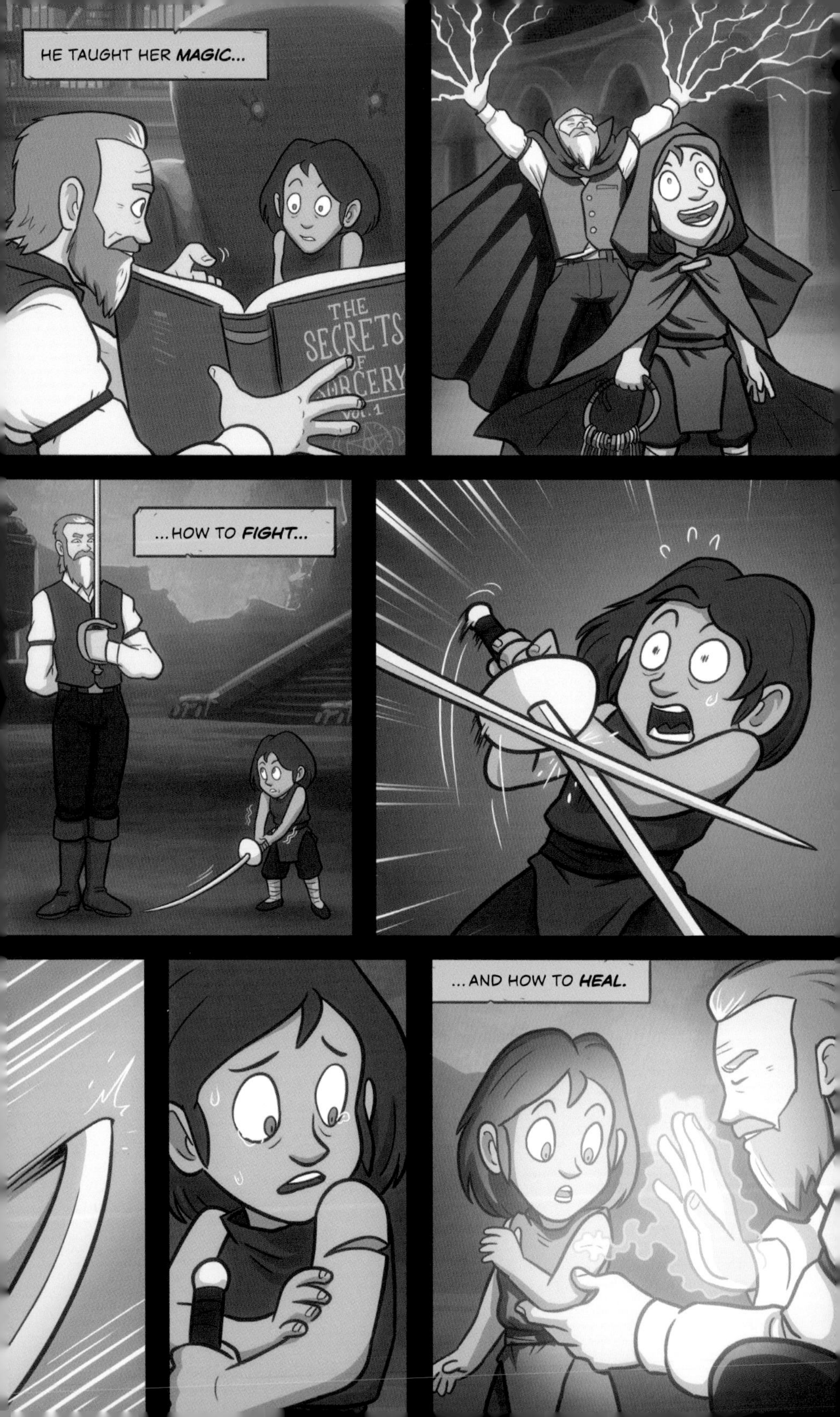
HE TAUGHT HER MAGIC...
THE SECRETS OF SORCERY VOL. 1
...HOW TO FIGHT...
...AND HOW TO HEAL.

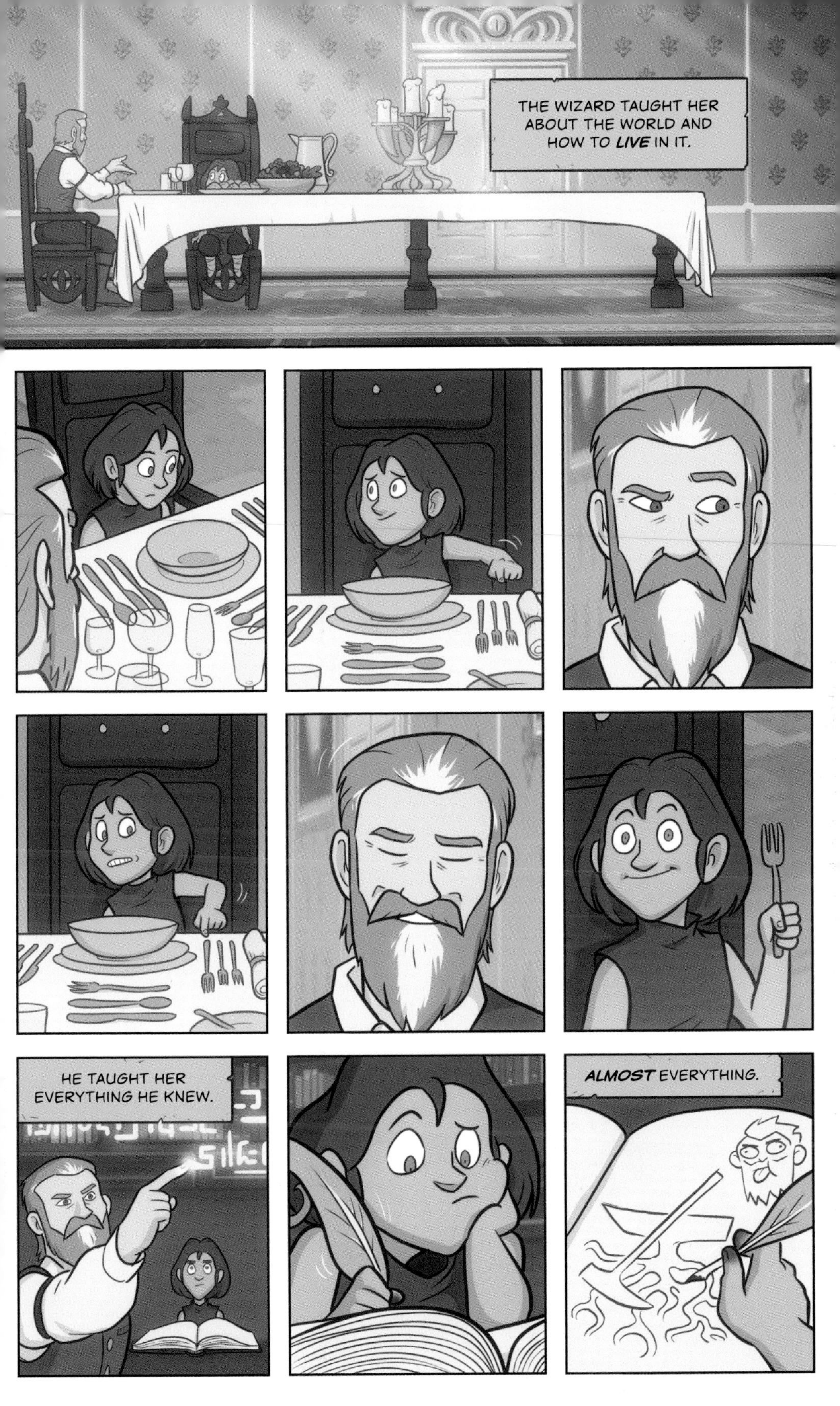
THE WIZARD TAUGHT HER ABOUT THE WORLD AND HOW TO *LIVE* IN IT.
HE TAUGHT HER EVERYTHING HE KNEW.
ALMOST EVERYTHING.

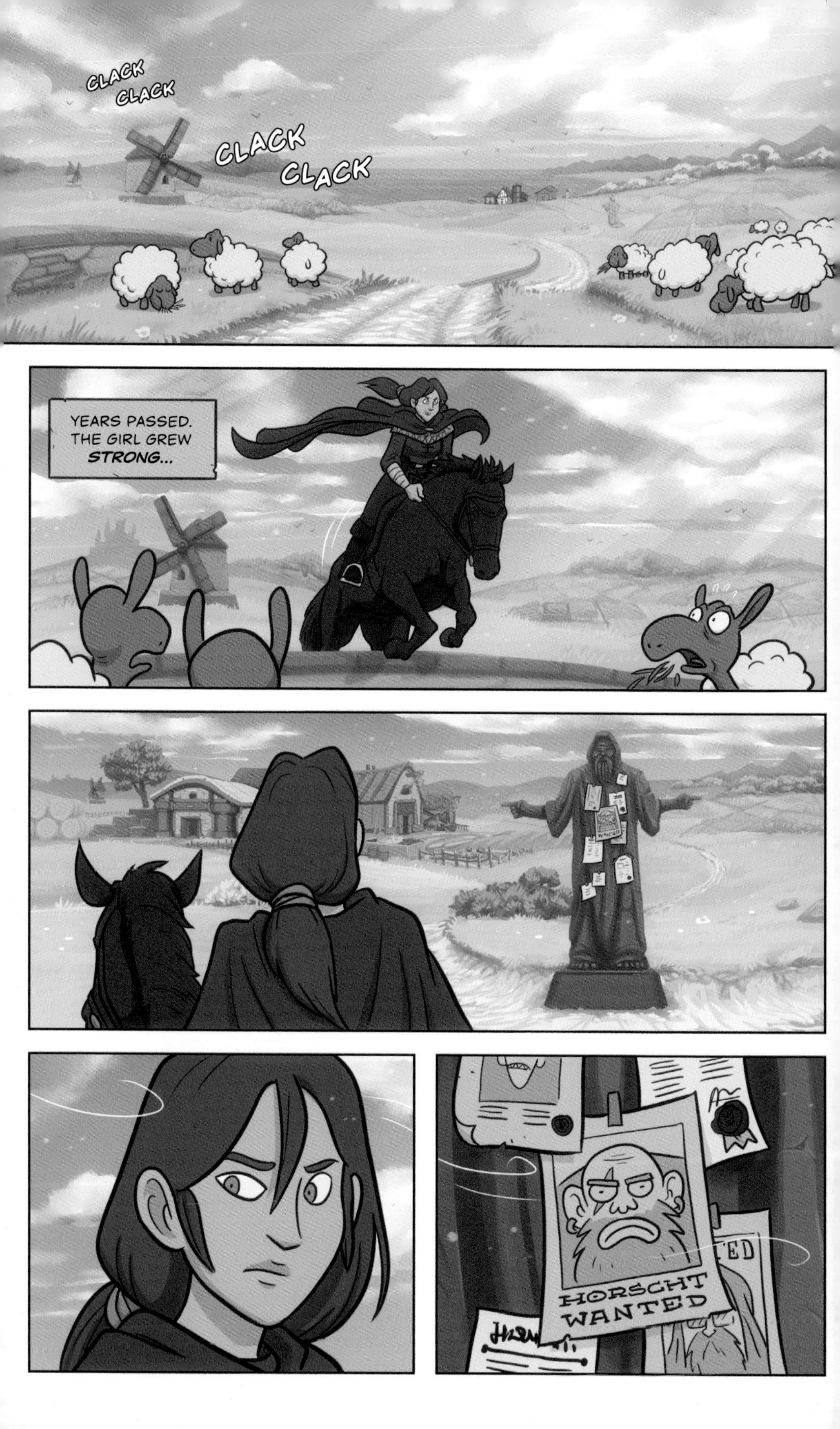
CLACK
CLACK
CLACK
CLACK
YEARS PASSED. THE GIRL GREW **STRONG...**
HORSCHT
WANTED

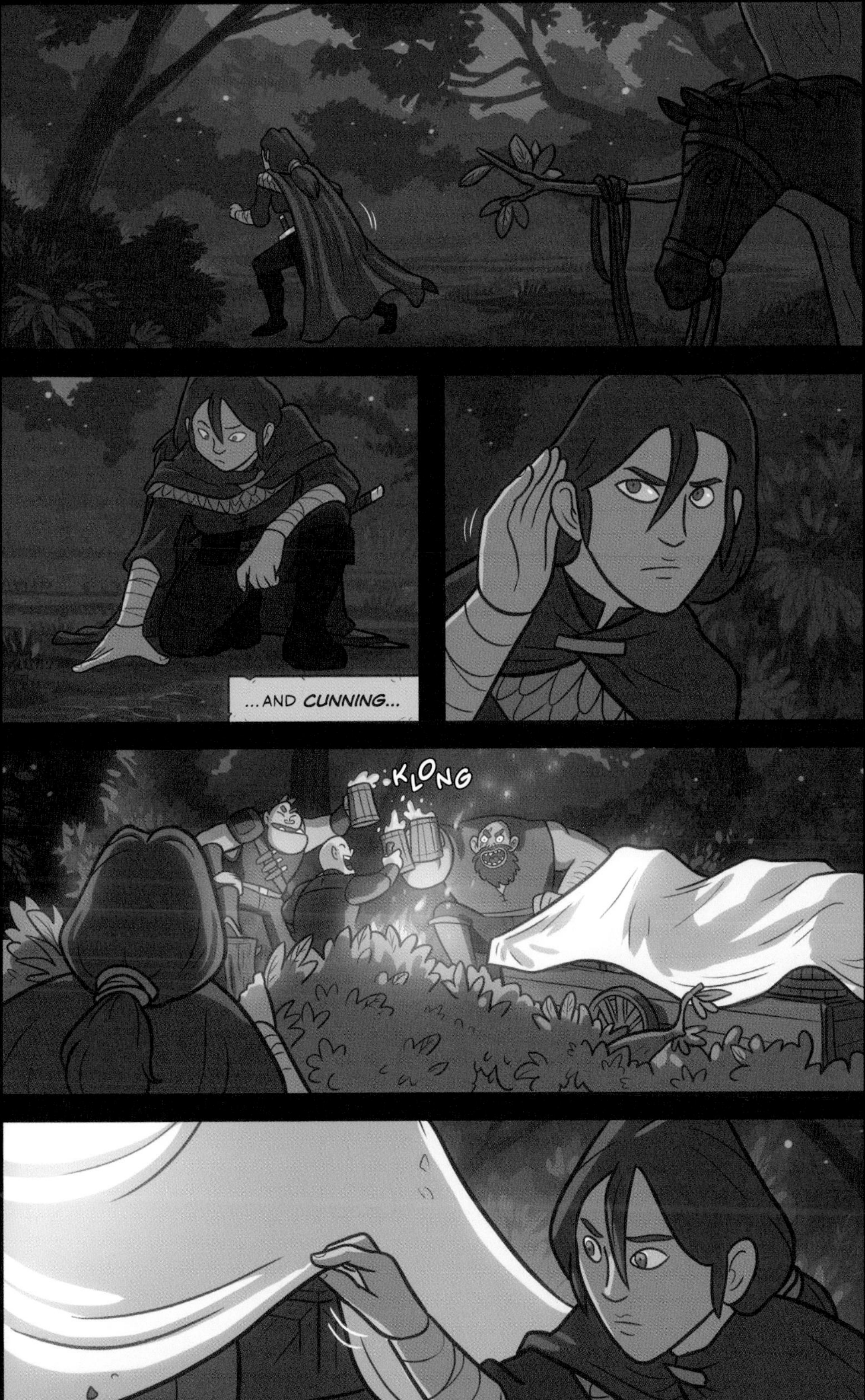
...AND CUNNING...
KLONG

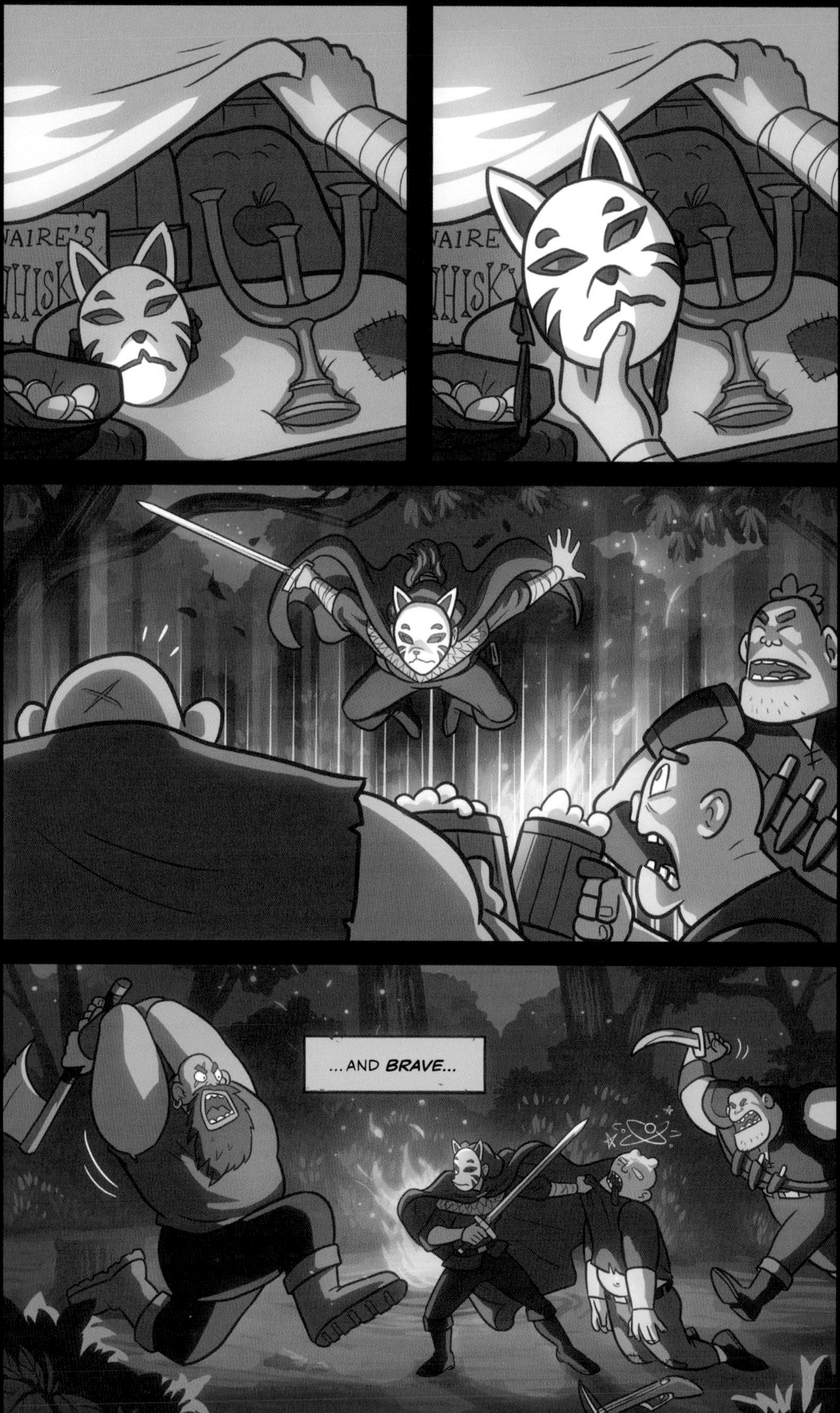

...AND BRAVE...

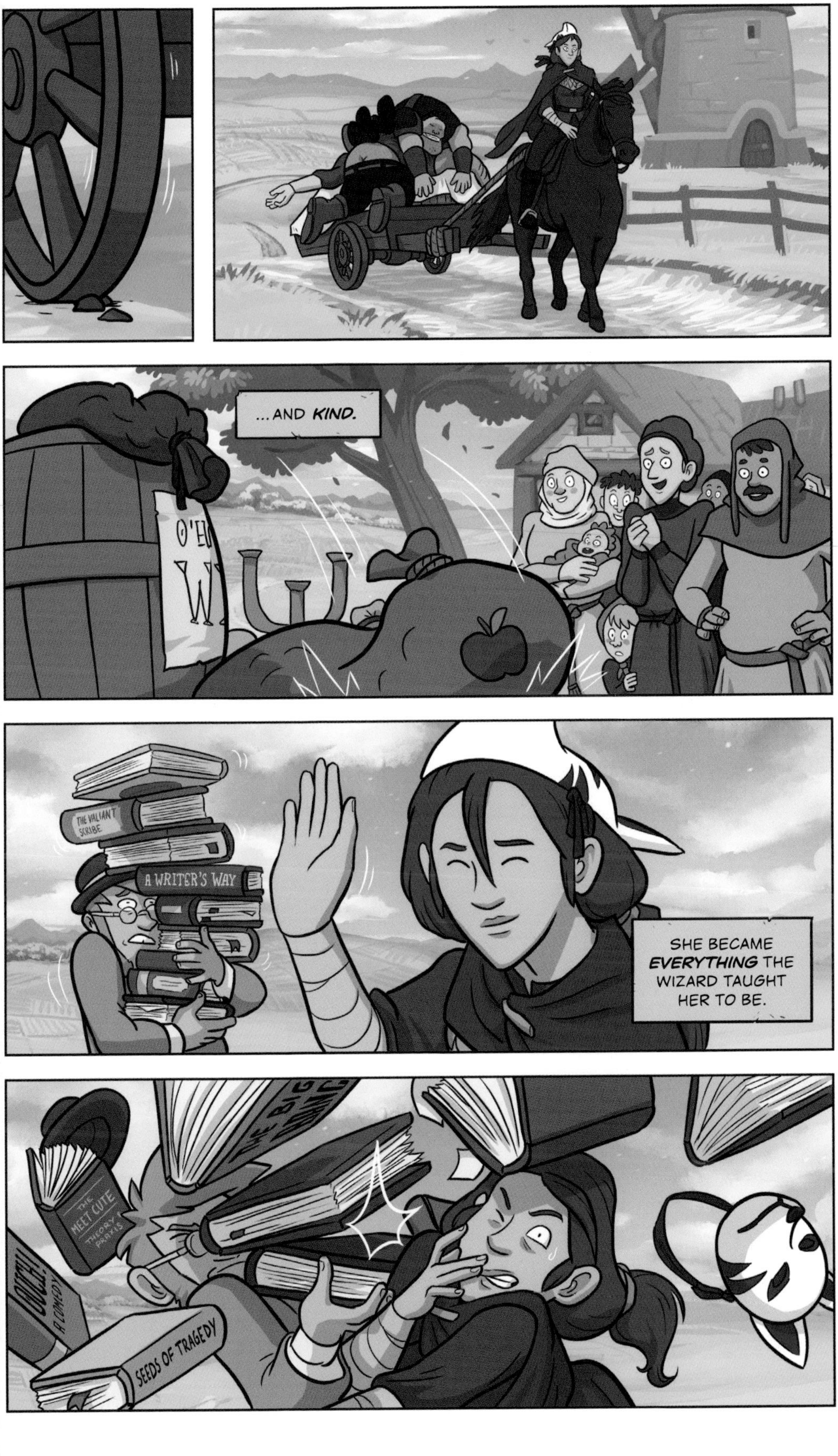
...AND KIND.
O'E
W
THE VALIANT SCRIBE
A WRITER'S WAY
SHE BECAME EVERYTHING THE WIZARD TAUGHT HER TO BE.
THE MEET CUTE THEORY & PRAXIS
OUCH! A COMEDY
SEEDS OF TRAGEDY

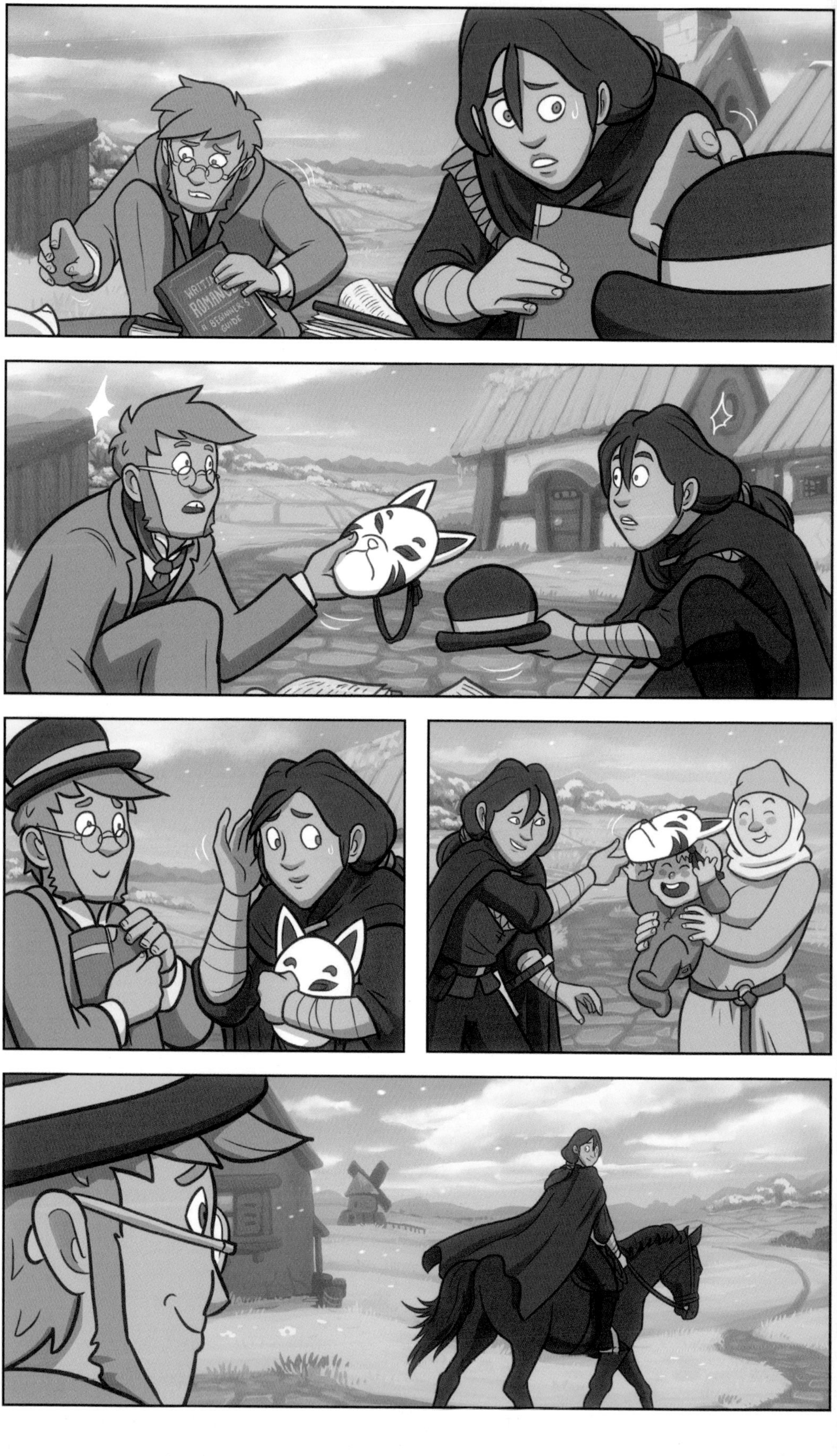
A BEGINNER'S GUIDE

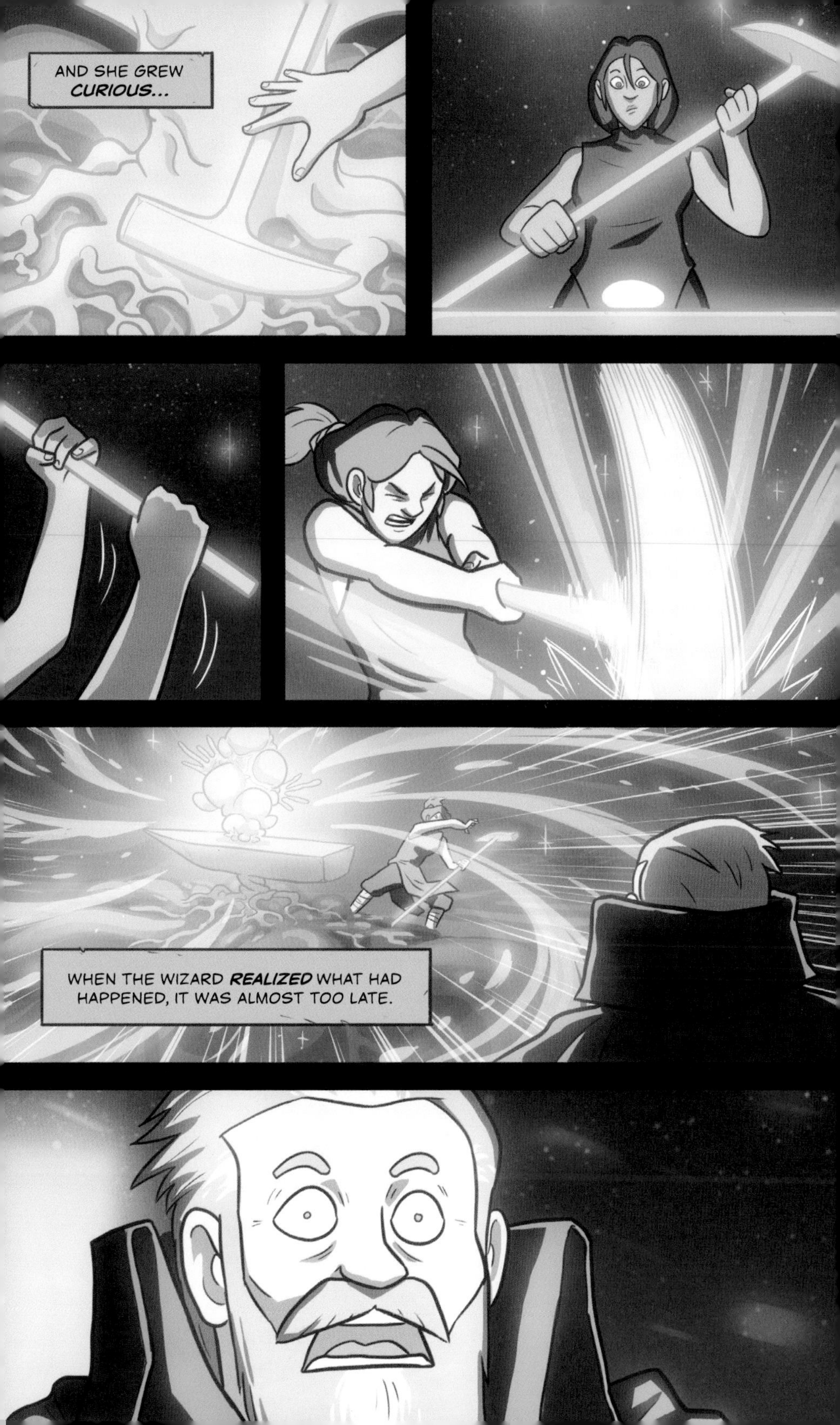
AND SHE GREW *CURIOUS...*
WHEN THE WIZARD ***REALIZED*** WHAT HAD HAPPENED, IT WAS ALMOST TOO LATE.

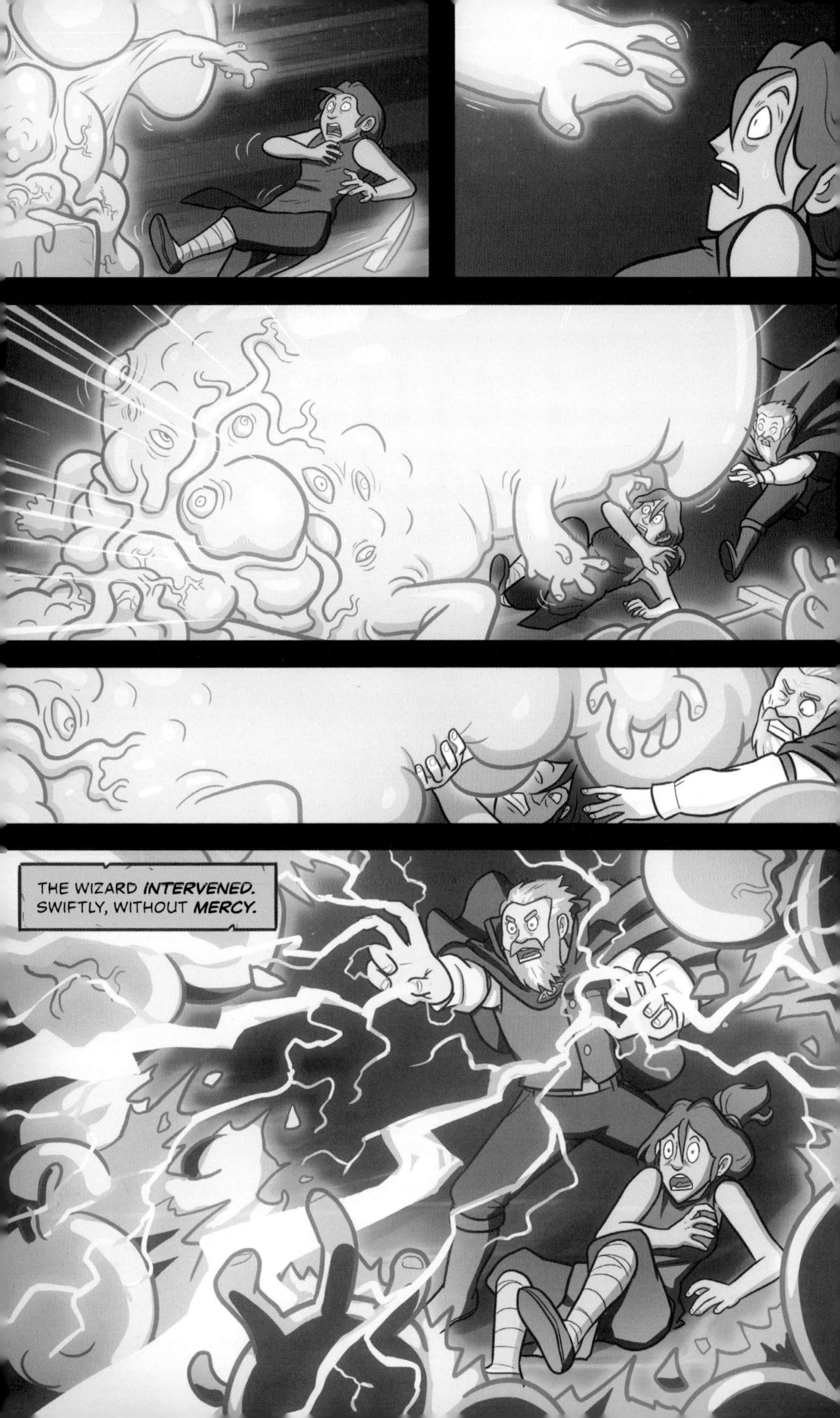
THE WIZARD *INTERVENED.*
SWIFTLY, WITHOUT *MERCY.*

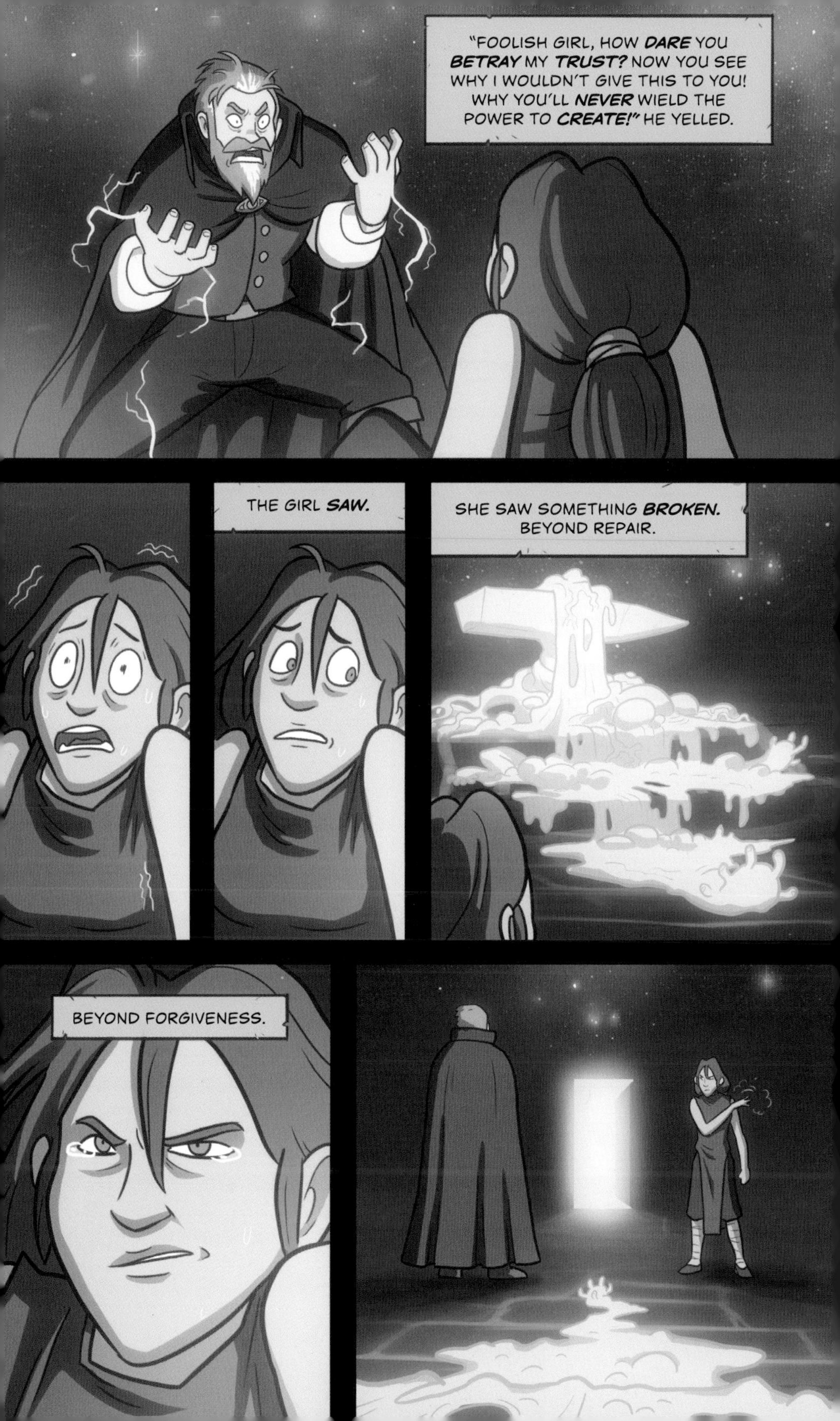
"FOOLISH GIRL, HOW **DARE** YOU **BETRAY** MY **TRUST?** NOW YOU SEE WHY I WOULDN'T GIVE THIS TO YOU! WHY YOU'LL **NEVER** WIELD THE POWER TO **CREATE!**" HE YELLED.
THE GIRL **SAW.**
SHE SAW SOMETHING **BROKEN.** BEYOND REPAIR.
BEYOND FORGIVENESS.

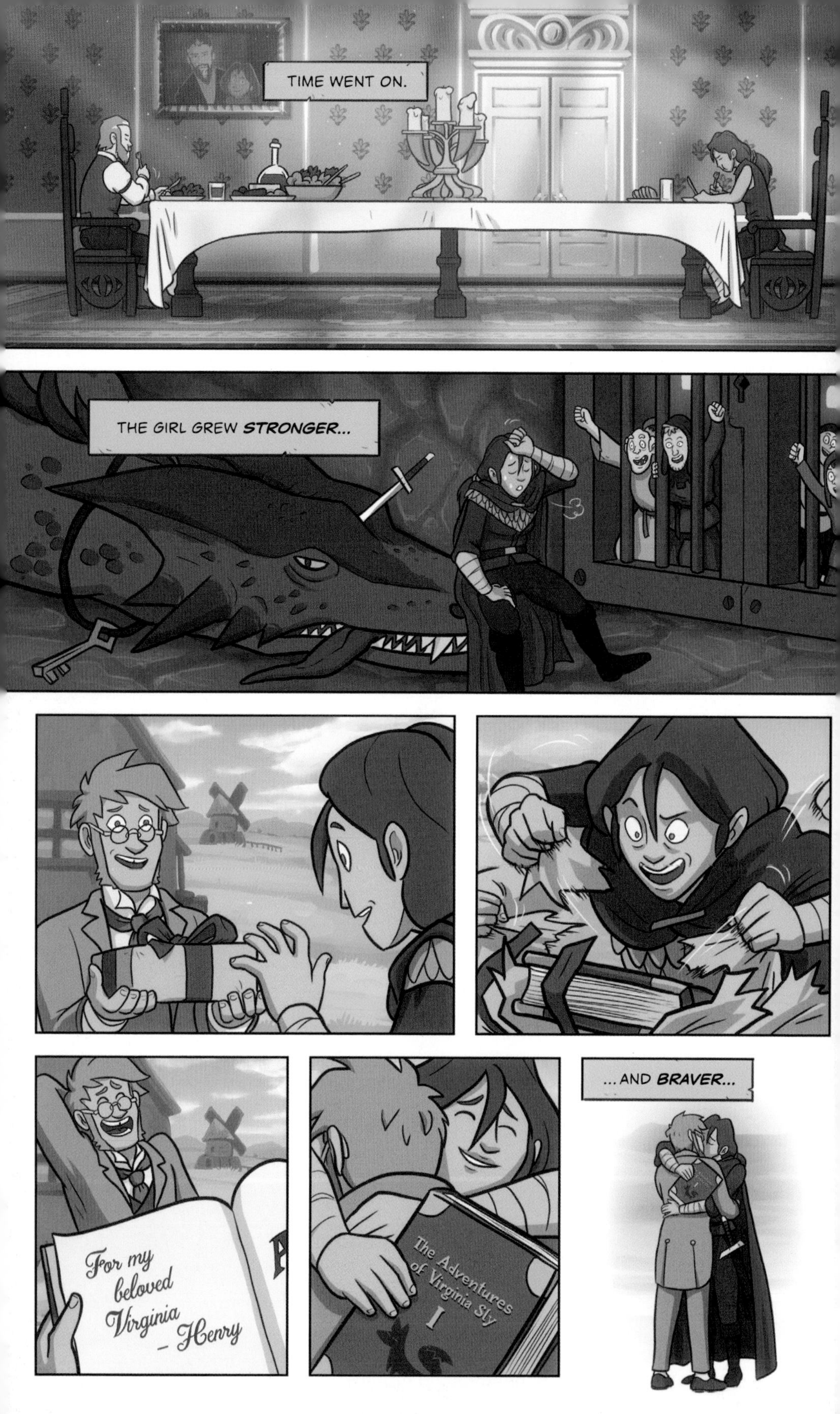
TIME WENT ON.
THE GIRL GREW STRONGER...
For my beloved Virginia - Henry
The Adventures of Virginia Sly
I
...AND BRAVER...

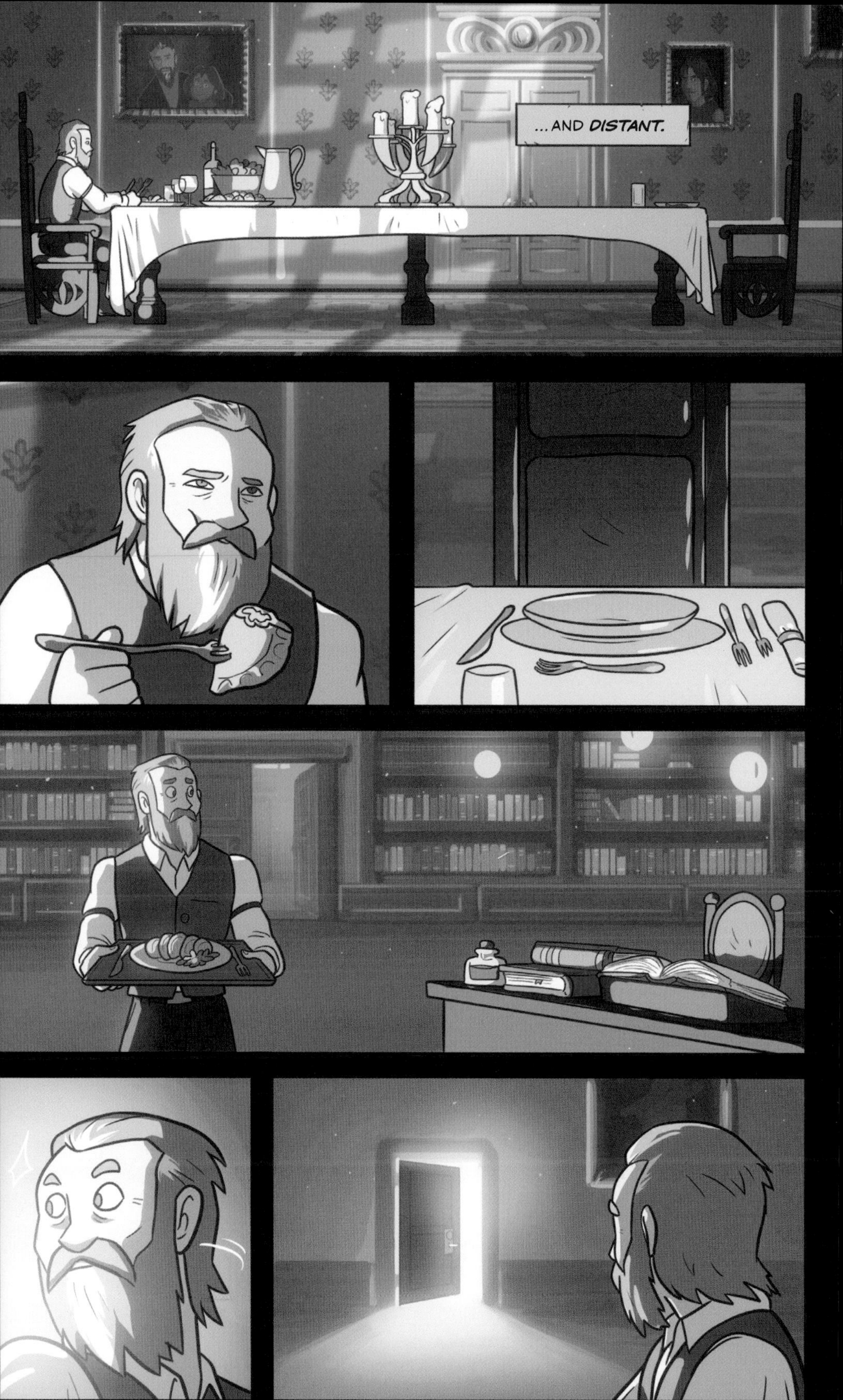
...AND DISTANT.

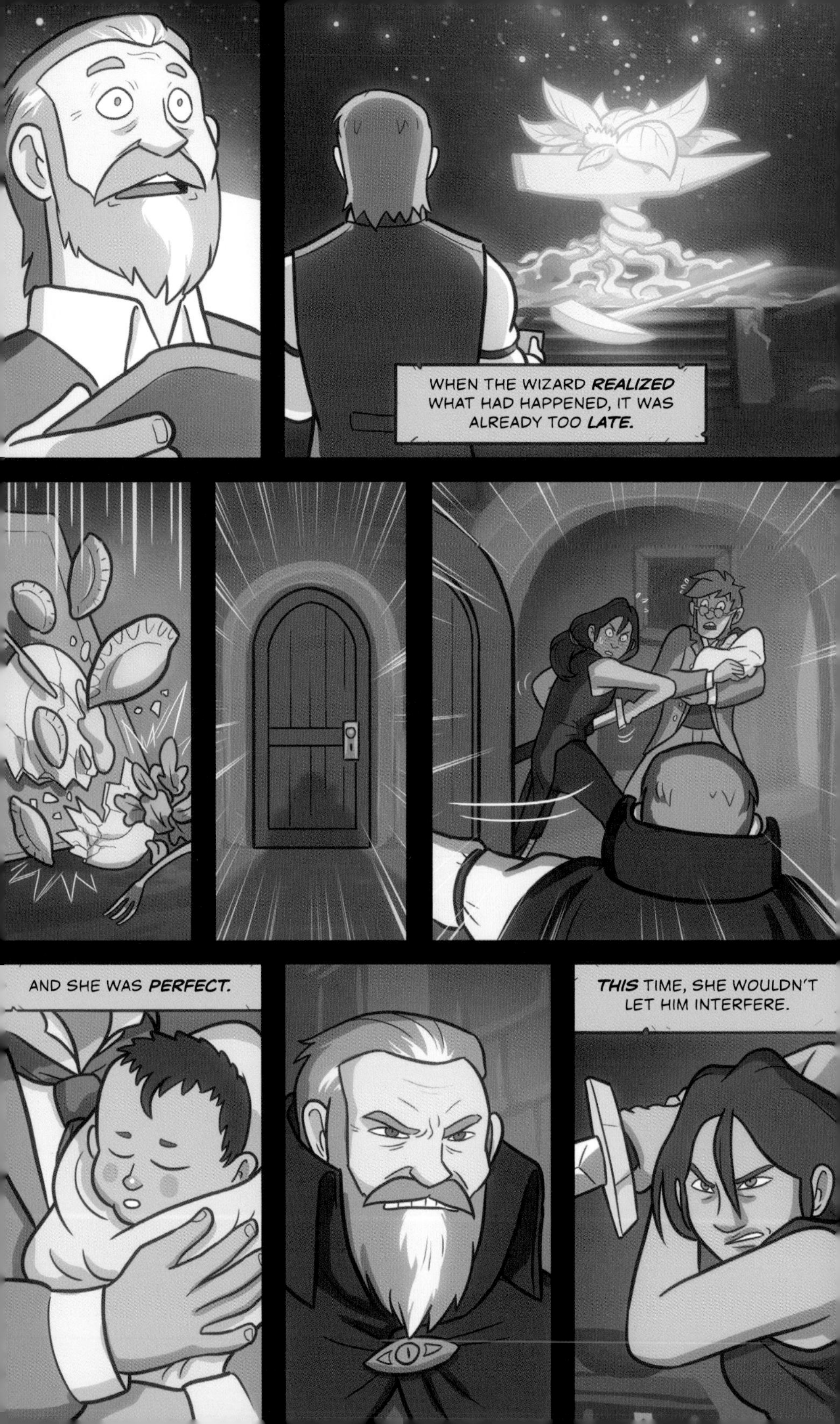
WHEN THE WIZARD REALIZED WHAT HAD HAPPENED, IT WAS ALREADY TOO LATE.
AND SHE WAS PERFECT.
THIS TIME, SHE WOULDN'T LET HIM INTERFERE.

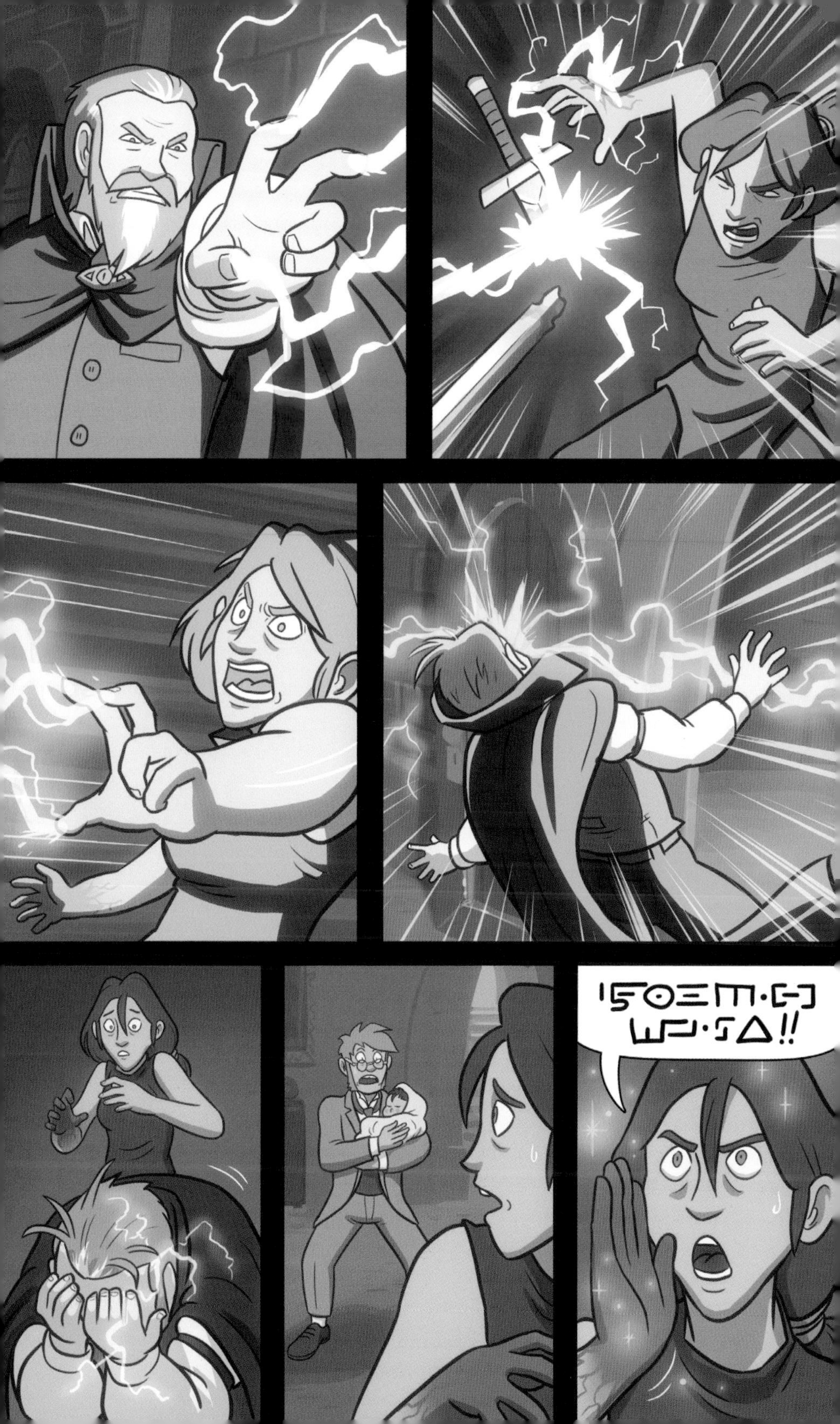

THE WIZARD TRIED TO PURSUE THEM, BUT HER TRUST WAS *BROKEN.* BEYOND REPAIR.

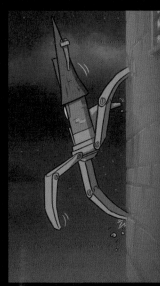

WHEN HE REALIZED WHAT HE HAD *UNLEASHED,* THE WIZARD VOWED TO UNDO HIS MISTAKE--WHATEVER THE *COST.*

AND SO, THE *WAR* BEGAN.

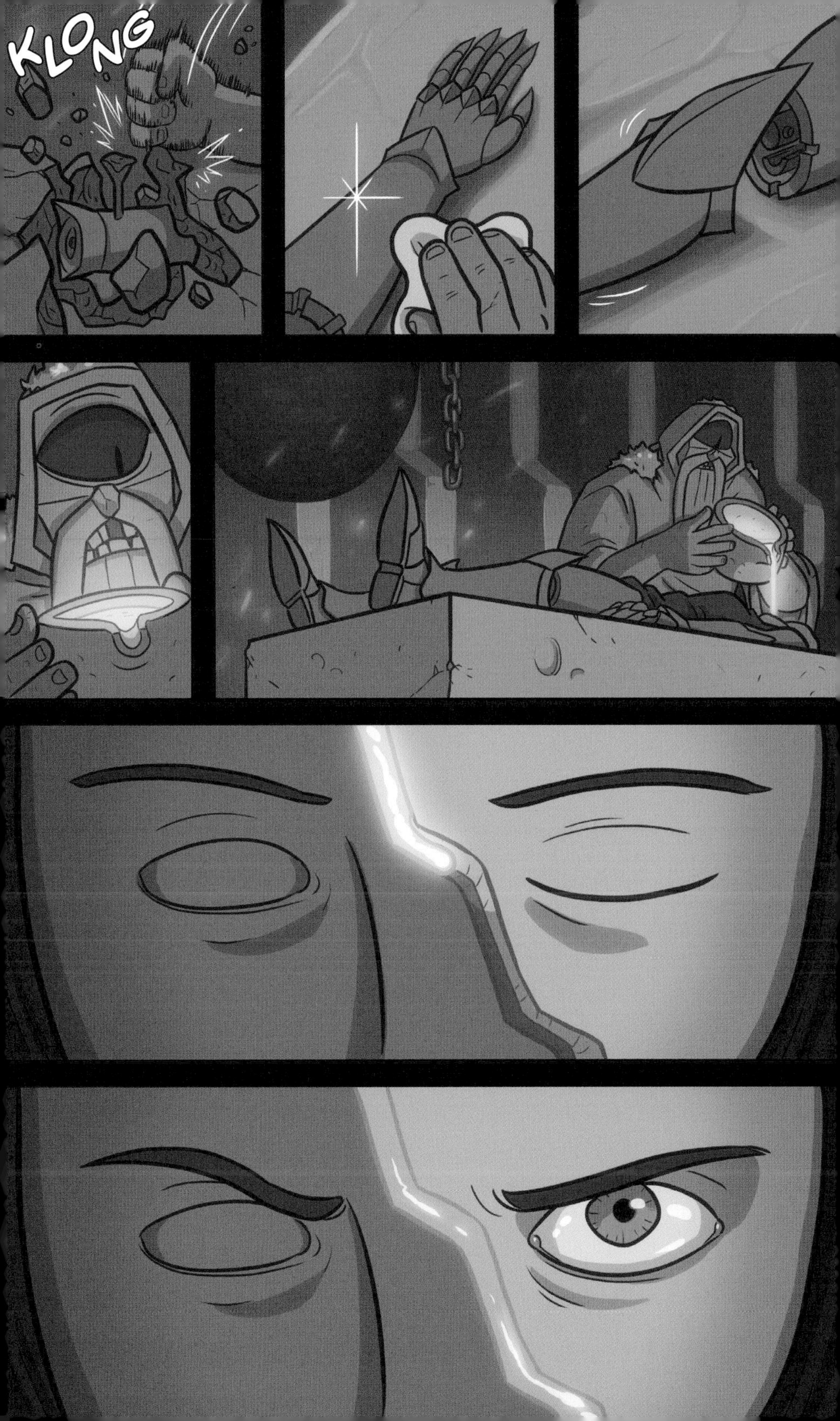
KLONG

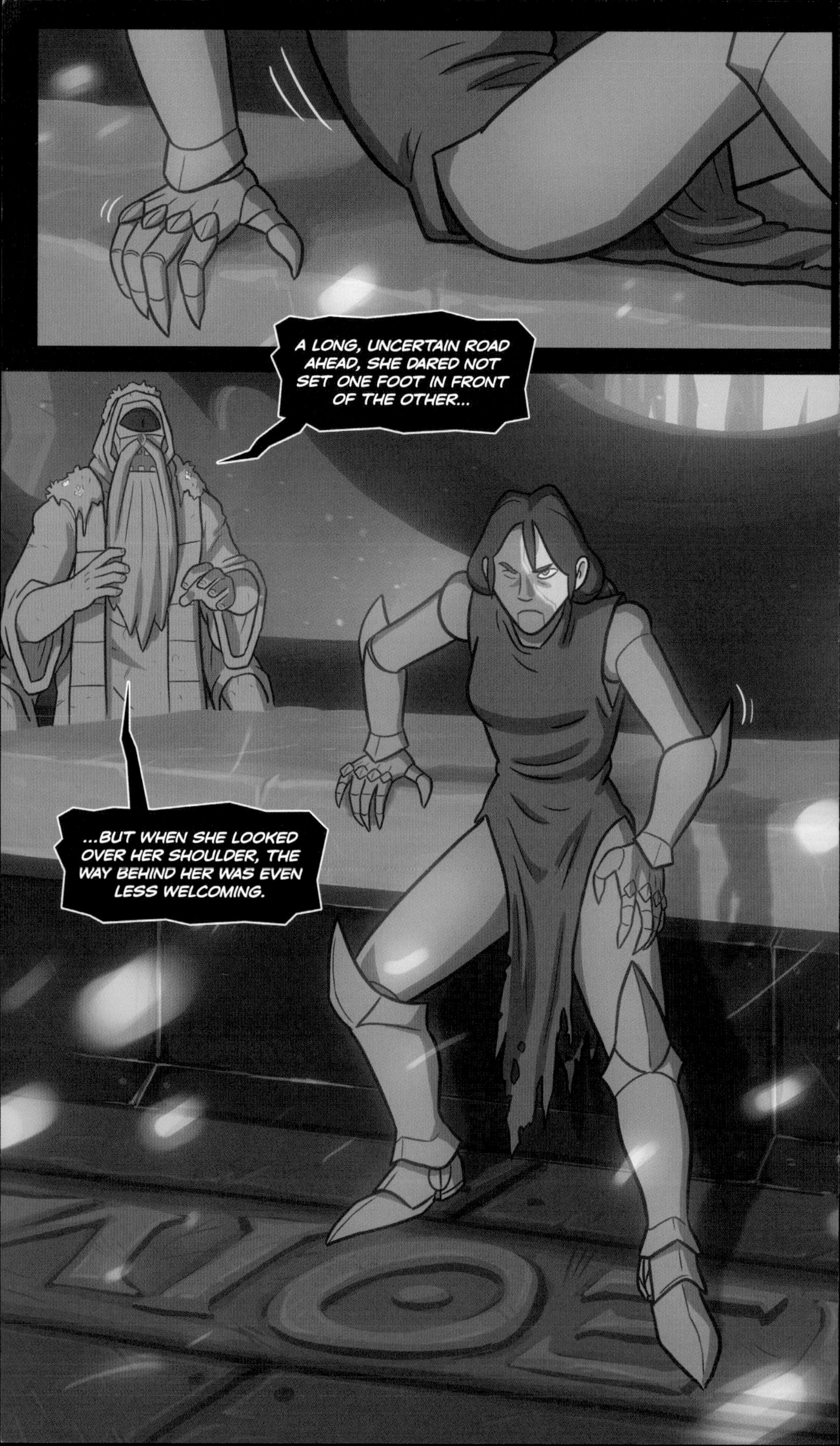
A LONG, UNCERTAIN ROAD AHEAD, SHE DARED NOT SET ONE FOOT IN FRONT OF THE OTHER...
...BUT WHEN SHE LOOKED OVER HER SHOULDER, THE WAY BEHIND HER WAS EVEN LESS WELCOMING.

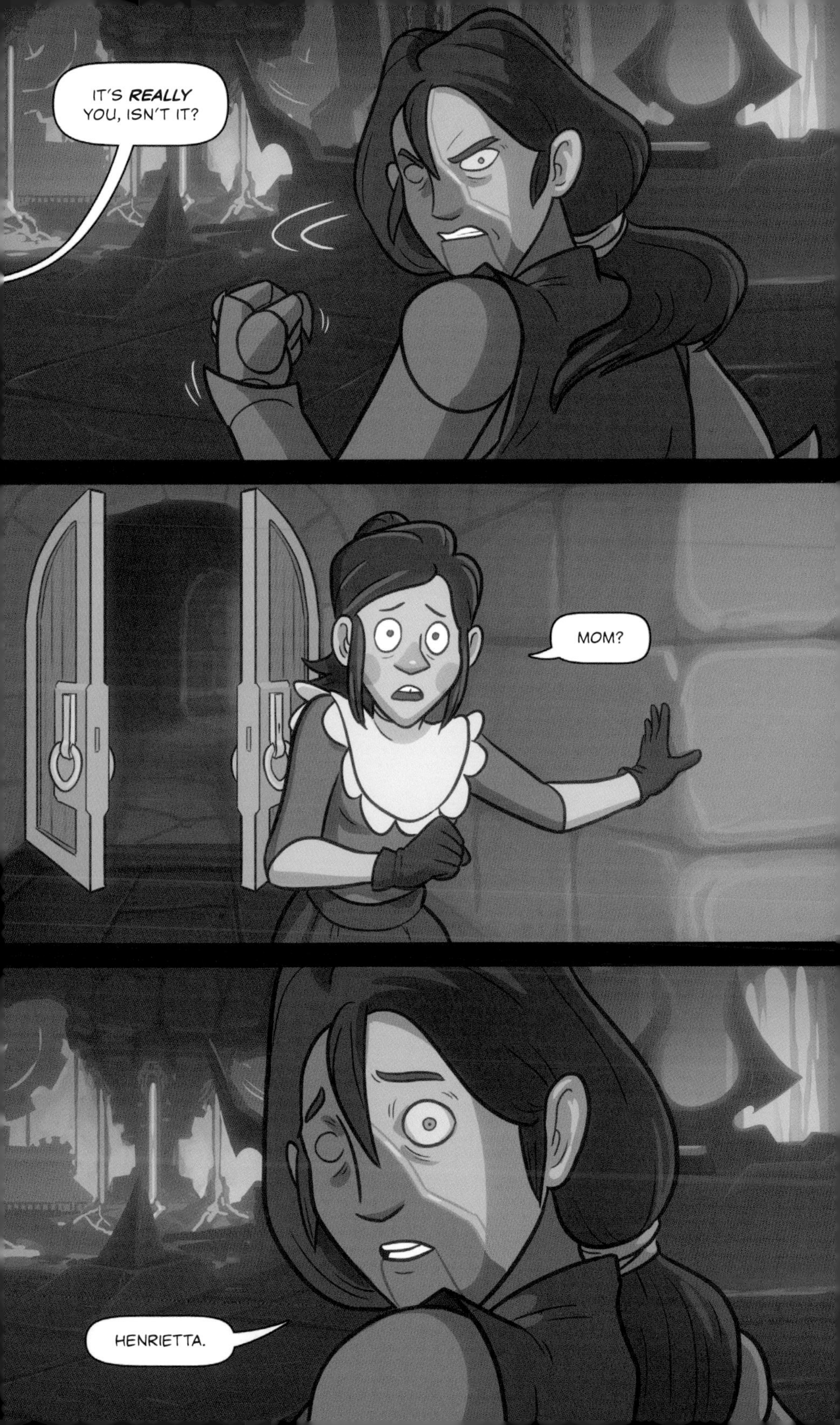
IT'S **REALLY** YOU, ISN'T IT?
MOM?
HENRIETTA.

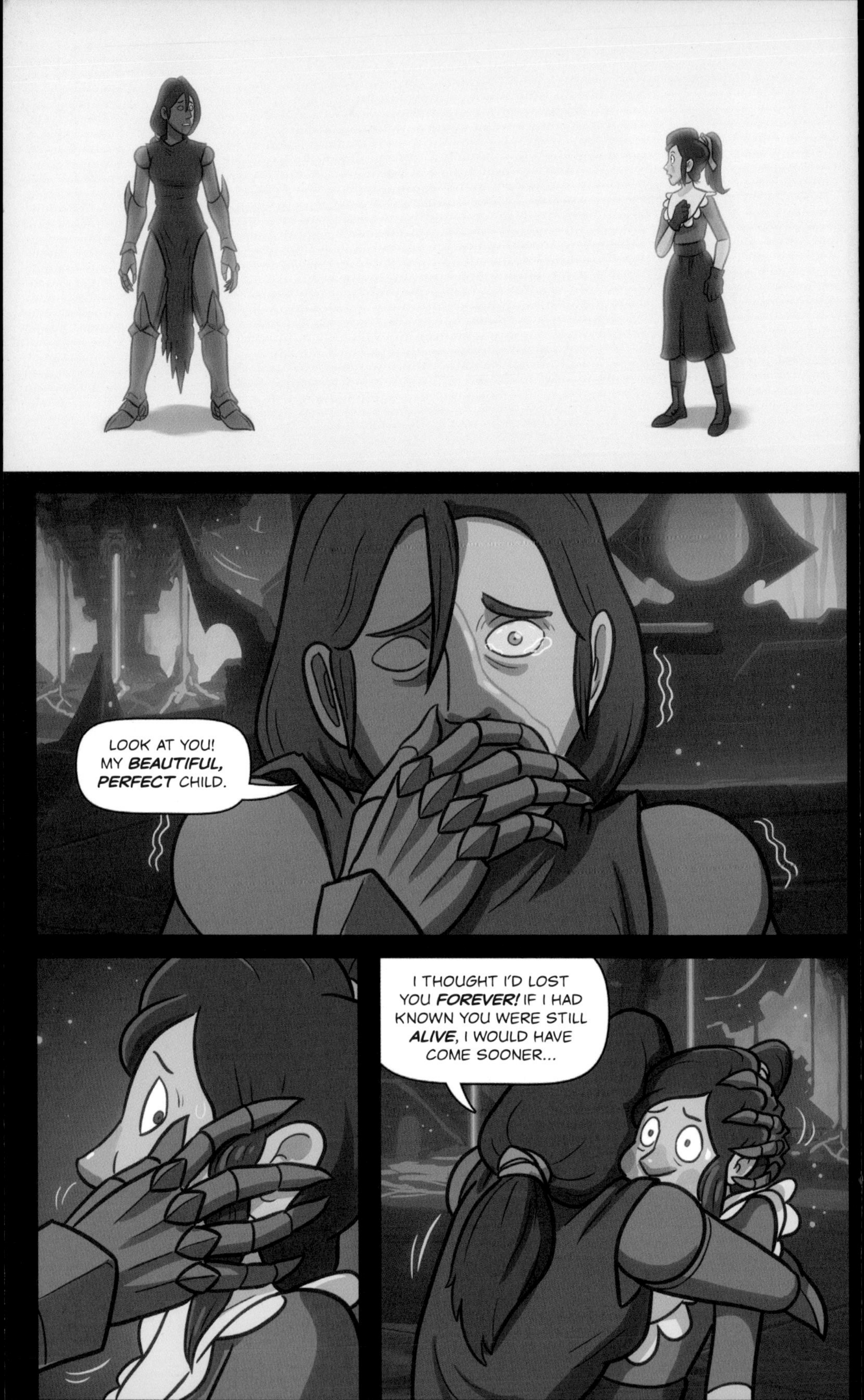
LOOK AT YOU! MY BEAUTIFUL, PERFECT CHILD.
I THOUGHT I'D LOST YOU FOREVER! IF I HAD KNOWN YOU WERE STILL ALIVE, I WOULD HAVE COME SOONER...

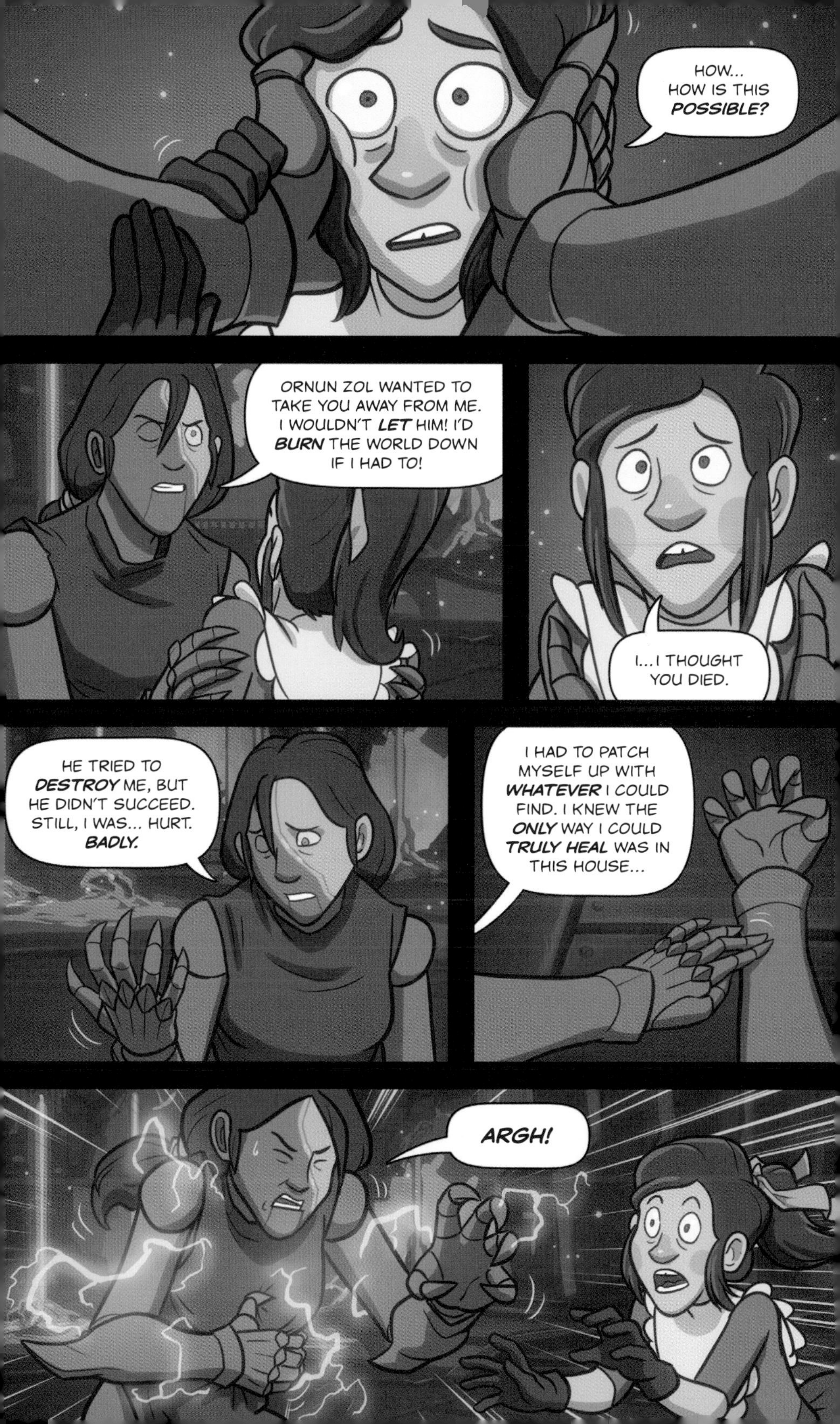
HOW... HOW IS THIS POSSIBLE?
ORNUN ZOL WANTED TO TAKE YOU AWAY FROM ME. I WOULDN'T LET HIM! I'D BURN THE WORLD DOWN IF I HAD TO!
I... I THOUGHT YOU DIED.
HE TRIED TO DESTROY ME, BUT HE DIDN'T SUCCEED. STILL, I WAS... HURT. BADLY.
I HAD TO PATCH MYSELF UP WITH WHATEVER I COULD FIND. I KNEW THE ONLY WAY I COULD TRULY HEAL WAS IN THIS HOUSE...
ARGH!

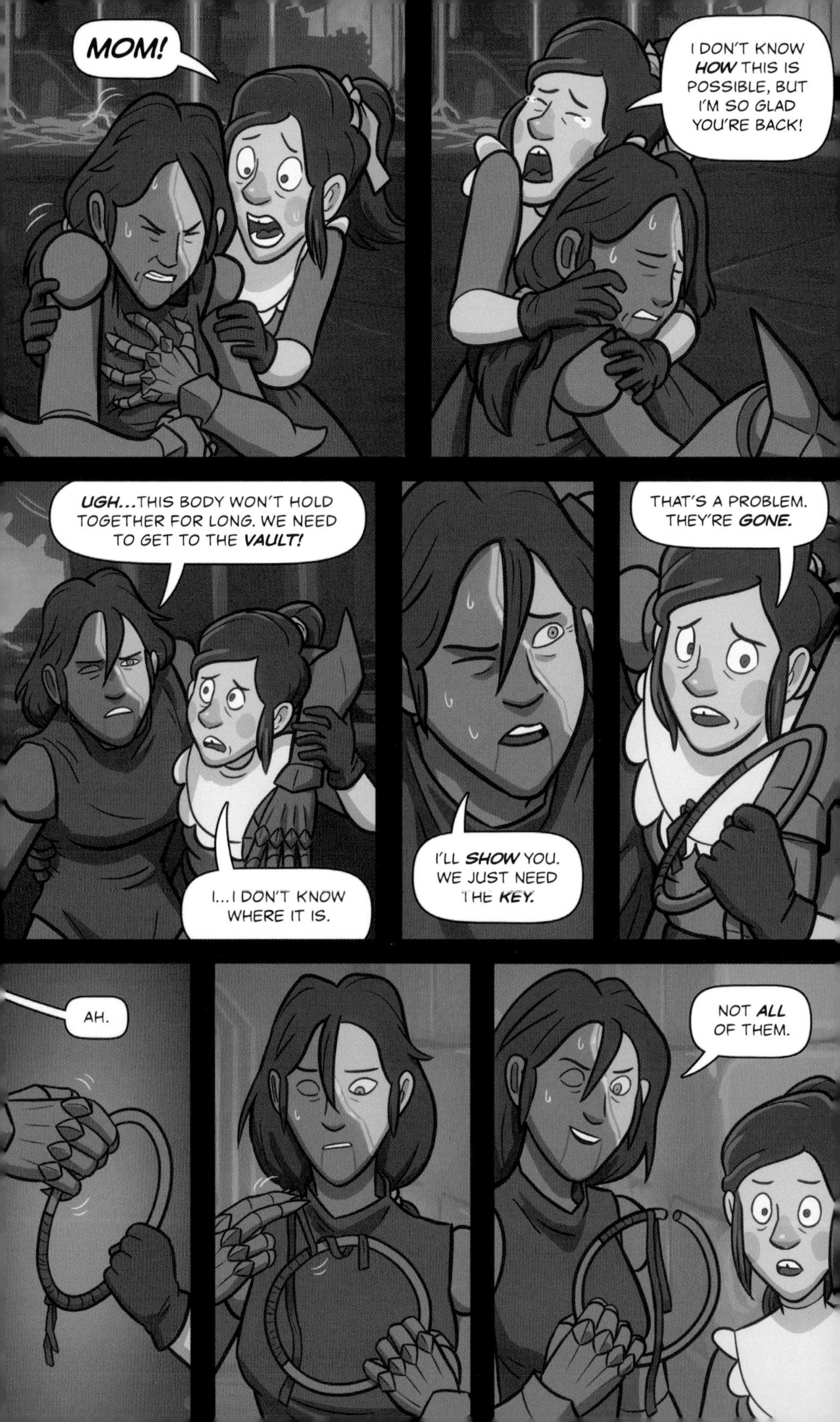
MOM!
I DON'T KNOW HOW THIS IS POSSIBLE, BUT I'M SO GLAD YOU'RE BACK!
UGH...THIS BODY WON'T HOLD TOGETHER FOR LONG. WE NEED TO GET TO THE VAULT!
I...I DON'T KNOW WHERE IT IS.
I'LL SHOW YOU. WE JUST NEED THE KEY.
THAT'S A PROBLEM. THEY'RE GONE.
AH.
NOT ALL OF THEM.

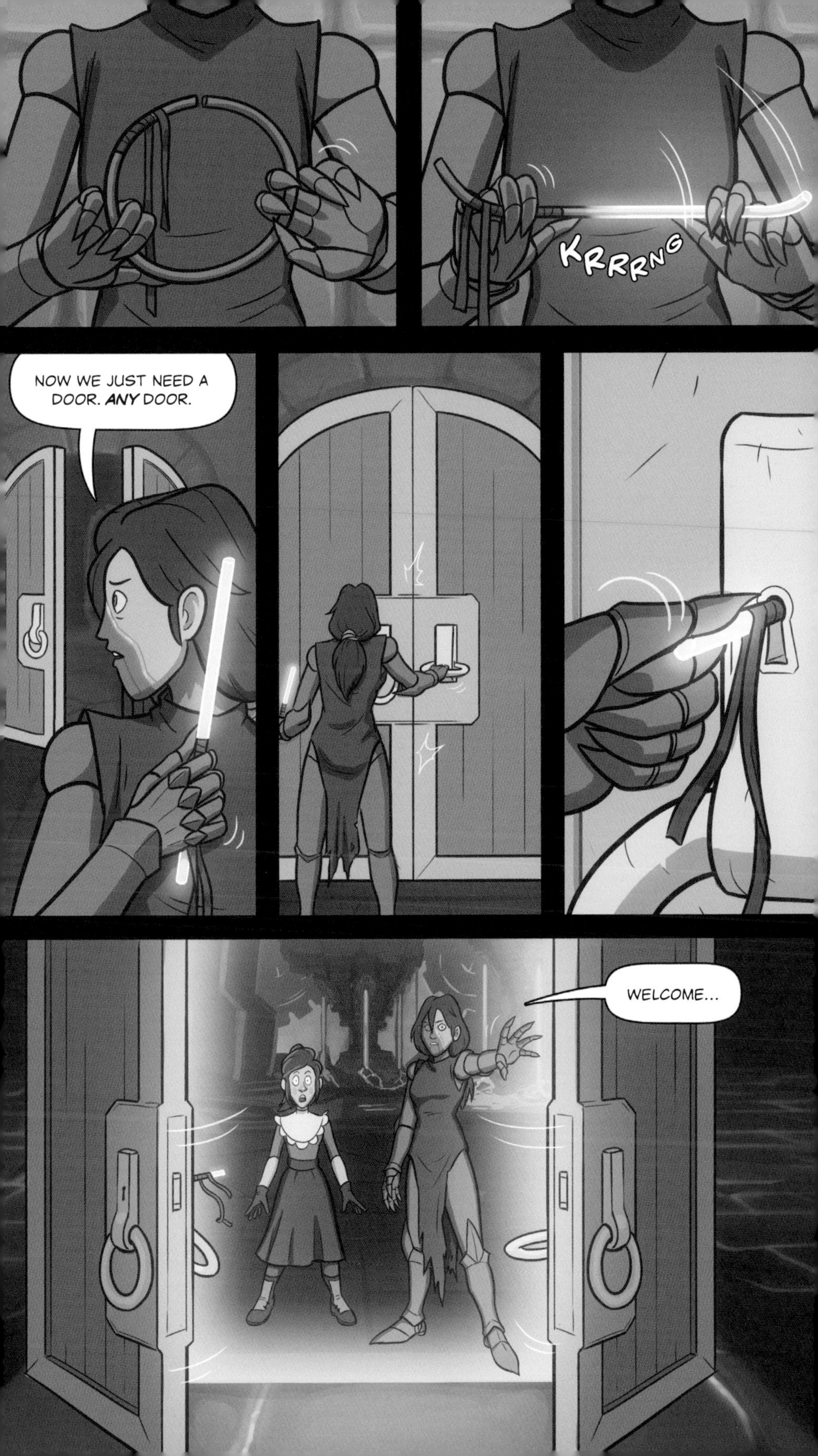
KRRRNG
NOW WE JUST NEED A DOOR. ANY DOOR.
WELCOME...

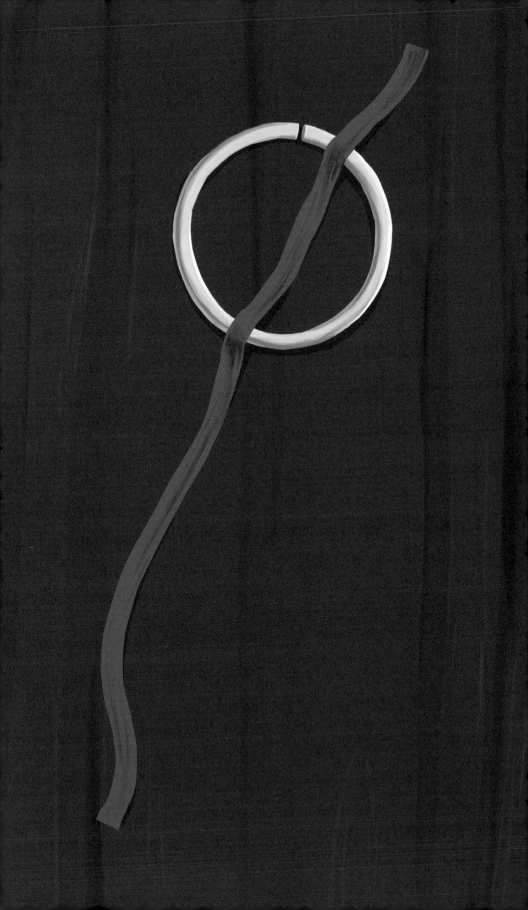

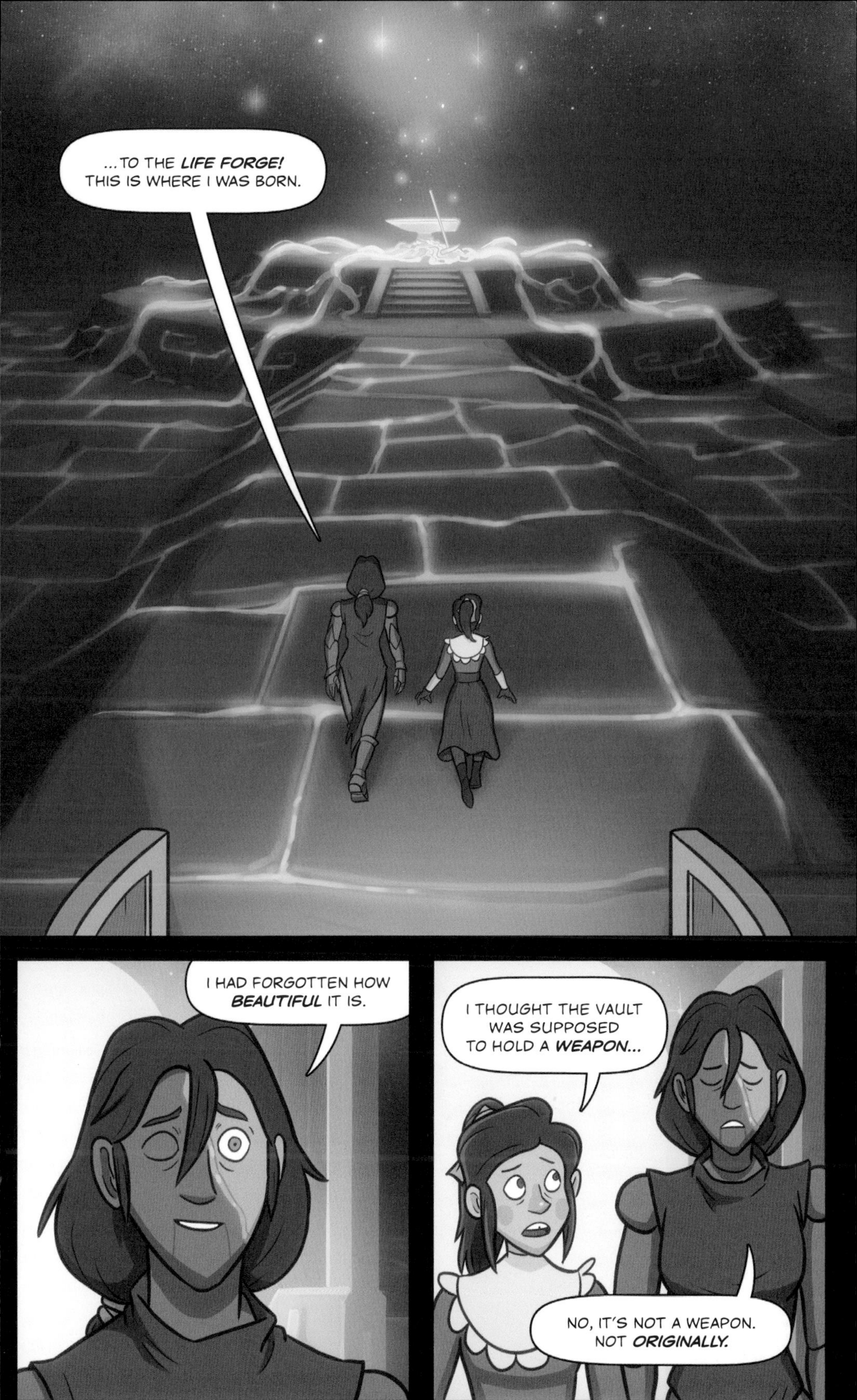
...TO THE LIFE FORGE! THIS IS WHERE I WAS BORN.
I HAD FORGOTTEN HOW BEAUTIFUL IT IS.
I THOUGHT THE VAULT WAS SUPPOSED TO HOLD A WEAPON...
NO, IT'S NOT A WEAPON. NOT ORIGINALLY.

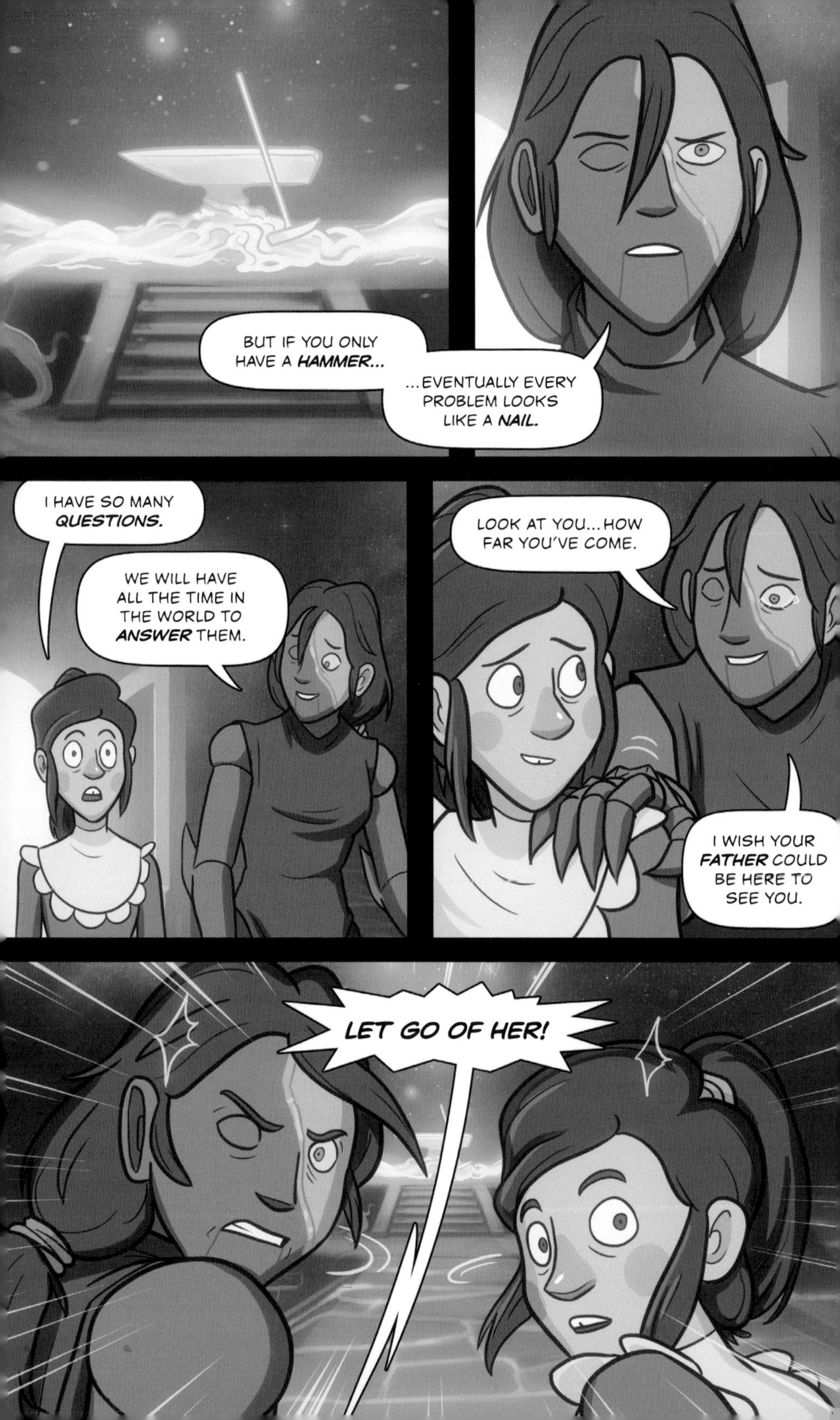
BUT IF YOU ONLY HAVE A *HAMMER...*
...EVENTUALLY EVERY PROBLEM LOOKS LIKE A *NAIL.*
I HAVE SO MANY *QUESTIONS.*
WE WILL HAVE ALL THE TIME IN THE WORLD TO *ANSWER* THEM.
LOOK AT YOU...HOW FAR YOU'VE COME.
I WISH YOUR *FATHER* COULD BE HERE TO SEE YOU.
LET GO OF HER!

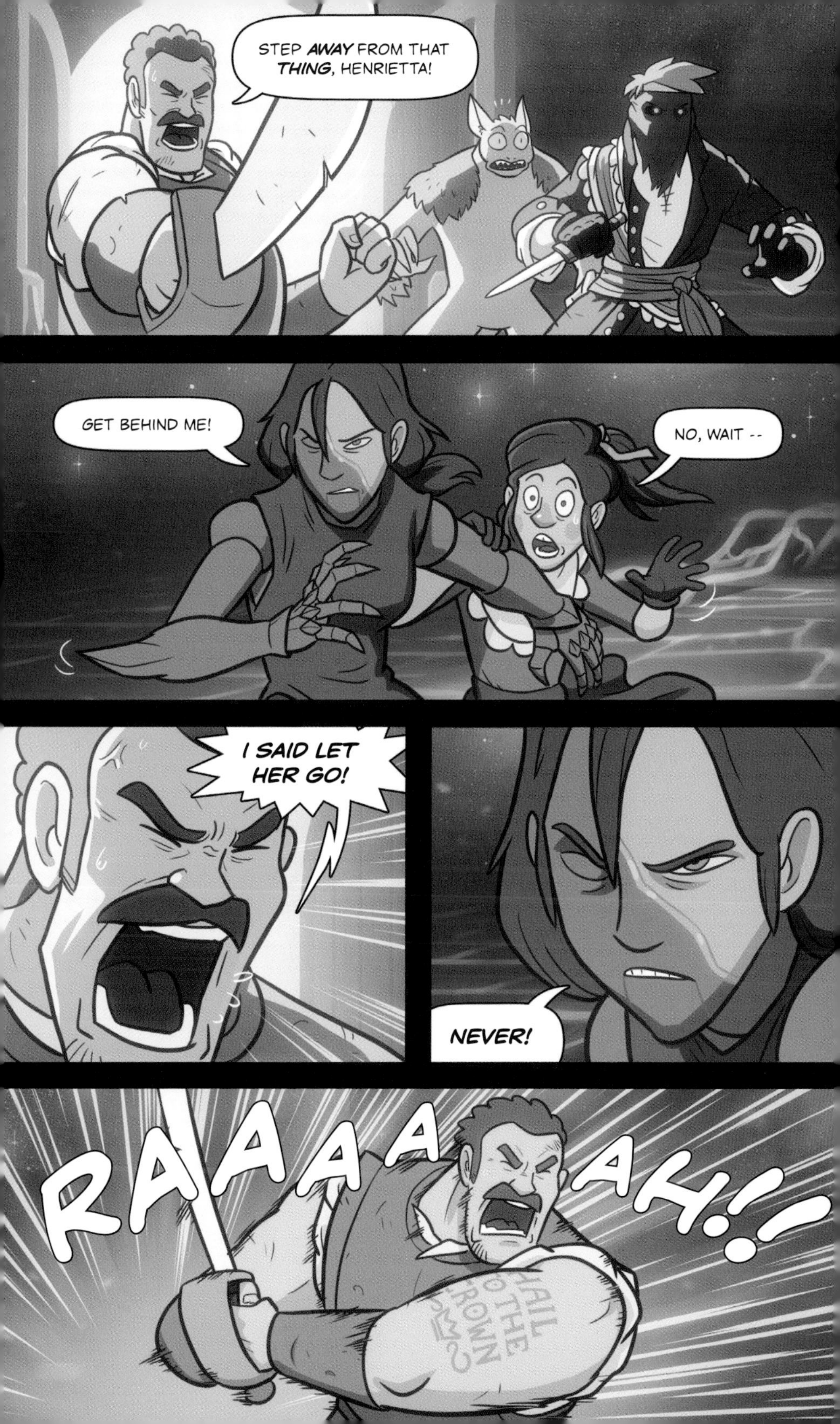

STEP AWAY FROM THAT THING, HENRIETTA!
GET BEHIND ME!
NO, WAIT --
I SAID LET HER GO!
NEVER!
RAAAAAH!!!
HAIL TO THE CROWN

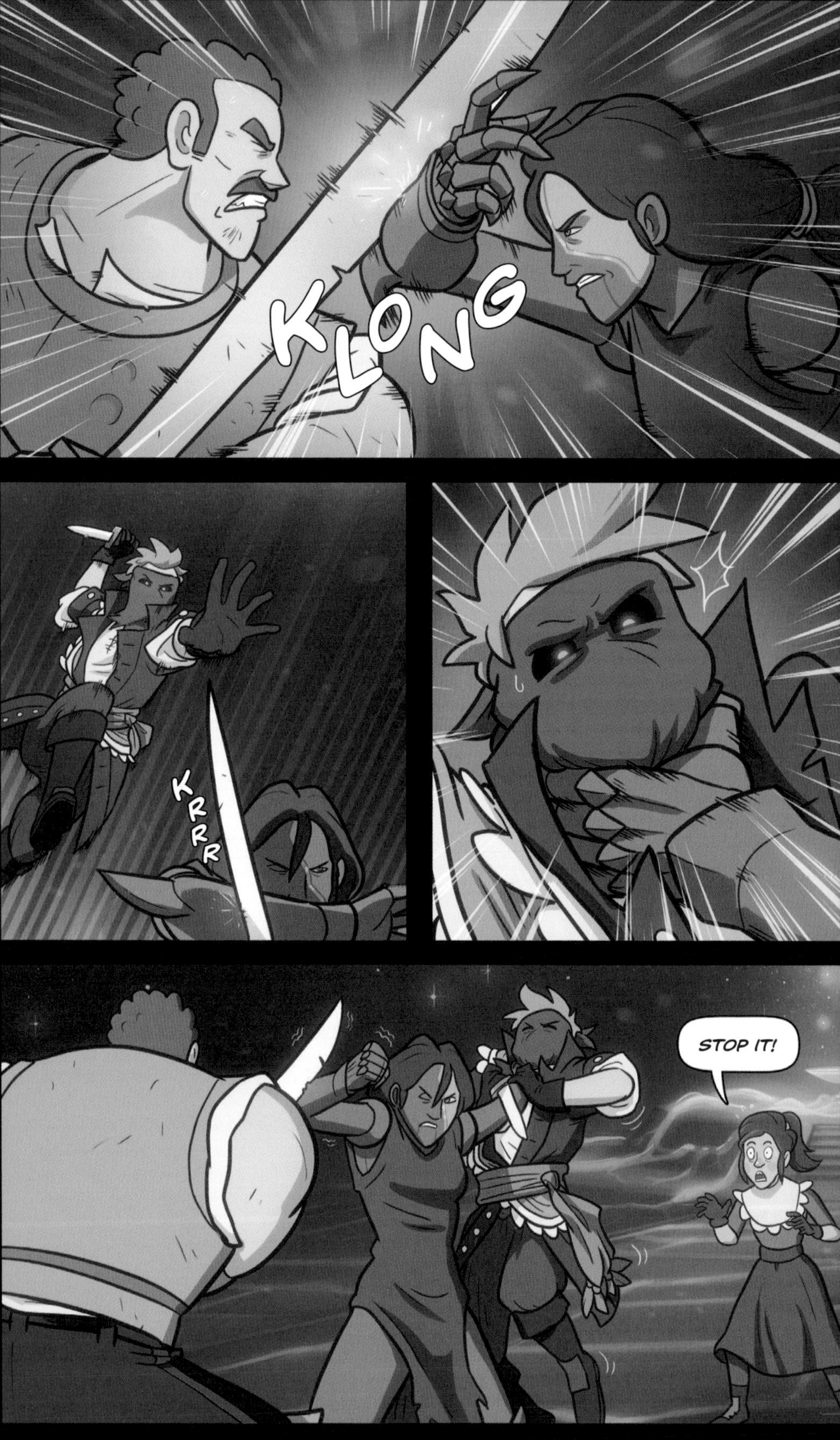
KLONG
KRRR
STOP IT!

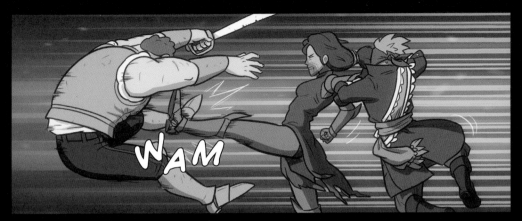

WAM

OOF!

STOP IT! EVERYBODY!

UGH!

GRIP

GO GET THE OTHERS! HURRY!

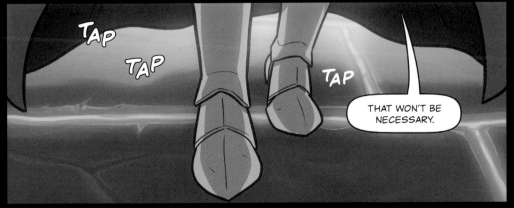

TAP

TAP

TAP

THAT WON'T BE NECESSARY.

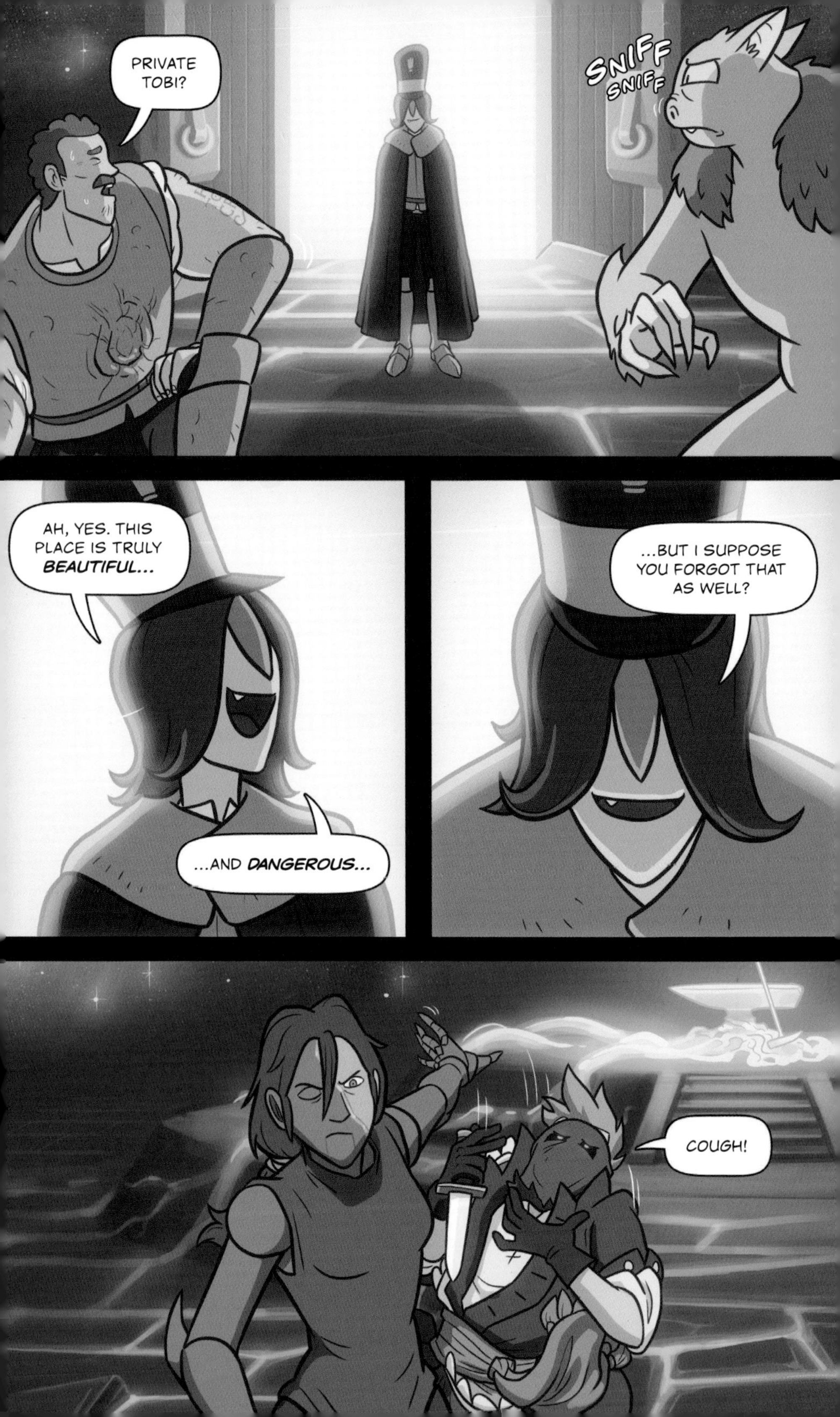
PRIVATE TOBI?
SNIFF SNIFF
AH, YES. THIS PLACE IS TRULY **BEAUTIFUL...**
...AND **DANGEROUS...**
...BUT I SUPPOSE YOU FORGOT THAT AS WELL?
COUGH!

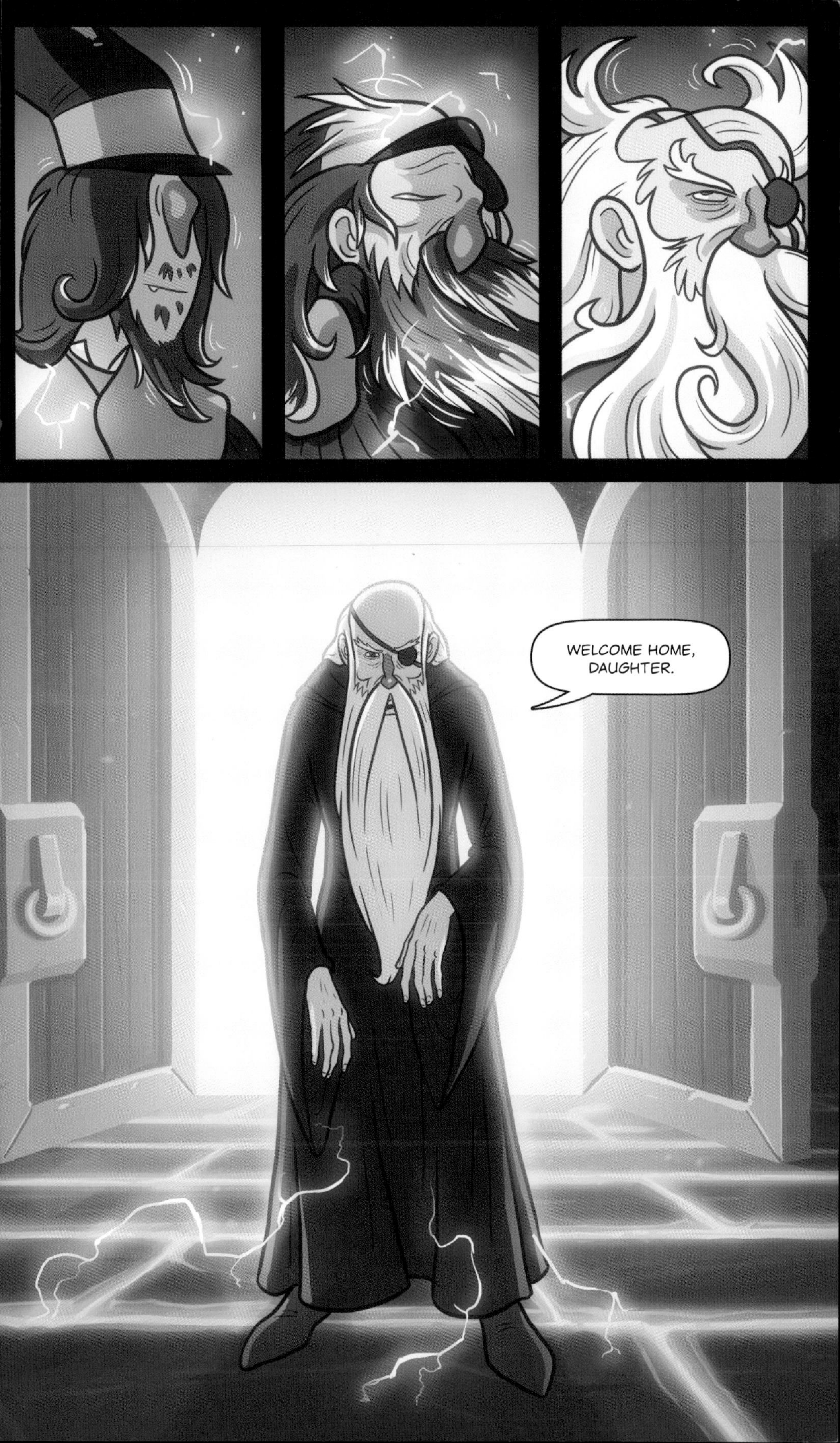
WELCOME HOME, DAUGHTER.

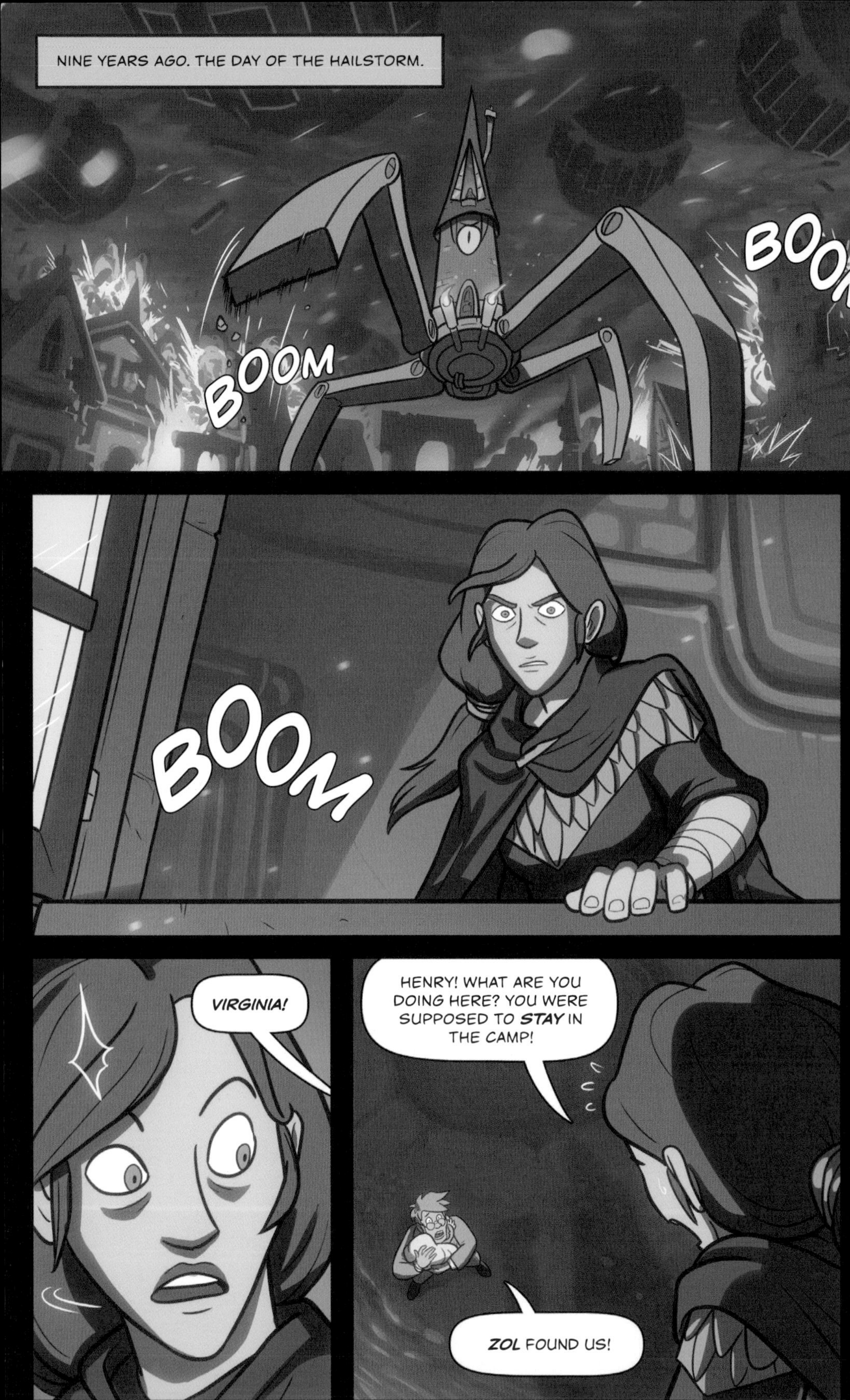
NINE YEARS AGO. THE DAY OF THE HAILSTORM.
BOOM
BOOM
BOOM
VIRGINIA!
HENRY! WHAT ARE YOU DOING HERE? YOU WERE SUPPOSED TO STAY IN THE CAMP!
ZOL FOUND US!

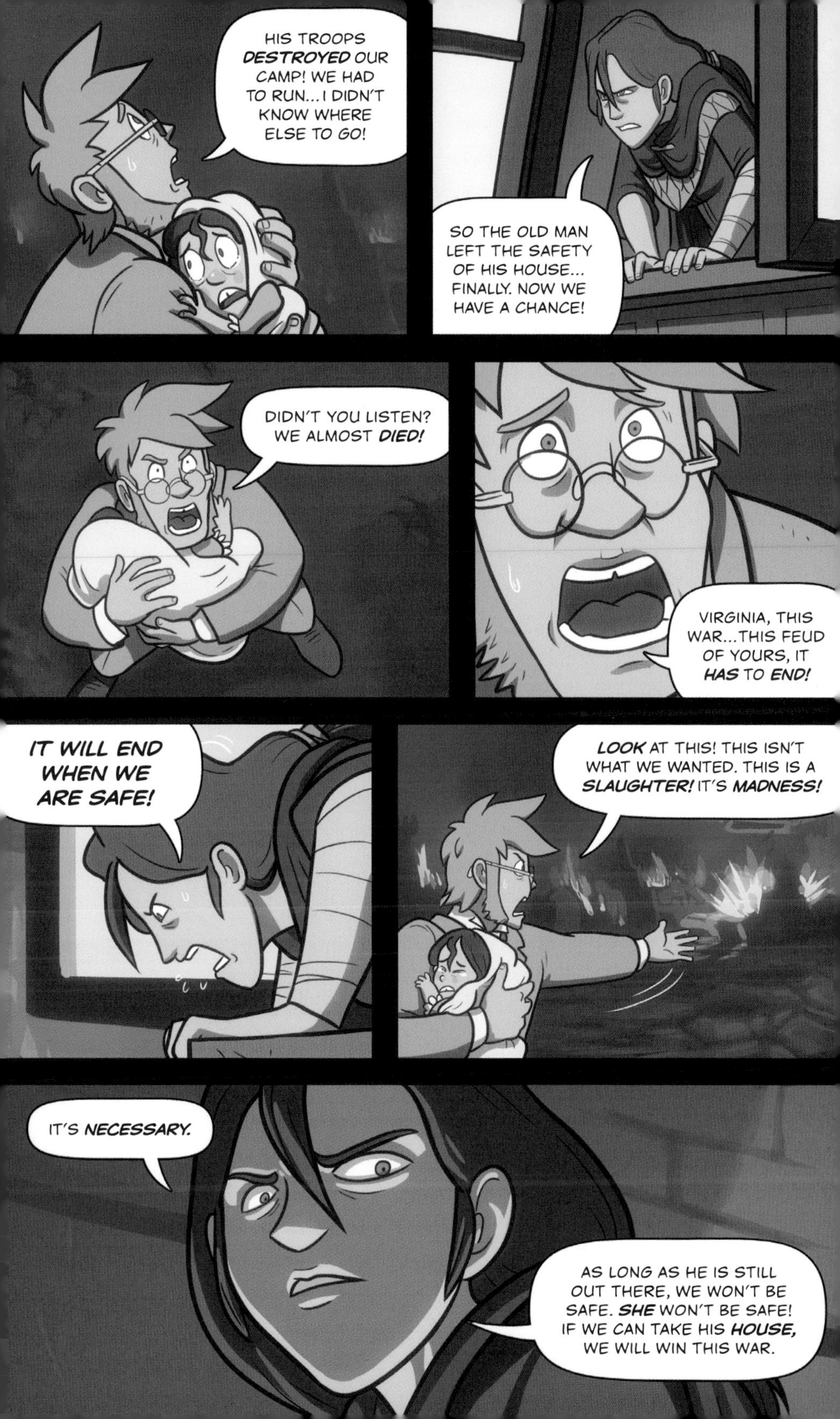
HIS TROOPS DESTROYED OUR CAMP! WE HAD TO RUN... I DIDN'T KNOW WHERE ELSE TO GO!
SO THE OLD MAN LEFT THE SAFETY OF HIS HOUSE... FINALLY. NOW WE HAVE A CHANCE!
DIDN'T YOU LISTEN? WE ALMOST DIED!
VIRGINIA, THIS WAR...THIS FEUD OF YOURS, IT HAS TO END!
IT WILL END WHEN WE ARE SAFE!
LOOK AT THIS! THIS ISN'T WHAT WE WANTED. THIS IS A SLAUGHTER! IT'S MADNESS!
IT'S NECESSARY.
AS LONG AS HE IS STILL OUT THERE, WE WON'T BE SAFE. SHE WON'T BE SAFE! IF WE CAN TAKE HIS HOUSE, WE WILL WIN THIS WAR.

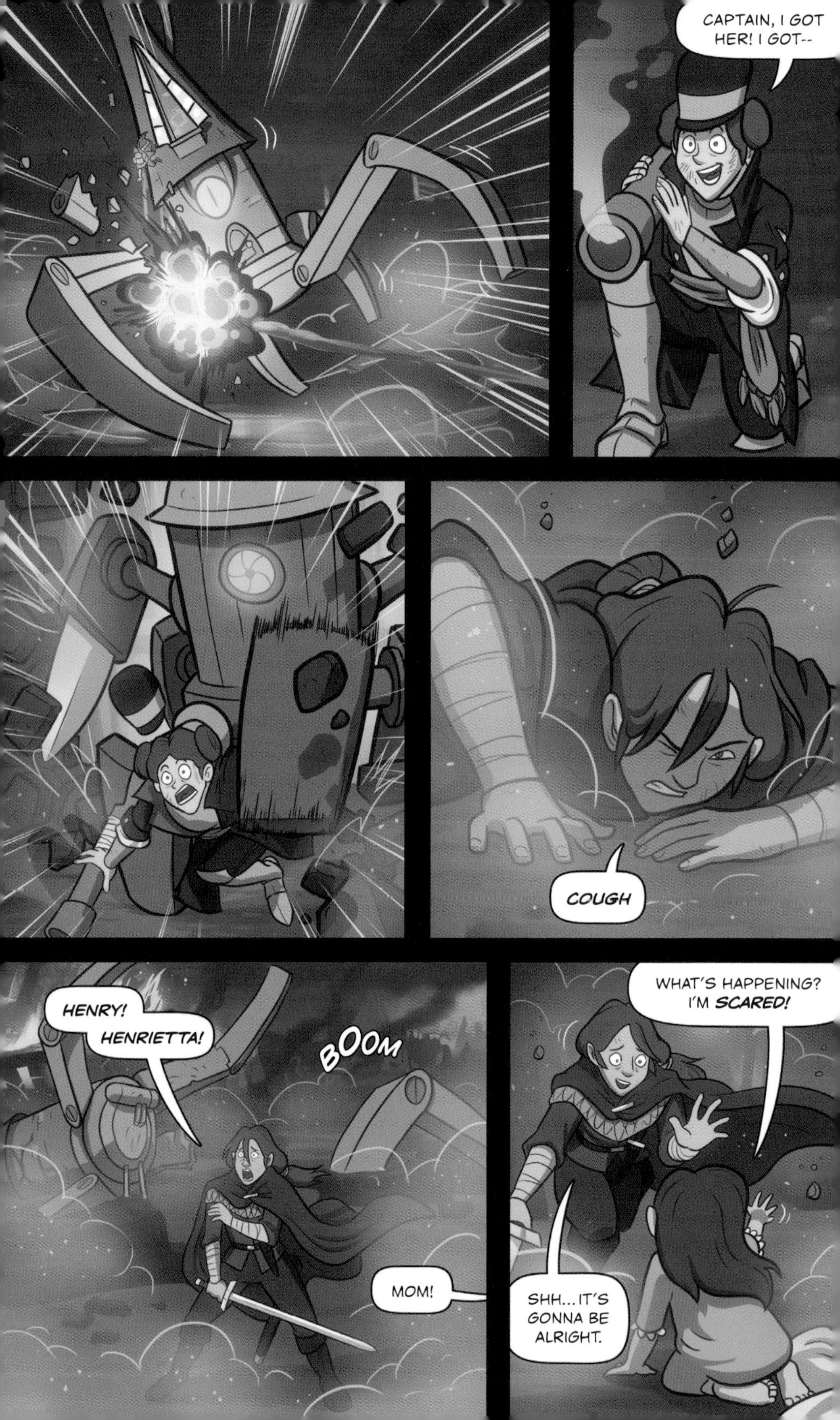
CAPTAIN, I GOT HER! I GOT--
COUGH
HENRY!
HENRIETTA!
BOOM
MOM!
WHAT'S HAPPENING? I'M *SCARED!*
SHH... IT'S GONNA BE ALRIGHT.

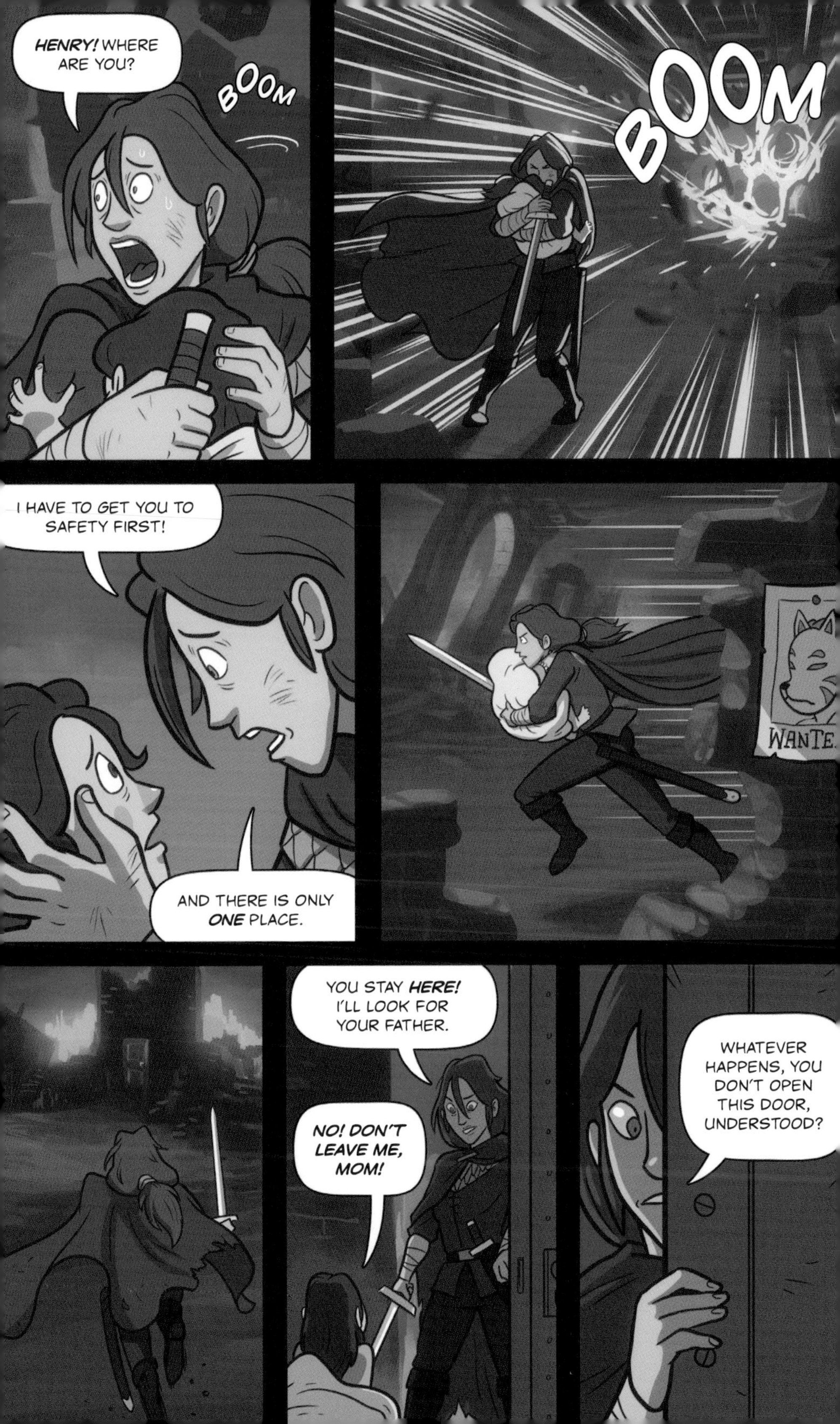
HENRY! WHERE ARE YOU?
BOOM
BOOM
I HAVE TO GET YOU TO SAFETY FIRST!
AND THERE IS ONLY ONE PLACE.
WANTE
YOU STAY HERE! I'LL LOOK FOR YOUR FATHER.
NO! DON'T LEAVE ME, MOM!
WHATEVER HAPPENS, YOU DON'T OPEN THIS DOOR, UNDERSTOOD?

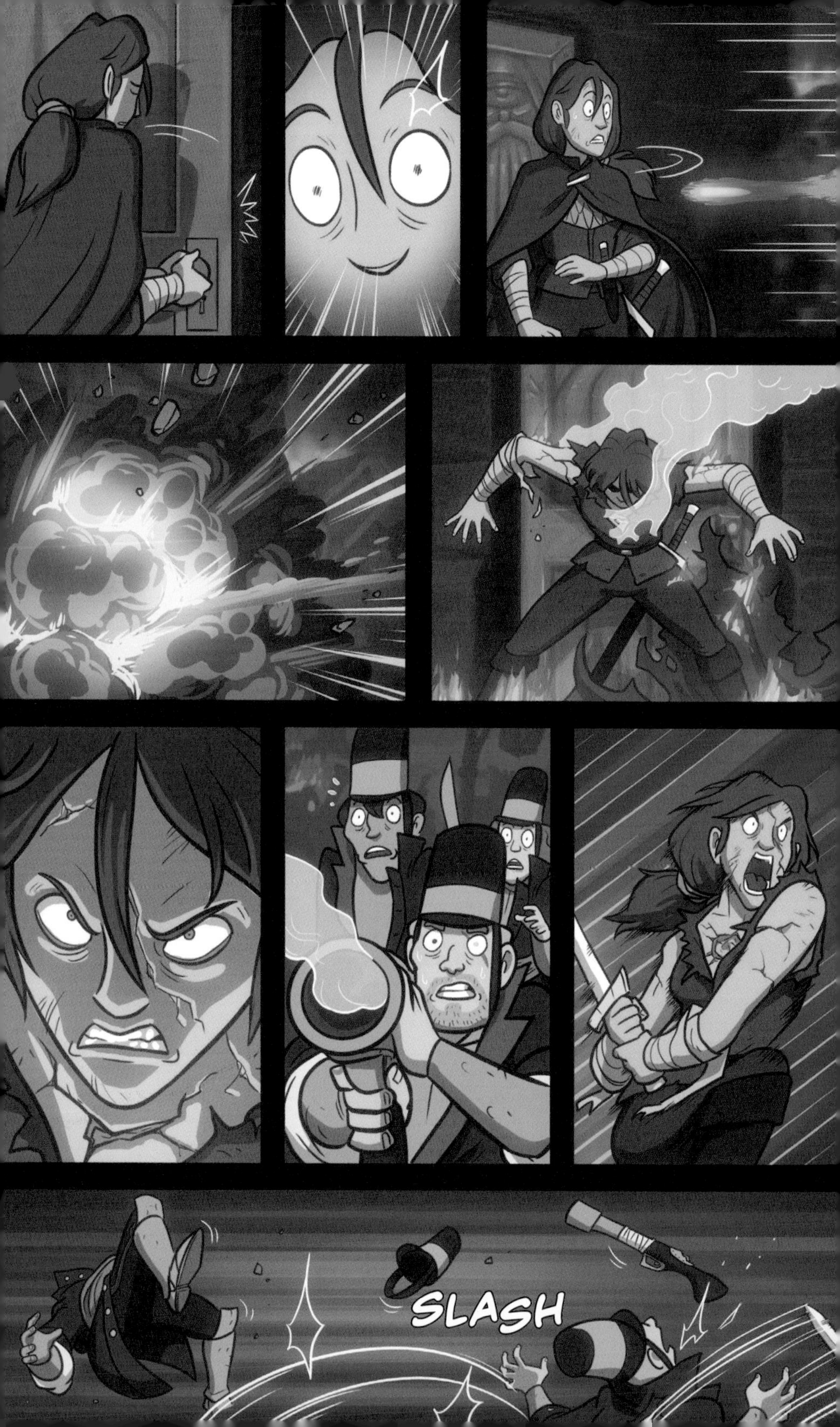
SLASH

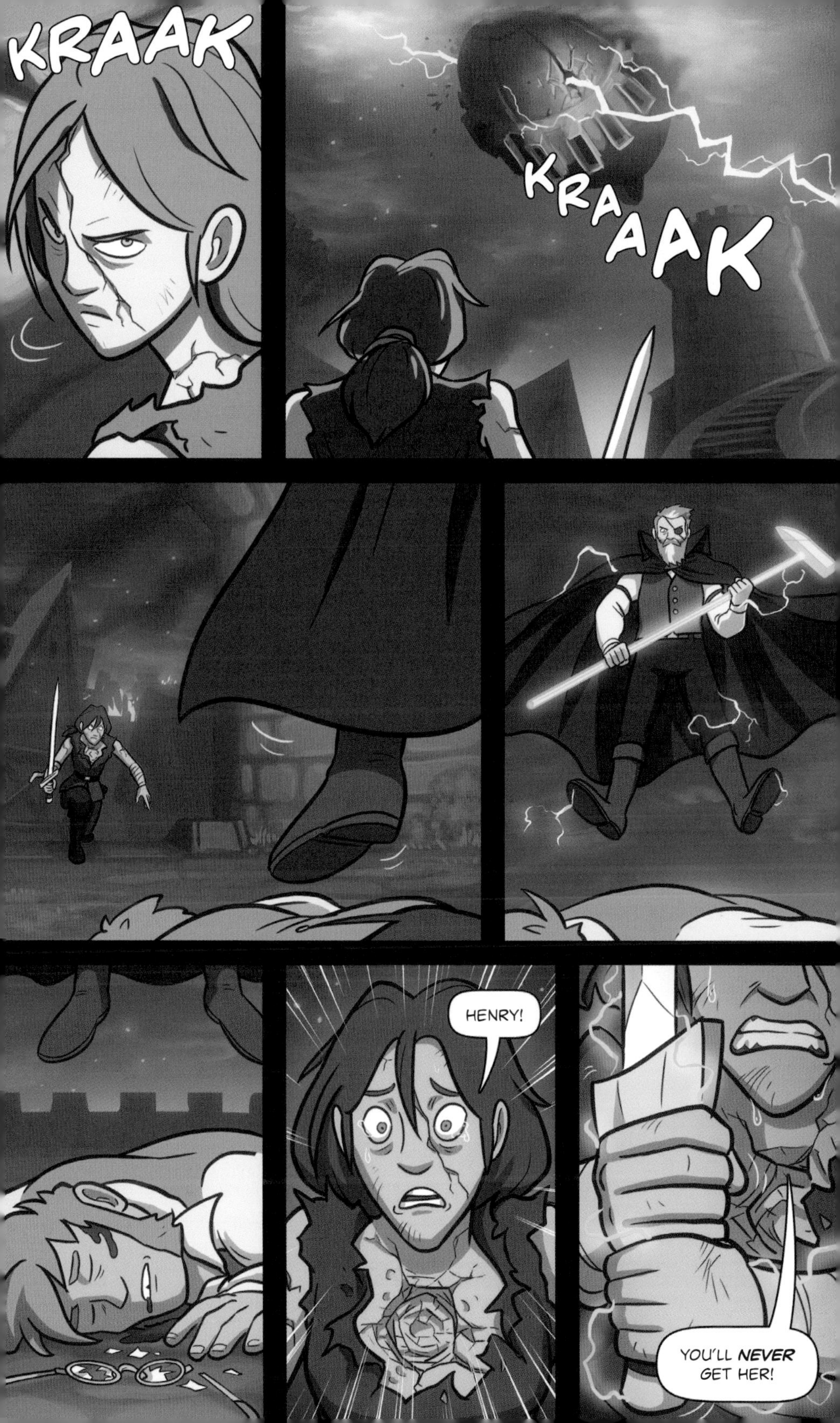
KRAAK
KRAAAK
HENRY!
YOU'LL **NEVER** GET HER!

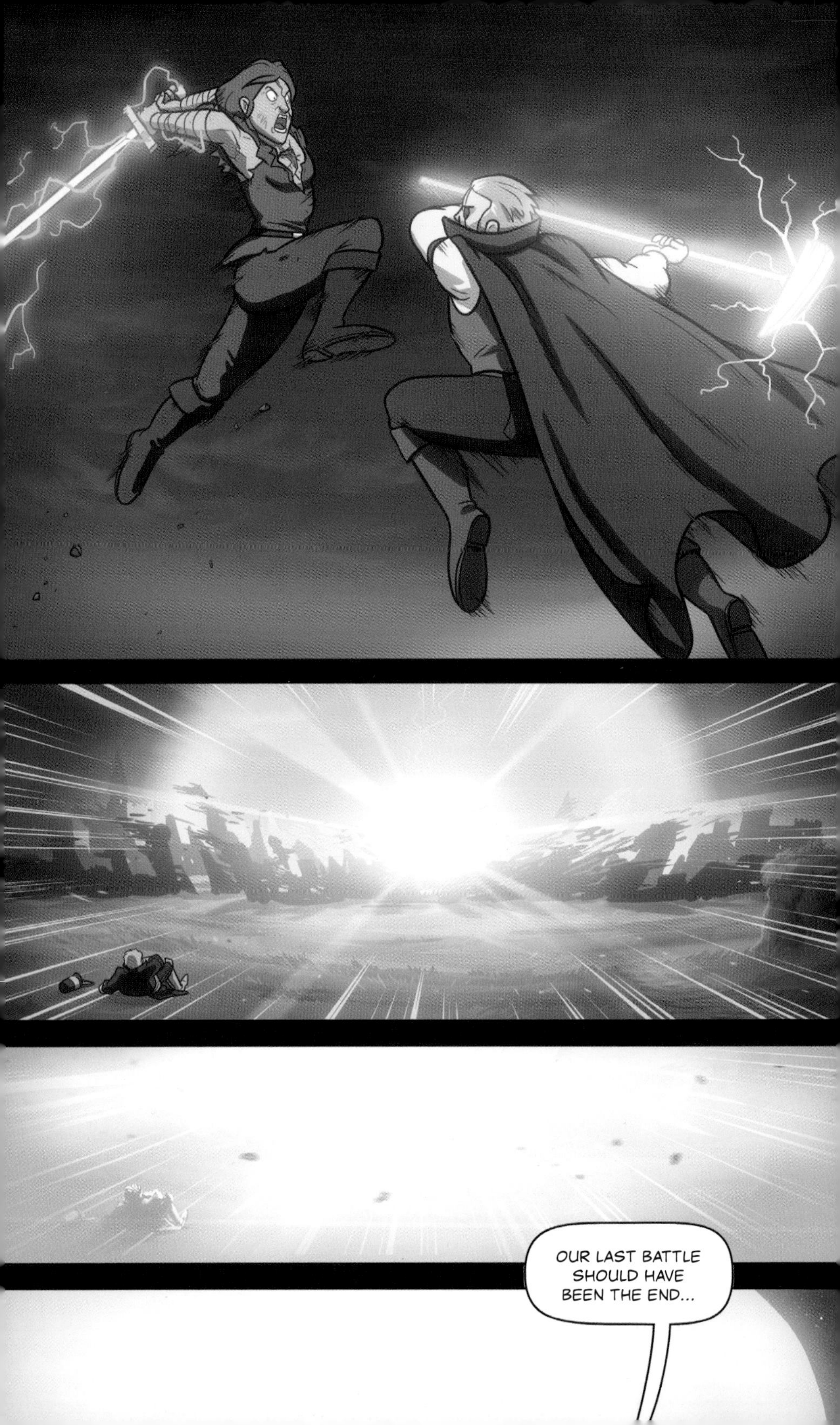
OUR LAST BATTLE SHOULD HAVE BEEN THE END...

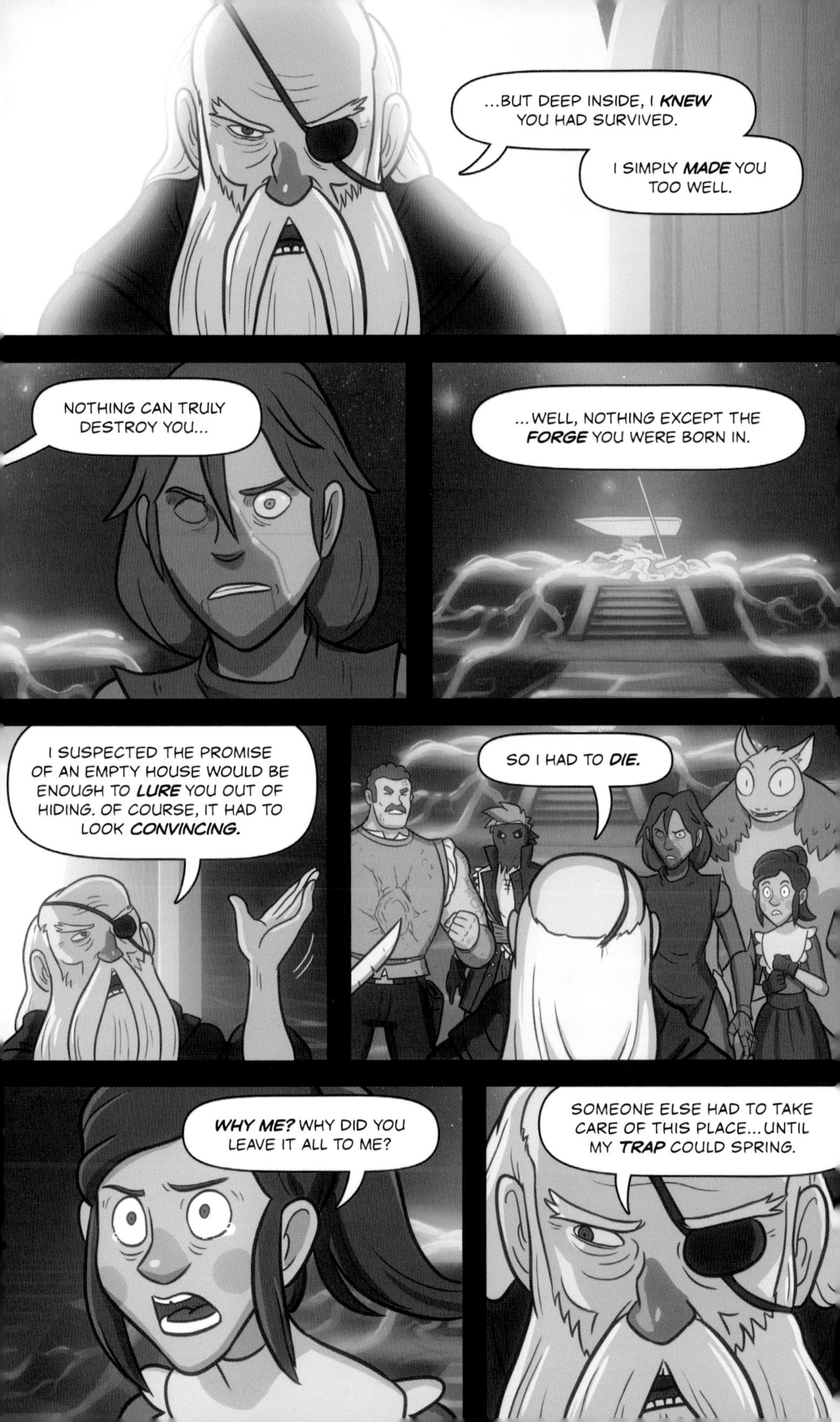
...BUT DEEP INSIDE, I **KNEW** YOU HAD SURVIVED.
I SIMPLY **MADE** YOU TOO WELL.
NOTHING CAN TRULY DESTROY YOU...
...WELL, NOTHING EXCEPT THE **FORGE** YOU WERE BORN IN.
I SUSPECTED THE PROMISE OF AN EMPTY HOUSE WOULD BE ENOUGH TO **LURE** YOU OUT OF HIDING. OF COURSE, IT HAD TO LOOK **CONVINCING.**
SO I HAD TO **DIE.**
WHY ME? WHY DID YOU LEAVE IT ALL TO ME?
SOMEONE ELSE HAD TO TAKE CARE OF THIS PLACE...UNTIL MY **TRAP** COULD SPRING.

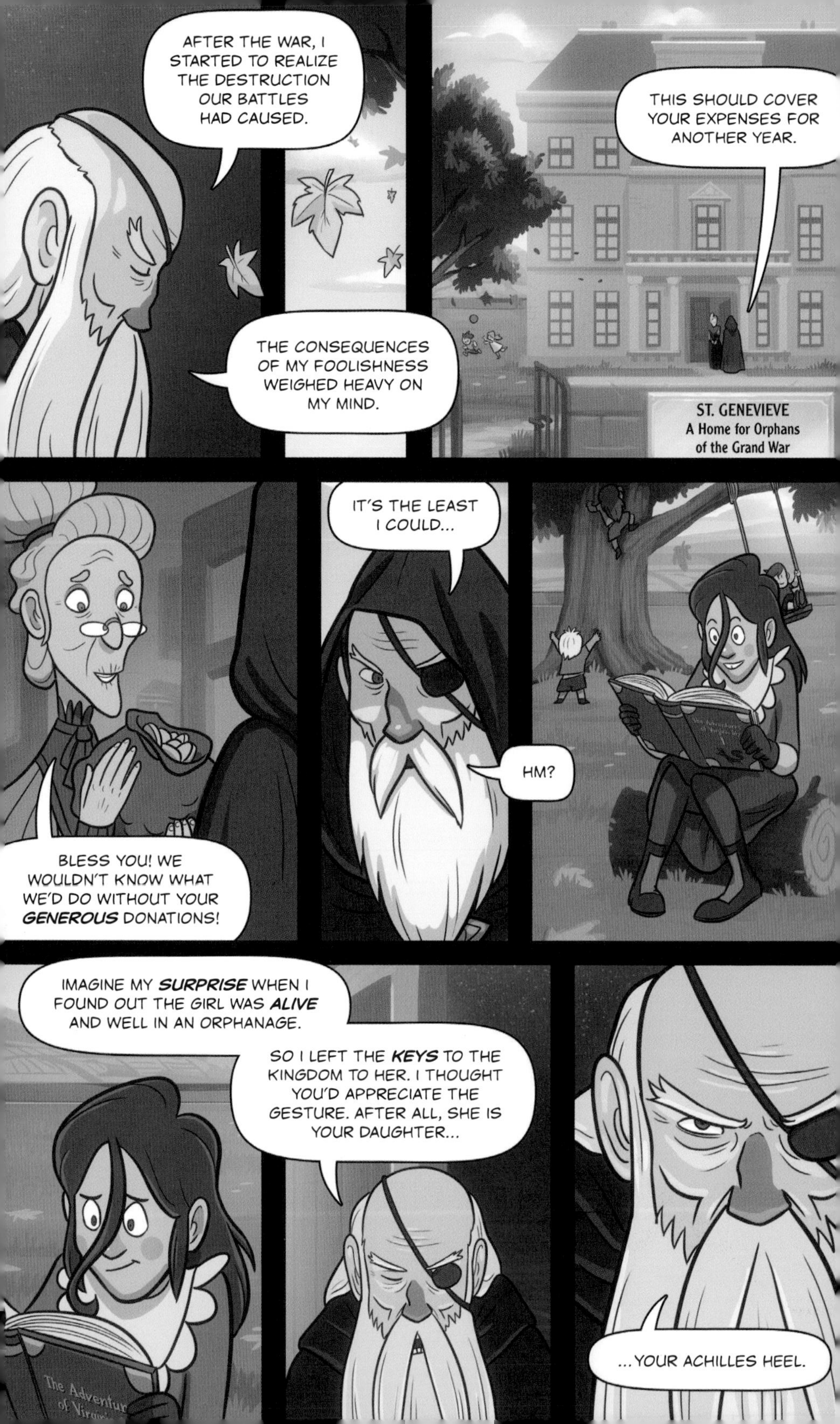
AFTER THE WAR, I STARTED TO REALIZE THE DESTRUCTION OUR BATTLES HAD CAUSED.
THE CONSEQUENCES OF MY FOOLISHNESS WEIGHED HEAVY ON MY MIND.
THIS SHOULD COVER YOUR EXPENSES FOR ANOTHER YEAR.
ST. GENEVIEVE
A Home for Orphans of the Grand War
BLESS YOU! WE WOULDN'T KNOW WHAT WE'D DO WITHOUT YOUR *GENEROUS* DONATIONS!
IT'S THE LEAST I COULD...
HM?
IMAGINE MY *SURPRISE* WHEN I FOUND OUT THE GIRL WAS *ALIVE* AND WELL IN AN ORPHANAGE.
SO I LEFT THE *KEYS* TO THE KINGDOM TO HER. I THOUGHT YOU'D APPRECIATE THE GESTURE. AFTER ALL, SHE IS YOUR DAUGHTER...
...YOUR ACHILLES HEEL.

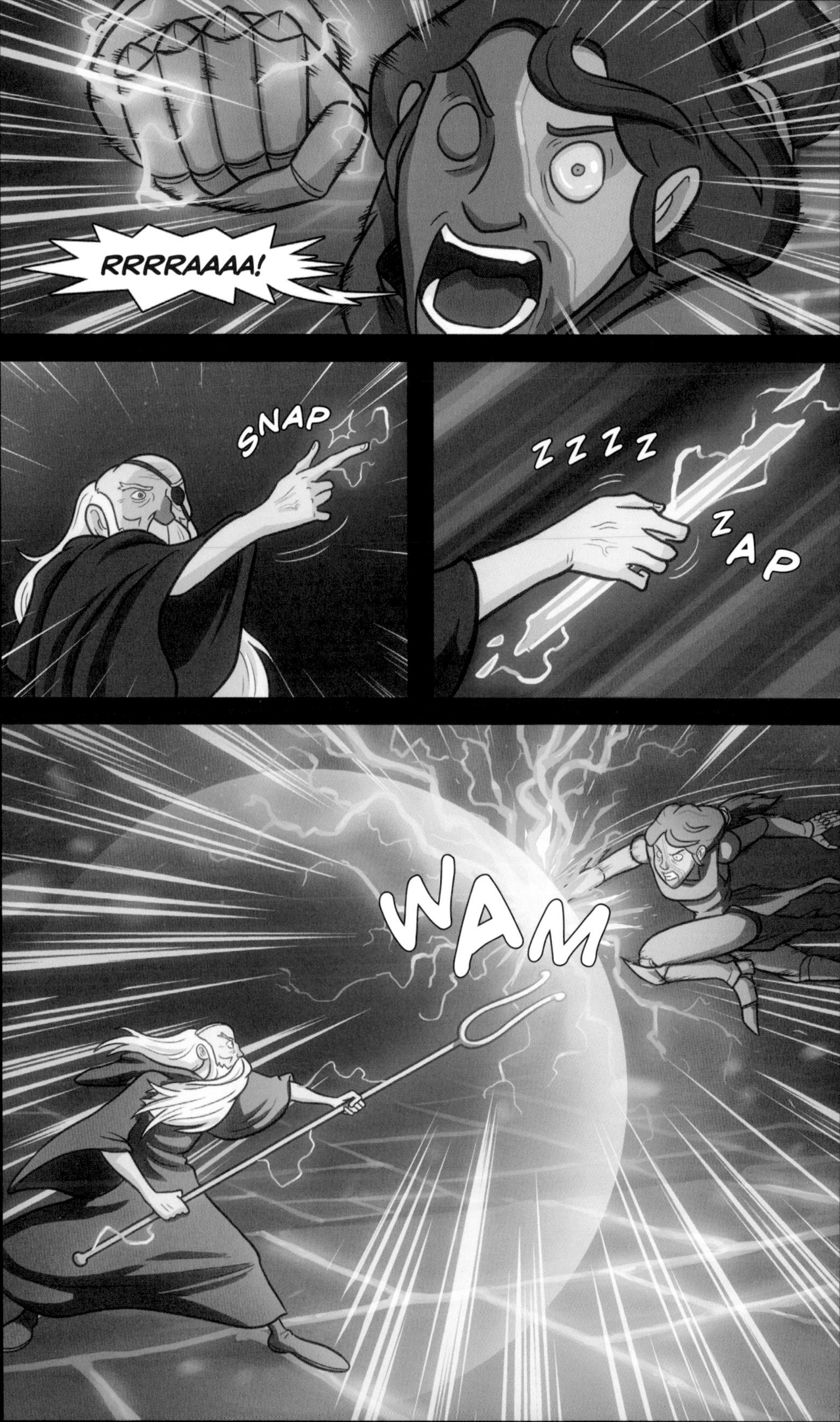
RRRRAAAA!
SNAP
ZZZZ
ZAP
WAM

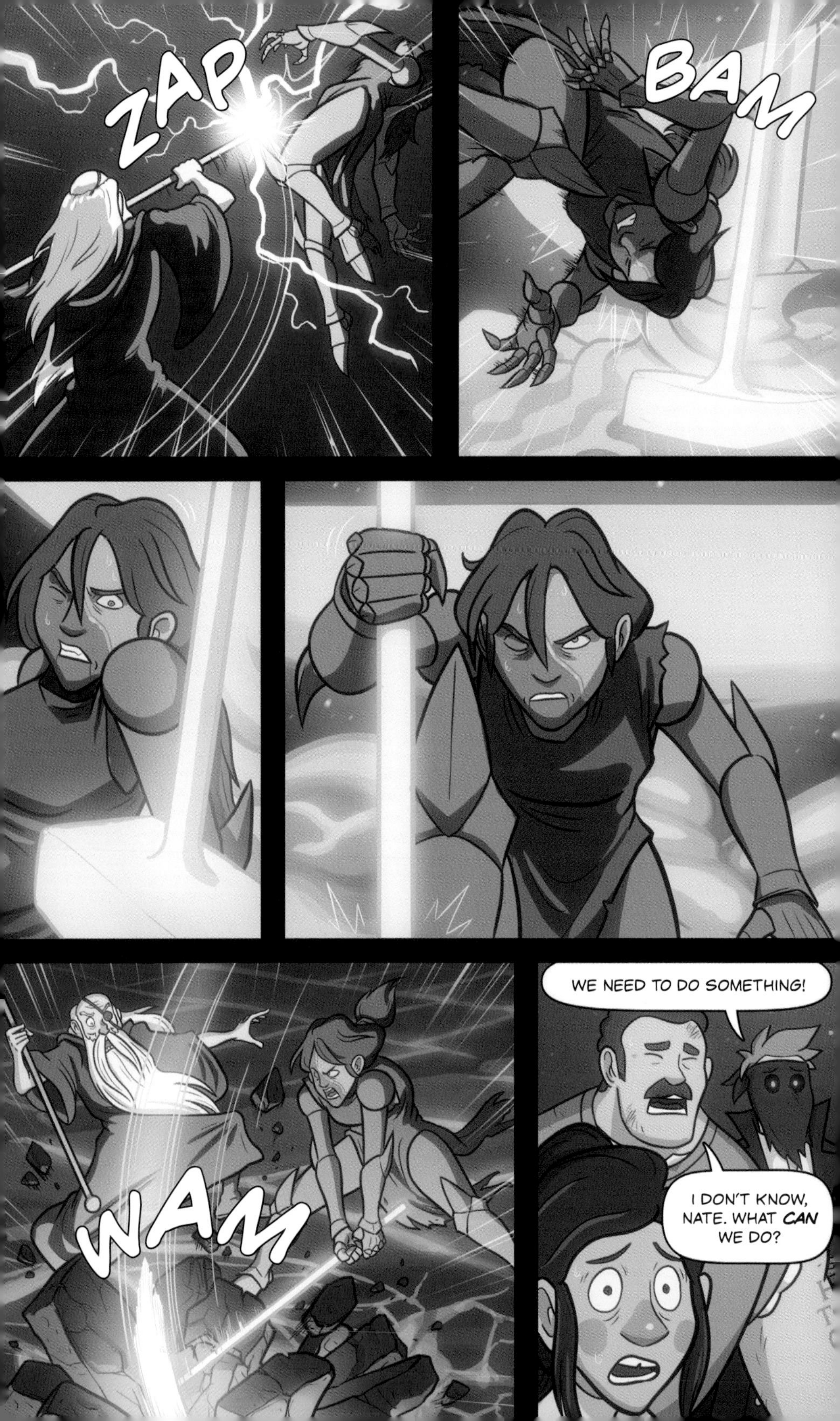
ZAP
BAM
WAM
WE NEED TO DO SOMETHING!
I DON'T KNOW, NATE. WHAT CAN WE DO?

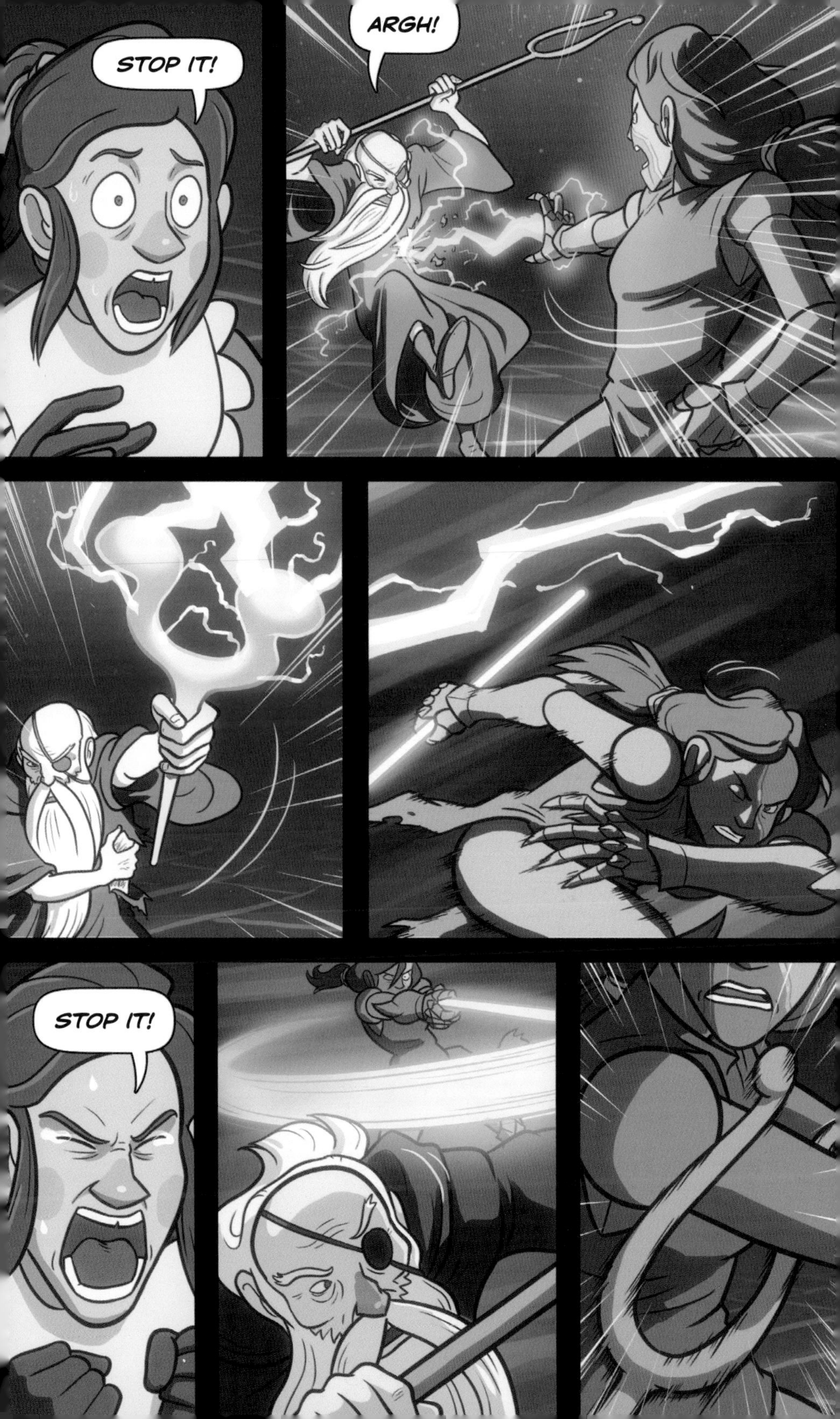
STOP IT!
ARGH!
STOP IT!

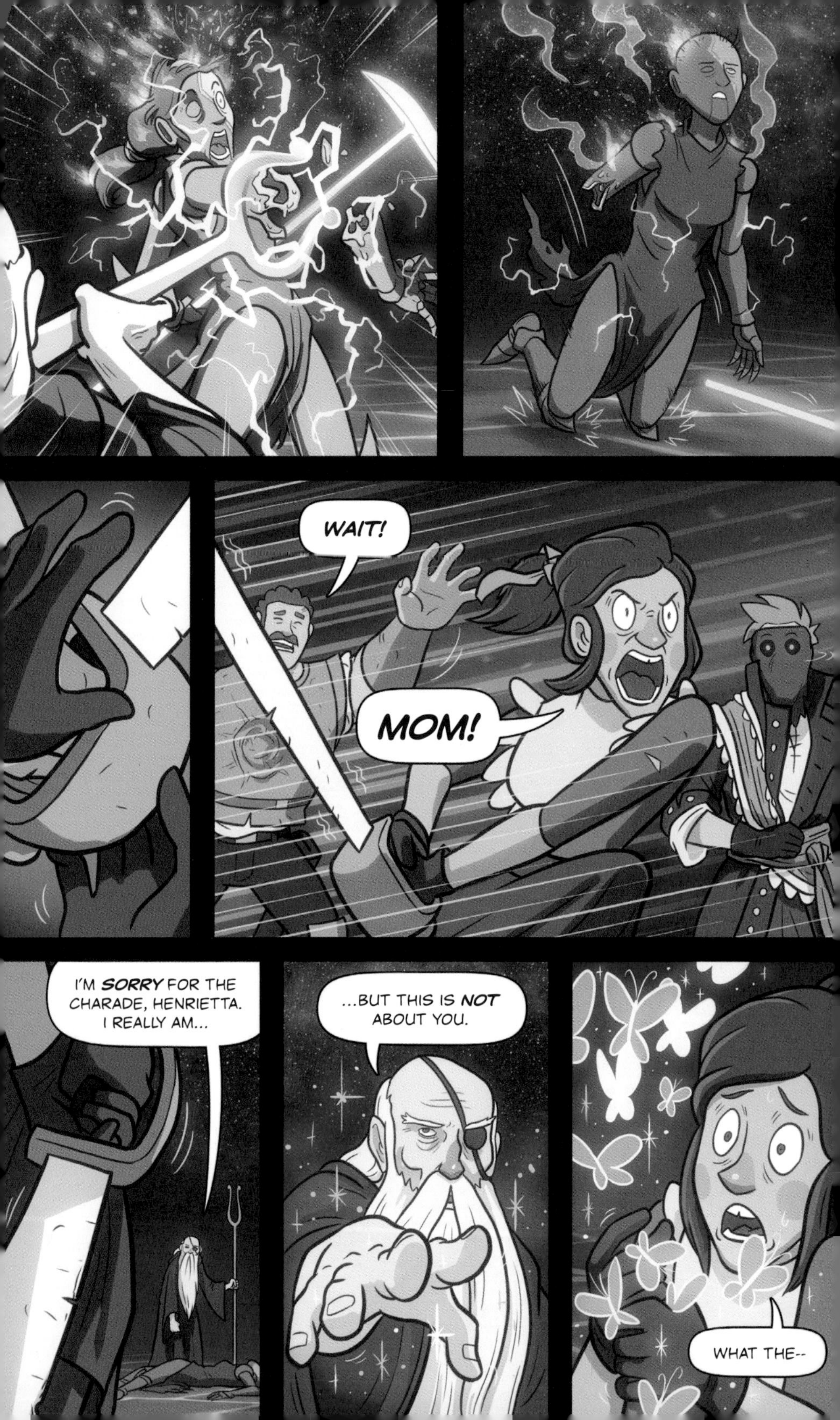
WAIT!
MOM!
I'M **SORRY** FOR THE CHARADE, HENRIETTA. I REALLY AM...
...BUT THIS IS **NOT** ABOUT YOU.
WHAT THE--

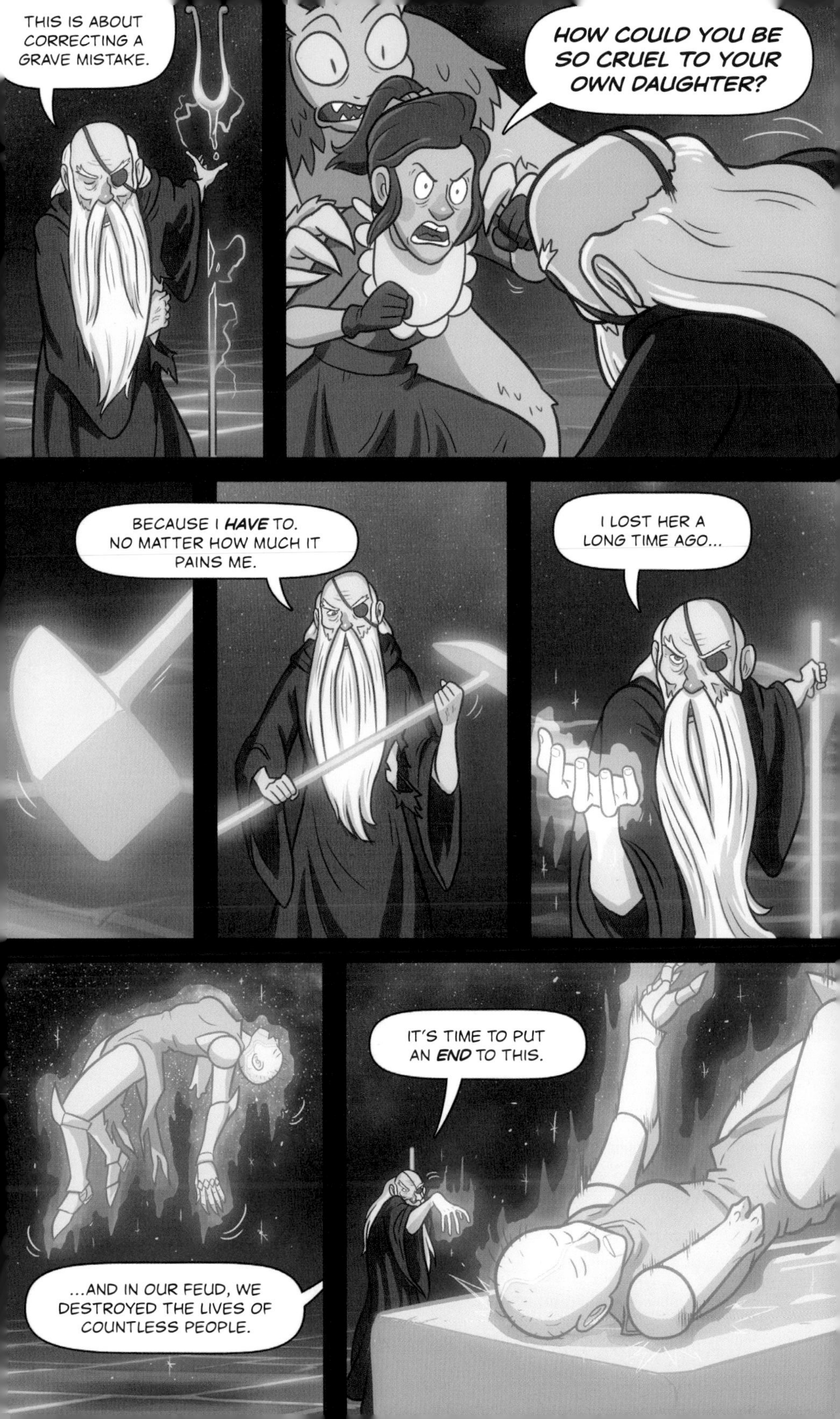
THIS IS ABOUT CORRECTING A GRAVE MISTAKE.
HOW COULD YOU BE SO CRUEL TO YOUR OWN DAUGHTER?
BECAUSE I **HAVE** TO. NO MATTER HOW MUCH IT PAINS ME.
I LOST HER A LONG TIME AGO...
...AND IN OUR FEUD, WE DESTROYED THE LIVES OF COUNTLESS PEOPLE.
IT'S TIME TO PUT AN **END** TO THIS.

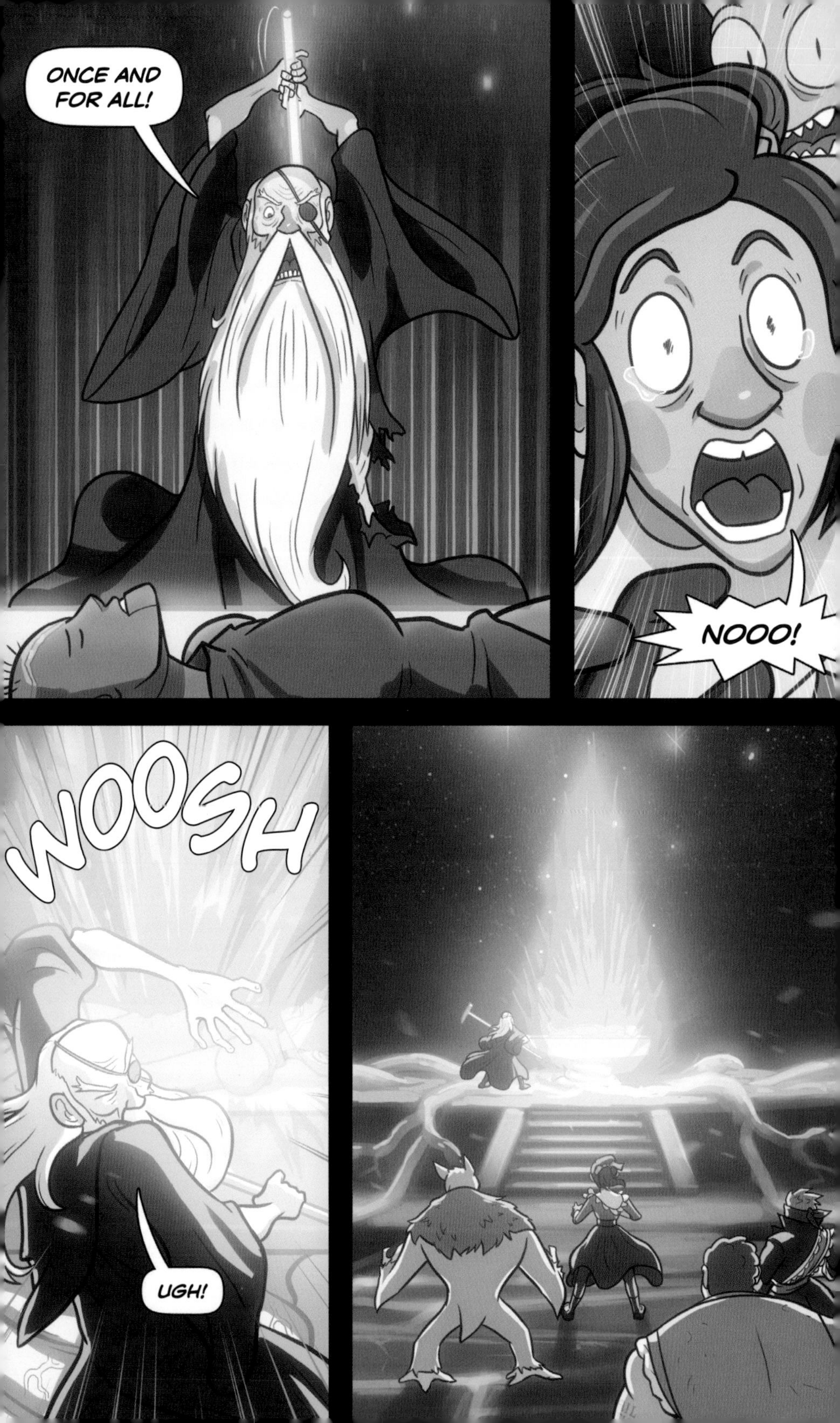

ONCE AND FOR ALL!
NOOO!
WOOSH
UGH!

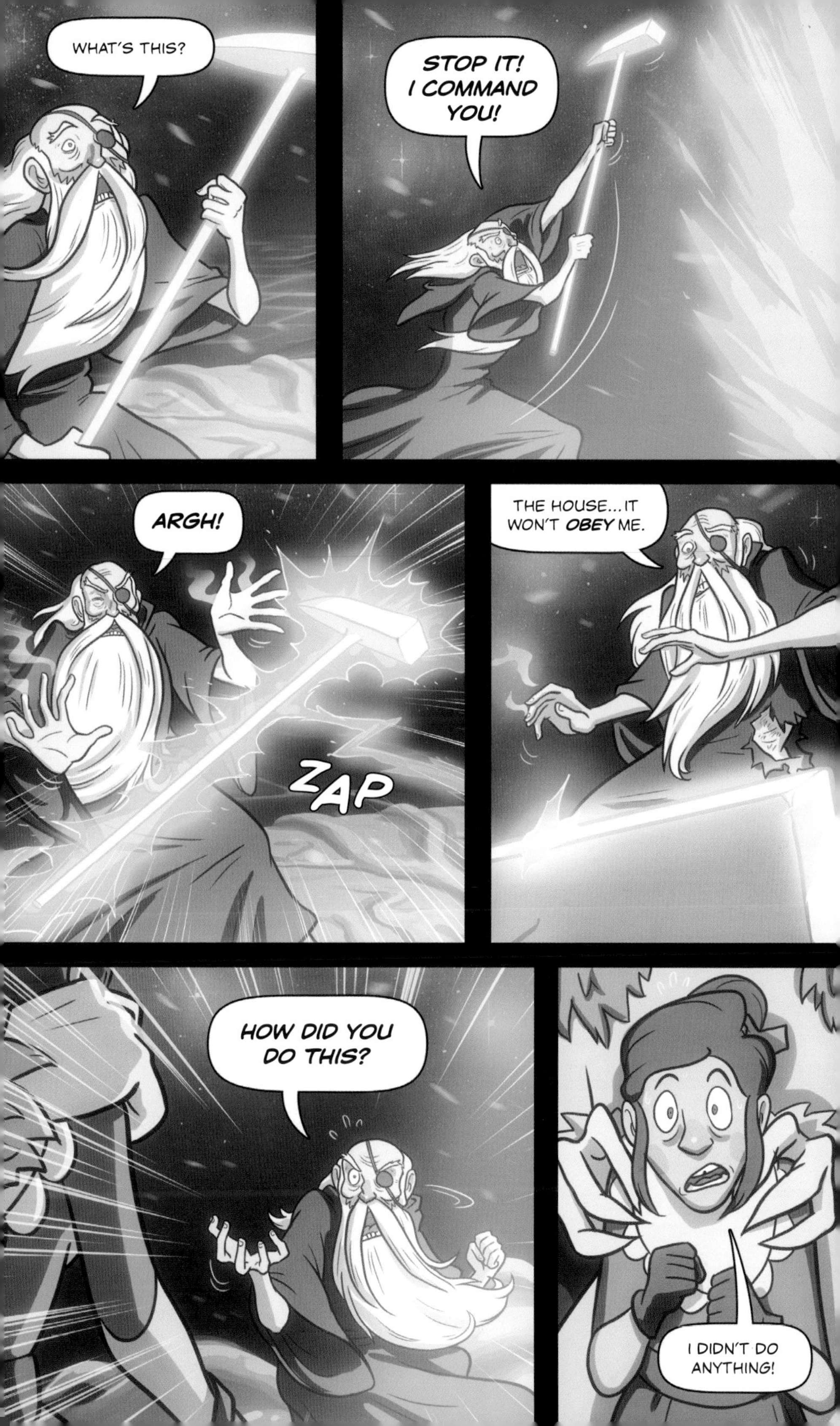
WHAT'S THIS?
STOP IT! I COMMAND YOU!
ARGH!
ZAP
THE HOUSE...IT WON'T OBEY ME.
HOW DID YOU DO THIS?
I DIDN'T DO ANYTHING!

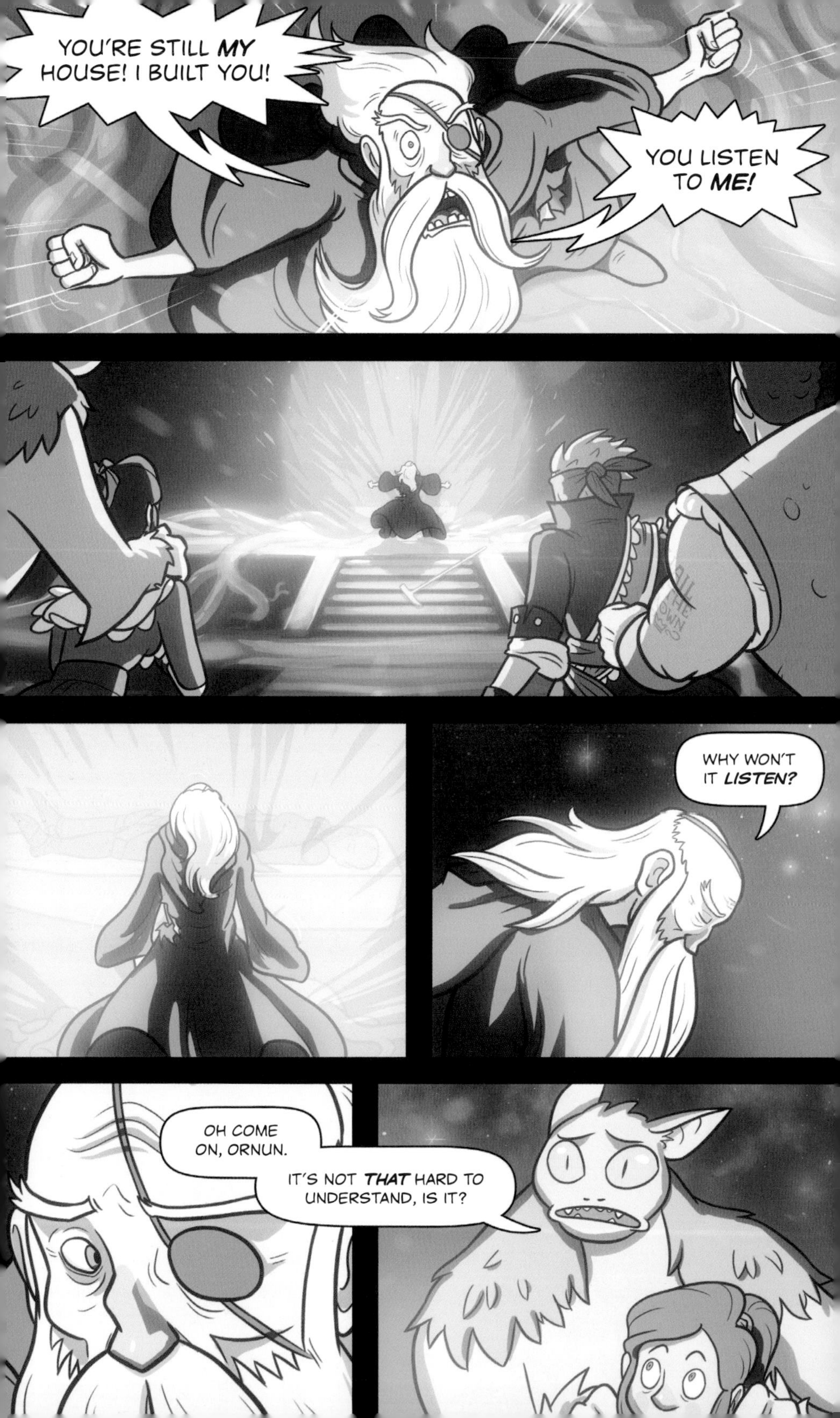
YOU'RE STILL MY HOUSE! I BUILT YOU!
YOU LISTEN TO ME!
WHY WON'T IT LISTEN?
OH COME ON, ORNUN.
IT'S NOT THAT HARD TO UNDERSTAND, IS IT?

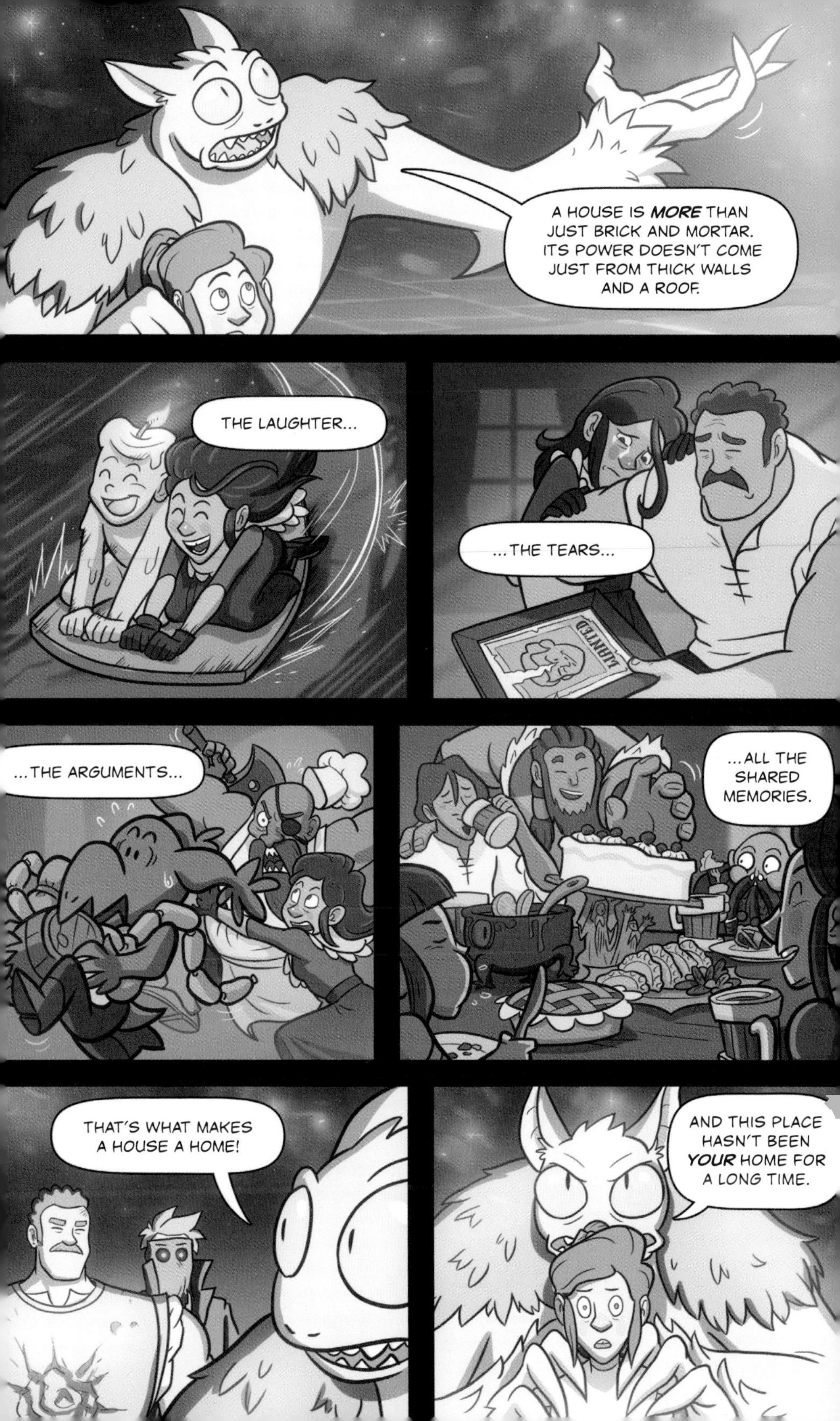
A HOUSE IS ***MORE*** THAN JUST BRICK AND MORTAR. ITS POWER DOESN'T COME JUST FROM THICK WALLS AND A ROOF.
THE LAUGHTER...
...THE TEARS...
WANTED
...THE ARGUMENTS...
...ALL THE SHARED MEMORIES.
THAT'S WHAT MAKES A HOUSE A HOME!
AND THIS PLACE HASN'T BEEN ***YOUR*** HOME FOR A LONG TIME.

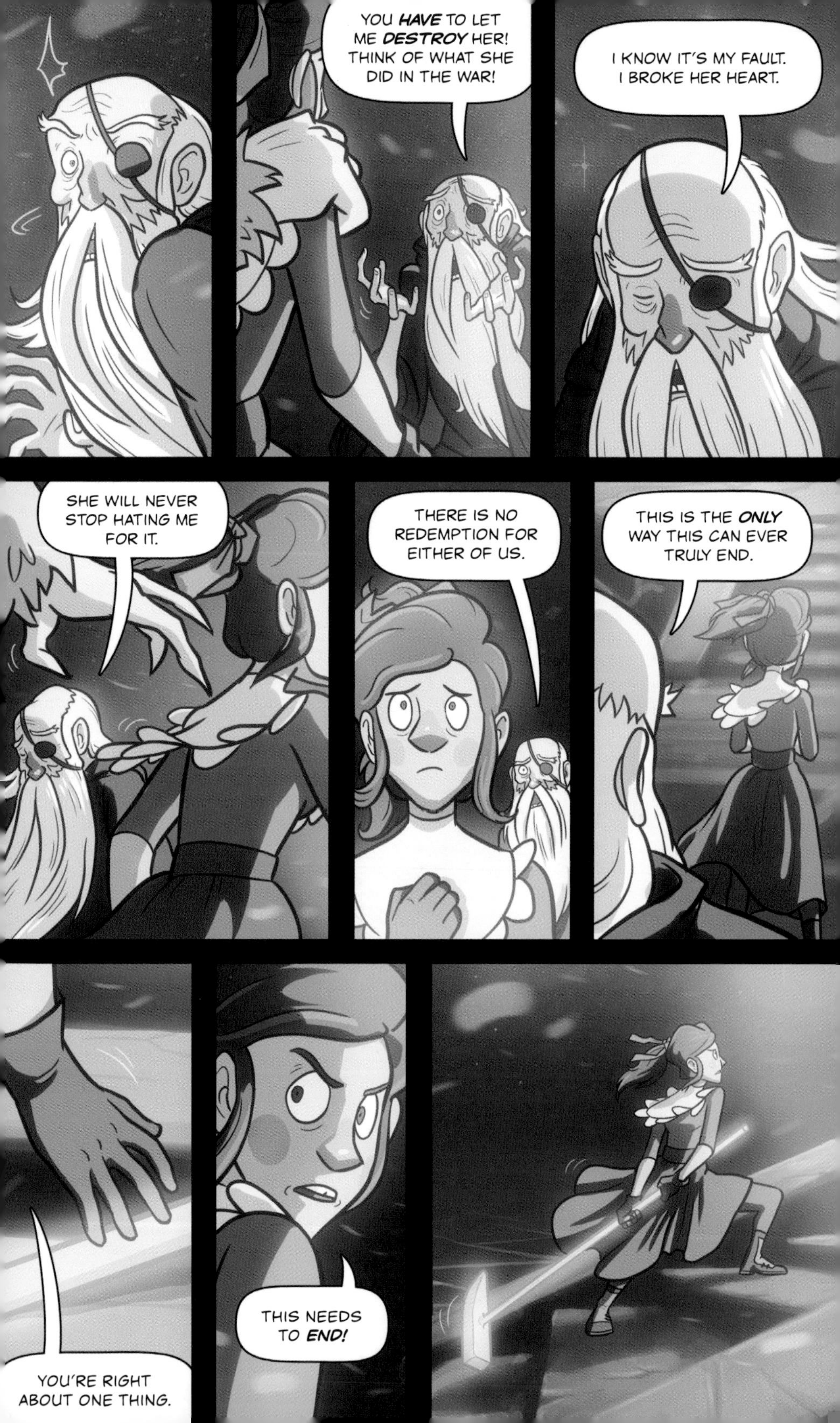
YOU **HAVE** TO LET ME **DESTROY** HER! THINK OF WHAT SHE DID IN THE WAR!
I KNOW IT'S MY FAULT. I BROKE HER HEART.
SHE WILL NEVER STOP HATING ME FOR IT.
THERE IS NO REDEMPTION FOR EITHER OF US.
THIS IS THE **ONLY** WAY THIS CAN EVER TRULY END.
YOU'RE RIGHT ABOUT ONE THING.
THIS NEEDS TO **END!**

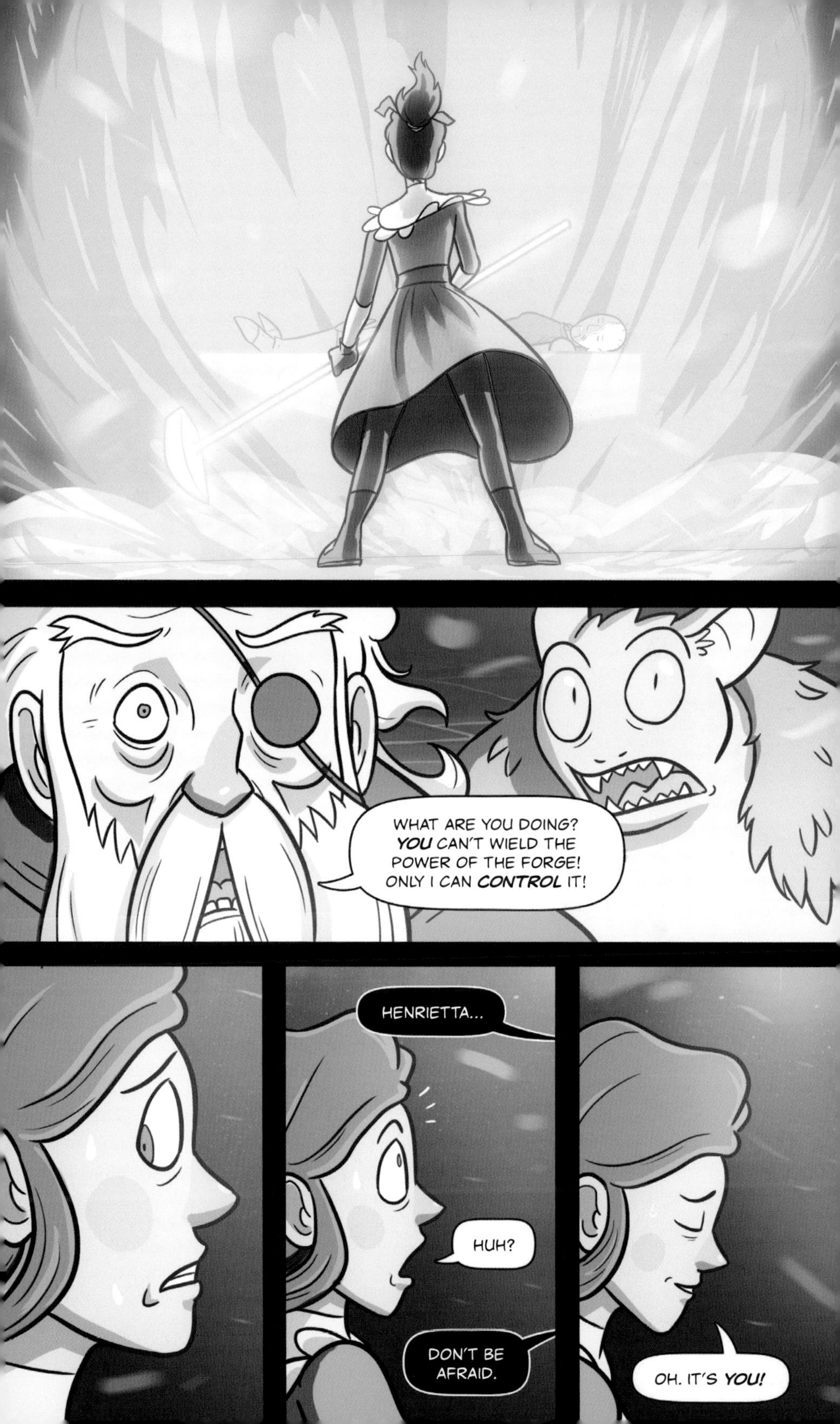
WHAT ARE YOU DOING? **YOU** CAN'T WIELD THE POWER OF THE FORGE! ONLY I CAN **CONTROL** IT!
HENRIETTA...
HUH?
DON'T BE AFRAID.
OH. IT'S **YOU!**

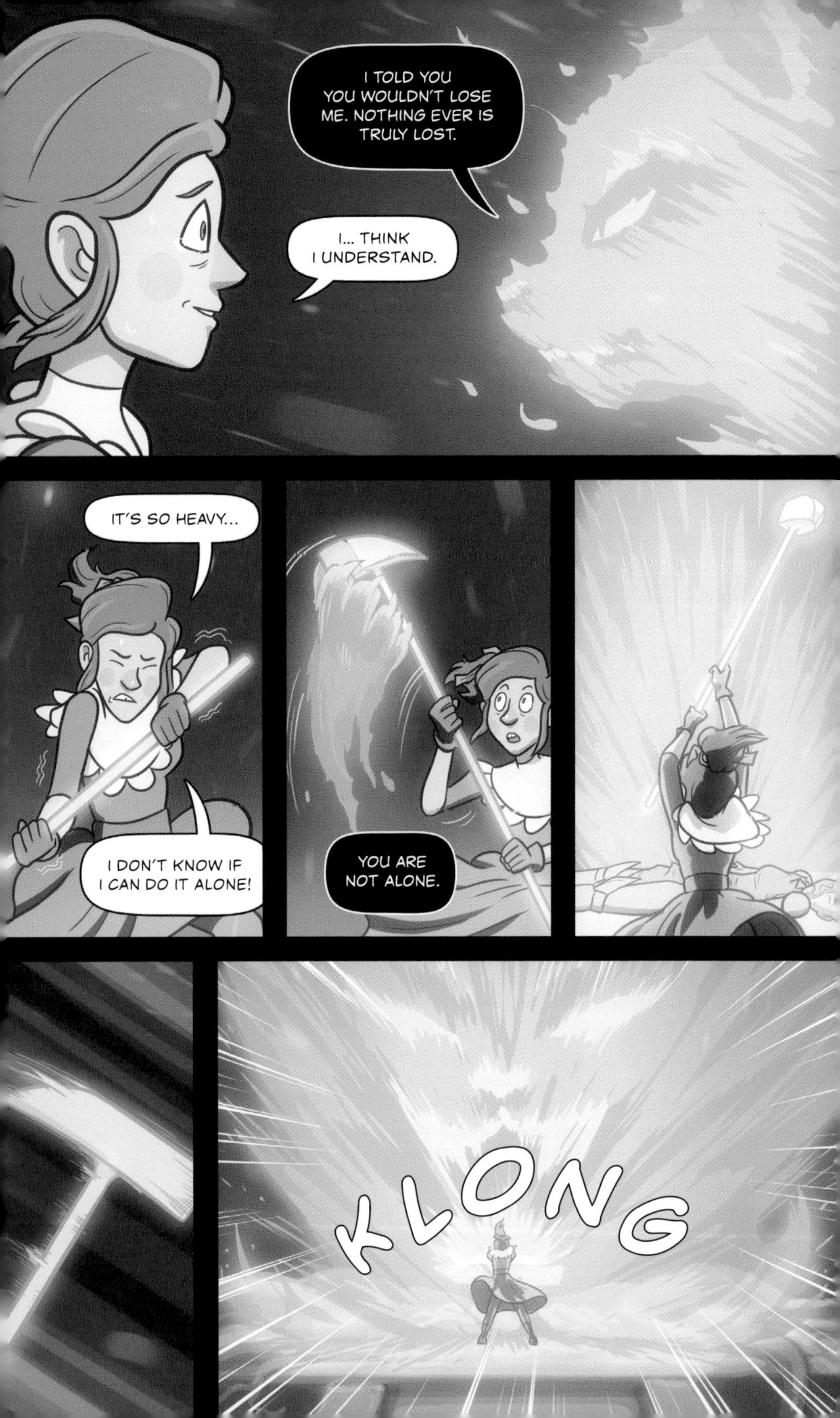
I TOLD YOU YOU WOULDN'T LOSE ME. NOTHING EVER IS TRULY LOST.
I... THINK I UNDERSTAND.
IT'S SO HEAVY...
I DON'T KNOW IF I CAN DO IT ALONE!
YOU ARE NOT ALONE.
KLONG

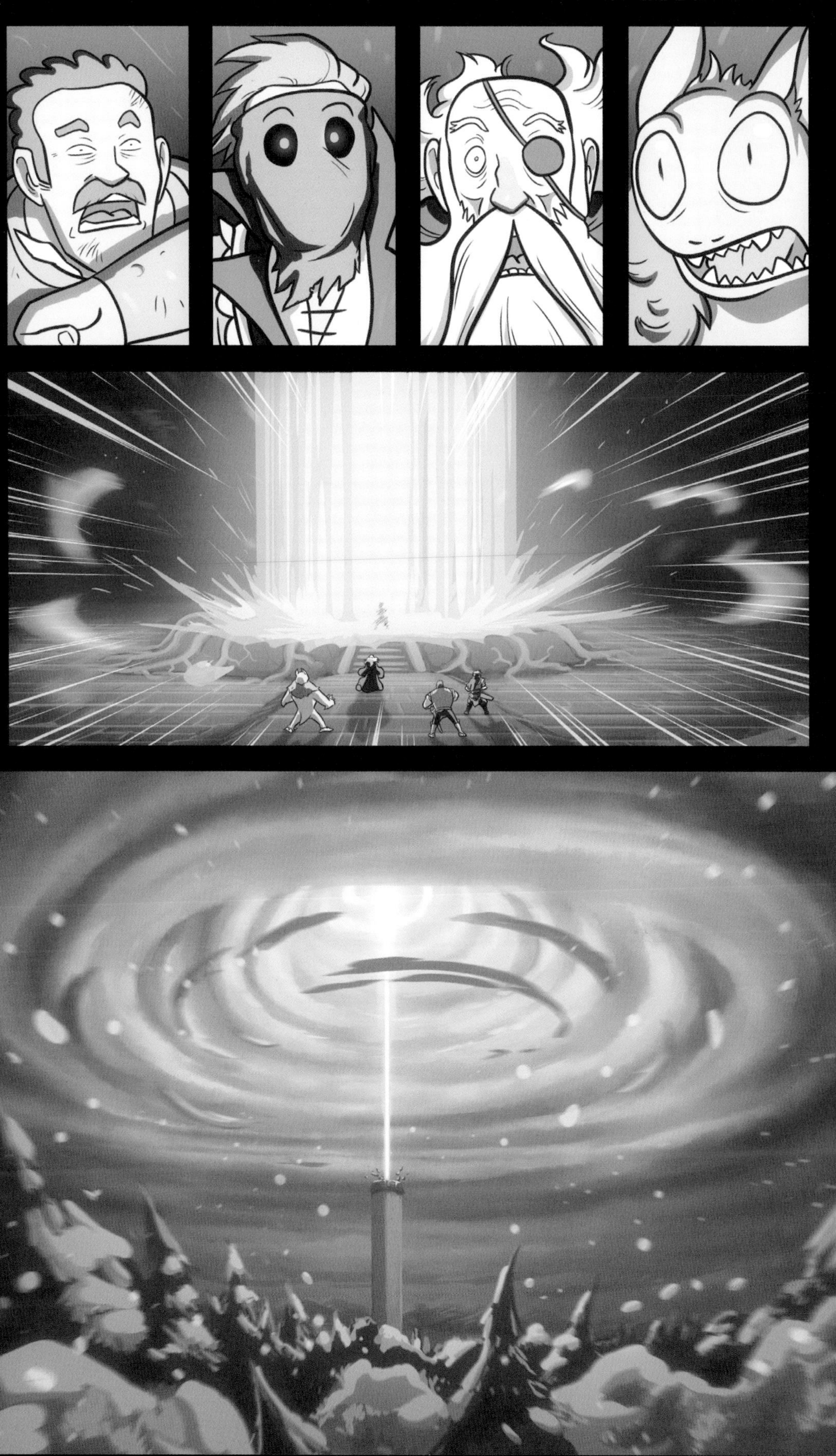

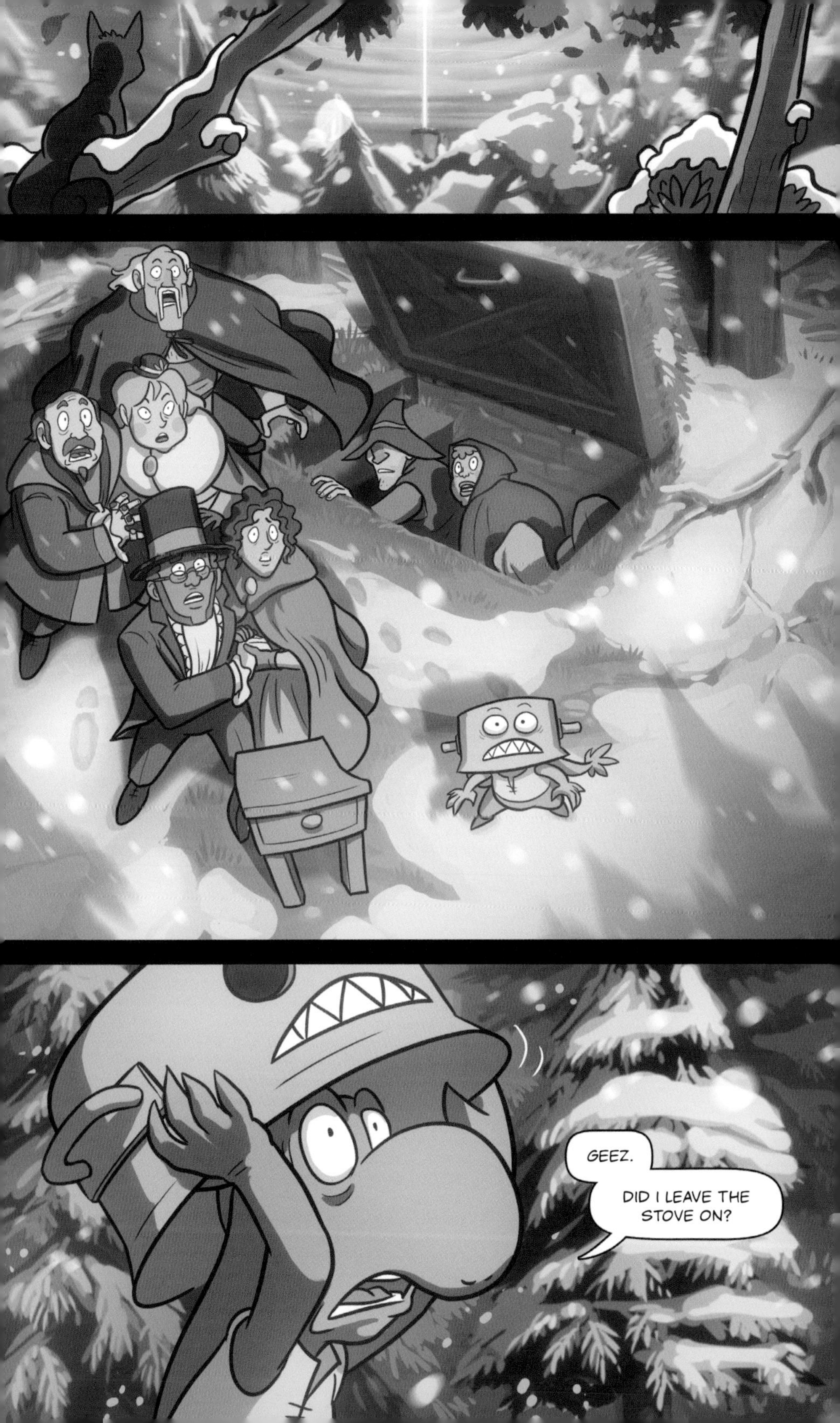
GEEZ.
DID I LEAVE THE STOVE ON?

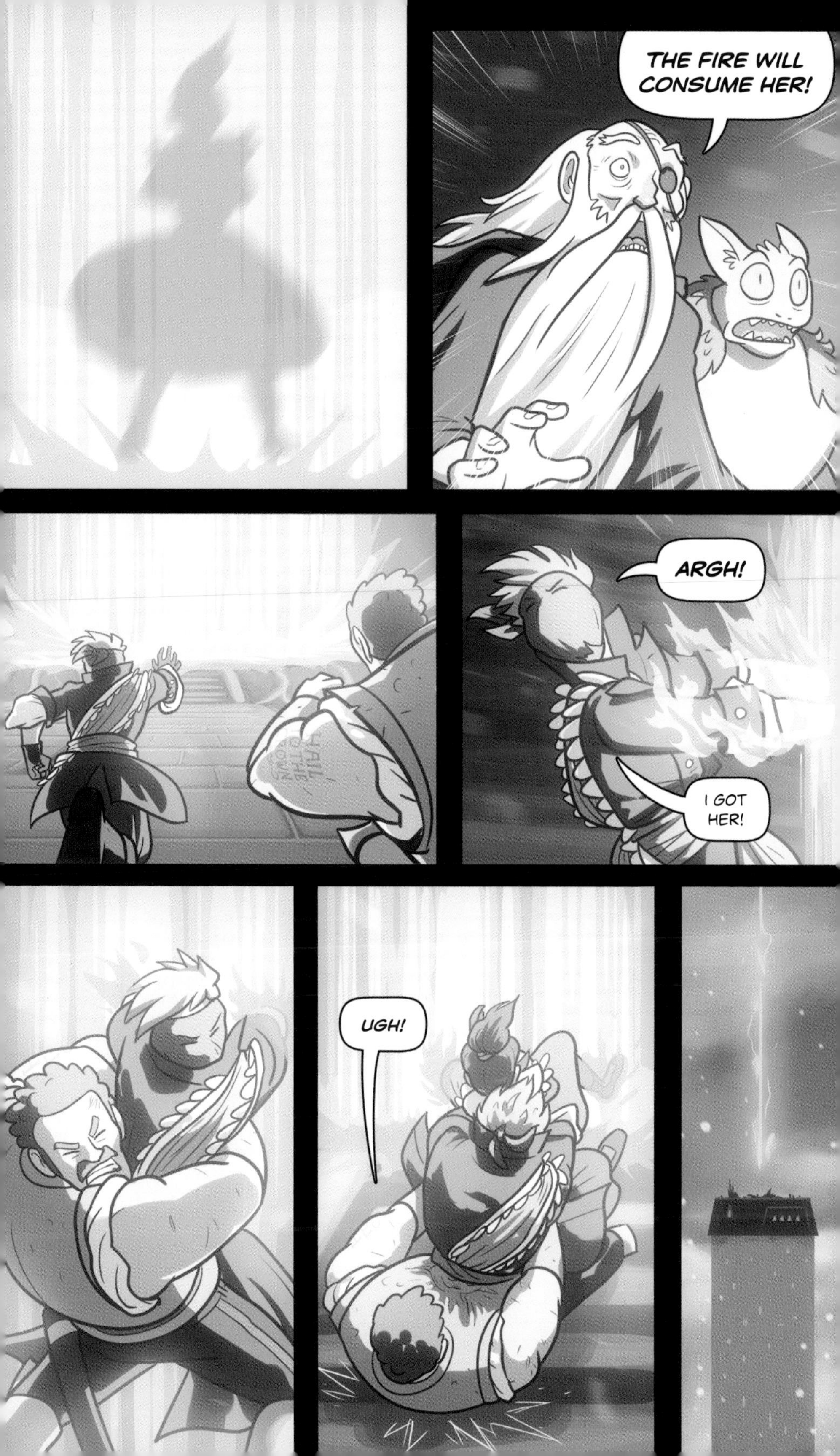
THE FIRE WILL CONSUME HER!
HAIL THE CROWN
ARGH!
I GOT HER!
UGH!

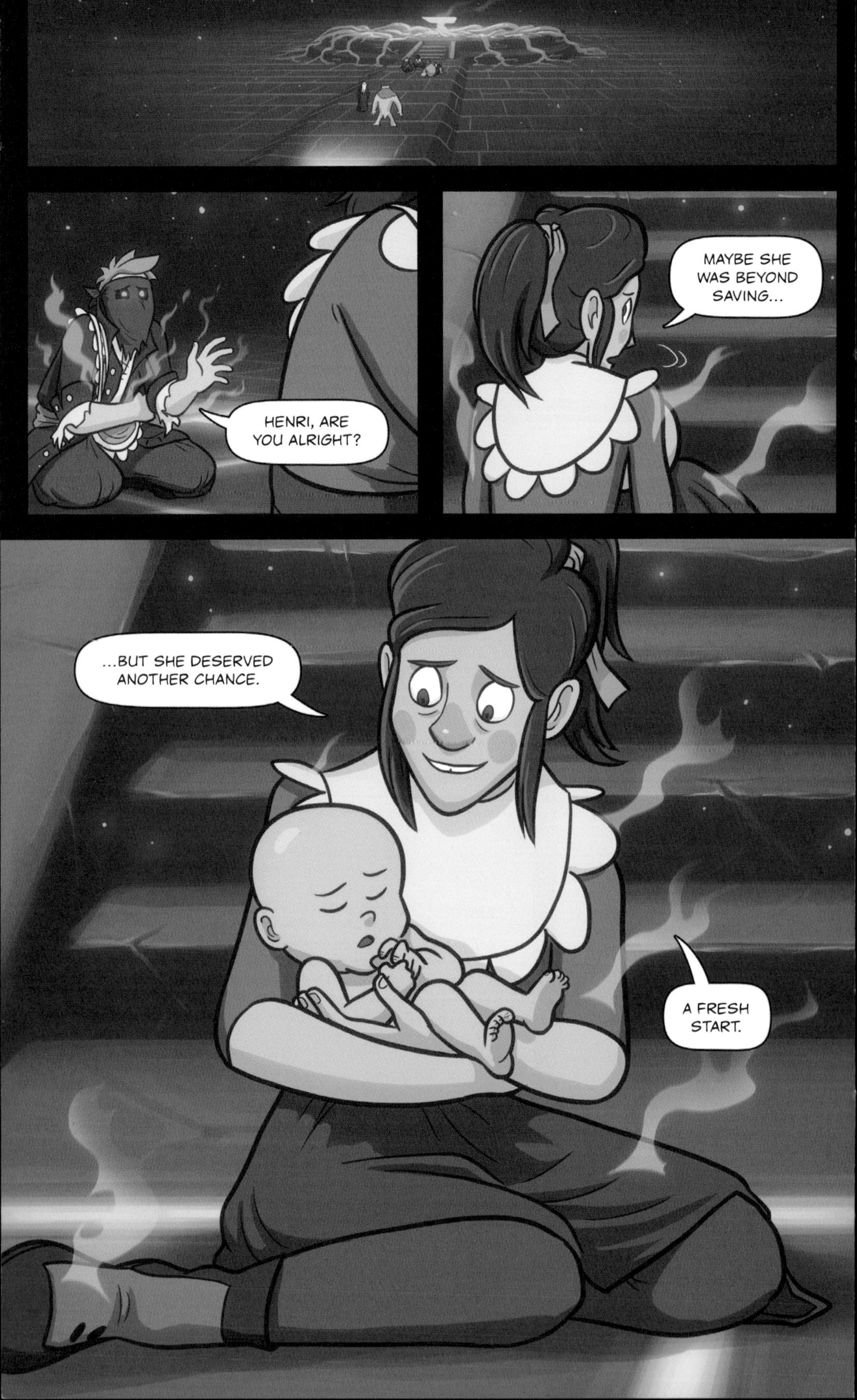
HENRI, ARE YOU ALRIGHT?
MAYBE SHE WAS BEYOND SAVING...
...BUT SHE DESERVED ANOTHER CHANCE.
A FRESH START.

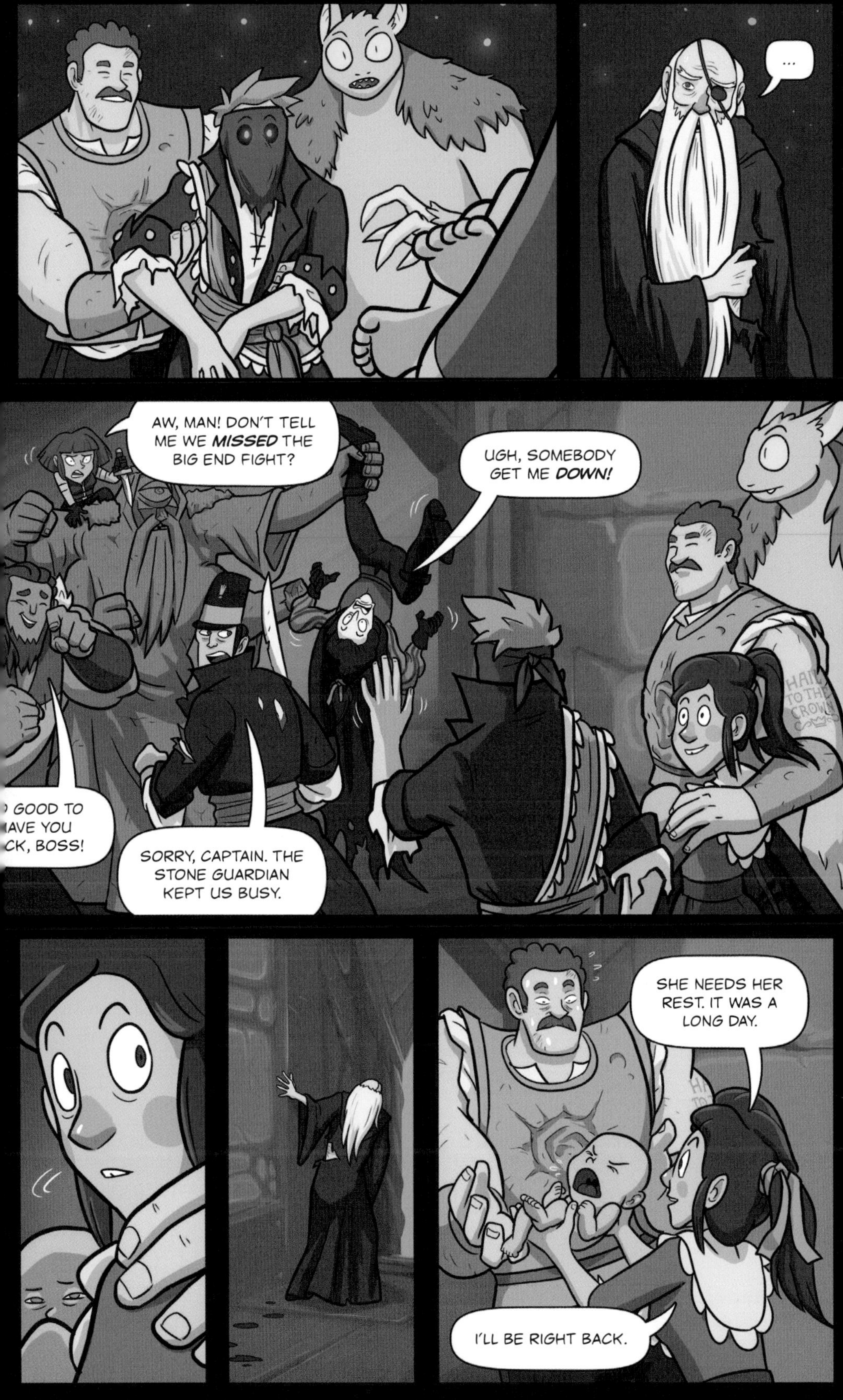
...
AW, MAN! DON'T TELL ME WE ***MISSED*** THE BIG END FIGHT?
UGH, SOMEBODY GET ME ***DOWN!***
GOOD TO
AVE YOU
CK, BOSS!
SORRY, CAPTAIN. THE STONE GUARDIAN KEPT US BUSY.
HAIL TO THE CROWN
SHE NEEDS HER REST. IT WAS A LONG DAY.
I'LL BE RIGHT BACK.

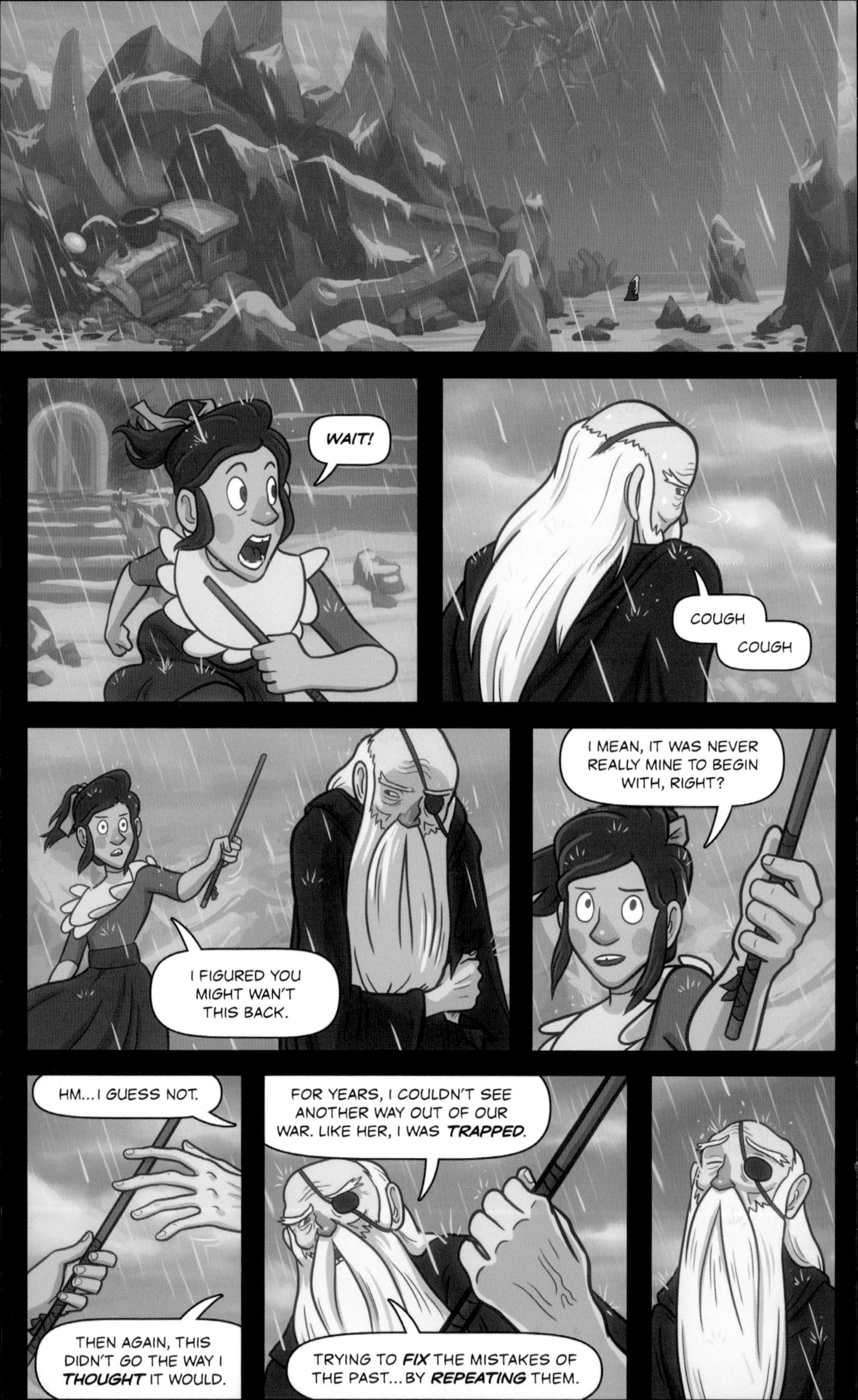
WAIT!
COUGH COUGH
I FIGURED YOU MIGHT WAN'T THIS BACK.
I MEAN, IT WAS NEVER REALLY MINE TO BEGIN WITH, RIGHT?
HM... I GUESS NOT.
THEN AGAIN, THIS DIDN'T GO THE WAY I THOUGHT IT WOULD.
FOR YEARS, I COULDN'T SEE ANOTHER WAY OUT OF OUR WAR. LIKE HER, I WAS TRAPPED.
TRYING TO FIX THE MISTAKES OF THE PAST... BY REPEATING THEM.

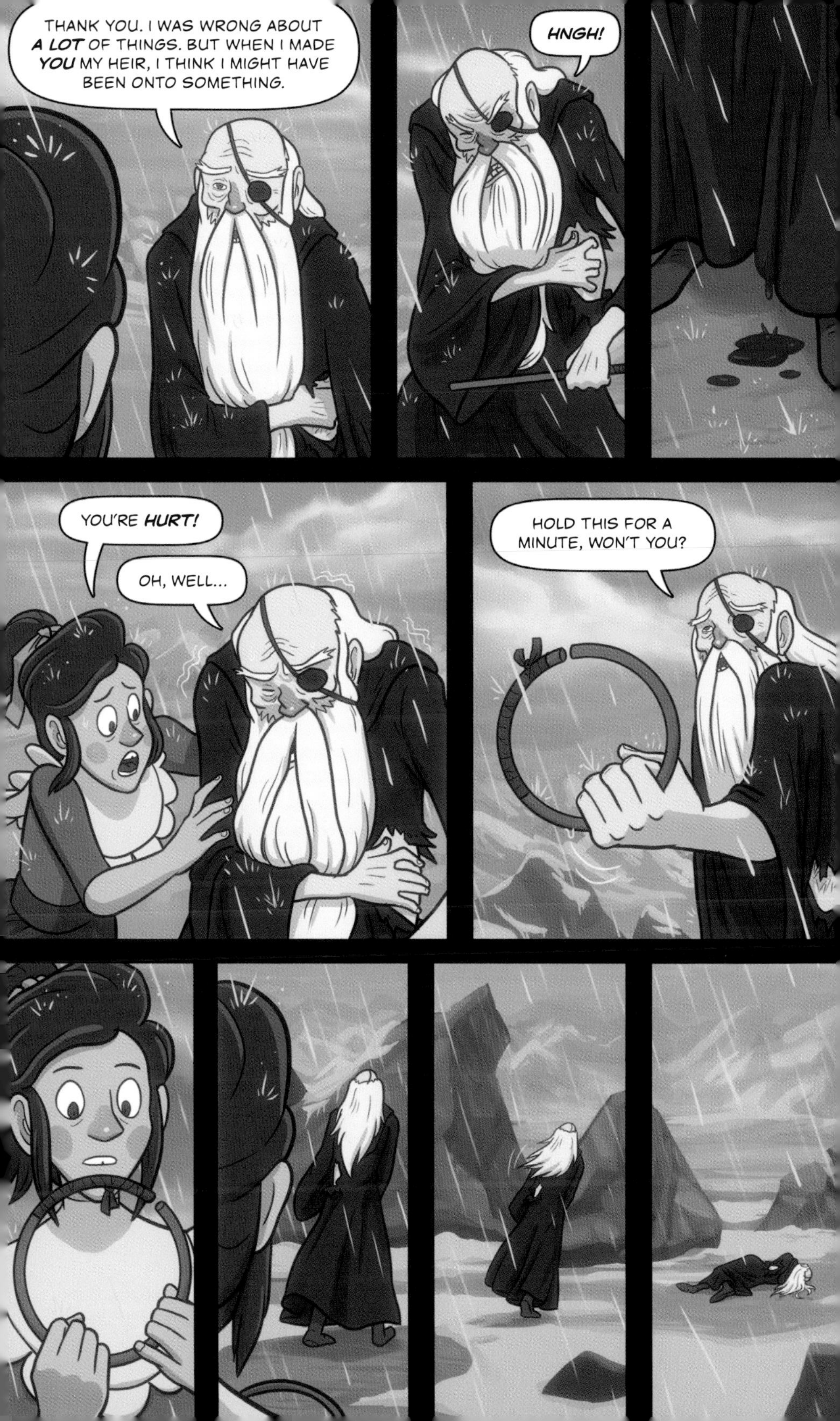
THANK YOU. I WAS WRONG ABOUT **A LOT** OF THINGS. BUT WHEN I MADE **YOU** MY HEIR, I THINK I MIGHT HAVE BEEN ONTO SOMETHING.
HNGH!
YOU'RE **HURT!**
OH, WELL...
HOLD THIS FOR A MINUTE, WON'T YOU?

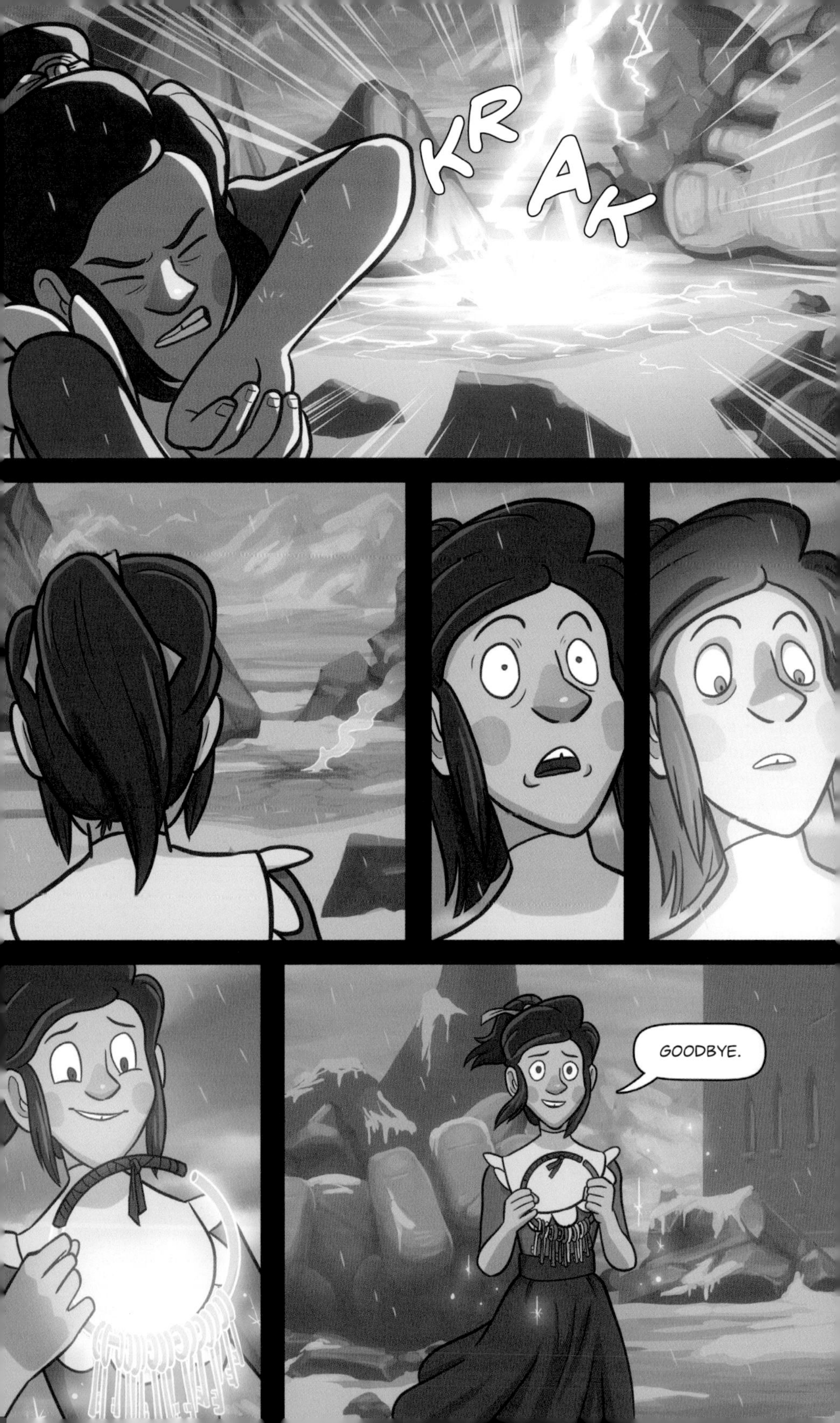
KRAK
GOODBYE.

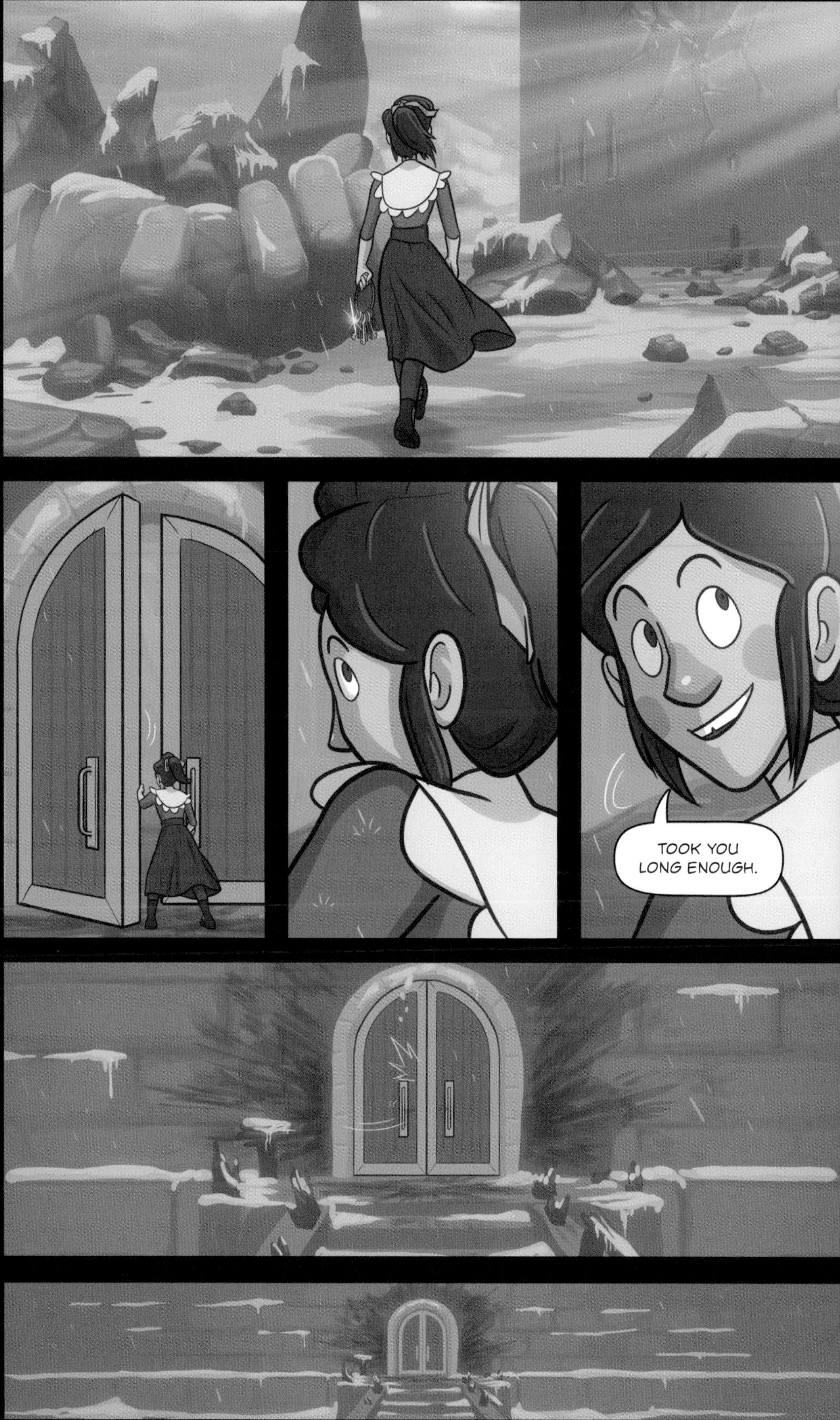
TOOK YOU LONG ENOUGH.

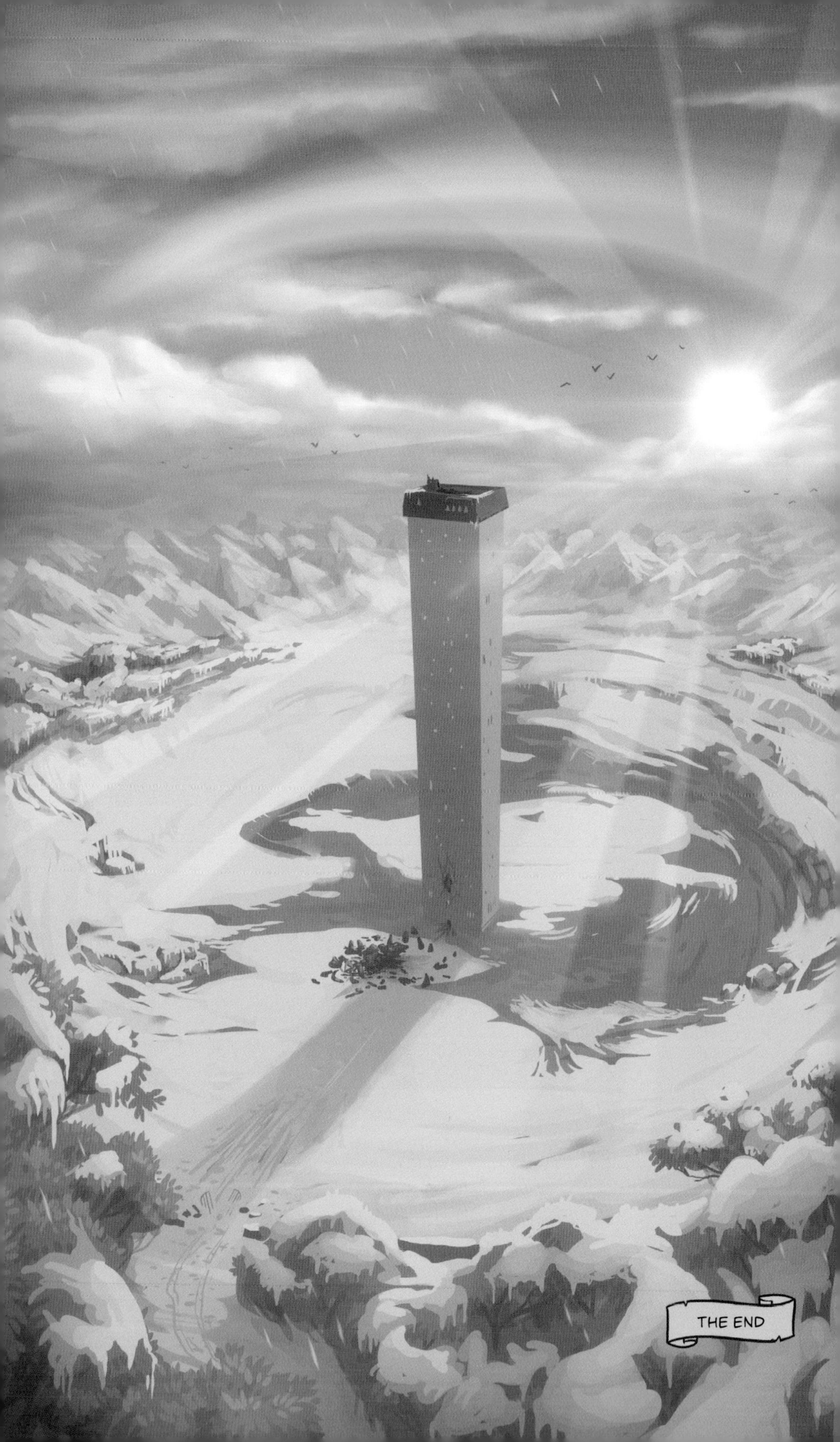
THE END

A HOUSE DIVIDED

created by

HAIKO HÖRNIG & MARIUS PAWLITZA

ACKNOWLEDGMENTS

So this is it. It's hard to believe we finally reached the end of the journey we started back in 2013. For the last eight years, working on A HOUSE DIVIDED has been a huge part of our lives, a constant fountain of joy and stress and pride and everything in between. We couldn't have done it without the support of our friends and families. It takes a village to raise a child, and roughly the same amount of people to finish a comic book series.

Many thanks are owed to Annelie Wagner, Eve Jay, Parvin Jahanshad, Elisa Hock, and Margarite Heimbuch for their coloring assistance and recipe illustrations. Big thanks to Julia Wagner and Edda Heue for the delicious recipes inspired by our story.

Thank you to Robert Wachs for his indispensable help on our website and his constant tech support.

Also big thanks to our dear agent Charlie Olsen for helping a small German title jump over the pond and reach a whole new audience.

Thanks go out to our great editor Greg Hunter, and the whole amazing team at Lerner for making such beautiful books.

And most importantly, a thundering THANK YOU to you, our readers, for joining us on this adventure!

We hope you enjoyed your stay in Henrietta's house just as much as we did.

Your pals,

Haiko & Marius

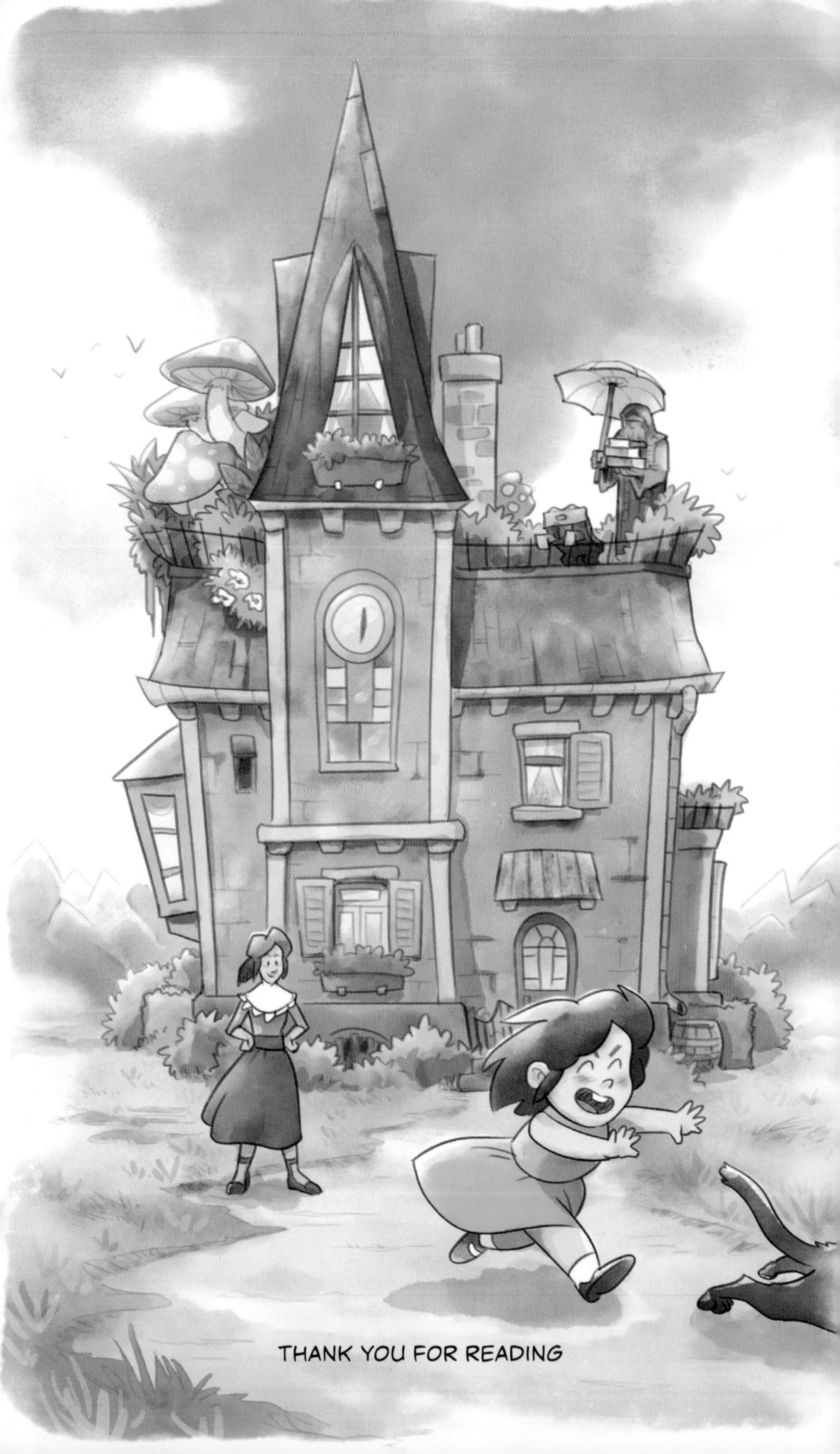
THANK YOU FOR READING

Ornun Zol's Enchanted Pierogi

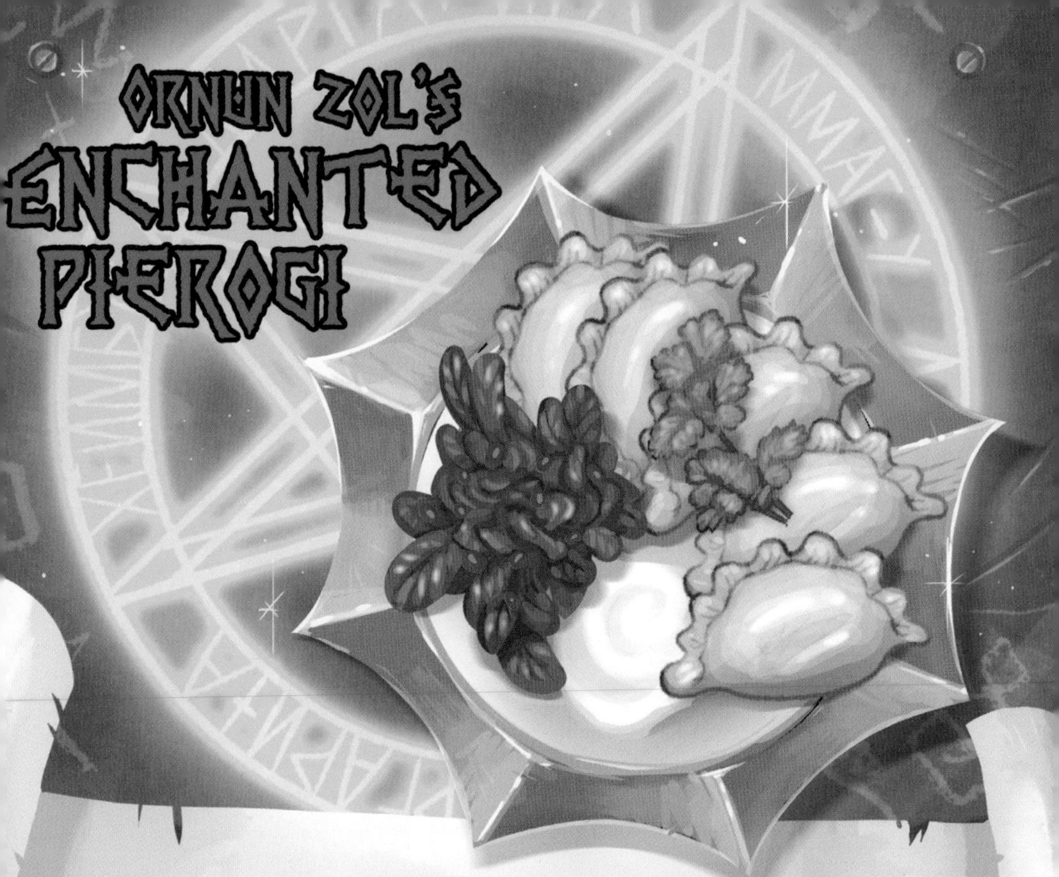

Dough

4 cups (500 g) flour
1 1/2 fl. ounces (45 ml) vegetable oil
1 1/2 teaspoons salt
1 cup (250 ml) warm water

1. Mix all ingredients well and knead the dough for five to ten minutes, until it is smooth and elastic.
2. Cut the dough in two and wrap one half in a clean, damp cotton cloth.

Filling

4 cups (600 grams) chopped potatoes
2 1/2 cups (300 g) diced onions
1 tablespoon olive oil
1/2 teaspoon smoked paprika
1 1/2 cups (300 g) organic tofu
1 to 1 1/2 teaspoons pepper
1 to 1 1/2 teaspoons salt
1 3/4 fl. ounces (50 ml) lemon juice
2 teaspoons vegan crème fraîche
5 to 6 tablespoons vegan grated cheese

1. Clean, chop, and cook the potatoes.
2. Cut the onions into *really* small pieces.
3. Give a splash of olive oil into a pan and fry the onions until they get brown. Then add smoked paprika and a pinch of salt.
4. Blend the tofu, mix it with the potatoes, and mash the mix together. (Note: Never, *ever* blend the potatoes!)
5. Add onions, salt, pepper, lemon juice, crème fraiche, and cheese. Set the filling aside.

Preparing the Pierogi

1. Sprinkle your pastry board with flour.
2. Roll out the dough until it is 0.2 centimeters (2 millimeters) thick.
3. Use a jar or a glass to cut circles into the dough.
4. Place 1 or 2 teaspoons of the filling on each dough circle.

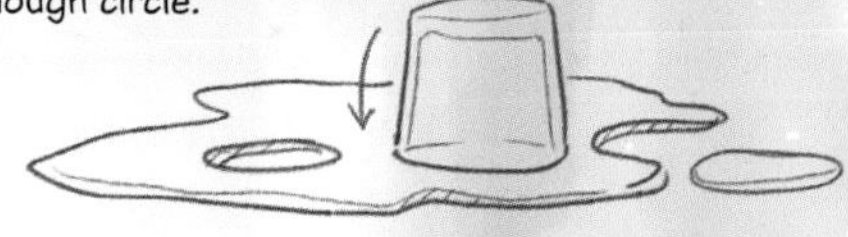

5. Close the circle by folding the dough and squeezing the sides together.
6. Use a fork to finish the pierogi with a little decoration around the rim!
7. Cover the pierogi with a clean cotton cloth and continue with the rest of the dough until it is all used up.

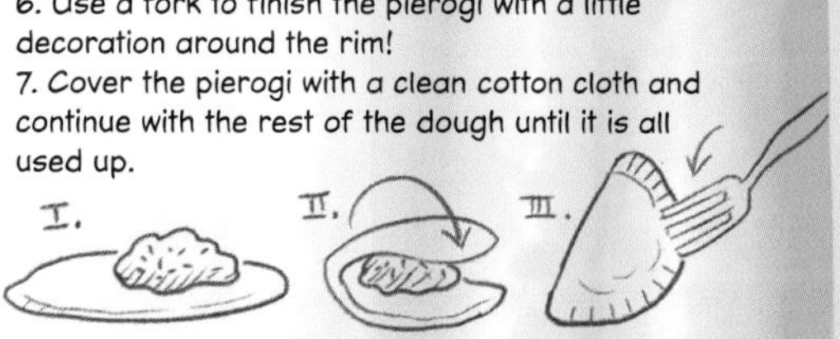
I.
II.
III.

8. Boil water with a little bit of oil and salt in a big pot.
9. Gently place the pierogi in the water and cook until they float on the surface.
Tip: Cook the pierogi in multiple batches so they have enough space within the pot.
10. Take the pierogi out of the water.
11. Serve pierogi with vegan butter, vegan yogurt, fried onions, or salt and pepper. Add a side salad or vegetables of your choice to complete the meal.

ENJOY!

THE ART OF

A HOUSE DIVIDED

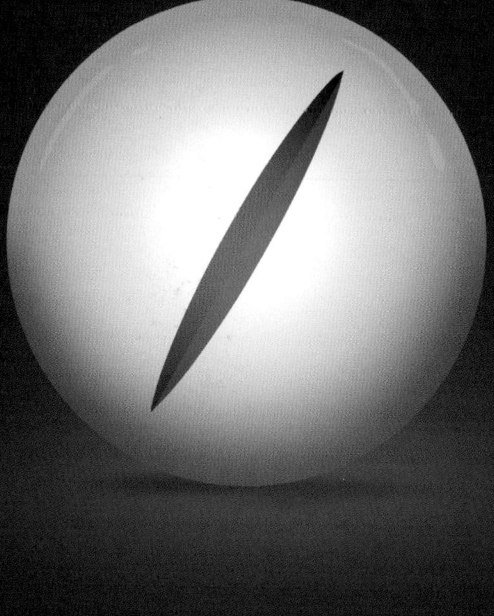

A FINAL LOOK INSIDE THE ATTIC

VIRGINIA, THE FIRST

The Firstborn, Virginia, has had many forms. The first was her original, human form we see back in *The Accursed Inheritance of Henrietta Achilles*, when Henrietta's mom saves her daughter from a bombardment. Then there's the battle-damaged version first seen in *The Winter of Walking Stone.* By this point, she has repaired herself with the help of scavenged parts.

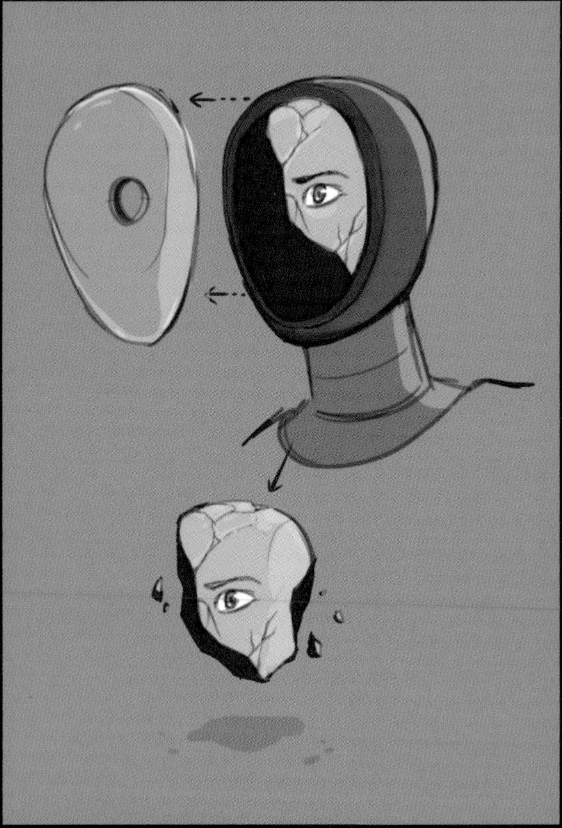

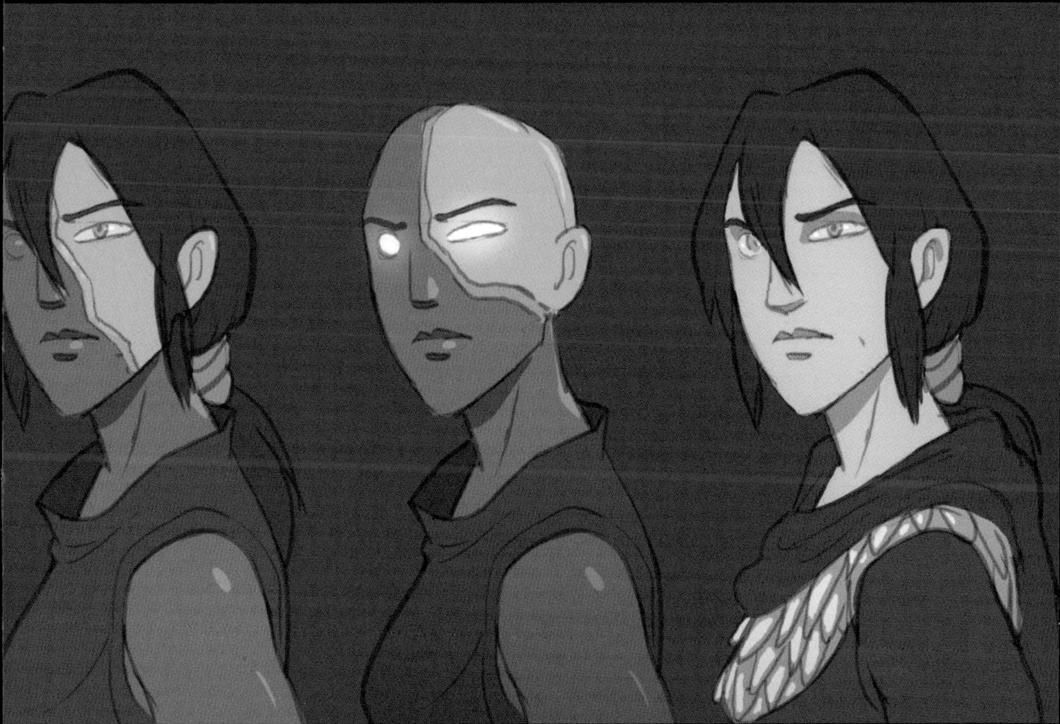

VIRGINIA, THE FIRST

Finally, there's Virginia's restored form, built by the last remaining stone guardian under her spell. For this evolution, we drew inspiration from kintsugi, the Japanese art of repairing broken pottery by filling the cracks with gold. By embracing the cracks and imperfections, the artwork becomes stronger and even more beautiful.

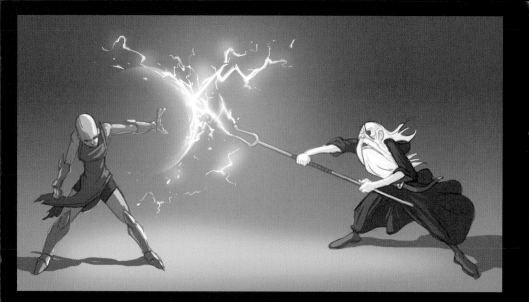

ORNUN ZOL

In the final installment of our story, the late Ornun Zol reveals himself to be very much alive. We wanted to have a clear distinction between his appearance in flashbacks and in present time, and also show that the war with Virginia had taken a toll on the once-powerful wizard. Much like his creation, this Ornun Zol is a shadow of his former self. The end result was a look vaguely reminiscent of an "evil Miracoulix." (That's right, we're dropping an Asterix reference.)

Old man Ornun Zol has still a few tricks up his long sleeves. For the climactic fight with his daughter, we decided to give him a weapon to channel his magic, a mix between a pole arm and a tuning fork.

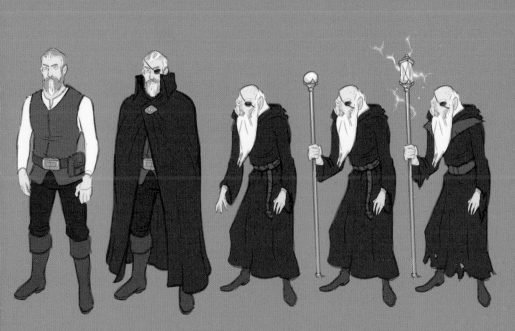

THE LIFE FORGE

The mystery of Ornun Zol's secret vault has been at the center of our story from the very beginning, although the actual design wasn't defined until we started working on book four. The vault--or Life Forge--is a pocket dimension within the house and in many ways its living, beating heart.

For the longest time, we thought the chamber would be a bright floral room bubbling with life and strange plants, but when the time came to set the scene and draw the showdown, we opted for a dark, abstract space filled with stars. After all, "we are all made of star stuff", as Carl Sagan once said.

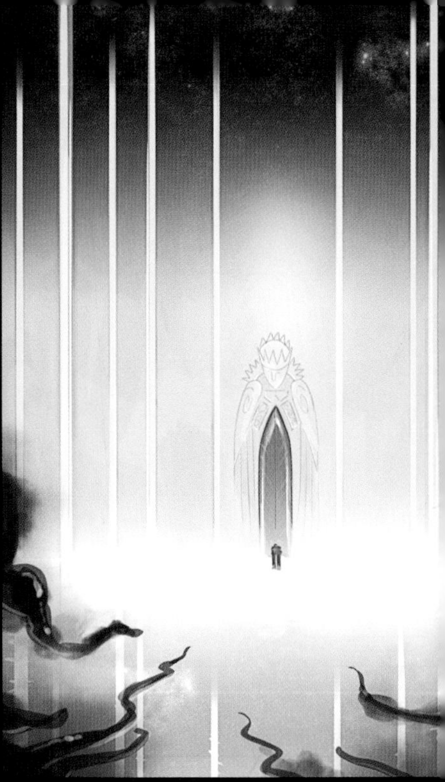

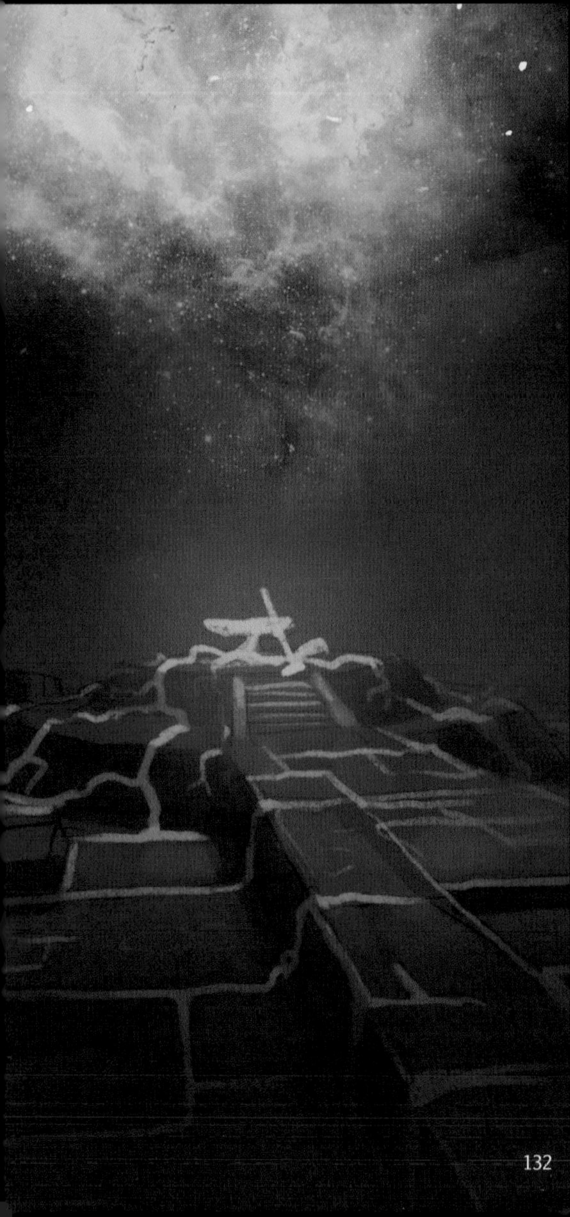

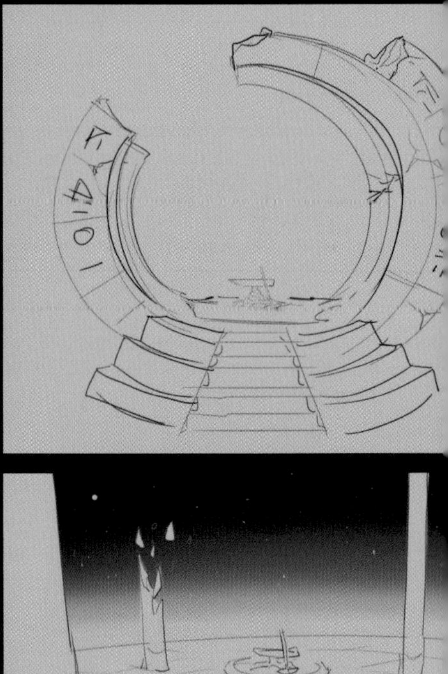

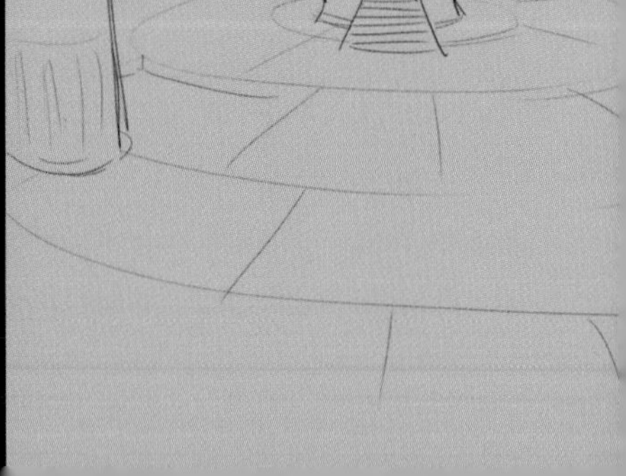

THE GUARDIAN

In the long process of making a comic, there are some ideas that can change drastically or get cut for various reasons. One was having a Guardian of the Lifeforge, an undead knight who would later be revealed to be the father of Henrietta, cursed by Ornun Zol to protect the mysteries of the secret vault. When it came to actually writing the script, we quickly realized that there wasn't a place in the story for another "returning parent" moment, and so the idea was scrapped.

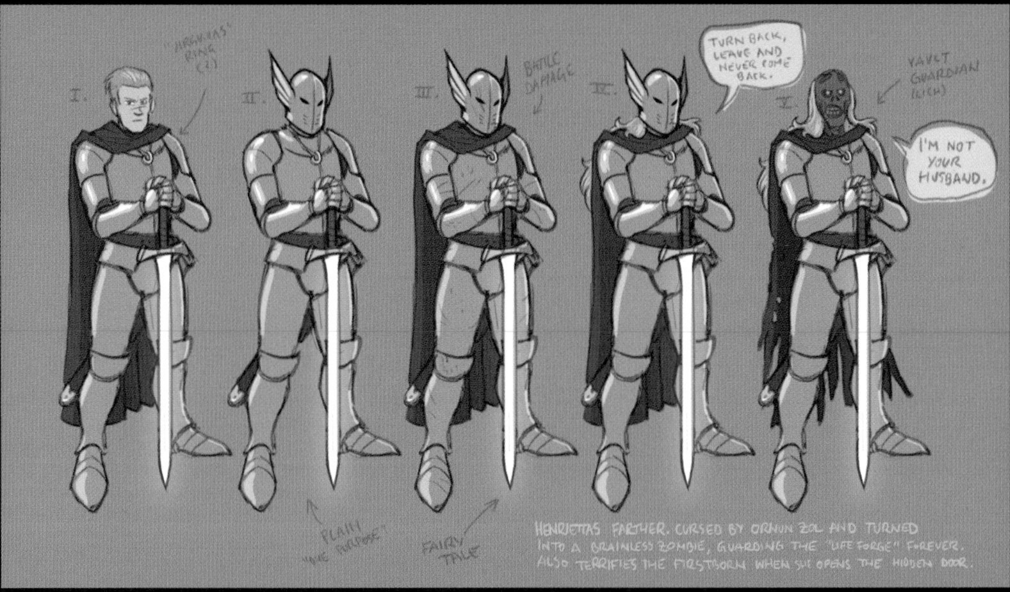
I.
II.
III.
BATTLE DAMAGE
TURN BACK, LEAVE AND NEVER COME BACK.
VAULT GUARDIAN (LICH)
I'M NOT YOUR HUSBAND.
FAIRY TALE
HENRIETTAS FARTHER. CURSED BY ORNUN ZOL AND TURNED INTO A BRAINLESS ZOMBIE, GUARDING THE "LIFE FORGE" FOREVER. ALSO TERRIFIES THE FIRSTBORN WHEN SHE OPENS THE HIDDEN DOOR.

FLEMMING REBORN

After Flemming's tragic encounter with the fiery wax golem, our dashing rogue lost not only his mind but also his good looks. To avoid getting too graphic, we wanted to give our boy Nate something to cover his face. We experimented with different types of bandages, and even a Skeletor-like plain ol' skull, but in the end opted for a pulled-up bandana.

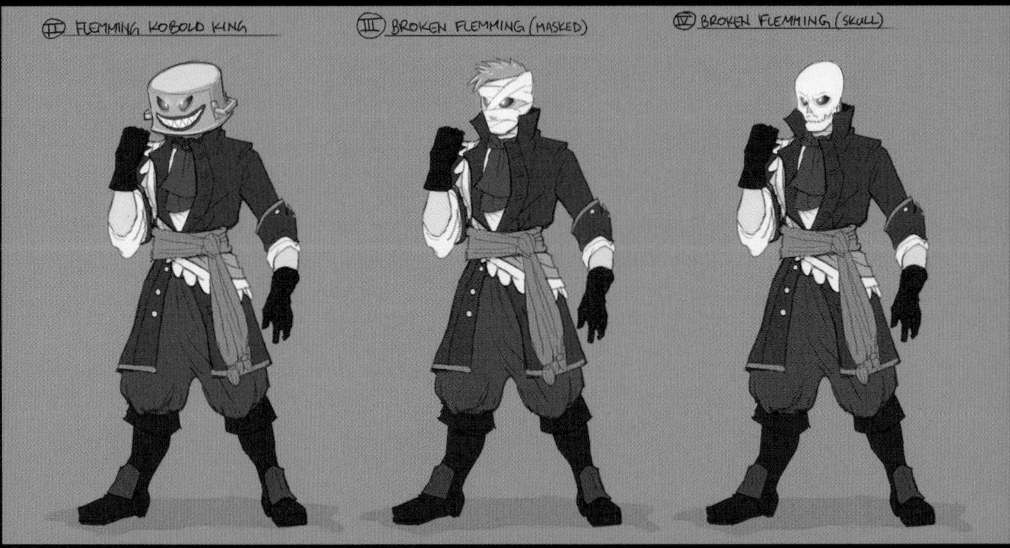
II FLEMMING KOBOLD KING
III BROKEN FLEMMING (MASKED)
IV BROKEN FLEMMING (SKULL)

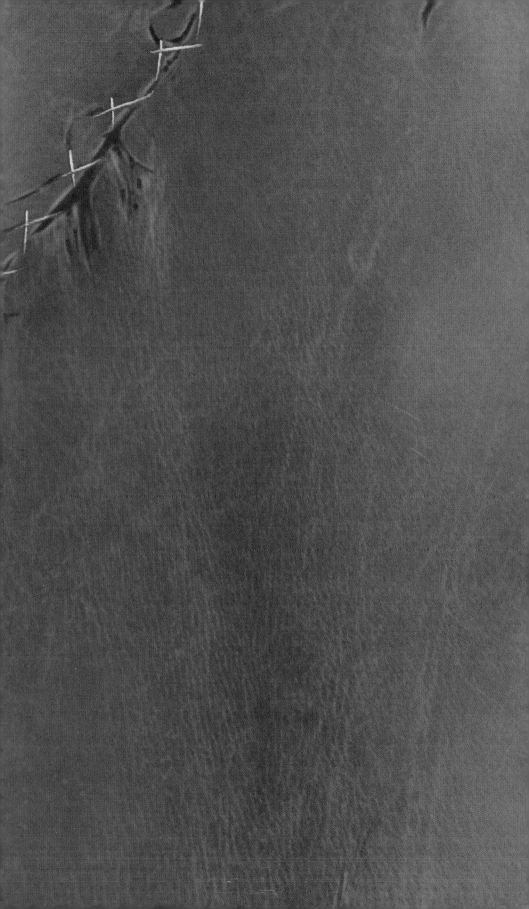

ABOUT THE AUTHOR

Haiko Hörnig spent his childhood in his parents' comic book store, where he developed a love for sequential art at an early age. In middle school, he quickly became friends with Marius Pawlitza. The two of them first enjoyed role-playing games together and later started to make comics. Since 2013, Haiko has worked as a screenwriter for animated shows and feature films. A House Divided is his first published book series. He is based in Frankfurt, Germany. He's also active on Twitter (@DerGrafX) and Instagram (@ahousedividedcomic).

ABOUT THE ILLUSTRATOR

Marius Pawlitza was born in Poland in 1984 and grew up in Ludwigshafen, Germany. Years later, he studied communication design in the German city of Mainz. It was a good excuse to spend as much time as possible playing video games and making comics with Haiko Hörnig. Since 2011, he has worked as an art director for different agencies and companies in Frankfurt, in addition to creating sequential art. On Twitter and Instagram, he's @pengboom.